The Aeonians

Thank you for supporting our

Dream Winter Show

The Aeonians

By

J.E. Klimov

HOLLISTON, MASSACHUSETTS

THE AEONIANS
Copyright © 2017 by J.E. Klimov

Cover Art by Sophie Edwards.

First printing November 2017
10 9 8 7 6 5 4 3 2 1

ISBN # 1-60975-209-0
ISBN-13 # 978-1-60975-209-5
LCCN # 2017950983

Silver Leaf Books, LLC
P.O. Box 6460
Holliston, MA 01746
+1-888-823-6450

Visit our web site at www.SilverLeafBooks.com

ABOUT THE AUTHOR

AUTHOR PHOTOGRAPH BY SVETLANA NESTEROVICH

J.E. Klimov grew up in a small suburb in Massachusetts. After graduating from Massachusetts College of Pharmacy and Health Sciences, she obtained her PharmD and became a pharmacist; however, her true passion was writing and illustration.

Ever since Klimov was little, she dreamed of sharing her stories with the world. From scribbling plotlines instead of taking notes in school, to bringing her characters to life through sketches, Klimov's ideas ranged from fantasy to thriller fiction. *The Aeonians* is her debut novel with Silver Leaf Books.

You can follow J.E. Klimov and stay in tune for news on her sequel among other things on her blog: http://jelliotklimov.weebly.com/, Twitter: @klimov_author, and Facebook page: @klimovauthor.

The adventure continues in...

The Shadow Warrior

As the last remaining Aeonian, Bence Brechenhad flees Deran with nothing but Isabel's ring and a black pearl. Even after sailing vast seas and trekking across exotic islands, the sins of his past lurk around every corner, haunting his every step as he journeys to find a new home.

❖ ❖ ❖

Isabel wakes up alone, without a chance to say goodbye to Bence. With a heavy heart, she assumes the Deranian throne as her people pick up the broken pieces from the Aeonian War. As the country falls back into balance, two visitors appear at the castle doorsteps days apart from one another: one is a complete stranger, and the other is an all too familiar face.

When Deran is sucked back into a vortex of violence and turmoil, Bence must decide whether to return and fight by Isabel's side once more or not.

For more details and information,
visit www.SilverLeafBooks.com

Acknowledgements

I would like to thank my parents and husband, who cheered me on throughout the process, and my late nana who is forever my muse. Also, I am eternally grateful to those that took the time to help me polish this novel so it could shine, including Becky Van Niel, Katie Van Niel, Tom Durant, and my dear friends from Scribophile. You know who you are. Finally, a huge thanks to Sophie Edwards who created fantastic cover art, and Svetlana Nesterovich, who took my author photo.

For Nikolai.

The Aeonians

PROLOGUE

The earth shuddered as a purple flash blinded Echidna. Releasing a primal scream, she squeezed her eyes shut. She refused to admit defeat. The rope that bound her wrists and feet rubbed her skin raw. A roar erupted in the air. The scent of soil filled her lungs. Echidna's mortal enemies were digging her grave.

A tenor voice interrupted her thoughts. "I, Karlyle, with my wife Olivia Deran, sentence you, Damian and Echinda Brechenhad, to eternal imprisonment for your war crimes."

Her husband growled and jostled about. "Shut up," she hissed, opening her eyes. Damian was on his knees beside her. His hair, stained red with blood, waved about in the summer breeze. He jutted his square jaw out in defiance as a lone tear escaped. Echidna's heart twisted when her gaze landed on his headpiece. His amethyst was gone.

Rotating her head slowly, she gasped at the sight before her. His stone of power had dissipated over a massive crevice in the ground. The pit, about a half mile wide, beckoned for her talisman as well.

"Your rights to command the precious stones that this Island grants to its residents have been revoked. They will be used to seal you away in this prison, Cehennem. There, time will never pass. And you will suffer the memories of what you have done for all time," Olivia exclaimed. Her voice, unwavering, cut through Echidna's skin like shards of glass.

The ring on Echidna's left hand weighed heavily as if begging not to leave her.

"Any last words?"

She shook ebony strands from her eyes. Karlyle and Olivia stood beside one another, both dressed in simple beige tunics. Olivia narrowed her eyes and brandished her three-pronged weapon at Echidna, pointing it at her right shoulder. Her lion paw tattoo.

"You. *Irellian.* Anything?"

"My name is Echidna," she said, baring her teeth at Olivia's condescending tone. "Mock my heritage, prissy princess. You think this Island belongs to you? Damian and I were here first. You stole everything from us and called yourselves heroes. You have my word, my husband and I will break free and take back what's ours!"

Her husband's voice rumbled to life. "And exterminate your bloodline."

Karlyle gripped the handle of his long sword, but Olivia waved her arm in front of him. Four figures moved forward and formed a horseshoe around the couple. One had the appearance of a man draped in a snow-white robe, but with iridescent hair and wings. The second stood knee-length, covered in blue fur with webbed hands and feet. The third figure, a reptilian creature three times Olivia's size, hissed at Echidna. The last one, wolfish in nature with copper fur, flicked its braided mane behind him and crossed his arms.

"We will see to it this will never happen," barked the

fourth figure. "You and all the traitors from our tribes."

The person in white pulled out a twisted golden object. Echidna eyed it curiously. He handed it to Olivia with a bow and whispered, "A gift from the leaders of all four tribes of this island as a sign of our alliance. This armlet possesses a stone of power from each of us. And may its first action be to seal this evil couple away."

"Evil?" Echidna spat as she muttered beneath her breath. "Just you wait." She jostled in her bindings once more but her bony frame was no match.

Olivia tucked her sun-kissed curls back and slid the armlet up her right arm. Echidna whipped her head in the other direction as light erupted from the woman. She could even feel the energy pulsing in waves, nearly knocking her from her knees.

Squinting, Echidna peeked back at Olivia. Opal, sapphire, amber, and ruby glowed proudly on that armlet. A quick sensation of intrigue trickled down her spine. Her skin crawled with invisible spiders. Echidna needed that armlet. That was the key to success.

Before she could blink, Olivia twirled her arm upwards and moved it about as if conducting an orchestra. A myriad of colors beamed from the armlet and shot towards Echidna's hand. The hand with her ring.

"No. No!" Echidna howled in agony. Wind whipped the hair from her face, choking her. The temperature rose, the heat searing her skin. Her husband cried out, but her focus was locked on her ring. The amethyst evaporated into a mauve mist.

"My talisman. That belongs to me!" She screeched in

despair. *Everything I worked for, all Damian and I sacrificed, now lost to some meddling brats.*

A gale wrapped its invisible hands around Echidna and her husband, lifting them hundreds of feet into the air. Karlyle, Olivia, and the other four tribe leaders shrunk into the size of insects. Rotating on the spot, she now faced the gaping hole that would be her prison for eternity. Hordes of her servants, her *Veijari*, were forced down the prison. They disappeared into darkness one by one while onlookers chanted.

"Traitors! Traitors!"

Echidna's blood boiled. This was it. When her last servant entered Cehennem, the gale hurled them downward, the entrance to the prison like a hungry mouth opening wide.

Black.

She landed with a thud. Moist earth gathered under her nails. A metallic smell filled Echidna's nostrils. Wailing and moaning filled her ears. Her husband sat up and didn't move. He just stared straight ahead, but Echidna looked up.

The mauve haze that was once her amethyst covered the opening with a *swoosh*. In seconds, thick metal bars materialized. The haze slipped through and entered Cehennem. For a brief moment, Echidna's heart leapt. Maybe it will return to her.

It swirled around everyone and released their bindings. Echidna rubbed her wrists, blinking in shock as her body glowed purple. The glow flickered. It faded. Then everything returned to black.

Darkness swallowed them whole, a blackness that absorbed even time itself.

CHAPTER

1

Releasing a breath, Princess Isabel let her arrow fly. It struck just outside the bull's eye. She tried to kick the dirt, but only managed to get her boots caught in her gown.

"Hey now, don't be so hard on yourself. Besides, the Queen wouldn't be too happy if you ruined yet another dress," exclaimed an armor-clad man with closely shaven white hair. He twisted his mustache as he stifled laughter.

"Shut up, Benjamin. I had it yesterday. Four bull's eyes. I don't know why I'm regressing." She pulled another arrow from her quiver and shot an icy glare at her target. Inhaling deeply, she focused on the scent of hay. Birds chirped rhythmically. Rays of sunlight spilled across the field. Pulling the arrow back against the string, she closed one eye.

Focus.

As soon as she released her grip, Benjamin jumped up, waved his hands and cried out. The arrow flew past the target and into the woods.

"What the hell?" Isabel growled.

"In battle, you may encounter many distractions," he said, falling quickly into a more serious disposition. "I'm not kidding around. You have already proven you can shoot an arrow faster and better than any female on this island, and you need to be challenged. Heaven forbid you ever need to use a bow and arrow to defend yourself, there will be chaos. Clashing of metal all around you—"

"I got it." Isabel wiped sweat from her forehead with her sleeve. "Thank you. I should be more grateful. You risk suffering the wrath of my mother finding out about this."

"And I have already suffered a few times. But I think she is softening up to the idea."

Isabel crossed her arms and sat on a flattened rock. She played with the hem of her dress. "I'm not looking forward to tomorrow."

Shining his helmet mindlessly, Benjamin said, "Why not? It's the armlet ceremony! An honor. Although, I don't think that our training sessions would be appropriate after tomorrow. You will be carrying such responsibility—"

"But my mother would still be Queen. I'm sure I can still find time to train with you and the others."

"What I meant to say was, you should make better use of your time."

When her mouth fell agape, Benjamin patted her hand. He locked eyes with her and shook his head.

Isabel jerked her arm away from his. "And who are you to tell me how to make use of my time?" Her words were laced with venom, then followed by a remorseful silence.

Benjamin's head dropped. He struggled for words as he adjusted his helmet.

"I'm sorry, I shouldn't speak to you that way. I just really enjoy my time here. I feel so carefree. You've taught me to wield a sword, maneuver with a hefty shield, and now fire an arrow. I don't want all of that to go to waste."

"We will see, kid." The lines around his eyes grew deeper. "The sun has begun to set. I think it's time to call it a day."

Isabel nodded as she pressed the bow into his hands. "Want to know the next weapon I want to master?"

Cocking his head to the side, Benjamin smiled. "What?"

"The royal sais!"

"No one has touched them since your great, great grand-mother Olivia during The Battle of The Storm. It's a treas-ured relic."

Her shoulders slumped. Isabel had eyed that weapon in its glass case in the chapel for years. The polished three-pronged silver weapon begged for some action, to be used again. Even if it was against a target stuffed with hay. Shak-ing her thoughts away, Isabel bowed. "Thank you for today. I have a long day ahead of me tomorrow." Anxiety filled her chest like a flash flood.

Benjamin bowed in return. "The royal army has com-plete and unbending faith in you. Even if there are others out there who don't. Remember that. See you tomorrow, Princess."

She bit her lip and nodded. Picking up the hem of her gown, Isabel scurried through the royal barracks. Her heels tapped against the cobblestone flooring until she reached massive mahogany doors. Pulling the copper handles, Isabel peeked back at Benjamin, now a speck in the distance, be-fore she took a deep breath and entered the castle.

The cold air shocked her back to reality. With only lanterns hanging from the stone walls, the west side of Deran Castle looked plain compared to the other areas. As she made her way towards the main hall, Isabel observed her tattered dress, trying to come up with an excuse for its condition. All her tunics were ripped beyond recognition, so she had to train in a formal outfit.

An idea popped into her head. She quickened her pace and took the stairwell up and around the main hall towards her room. She called her maids, who were sewing her tunics. The foremost maid clasped her hand to her mouth when she laid eyes on Isabel.

"I know, I know. I went practicing in a dress. Is there a spare I can change into before dinner?"

"Yes, yes. Here's a green taffeta gown. Let's get you dressed quickly."

While the other two maids fussed over Isabel, her line of vision fell onto a satin dress with lace trim that hung prominently on a wooden mannequin. This lilac gown dripped with pearls. It was the gown she would wear for her armlet ceremony. Isabel dreaded the corset that would soon suffocate her. When she had first tried it on, all her mother and her maids could do was coo at how it complimented her hazel eyes.

She snapped from her reverie as the maid yanked a ribbon around her waist. "Thank you," she said.

"Of course, Princess. We will, uh, see if we can fix this up for you," the second maid said, trying to disguise her cringe.

With a wink, Isabel whispered, "It's pink. I will be fine if I never see this dress ever again."

The two maids glanced at one another, faces blank.

"Okay. Thank you, ladies," Isabel said, backing away slowly. After a quick curtsy, she rushed out the door.

A burst of giggles erupted from her room. Isabel paused. "What a joke, Christiana," whispered one of the maids.

Isabel balled her hands into fists. She inched back against the wall and leaned towards the door.

"Hush, Agnes. It's true, Isabel isn't very... ladylike, but it's not our place to pass such judgments. What if someone hears and tells the royal family!"

"Just look at what she did to this dress!" Agnes huffed. "Victoria was so different."

Biting her lip, Isabel's heart twisted with guilt. Her sister had passed away a year ago, and even to this day, she lived underneath her shadow.

"But it doesn't change the facts. We have only Isabel now, and tomorrow, the family heirloom will be passed down to her instead—"

"The armlet should not be given to someone as careless as her. Isabel is not fit for the title."

Tears welled in her eyes as Agnes' voice faded into the back of her mind. Last year, Victoria was elected to receive the armlet by the four tribes when she turned eighteen years old. She was a quiet, graceful young woman. She also was very calculating, excelling at the art of diplomacy.

Isabel looked down at her callused hands. A frown stretched her lips. Even as the older sister, she had always been second in line, destined to marry some lord, bear children, and oversee insignificant duties within the castle walls. While serving her sister, of course. That was the plan until the day Victoria fell.

Each time Isabel blinked, a tear drop fell, and the image of her sister reaching out to her flashed before her. Isabel wrinkled her nose, trying to push the memory away. Victoria had been cared for by the family nurse for weeks, but nothing stopped her fever. She recalled visiting her sister every day since the accident, watching over her bloated, unpleasantly warm body. When sepsis had set in, it was only days until she witnessed her sister's last rattled breath.

Chewing on her fingers, Isabel winced as images from the funeral played before her eyes. It was a blur, but guilt and sadness pricked her skin as strongly today as it did a year ago. And ever since then, fear of failing to fill her sister's shoes never left her. While the responsibility of the armlet transferred from Victoria to her, she never got used to the idea of it.

Giggling broke her train of thought. The two maids waltzed from her room. Agnes held the dirtied pink gown against her and twirled. When Isabel locked eyes with her, Agnes froze. Christiana swallowed and bowed so low her hair touched the ground.

Isabel's heart pounded loudly. She could barely hear the gibberish Agnes was spewing. The guilt and uncertainty that simmered beneath her skin transformed into boiling anger. She snatched her dress with lightning speed and clutched it to her chest. "I am not the perfect royal heir like Victoria was, but I'm the one alive," Isabel said, voice wavering. Her hands trembled violently. "After tomorrow, I will prove to everyone that I can handle the powers of the armlet."

Casting the dress onto the floor, Isabel rushed past her maids and headed towards the castle chapel, the room where the royal sais were kept.

CHAPTER

2

By morning, the sun had chased the gray clouds away. Ribbons of purple, silver, blue, amber, and red flowed down the receiving hall. The smell of roasting turkey wafted everywhere. A golden chandelier, holding hundreds of candles, dangled from the vaulted ceiling. The stone walls displayed relics and paintings that celebrated the different cultures of the tribes. The voices of Isabel's parents flowed through her ears.

"My maids have picked up some lovely tapestries on the West Royal Trade Post. I think the receiving hall should have a touch of elegance to balance the hall out. Make it feel more welcoming," Febe whispered.

Hadi grunted. "Whatever you wish, my love. I took your last name, didn't I?" He released a chuckle and placed his hands over Febe's.

Isabel rubbed her eyes. When she had reached the chapel last night, all she could do was stare at the legendary sais, wishing her life was different. For hours. She just couldn't sleep. As servants bustled about, she tried to focus on their small talk and quell the bubble of anxiety that expanded in her gut.

"Yes, I don't think your family appreciated that."

Slurping the wine from his goblet, he tapped his ring finger against the armrest. "Ah, yes, I recall the look on my father's face. Typical Norelander. So much pride in passing down the family name. But I think he forgave me after realizing I would rule a country of my own."

"And that's why I love you. Thank you for respecting our tradition. You know, we should make a trip up there soon. It's been a few years since we've been to visit your family."

Thoughts of sailing on the open ocean beneath the two moons inched into her mind. Isabel hummed as her people, the Deranians, milled about. Their chatter created a low buzz around the room. A person would occasionally glance at her, redirecting her anxiety.

This is it, sis. This was supposed to be your big day.

Heat flushed up her collar as guilt grasped its hands around her neck. A soldier clad in leather armor and chainmail marched forward and saluted them.

"The first of the tribes have arrived, King Hadi and Queen Febe." After bowing, he looked up and winked at Isabel. "How are you feeling today, Princess?"

"Alright, Benjamin. Although I would rather be at archery!"

He chuckled and stroked his mustache. "We miss our little tomboy, but you are far from that now."

Glancing down at her dress for a moment, she sighed. "I

guess so."

"Bring them in," her father boomed to her left.

With the clang of his armor, Benjamin puffed out his chest and cleared his throat. "Presenting the Tuuli from the district of Buryan."

Isabel stood with her parents. Nearly tripping on the hem of her dress, she swung her arms to steady herself, cursing silently as the weight of the gown strained her shoulders. Febe threw her a sideways glance.

As soon as Hadi raised his hand, trumpets sounded and both doors opened. A tall, slender figure appeared, followed by a sizable crowd. Isabel craned her neck to get a better look at everyone's silver and blue garments that seemed to sparkle in the rays of sun that shone through the high windows. They glided forward as if floating on air. Despite the easy, effortless grace with which they moved, it was hard to believe they weren't human, like the Deranians. Isabel searched for their only distinguishing feature: wings. When she didn't spot any, she sighed.

I wonder how many of them still have them? There must be some. Maybe they are hidden beneath their outfits.

It was a mystery to Isabel as to why they would hide such a beautiful trait here in Deran when the Tuuli on the mainland displayed them proudly. She always daydreamed of having wings.

When the foremost figure reached the steps, Isabel's heart raced. Despite the fact he was only one year older than her, his face was boyish. He looked far too young to be the leader of a whole tribe. Yet, there he stood, head high and shoulders back.

His hand floated to his smooth chin as he bowed to Hadi and Febe. "Dante Roril. My people and I are honored to be here." Isabel tried to look away but her eyes were glued to his face.

Curtseying, Febe smoothed her magenta gown, decorated with cream colored lace. "Welcome."

"My friend! How are you?" Hadi boomed as he slapped Dante's back. His crown, bejeweled with various precious stones, slid back when he raised his empty goblet.

"My Queen. My King, I am well." He paused. "Greetings, Princess."

Isabel twisted her lips. She hated formalities between friends.

"Hello, Dante. It is a pleasure to see you again," she said, releasing a smirk. Even after knowing him for years, his wispy blonde hair that danced around his baby blue eyes still made her heart flutter.

"Excited to receive the armlet today? This is a big moment. Time for you to be a grown up!" he exclaimed with a twinkle in his eye.

Before Isabel could fire a witty response, three Tuuli in silver robes joined Dante's side. Their platinum blonde hair outshone Dante's dirty blonde locks. After bowing to Febe and Hadi, they too, acknowledged Isabel.

"We are so proud of you," one said. Even though wrinkles stretched from the edges of his eyes to his lips, he remained handsome.

The Tuuli are blessed to maintain such beauty even at an older age. From their fair hair to their porcelain skin. With soft spoken voices and a reverence for manners, they seem more civilized than their human counterparts at times.

"Thank you, Elder Lief," Isabel replied, snapping from her thought. Her attention was immediately drawn to his wings, and her mouth dropped in awe. "I see that you are the only one displaying your wings today."

Lief flicked them up and down. They resembled bird wings in shape but were translucent and had no feathers. "I am very proud of them, even though it may not be the trend around here anymore." Ice laced the last few words. He turned to Dante, stone faced.

Dante flushed as he twisted his opal ring. "As you know, it is legend that humans descended from the Tuuli. The Tuuli and humans had always maintained a peaceful relationship, and at times, they would even intermarry—"

Isabel blushed at the thought.

"And I think it is about time to be more like our fellow humans. Tuuli wings have become obsolete anyway. Many cannot even fly long distances with them. Lief, we had this discussion before, and we can agree to disagree." Twisting his ring faster, he gave a tight-lipped smile.

"Of course, my apologies if I seemed rude, especially in the presence of the royal family."

Febe waved her arms. "There is no need. Everything is fine. Please make your way to the main hall and enjoy yourselves."

Emitting a warm smile, Lief gestured for the other elders to follow him down the steps. Dante's fingers played with the hilt of his sword as he bowed once more, hair cascading over his face.

"See you in a little while, Isabel."

Flushing, Isabel hid her face as the Tuuli were escorted to the ballroom. Her mother suppressed a giggle. When the pitter-patter of their footsteps echoed past her, she peeked up to see Dante's head shrink in the distance.

As soon as the Tuuli left the receiving hall, a massive form ducked through the entrance. A rhythmic pounding had shattered the silence. Benjamin scrambled out of the way. Scores of reptilian creatures banging on leather-bound drums poured through the door, ranging from twelve to twenty-four feet tall.

"May I present Adem and his people, the Dunya."

The largest reptile stood on his hind legs and stretched his arms, covering the windows and casting a large shadow over Isabel. "Good morning, and congratulations! Going to put that armlet to good use? Are you *sure* you can handle such power?"

"Yes, I'm ready." Isabel said, biting her cheek.

At least I think I am. Do the tribes really lack confidence in me?

Adem roared as he narrowly avoided hitting his head on the chandelier. The Dunya mimicked him, flailing their arms and twitching their tails to the beat of the music. As they paraded around the receiving hall, they showed off the piercings that lined their backs. Some were made of gold. Others were decorated with diamonds and amber. The Dunya were exceptionally proud of their body jewelry; the type and quantity were indication of rank. When the sunlight hit their scaled bodies, the room exploded with color.

"Princess Isabel. It is an honor." A Dunya half Adem's size stomped to the front of the crowd. "Do you remember me?" The rest of the reptiles bowed as they backed up to give her space. The silver rings that adorned her snout clanked as she snuffed out a greeting.

"You are Adem's daughter, Avani," Isabel said with a warm smile.

"My apologies for not bowing, Princess. My body has been troubling me lately."

"Don't worry at all. I will have someone escort you to the main hall," Isabel replied.

Avani chortled. "If I were to faint, I am sure I would crush him!"

"Very true!" Joining in on the laughter, Isabel curtsied. While commonly irritated by the Dunyans' boisterous personalities, Isabel found their sense of humor refreshing today. She even found herself bobbing her head to the beat. "How is it in Zeyland?"

Adem opened his jaws to speak, but Avani threw her claw in front of him. "The drought continues. But we pray faithfully every day."

"To… Maz?"

The drumming stopped. Every reptile's eyes landed on Isabel. When they nodded, she exhaled. The Dunya worshiped three gods, and she was relieved she got the name of their 'earth' god correct. Isabel had taken many classes growing up, and her least favorite was cultural studies. That was when she learned all the tribes' religions, and the Dunya were the only race that still practiced polytheism.

"Isabel. My people and I have a gift for you," Avani said.

Adem stomped past his daughter and dug into his satchel. When a package squeezed between two sharp nails appeared, Isabel's stomach did a somersault.

"Oh! Oh! What is it?" Hopping on her tip toes, she reached for the package. Adem dropped it into Isabel's hands then offered her a handshake. While his claw completely covered her hand, his grip was gentle.

"Isabel." Febe let out an uneasy laugh. "Please act your age."

"Come now, Queen Febe. She is. She just still knows what it's like to experience pure joy over simple things. I envy that. Growing old is a sad business."

Glancing sheepishly up at Adem and her parents, Isabel unwrapped her present as daintily as she could. But excitement burned at her fingertips. Underneath was a sleek drum with a hollow log frame, sanded down to a smooth finish. Rawhide stretched tightly across opposite surfaces. Isabel struck it, and the instrument vibrated. Her chest swelled.

"Thank you very much. I can't wait to play with you guys. As long as you teach me," Isabel said.

"You are welcome anytime, Princess," Adem bellowed, exposing hundreds of razor sharp teeth. His breath, which smelled like rancid meat, rolled from his tongue.

She scrunched her nose and tried to hold her smile. When Avani tugged at Adem's arm, he turned away and Isabel released her breath.

"Father, let's get a move on. We are holding up the receiving line!" Avani hissed.

When the Dunya marched past Isabel, she waved, and they each nodded their heads in return. As they disappeared into the next room, the drumming faded. Adem decided to go last. He tucked his tail between his legs, carefully contorting his body through the archway. When he turned to give one last wave, his elbow hit a marble column, causing it to crack down the middle.

Isabel's hand flew to her mouth, her belly aching with laughter. Her mother sighed, and her father snorted.

"Carry on, Adem," he said. Turning to one of the servants, Hadi pointed at the column. "See that it gets attended to. Oh, and I am out of wine."

Leaning to her left, Isabel could barely make out more guests at the entrance of the castle, led by Benjamin. She placed her present down by her feet and took a deep breath.

"Presenting the Foti from Ogonia City and Kai from Pekas Bay!"

Two beings of contrasting appearance led the massive group. Covered in copper fur, one looked like a wolf on his hind legs. He wore a red sash draped from one shoulder to the opposing hip and dark pants. A picture of a wolf's skull with fire erupting from the top was stamped front and center of the sash. His people looked and were dressed identically. However, it was his mane that screamed he was the leader. Longer and thicker than the rest, he carried his braided and decorated mane on his left arm.

I can't imagine how heavy it must be. There must be at least a hundred rubies woven into the braid. That's Hakan, alright.

He grunted to a stocky blue figure who could have been no taller than Isabel's thigh. He too, was covered in fur, but it was groomed short. With each hop, he struck his cane against the floor. The *clack clack clack* filled Isabel's ears with familiarity.

I can't believe Dover is 273 years old. He is so energetic.

The irony of their friendship amused Isabel, since one was more like fire, and the other like water. As he continued to hop alongside Hakan, Dover's rabbit-like ears flopped around. When Isabel squinted her eyes, she could barely make out the gills within them. Like the rest of the Kai, their fin-like tails swished back and forth to maintain balance.

When the pair reached the steps, Hakan paused. Smoothing his fur with his claws, he purred a greeting.

"Hello, King Hadi. Queen. It is a perfect day for a celebration."

Isabel cleared her throat.

"My apologies. We are here ready to honor you, Princess."

"It is a pleasure to see you again." It was hard for Isabel to not stare at his yellowed fangs. "And greetings, my proud Fotians."

One by one they howled until it fell into a melodic unison. A slight chill resonated in her bones. There was something haunting about the way they sang, yet hypnotic at the same time.

When they finished, Dover hobbled up to Isabel. His ears drooped over his eyes. Dover focused his attention back on Isabel and her parents. "What a thrill to have the ceremony finally!"

Finally?

Her mind raced.

Dover meant nothing by it. I mean, this ceremony has already been rescheduled once since Victoria's death.

Shaking her head, Isabel focused on a Kai elder who arrived with water for Dover. "It's nice to see you, Bo. You too, Sachiel. Calder."

The three elders greeted her in unison. Sachiel and Bo's faces were weathered, and their whiskers were thin, like Dover's. Calder, on the other hand, was much younger, and stood almost up to Isabel's chest. Coral bangles decorated their wrists, shimmering with each movement.

A hand cupped Isabel's shoulder. Her father jerked his head towards the main hall. "We can socialize with everyone once the formal introductions are done," he said.

"Of course," Isabel replied.

After Dover and the elders exchanged greetings with Hadi and Febe, they herded the rest of the Kai into the next room. Their bodies disappeared in the crowd, all dwarfed by the size of Foti, Tuuli, and Dunya.

Isabel sighed dramatically. Her muscles loosened now that there were no eyes on her. She never felt as comfortable in the public as eye as her sister had.

But I made it. Part one is over.

"Is the entertainment here?" Hadi called out to Benjamin.

"Yes, they just slipped in when the Foti and Kai presented themselves. I directed them to their quarters to get ready."

Febe clasped her hands together as her lips curled upwards. "Fabulous. Please see to it they are served something good to eat, too."

When Benjamin saluted, Isabel's parents signaled her to follow them into the main hall where their guests intermingled. She waited for them to walk a few feet ahead of her so she wouldn't trip on her father's fur cloak that was longer than her mother's train.

Okay. Phase two. Let's get social.

Isabel hiked up her dress so she could navigate the stairs with her four inch heels. When she reached the bottom step, her left ankle buckled. Throwing her arms out, Isabel caught the railing.

"Stupid heels," she grumbled, checking to make sure the heel did not break. "My mother would kill me if I ruined her shoes."

Benjamin rushed to her side and offered a hand. "What? You have no shoes of your own?"

"Very funny. For your information, I own tons of... boots and flats. The few heels I have are unfortunately all at the cobbler."

"Hm. I wonder why," he replied with a twinkle in his eye. Extending his elbow, he insisted on escorting her to the main hall.

As they walked, Isabel paid attention to each step she took. The noise from the next room grew louder and stirred up her anxiety once more. Hundreds of figures conversed, all waiting to witness her initiation into adulthood.

She had gone over the reality of it all the night before and managed to scrape by with a few hours of sleep. And when she had woken up, the responsibility of it all still felt misaligned. *What will my life be like once I receive the armlet? Will I be able to still do the things I want to do?*

"Listen. I'm thinking of shooting some arrows tomorrow. How about it?" Isabel blurted.

Benjamin's footsteps faltered. Clearing his throat, he struggled to reply. She stared at him, begging for him to look at her. She needed this. Just a little escape to help cope with her major life change.

They arrived at the archway that opened into the main hall. A few servants scurried back and forth with a ladder and rope to secure the cracked pillar. Dust swirled about, blurring the scene before her. Isabel took a deep breath, pushing against her corset.

"Princess Isabel." His voice was soft.

"Yes?" Isabel replied, eyes glazing over.

"My men will be practicing archery tomorrow and would be honored for you to join us."

Her eyes refocused. "Really? Thank you."

"It's our pleasure. Now, go. Your people are waiting for you."

"My people... Yes."

Isabel lifted her head and took a step forward.

CHAPTER

3

Even though flowers were strewn across the walls and crowds dressed to their best danced to string instruments, it was just another day to Isabel. Maybe it was because she knew that the armlet was never intended for her. When her chest tightened, she focused on deep breathing. The main hall became so crowded, people spilled into the ballroom. Many of the Dunya made their way outside to the courtyard so they could stand comfortably.

Isabel made her way to the ballroom as well. The columns stretched towards the ceiling, which was covered with stained glass. Bursts of light scattered the area, showering its guests with color. Rectangular tables with plum colored tablecloths mixed with round ones, and candles peppered every corner. And yet, her thoughts continued to ebb in and out like ocean waves.

Nodding her head to the rhythm of a waltz, Isabel watched the servers, holding steaming hors d'oeuvres weave in and out of the crowd. There was no shortage of duck wings, seasoned lamb chops, and colorful sauces that oozed over freshly baked bread, the wheat harvested from the great fields of Stopping Valley. However, even the tantalizing scent seemed unable to lift Isabel's mood. One Foti ripped into his duck wing and gulped it hurriedly, bones and all, while conversing with a Kai, who pecked at his vegetarian dish. Candles stood on their three-pronged holder, flickering to the direction of their voices. The flame highlighted the Foti's jaw, angular and long while it accented the Kai's protruding brow.

As she drummed her fingers against her arms, Isabel wondered how much time has passed. Wax already seeped onto the polished table.

It shouldn't be much longer until the ceremony.

Isabel's breathing grew shallow as each passerby nodded to her and raised his or her glass with a pitying smile. She squinted at the windows high above her, imagining herself breaking through one of them.

"There you are. I've been looking for you." The sound of Dante's silky voice filled her ears. "Why is the beautiful princess sitting all by herself?"

When he appeared by her side, she flushed red. "Just reflecting."

"I think it's time to stop reflecting and start enjoying your night."

Dante held out his hand and waited for her to take it. As he led Isabel to the center of the ballroom, the spectators parted. Within moments she was in his arms, twirling on the spot. When Isabel looked into his eyes, her heart squeezed.

He seemed so gentle, yet firm.

"You dance very well, Isabel," Dante said. He leaned in to kiss Isabel's forehead. "I feel that no matter what problems our country encounters, you will solve them efficiently, and bring prosperity to all of Deran. I will forever envy that."

"I feel far from a leader. I am twenty-two, way past the age when a princess usually receives the armlet. It makes it so obvious that I am only here because my sister could not be. I am not believed in… other than by you and the castle guards," she replied, frowning. "Why would you believe in someone who has not accomplished anything? You single handedly took up leadership for the Tuuli at such a young age."

"It is never so easy, especially for me." A crooked smile crossed Dante's face. "But you, you are strong and powerful. You just do not realize it yet. And besides, I always liked you more than your sister."

Isabel's shoulders relaxed.

"If you ever need anything, I will be at your side in a heartbeat." A comfortable silence stretched around them. She squeezed Dante's hands. Now he was the one who was blushing.

The festivities continued until the food disappeared and bellies became full. Everyone danced to a tune or two, then began seating themselves. Dante escorted Isabel back to the platform where Hadi and Febe waited. Drumming her fingers against her knee, Isabel eyed her mother. A flutter formed in her stomach.

Her mother's left arm was bare, yet faint white lines

hinted at something that had been worn for years. The King bowed to his wife, who walked a few feet to a raised pillar which held the armlet. The golden armlet twisted like a snake and bore four stones: opal, sapphire, amber, and ruby. Each glowed to life at the touch of Febe's hand. When Isabel laid her eyes on the armlet, she sighed in wonder. The most valued treasure in all the land. The opal touched Isabel the deepest because it was the Tuuli's stone. Febe beckoned Isabel, breaking her from her thoughts. The princess stumbled as she approached her mother but quickly righted herself. They both stood in front of the entire audience, entranced by the magic of the moment.

"Opal, sapphire, amber, and ruby are but lifeless stones harvested from the earth to the naked eye. Mother Earth has blessed the land of Deran to produce these fine jewels and granted them mysterious powers. Symbols of peace and friendship, a piece of history is passed down from mother to daughter, from Queen to Princess, in this armlet containing these four stones."

Many in the crowd nodded and waited eagerly for her to continue.

"Let us not forget what happened two hundred years ago. My great grandmother, along with her betrothed arrived in Deran to witness a civil war among four tribes. All unknowingly, they emigrated here, chasing a myth about an island in the far east, isolated by vast oceans. It was believed that this mystical place harbored precious gems. But not just any gems. When held by someone truly connected with nature, it granted a power that amplified the elements he or she most deeply represented. The Tuuli, power of air. The Kai, water. The Dunya, earth. The Foti, fire."

Isabel caught Dante's eye. He nodded reassuringly as his hand traveled to the hilt of his sword where a large opal was embedded. It glistened in the light innocently, but Isabel knew that was the source of his elemental abilities.

"Myth transformed into reality. But, no discovery of the incredible goes without breeding greed and conflict. All were immigrants to this island. Some came to mine these mythical stones. Some came for freedom. But in the end, all were caught in the deceitful web of Damian and Echidna, an evil pair whose sole desire was power. As the war raged on, named *The Storm* in its infamy, my great grandmother and grandfather fought to end the bloodshed. Eventually they sealed Damian and Echidna in an underground prison, Cehennem, with the help of the tribal leaders' stones of power. In this hell, time does not pass for those who deserve eternal punishment. Certainly a punishment worse than death. They are the *Aeonians.*"

Febe paused for effect. Tribal elders shuddered, and little children gaped in awe.

"My great grandmother taught her daughter to preach peace, and the two traveled around Deran, weaving the threads of diplomacy so peace could blossom.

"They were successful in establishing a united government. The four tribes were provided a portion of the island to live on. The Queen and Princess called themselves Deranian, and they pledged to only intervene when the laws of peace were violated. They cherished the talismans in this armlet. Talismans that granted the Queen and Princess the power to harness the elements that represented each tribe.

This armlet also represented a pact that was made to prevent the misuse of powers from anyone ever again. It arrested the magical powers of all other stones if they were to fall into the hands of any citizen of Deran, except for the owner of the armlet, and the four tribal leaders.

"And so it has been established that every generation a female is born, she will be chosen to receive the armlet and be appointed successor to the kingdom. So I, Queen Febe of Deran, bestow my armlet to my Princess, Isabel, with a blessing of great love, wisdom, and faith."

Queen Febe solemnly kissed the armlet and slid it up Isabel's right arm. The cold metal warmed upon contact. The stones radiated brightly. The Queen embraced her, and the crowd erupted into applause.

Adem raised his claws as his scaly followers raised their glasses in unison. "To the continued reign of peace and prosperity!" Their roars shook the ground. The Foti dug their hind paws into the dirt as they glanced at them in irritation.

The Kai hopped around embracing one another, except Dover, whose eyes were fixed on the stage. The Tuuli, not used to being last, raised their glasses.

Flushing, Isabel was about to excuse herself when her mother cleared her throat.

"Is there anything you would like to say to your people?"

Sweat formed at the nape of her neck. Isabel laughed nervously as she surveyed the sea of eyes that were glued to her. The corset seemed to squeeze her even more tightly. "Yes. Um. Sorry. Thank you, everyone resting your trust in me."

I wonder how many of them are thinking 'We really trusted Victoria. But you will do.'

"I will do my best not to disappoint. I will shadow my mother's work and promise to visit each of your tribes more often. My goal is to keep this country safe and prosperous."

Dante was the first to break into applause. Isabel smiled gratefully as the rest of the room followed. Her parents clicked their glasses behind her.

"Everyone enjoy the rest of their night!" Hadi announced.

Relieved, Isabel bounded into the crowd, right for Dante.

"Congratulations!" He wrapped his arms around her waist.

"Thanks. I'm glad it's over."

"See? Everyone is happy for you."

"Maybe I shouldn't doubt myself so much," Isabel said. "Anyway, I probably should thank the other tribal chiefs."

Even though they would have preferred Victoria.

"Very well, then. Meet me when you are done."

Isabel wanted to stay by Dante's side, but for her first night with the armlet, she wanted to make a strong impression with Dover, Adem, and Hakan. Now that the armlet belonged to her, she was officially on the path to the crown. Stopping by a table, Isabel flagged a waiter.

"Wine, please."

He was back with a glass within minutes. Isabel swirled the glass over and over, staring into the dark red liquid. After a swig, she scanned the room. Wolf-like Hakan and Adem, the massive Dunya, were chatting out in the courtyard. She picked up her glass and made her way there.

"Victoria was much stronger."

She stopped a few feet away from them. Their heads were bowed close together.

"Isabel cannot handle such responsibility." Hakan's voice cut through the air more sharply than anyone else's. "There is a reason why all four tribes *elect* the bearer of the armlet. It would be better that it remains with Febe until we find an outsider—"

"Now, there is no need of saying this where she can *hear.*" Adem leaned in and nudged him with a scaly shoulder.

The pair blinked at Isabel, who bit her lip. She couldn't find any words. All the confidence she mustered was already shot down.

"This is why my people built our great fortress around Ogonia." Hakan paused, as if seeking for more ears to listen. "Because we can rely on no one for protection."

"Hakan!" Adem hissed.

"You ignorant reptile, what do you know?" Growling, Hakan got on all fours, as if ready to pounce.

Adem flicked his tongue. "What I know is that your temper matches your element *perfectly.*"

Dover hopped past Isabel and stepped in between them, waving his cane in warning. The two fell back without another word.

Tears welled in Isabel's eyes, but she held them back. She balled her hands into fists. It took all her strength to unhinge her jaw from its clenched state.

"Hakan. If you had a problem with me, then you should have addressed that before I received the armlet."

Before he could respond, she excused herself and made her way to her parents. Salty liquid fell onto her lips.

"Mother, may I be excused? For the night?"

When Febe did not answer, Isabel looked up. A frown was etched on her mother's face. It struck Isabel in an odd way. She suddenly seemed much older, skin hanging loosely from her frame from all the years of gravity taking a toll on her.

"Are you alright, my dear daughter?"

"Yes. Just not feeling well."

Her mother glanced at Hadi, who simply drummed his fingers on the armrest.

"Of course. Just say good bye to the tribal leaders—"

"I already did," Isabel blurted. She crossed her arms and looked away. Everyone in the room was chatting away, oblivious to her microscopic breakdown. And that was how she wanted it.

"Very well. Good night."

She turned around and skirted towards the southern part of the castle, past the receiving hall.

"Where do you think you're going?"

Panic clogged Isabel's throat. She turned and saw Dante, stone faced.

Did he see me crying?

Taking Isabel by the hand, he gently escorted her to the corner of the room. He turned his head both ways before leaning close to her. When he stroked her hand, Isabel's heart raced. The two moons cast a soft glow over them, and for a moment, it felt like they were the only ones in the room. They sat together in silence.

The moons must be at their peak. The party will end soon.

She opened her mouth, trying to find words. "I'm sorry that was I about to leave without saying goodbye—"

"I understand. This has been quite a night for you," he said.

Folding and unfolding her hands, Isabel scanned the room. "I hope you enjoyed yourself."

"It was wonderful. But it would've been better if I had gotten another dance out of you." Dante adjusted his silver robe and scooted closer to her.

"Please," she said, scoffing at his comment. "You're trying too hard to be charming."

As Dante twisted his opal ring, he winked. "Maybe."

Lief appeared at the corner of Isabel's eye. He chatted with Sachiel, who stood on his hind legs to admire his wings. When he fluttered them, Sachiel hopped up and down. The Kai elder's floppy ears waved about wildly, giving him a cartoonish look. Lief turned his head and spotted her giggling. Heat rose in her cheeks as he lowered his wings.

I hope he doesn't think I'm laughing at him.

Turning her attention back to Dante, Isabel said, "So, how has it been going with your 'wingless campaign?'"

"It's more popular than you think. Just take a look around you. The majority of the Tuuli here don't have them." Dante twisted his ring faster.

Isabel observed his sword. "So, is *that* how you do it?"

As Dante unsheathed it, the blade glowed white. Light pulsed from the opal, increasing its intensity as he swished the sword around. A few passersby stood and stared. One

Dunya crouched and rested his chin on a claw while a Foti crossed his orange-furred arms. Isabel swore he mumbled 'show off.' Tuuli that were nearby merely paused before carrying about their business.

"Yes," he said softly. "By simply tracing their backs, my stone of power can seal the wings away. All that's left... a simple tattoo."

"Does it hurt?"

"It didn't hurt me."

"Ah." Isabel recalled the first day she saw him wingless a couple of years ago. His back seemed so flat, so naked without those wings. She had been speechless for one painfully long minute.

"Of course, it is still in its voluntary phase. I plan on making it mandatory, but Lief objects."

Her eyes bounced back to Lief who was approaching them. "Obviously."

"Excuse me, Princess," Lief said with a polite smile. Turning to Dante, his smile faded. "I'm afraid it's getting late. I advise that we take our leave."

"I agree. Please make the announcement. Let me say my good-byes to the Princess," Dante said. He put his sword away with an assertive click.

"As you wish."

Isabel bit her lip, watching Lief float towards Hadi and Febe. "I feel so bad. I hope he didn't think I was laughing at him. It was Sachiel, really—"

Dante held a finger to her lips. "It's time for me to leave. I had meant to give this to you earlier, but I feel like now is more appropriate. I hope that I may see you again soon.

THE AEONIANS • 45

Now, let me say farewell to your parents." Dante placed a hard substance incased in a cloth pouch in her hands, then kissed her forehead and backed away. He waved to his people, who gathered at the entrance.

Everyone strained to catch a glimpse of Isabel. Warm smiles painted many of their faces. Isabel waved at them, and they bowed in return. After exchanging words with her parents, Dante joined his people. Before he disappeared into the crowd, he turned to her and mouthed the words, 'I believe in you.'

The Tuuli marched out, bottle-necking at the front door. A handful of wings stuck out of the crowd. Even from a distance, they glistened as if a perpetual light shone on them.

Isabel gratefully retired to her boudoir. Her servants had already drawn a warm bath. After excusing them, she slipped into the welcoming waters. She sank her body as deep as she could, leaving only her eyes and nose exposed. Her tense muscles relaxed. Her thoughts slowed. Yet, the weight of the armlet made its presence consistently known.

The gold was brilliant, but not as much as the four talismans that decorated the armlet. The four tribes had surrendered their most powerful stones ever mined. Dante, Dover, Adem, and Haken did not possess anything close to this. The amount of trust for her to wield this power, however, did not reflect the attitudes she witnessed today.

Controlling the elements. Seems like some wild tale.

When Isabel lifted her left arm out of the water and twirled her finger, the sapphire on her armlet glowed softly. The water she sat in sloshed around, imitating the direction of her action. She flicked her index finger from her thumb, and tiny spouts of water shot up into the air. Isabel giggled in childish amusement. After sitting up, she used the same finger to draw a heart on the surface of the bath water. Lifting both hands, up came a liquid silhouette of a heart.

"Dante. If I were to have a King, I would marry him in a heartbeat. Oh! His gift. I wonder what it is!"

She sprung from the tub, wiped herself clean, and jumped into her nightgown. Isabel fell into bed and observed the satchel that sat by her door. She hummed and squinted her eyes. The opal now flickered to life. A soft wind, from a source undeterminable, pushed the satchel up and into her hands.

"Extraordinary…"

When Isabel opened the bag, she gasped in delight. Inside were a handful of pure white crystals, mined in the hills of Buryan. She touched their smooth yet chalky exterior. They caused pleasant dreams for those who slept near them. Isabel squealed and held the crystals near her heart.

That night she dreamt of Dante.

CHAPTER

4

Bence lay his weapons on the ground. There were two daggers and a broadsword. After a second of staring at them, he tapped the handle of the sword so it would line up parallel to the daggers. He scowled at the fingerprints smudges all over the blade.

'The monsters are outside. The monsters are outside waiting to kill you and your family.'

All his life, the shadows of Cehennem had polluted his mind with those two phrases. They filled his dreams with the people who lived beyond the prison, bodies warped and thirsting for his blood. He adjusted his shin guards methodically, allowing no room for the haunting words to enter his mind again. They mean nothing to him now because he was standing, free from imprisonment and ready to face his enemies. These monsters.

"Bence." A baritone voice rumbled nearby.

He tucked his daggers back into place, one into a pocket on his boot and the other onto his belt. Before he sheathed his longword, he took the edge of his cloak and wiped it carefully. When he was done, Bence approached his father.

"Look at the land before you. None of the inhabitants know that the balance of this island will be overturned soon by our hands." His father lowered his hood, revealing a hawkish nose and weathered skin. A headpiece rested on his hairline, but the setting was empty.

"I am honored to work as your right hand."

Brushing his blood orange hair from his eyes, Bence took a deep breath. Ice cold air funneled through his nose and filled his lungs. He surveyed the rolling plains around him. The environment was new to him. Trees with knotted branches were scattered about, and their golden leaves rustled in unison. The Castle of Deran was a mere dot in the distance.

"You were first from the womb by a matter of minutes. Your wit matches mine, and your skills exceed your siblings'. I am proud for you to lead my army."

Bence glanced at his brothers and sisters, standing in a wedge formation, clad in dark violet armor. Not an inch out of place. Grotesque creatures were littered among his human siblings, bearing clubs and grinning viciously. Everyone bore the same mark on their body: four vertical lines, with a fifth line striking the other four horizontally.

His mother approached them. Raven hair peeked from her hood and cascaded down to her hips. She crossed her arms, exposing a tattoo of a lion's paw on her right forearm. Various hemp bracelets clung to both her wrists, and a lone ring sat on her left ring finger. After taking a second to admire her reflection on the ring's large amethyst, her lips curled. "Damian. It is time."

Damian embraced his wife. "Yes, Echidna. We have

been imprisoned in this hell for far too long. And the fruits of our labor, they have grown up to be formidable warriors."

"They sure have. Once we achieve victory, I'm sure we can salvage your amethyst talisman."

"With the powers of the armlet, I will have no need for it."

"Let's move forth! Bence, my son, are you ready?" Echidna's shrill voice rang out, directing her pointy nose past her husband.

"Yes, mother." He turned his square, dark face toward the army behind him. "Brothers, sisters, and the Veijari. It's time to leave Cehennem in the past! I need not make a speech of motivation, as our nightmares are motivation enough. We will storm the castle and reclaim the land of Deran, the land Damian and Echidna spilled blood for two centuries ago! History's wheel of fate now turns in the Aeonian's favor!"

The crowd roared. The Veijari, traitors of the Tuuli, Kai, Dunya, and Foti from the Battle of The Storm, stomped their feet, while the sons and daughters of Damian and Echidna raised their hands in the air.

When Bence beckoned the Dunyan Veijari to the front lines, the earth beneath his feet shuddered. They towered over the tallest tree. Rearing their heads, they gnashed their jaws. Scales were chipped from their hides at places where their piercings were ripped out.

Nodding in approval, Bence directed them to his side. He brushed his hair from his emerald eyes and pointed his finger towards the castle entrance.

"Charge!"

CHAPTER

5

Princess Isabel snapped awake, gasping for breath. Her eyes darted back and forth as they adjusted to the darkness. When she ran her hand through her chestnut hair, crumbled bits of wall gathered at her fingertips. The castle's foundation shuddered, tossing Isabel from her mattress. Landing on her shoulder, she cursed through gritted teeth. The walls swayed, sending the contents within her stomach sloshing around.

Deran never has earthquakes. Something's wrong.

Isabel reached for her lantern on her bed stand. She blindly felt for matches.

Wait. I don't need matches anymore. Here goes nothing.

When she finished her thought, the golden armlet warmed her skin. The ruby glowed to life. Sparks flew from her fingertips when she snapped. She tried again, trying to ignore the increasing magnitude of the quake.

Come on. Focus.

With another snap, a small flame danced on her index finger. Breathing a sigh of relief, she lit the lantern and scurried towards her door. Her hurried footsteps echoed down the stone hallway. Anxiety boiled in her chest as thoughts raced through her mind. The earth had come to life like some dark omen. It was as if she angered the heavens when she received the armlet.

A deafening explosion roared from what seemed to be the entrance. Shouts erupted, both male and female. Isabel broke into a sprint. "Mother?" she shouted, "Father?" When she reached the spiral stairwell, she crashed into someone with a petite frame.

Looking up, Isabel cried. "Oh, mother! You are safe. This can't be an earthquake, can it?"

Queen Febe steadied herself against the wooden railing and furrowed her brows. Gray strands escaped from her loose bun. "Honey, I was about to check in on you. Are you wearing the armlet?"

"Uh, yes," she replied, tracing the object with her opposite hand. Isabel stared at her mother's vacant arm.

"Good," she replied as she lifted the hem of her satin night gown from the floor. "We need to find your father."

"He's not with you?"

The castle rumbled once more. Febe lost her balance, but Isabel reached out and snatched her mother's hand with lightning speed.

Pursing her lips, Febe said, "No. I bet he was at the chapel."

Without another word, Isabel followed her mother down the stairs. The closer she approached the first floor, the more oppressive the air grew. An arrow zipped by Isabel, tip aflame. It pierced a deer head mounted on the wall.

"Gracious, what on earth?" Febe shrieked, pulling her back a few feet.

Isabel scanned the room for the assailant. Her mouth hung askew as she surveyed the foyer. The chandelier had crashed onto the floor. The flames from the candles licked the carpet. Tapestries were ripped from their places and strewn about. Shelves that contained her father's prized hunting trophies lay face down.

Someone screamed to her left. Howling erupted to her right. She couldn't identify the archer. But when she focused straight ahead, where the entrance stood hundreds of feet away, Isabel froze. A lump formed in her throat at scores of bodies clad in armor bearing the crest of the royal family, the Phoenix.

"We're being attacked," she uttered. "But by whom?"

Isabel noticed a gaping hole through the top corner of the door, wondering if that was where the invaders entered. She rushed closer, but a rattling noise stopped Isabel in her tracks. Something clawed its way up. Grunting, panting, something was hungry to join the bloodshed.

A hand tugged at her sleeve. Jumping, Isabel jerked her head around. Her father, King Hadi looked her dead in the eye. His chest heaved, desperate for air. His face dripped with sweat.

"Isabel," he exclaimed. "I'm so glad I found you both."

"What's going on?" Isabel stuttered. Her body trembled, unable to control the spread of fear.

King Hadi struck the sword against the ground. "I don't

know." He turned to Febe. "I was praying to our ancestors when I felt the first quake. By the time I made my way out here, chaos had erupted throughout the castle. The only soldiers I have run into were dead ones! The watchtower had collapsed. I have yet to encounter any foes. None of this makes any sense!" His baritone voice rumbled with frustration.

The creature rammed against the door, but the tiny hole did not allow its entrance.

"We should head back to the chapel. We will use the back door leading to a private garden," he said.

"What about everyone else?" Isabel replied.

"My family is priority. And you possess the armlet. No one must get their hands on it!" he bellowed.

Isabel's heart raced as he finished his last sentence. Febe urged her to move, but her feet weighed down like stone. Struggling to lift each leg, she followed her parents to the other side of the foyer. She swerved around the smattering of glass and porcelain. Large mahogany doors that stretched to the ceiling greeted her. It creaked as Hadi kicked it open. A marble corridor with an arched ceiling greeted them. Picture frames littered the floor. Lamps on the walls flickered. When Isabel closed the door behind her, everything fell eerily quiet. Her father led the way, keeping one hand out in front of them and the other on the pommel of his sword.

"Hadi. Who would attack us? The four tribes surround us. We would have been notified of an invasion!" Febe exclaimed.

He towered over his petite wife, but struggled to respond. His hazel eyes shined with dread. His broad shoulders slumped forward as he clenched his jaw. "The only conclusion is an attack from within."

Isabel narrowed her eyes. "But father. We are in a state of peace—"

When they neared a corner, her father held out a hand. "Wait here," he whispered as he disappeared with a flick of his floor-length robe. After a second he called, "The path's clear."

Isabel and her mother didn't waste any time in following after him down the deserted hallway.

"Why haven't we run into our intruders yet? They seemed to do a good job destroying the main hall, so they have to be inside somewhere," Isabel said.

A chill shot up her spine as her father gripped her shoulder. He lifted his fingers to his lips. "Whoever *they* are… they are after us. They are after your armlet. Doesn't matter where they are now. What matters is that we escape unnoticed."

Isabel held her breath when she spotted the chapel at the end of the corridor. The entrance was already broken. As her fingers grazed the armlet, goose bumps erupted on her skin.

Febe ran past her to pry the splintered door open. Stained glass windows were shattered. Nine porcelain urns lay broken on the floor. As Febe drew her breath, Hadi lunged to stifle her screams. Numbness consumed Isabel. She refused to believe the sight before her. The dust of her ancestors and her sister, Victoria, were scattered about, mixing in with the dirt of the earth.

A loud bang interrupted the moment of mourning. Isabel

turned towards the chapel entrance. Soldiers clad in chain-mail stood before her, swords drawn. One removed his helmet, revealing a man with disheveled white hair.

"Benjamin!" Isabel cried as relief washed over her.

"Report! What is going on?" Hadi's hands fell to his knees as his breath grew labored.

"We were attacked from multiple parts of the castle at once. Beasts, twisted, corrupt versions of the tribes but twice their size, beat through us like wooden pawns. We have yet to find their leader, but they are moving quickly."

"How many soldiers are left?" Isabel asked.

Benjamin gripped the pommel of his sword, agitated. "It is just me... these two men, and probably no more than a dozen other soldiers who have scattered to various parts of the castle looking for you!"

The room went silent as everyone looked toward the door leading to the private garden. One soldier sprinted to the exit, poked his head through the door, and the second solider retreated a few steps to check the hallway. After signaling with his two men, Benjamin nodded.

"Go!"

Isabel gave one last look at the urn that once contained her sister's ashes, and then followed everyone towards the exit. When she rounded the last pew, she tripped over an object and crashed onto the ground. Lights exploded from her eyes as she wrapped her hands over her head.

"Princess. Princess! Are you okay? Get up! Hurry!" Benjamin's voice echoed through her ears. Vertigo consumed her and she emptied the contents of the night's feast from her stomach.

"Fine," she hacked.

His arm hooked around hers, pulling her up. Everything was blurry. Isabel blinked until her eyes could focus.

"Isabel! Isabel! I need you to focus. I need you steady on your feet!"

She shook her head and nodded. When he released his grip, she wobbled, but managed to follow behind at a steady pace. Noticing her mother and father were already out the door, she broke into a sprint.

CHAPTER

6

Lightning illuminated the sky. Thunder drowned out various battle cries echoing from the dying castle. The garden was long, but Isabel knew there was a walkway at the end that led to the castle gates. However, her lungs burned, and she slowed down.

The world around her swirled like paint on canvas. When she stumbled over a rosebush, she cursed as the thorns scratched her. Getting back up, she continued with a slight limp. Her gown tore with each step. The night's chill swirled up her legs, invigorating her as she pushed thoughts of pain out of her mind.

Shouting erupted somewhere from behind. Her heels dug into the mud, and Isabel fell. After pushing herself up, she looked around. A ball of fire in the distance caught her attention. The light inched towards her until she could see her father, kneeling on the ground next to her mother. The ball of light was actually a torch, held by a giant reptilian beast.

It looked like a member of the Dunyan tribe, and yet, something looked off…

It towered over them, a wild toothless grin forming on its face. In place of opulent earrings were grotesque scars. As the monster dropped the torch, a fire ignited in a ring around the royal company.

It looks like a Veijari. But those were traitors from The Storm. There's no way they'd still be alive.

Benjamin lunged at the giant and with a swing of his sword, he ripped into its flesh. He slashed and stabbed until the beast's rocky tail knocked him to the ground. The creature hovered over Benjamin and unhinged its jaws while emitting an unholy cry. Benjamin flipped onto his stomach and drove his sword into its foot. The creature stumbled backwards and into the flames. He let out a whoop as fire consumed its body.

With a sigh of relief, Isabel approached her parents. By the time she reached them, she gasped as if the air was sucked out of her lungs. Four dark figures on horses leapt over the flames. The ground trembled as the hooves made contact. The figures, three men and one woman, eyed Isabel with a familiarity that confused her.

"Should I know you?" Isabel said in a clipped voice.

Hadi drew his sword, appearing by her side. "Damian! Echidna! It cannot be."

Isabel eyed the older man and woman in disbelief. The man her father called Damian was burly, muscles so large as if ready to burst from his clothing. His hair was like fire, blowing in the wind as his black eyes bore down at her. Echidna, too, looked down at her from her pointed nose.

Her thin eyebrows pinched together as her purple lips curled.

I don't understand. They are supposed to be a legend. They look like they have not aged a day.

The two other men were much younger. One had a leaner build and blue eyes. He slouched forward, smiling maliciously while fondling the silver hilt of his sword. The other sat up straight as if a plank was tied to his back. His emerald eyes observed her with deep curiosity. When Isabel spotted gold on the hilt of his sword, she knew he must be first in command.

"Hello, Princess." The green-eyed youth exaggerated a bow.

"And who might you be?" Isabel exclaimed, eyeing him up and down.

"Never mind me. I would like to formally introduce you to my parents. I'm sure you have heard of them before. I believe they are quite a legend among the creatures that inhabit this island. Even two hundred years later, your royal folk tell and re-tell their story. I must say, I feel honored."

"You?" Hadi snarled, turning to Damian. "*You* produced children while you were imprisoned? You disgusting pig—"

"And my name is Bence," barked the young soldier, ignoring Hadi. Observing him closely, Isabel could tell without a doubt he was their son. He shared his mother's olive skin and stocky build from his father.

"Beside me is one of my brothers. Twin, actually. A lethal warrior. I am here with him and the rest of my brothers and my sisters and the Veijari to destroy you. Your family. Anyone that poses a threat to us." He pointed his finger at

Isabel. "And that armlet belongs to my mother and father!" He dismounted and cracked his neck. Benjamin and his two men charged at him, but with a snap of his fingers, he flung daggers that struck the three soldiers square in the chest. The daggers glowed a strange purple as they dug past the chain-mail and into their flesh.

Blood curdling screams filled the air. Isabel crawled towards Benjamin, who writhed in agony. He arched his back and groaned. The purple glow faded. When his eyes met Isabel's, he gripped the handle, and yanked the dagger out.

"Maybe all your training had prepared you for this moment." As he tossed the dagger her way, Benjamin broke into a hacking cough. His body seized for a few seconds, then went still.

When her hand flew towards the weapon, a boot slammed down on her wrist. Isabel screamed as searing heat shot up her arm like streaks of lightning. Her fingers wriggled, but she was still inches away from the dagger. Bence stared down at her, shaking his head. He kicked it away.

"Tsk-tsk."

Isabel froze, choking on her own fear, forgetting she had the power of the royal armlet now. Her mother's faint groaning brought her back to reality.

Raising her other arm, she attempted to push her opponent away with a blast of violent winds. But the effort died as the pain in her side grew.

Air.

If only she could focus, she would send a torrential downpour and drown him.

Water.

If only she could focus, she could open up the ground below him, and send him into the bowels of the earth.

Earth.

If only she could focus, she could burn that smug villain. Engulf him in flames.

Fire.

But without precise concentration, Isabel might also incinerate her family, bury them, or wash them away never again to be seen. There was no practice, there was no test run. Isabel realized she was given something she did not even know how to control. And now death was staring her in the face.

"It's too bad. You're so pretty," Bence whispered into Isabel's ear, pushing her down into the mud. Then, without a moment's pause, he drew his sword and struck down. Instead of meeting skin, the loud clang of Hadi's sword greeted his own.

Her father pushed against the young warrior. "You shall not harm my daughter!"

Bence's gaze flickered over to his parents, and they nodded before his gaze returned to Hadi. A wicked grin spread across his face. "As you wish, my lord."

In one swift movement, he kicked Hadi's arm, forcing him to release his weapon. The hilt of Bence's sword came down on the back of the king's skull with a sickening crunch. Isabel's mouth fell open in horror, unable to form words as her father fell to the ground in a motionless heap.

Bence took the bow that had been slung across his back and drew a black feather arrow, taking aim at the fallen king. "No!" Isabel tried to push herself up, but collapsed to the muddy ground as energy drained from her limbs.

This can't be happening. I have to stop him.

Bence lowered his bow and leaned over. He took her chin in his hand, grinning. "Don't worry, princess, you'll have your turn." Isabel spat at his face, hitting his cheek. Rage burned within. Never had she longed to kill, but this man... he would die. She would make sure of that.

As he wiped his cheek, Bence chuckled and raised his bow once again. "I like your spirit, but it won't save you. Or your parents."

Echidna's voice erupted in the darkness, shrill and laced with lunacy. "Kill them. Kill them all!"

"I know *that*," he muttered. When Bence turned towards Hadi, he drew an arrow and breathed deeply.

Two arrows flew in quick succession. An arrow struck the king's lifeless form in the back while the second pierced the Queen's chest.

"No!" Isabel screamed until she was hoarse. Her whole body shook as if she were electrified. Her tears mixed with the rain. An unspoken sorrow flooded her soul as she watched the light flicker from her mother's eyes.

"Farid, what the *hell* are you doing?" Bence's voice bellowed.

Isabel tore her eyes from her parents for a split second, glancing first at Bence, then at his brother. Bence's arrow was still drawn.

"You hesitated, brother," Farid exclaimed. He pumped his bow in the air. "I know how to get things done quickly."

"You pompous brat! I was simply taking aim, and you feel like you could steal my thunder?" Bence spat. With a growl, he faced Isabel. "Farid, I will deal with you later."

Desperation clawed within Isabel, like a wild animal trying to escape.

How can all this be happening?

Her body went numb.

How?

Drawing his arrow once more, Bence clenched his jaw. He blinked through the rain drops that fell onto his lashes.

"Good bye, Princess."

Everything went dark.

CHAPTER

7

The Princess' body crumpled like a paper doll. But Bence still had his arrow drawn. Blinking in shock, he rotated on the spot to find his twin slinging his bow over his shoulder with a smug grin slapped over his pale face.

"You," Bence said with a low growl.

"Me? What about me?" Farid said. He extended his arms as if gesturing to an audience.

Bence ripped his cloak off in frustration. He flung it over his horse. "Isabel was mine!"

"The lives of the royal family belong to those who work swiftly," Farid said. He snickered and turned to his parents, "Right?"

"Enough," Damian bellowed. His voice rumbled louder than the thunder. He dismounted his horse and made his way next to Bence. Echidna followed suit.

Bence stared down at the Princess, waiting for his parents' next command.

"That was too easy," Echidna squealed as she tapped her nails together. The beads on her hemp bracelets clacked with glee. "Son, you have no idea how long your father and I waited for this moment."

Damian knelt over the Princess and observed her. Turning her on the other side, he nodded at the sight of the armlet. "Bence, I commend you for leading the army into a successful invasion. And Farid for neutralizing the threats." Bence crossed his arms. Ignoring the rain soaking through the crevices of his leather armor, his irritation towards his over-achieving twin had taken the form of a massive headache. His head continued to throb as Farid squawked his usual self-praise.

"Well?" Bence cleared his throat. He drew a dagger and stared at the glistening metal. He rubbed his forearm against a smudge he found. When satisfied, he extended it to his father. "We are here to take back these talismans?"

Damian exposed his yellow teeth through cracked lips. "Their power is key to getting my amethyst and dissolving Cehennem once and for all. And from there—" His eyes lit up, "—the possibilities…" He took Bence's dagger and focused on the first stone: a glistening opal.

As soon as the tip of the blade found a groove in between the stone and setting, a white light flashed from the armlet. An ear-splitting ringing erupted from the armlet as the earth shook. Damian fell back as the opal rocketed into the sky, leaving nothing but a blinding streak behind it. The opal circled in and out of the clouds three times before disappearing west.

Shock stung Bence like a slap in the face. "What the

hell—"

Before he could finish his sentence, the sapphire, amber, and ruby ejected from the armlet and zipped through the skies in various directions.

His mouth fell askew. Silence blanketed the area, minus the *pitter patter* of rain. Avoiding his father's gaze, Bence fixed his eyes on the now barren armlet.

CHAPTER

8

Dante lay in bed, stripped of his celebratory garments, gazing up at the ceiling. Waning in and out of sleep, he was restless from the ceremony at Deran Castle today. His stomach fluttered. Isabel looked nothing short of stunning.

He remembered the day he met her. It was years ago, yet the memory still made him blush.

"Whatcha got there?" A timid voice had snagged his attention.

It's the princess!

He nearly dropped a large wart-covered toad from his hands.

"Please, Victoria. Princess Victoria. Do not tell the elders, or Vindur—"

The girl in front of him frowned. She jammed her hands

at her hips, wrinkling her gown. Strands of brunette hair fell from her bun and danced around her shoulders, and her shoes were caked in mud. The only elegance about her was an opal necklace and matching ring that seemed too big for her.

"I am not Victoria. There are *two* princesses you know!" She folded her arms.

Dante straightened up. "Oh, right! Then you are—"

"Isabel!" She huffed and silently drew lines in the dirt with her toe.

"I have a toad. I found it." He held it out for inspection.

Her mouth fell open. "Wow!" She waved her hands into the air, uncharacteristic of royalty. Isabel squealed in delight as she seized the toad. "So, what were you supposed to be doing?"

"Fetching some water from the mill. For Vindur." Every syllable was difficult to utter. Dante never had direct contact with the princesses, King, or Queen before. His hands were sweating. Dante rubbed his palms against his tunic, smearing dirt all over the once white fabric.

"That is your leader, right? My father and mother are meeting with him today." Isabel's eyes grew bigger, gripping the struggling toad tighter.

"Yup." Dante grabbed the pails of water as if the chore became urgent.

"Well, you cannot go in there looking like that!"

Isabel dropped the toad and lifted her dress suddenly. He gasped and dropped the pails to cover his eyes. After a moment of silence, he peeked through his fingers. She dipped the hem of her gown into a pail. Cool water touched his face.

"I-I am just a servant. You are a *princess*!"

"Nonsense." She pushed his cheek the other way as she scrubbed.

When the sound of other feet stomped against the ground, Dante looked up and saw another young girl in a similar dress as Isabel. While Isabel's blue gown was wrinkled and now stained with mud, this girl's pink dress looked flawless.

Victoria.

Dante and Victoria's eyes locked. She did not blink, and her lips were a flat line. He could not tell if she was impatient, angry, or intrigued. He nudged Isabel, and inclined his head towards Victoria.

"S-sis!"

"What are you doing?" Victoria asked, still emotionless.

Picking up the toad, Isabel held out her new gift.

Victoria's face contorted to disgust. "Put that down. It has germs!"

Dante's eyes fell to his feet, flinching at her high-pitched voice.

"If you do not clean yourself up, Isabel, I am going to tell Papa and Mama!"

"But sis, what harm is it?"

Victoria held her ground. "You should be in the chateau attending the meeting. If you want *any* chance at being the chosen one for the armlet—"

"Aw, you're gonna get it anyway. I will probably be a nun or something!" Isabel growled.

When she did not respond, Isabel shoved the toad in

Dante's hands and stormed off. He dropped the toad as Victoria approached him. His hands shook as he grasped the pails once more.

"I am on my way, Princess Victoria."

"You know that if you work hard, you can lead the Tuuli when you grow up," she said.

"Excuse me, Princess?" Dante's face grew hot, suddenly uncomfortable. "I am not immediate family to Vindur, so that would be impossible."

"My papa and mama told me if you work hard, anything is possible," she said. "Vindur has no children. Maybe when you grow up, you can be my prince!"

Victoria leaned forward. She was so close, he could see his reflection in her fierce blue eyes. Victoria curtsied and ran off after her sister. Dante, the little dirty servant boy, stood there, forgetting all about his chore.

Dante rolled over in his bed to dispel his memory. He had followed the nine-year-old Victoria's wise advice, accompanying Vindur in his travels around the island and attending diplomatic meetings. Dante became refined, cultured. When his servant father died, Vindur accepted him like a son he never had.

Closing his eyes, fragments of another memory seeped into his mind. He couldn't shake the thoughts of Isabel and Victoria.

Dante strolled idly in one of the Deran castle courtyards, filled with open space and shrubs that lined the circular wall. A marble statue of a regal couple stood in the center. Dante always believed it was of the first king and queen. His attention shifted to a slim figure leaning against a stone archway.

"Dante!" Victoria gasped, approaching him. Her peridot necklace and ring glistened in the sun like dewdrops on shrub leaves. She paused near the statue and buried her nose in a white rose. It paled against her porcelain complexion. "You have come to visit me!" Her lips twisted into a smile.

Dante's eyes roamed the courtyard. With no one else around, he nodded and accepted her embrace.

"You look so regal," she cooed, tugging at his collar. Dante grew hot, despite the brisk autumn day. "And to think you took over leadership of the Tuuli. Just as I predicted! You know, I will be coming of age soon, and I think it would be fitting that you and I wed."

His mouth hung open as he struggled to find something to say. "You are an ambitious woman."

"When I know what I want, I take it."

"That is to be admired. Let's wait for your armlet ceremony in a year or so, and move from there," Dante said, running his hand through his hair. He stumbled on a cobblestone and caught his hand on the cool castle walls.

"Do you think I am pretty?" Victoria asked as she studied her nails.

"Of course," Dante answered.

"Do you think I am prettier than Isabel?" She leaned closer to him.

"I don't think that is a fair question," Dante gulped, eyes

darting around, looking for a way out.

A glimmer of blue appeared at the corner of his eye. It was Isabel. He sighed with relief and ambled towards her, freeing himself from Victoria's cornering attack.

"Princess Isabel! You look ravishing in that dress. It captures the beauty of the sky."

She gave him a tight hug. "Just Isabel, please."

"Of course," Dante nodded.

"Are you done meeting with my parents?" Isabel waved at her sister in greeting. Victoria nodded, without taking her eyes off him.

"Yes, we just had a little talk about the Tuuli's souring relationship with the Foti. It seems Hakan is as stubborn as ever and will not reconsider a treaty to build an irrigation system from the Golden Falls."

"Ah! So young men can stop toiling at the mill!" She nudged Dante with her elbow.

He smirked. "And I would know personally."

"Well, if you're done smelling the roses, Dante, will you join me at Lake Hama to throw some stones?"

"I would love to."

"Great," Isabel piped. "I am going to change out of this dreadful dress. Meet you there in a few minutes!" She punched his arm and ran off.

Dante swayed in place, smiling. He turned to Victoria and bowed. As he turned to walk out of the castle, he heard her voice, cool and calm.

"Isabel will not get you the *crown*."

Dante didn't think about that. He ran almost the whole mile to Lake Hama. Golden leaves swirled about him. His breath curled into the air. He stopped short of the lake and tore his shoes off. Dipping his feet into the icy waters, he shuddered with delight. *Victoria would never do something like this.*

"Dante!"

Isabel plowed into his back. He teetered towards the water, but she pulled him back. They both lost balance and toppled onto the sand, bursting into laughter.

"Thanks so much for coming out with me. It was getting dreadfully dull inside." Isabel sighed.

"No problem."

He sat in silence for a beat, listening to the lap of water a few feet away.

"What did Victoria talk to you about?" She twirled her finger in the sand.

Dante bit his cheek. "Uh, nothing."

Isabel screwed up her lips, tilted her head, and regarded Dante down the length of her nose.

"Okay, she was making another pass at me."

"As I expected." Isabel snorted.

"She bribed me with the crown." He turned to face Isabel, expecting laughter, but only encountered silence. "What's wrong?"

"Well, maybe you should be with her then. She has more to offer. You have gone from servant to tribal leader. Now, you have a shot at the crown!" Isabel's voice faltered. "I cannot offer you more than a few crass jokes."

"I know it may scare you, but my goal is not to be like previous Tuuli leaders. I want to be the first to say enough is enough."

Isabel stared at him blankly.

"We migrated here for the sole purpose to mine the stones of power. The Dunya escaped slavery and the Kai — religious persecution—"

"—the Foti came here to claim more land for themselves. What did they say? To better themselves and prove to humans that they were not animals." Isabel smiled as she finished her sentence.

They broke into laughter.

"We jest, but I mean it. Vindur is a great man, but he is a bit imperialistic and most of all, I want to show you that I wish to be with the girl who has my heart, not the keys to power."

Dante spoke no more, but moved his hand over hers. And they lay on the sand until the sun fell.

Dante awoke with a smile.

Looks like you can offer more than a few crass jokes now.

His smile faded. His face grew dark. The events that had followed were anything but pleasant. Dante shook his head. He did not want to remember anything else.

The morning sun streamed through the window and washed over his bed. He wondered how Isabel was feeling, certain that she would be scared and perhaps grumpy. She grew up knowing the armlet was meant for Victoria.

Dante threw his feet on the ground, his toes cooling at the touch of the slate floor. He stretched his arms up high, drawing in the cool air. As he exhaled, he focused on the sound of his breath.

Catching his reflection in a mirror on the opposite wall, Dante ran his hands through his hair. It had been a dirty blonde all his life, unlike the rest of his peers who had perfect platinum locks — a signature mark of the Tuuli. He couldn't figure why he looked different, and he certainly didn't think it mattered.

'Dirty.'

Shaking his head, Dante looked away. That was the word he had heard whispering around him as a boy. Maybe it had something to do with his unceremonious birth. He glanced back at the mirror, then at the portrait besides it.

An oil painting of a woman filled the frame. Her luscious locks curled around her plump face, and her wings were specked with dew drops. Ice blue eyes popped above her rosy cheeks. A hand draped across her chest.

Dante walked up to the painting and traced his fingers along the woman's face. He wasn't one-hundred percent sure what his mother looked like, but he did his best with the details he gathered. His heart ached to meet her.

Why did she have to die on the boat?

Dante had been told it was right after she gave birth to him, on route to Deran from her home country of Waaken. He was born with no status, no real home. "But, I'm climbing my way up, mother. You'll be proud," Dante murmured and turned around. Walking to his shelf, he picked through his clothes.

I have to start planning my day. Maybe with a walk to Buryan Temple. Or draft another proposal for the irrigation system that Hakan continues to deny.

Pounding at the door snapped him from his trance. He opened the door. His servant, Aysu, hopped up and down in a fury, tears streaming down her face.

"What? *What?*" he begged.

"We are under attack!" she coughed before collapsing to her knees.

Dante pulled her up before tearing through the hallway and down the stairs. The Tuuli elders stared up at him from the bottom floor like lost sheep. The ground began to shake.

"Do we know who? Do we know what country…"

Lief stepped forward, resting his hands in his sleeves. "The attack did not come from shore. Word is they come from within the island!"

"That is insane." Dante continued to the main door and ripped it open, shaking away those that tried to restrain him. Heart sinking, he surveyed the area. Arrows flew in all directions. His people filled the narrow cobble stone streets, seeking cover. Many thatched roofs of Tuuli cottages were aflame.

"Take cover here!" Dante shouted to a family of four that veered towards the gates of his manor.

I have to get my horse and get out there.

The family was a hundred feet from Dante when the father flew forward, a spear protruding from his back. His wife screamed and covered her two children's' eyes. Dante sprinted to them.

"You've got to get indoors. Hurry!"

As he pushed them towards his manor, Dante noticed gash marks all over the mother's legs. Blood poured liberally from her wounds. Her son, who was no more than six years old, clung to them. He wailed as his arms were painted red.

"Lief. Help! Bring the children indoors!"

When the elder flexed his wings, he sprung towards the children with lightning speed. "There is still use for these wings."

Dante grunted. "Just hurry. I have the mother."

As Lief gathered a child in each arm, he looked past Dante's shoulder. His eyes widened in horror.

"Lief. What are you doing? Don't stop!" Dante yelled, his voice growing raw. "I got this."

Lief flew back to the manor as Dante reached for his sword. He gazed into the mother's eyes and said, "I'll protect you. I won't let you die." Dante drew his sword and whirled around. The opal stone on his weapon flashed, and the air whipped around them.

A young woman draped in a violet tunic charged at them. Human. But unlike any Deranian he had ever seen. As she approached, he noticed scars beneath her sunken eyes. She was more solidly built than him; her body pure muscle. Her tangled hair flew about in the wind.

"Who are you?" Dante shouted.

The woman didn't stop. She reached for another spear strapped on her back and licked her lips. Pushing against the wind-barrier Dante created, she was only a few feet away.

"I'm warning you!"

She broke into shrieking laughter and aimed for the mother on the ground.

Dante hurled his sword, commanding the wind to thrust the blade forward with the strength of a hurricane. As the massive woman released the spear, Dante's sword slammed into her chest. The metal disappeared into her flesh, and blood exploded from her back. Her body flopped onto the ground.

Kicking the woman onto her side, Dante knelt to observe her face. "Who are you?"

All he could hear was the sound of the mother's moan behind him. Dante's blood boiled as he shook the warrior again. "I don't have time for games."

Coughing, the warrior flashed her gray eyes at the sword in her chest. She released a cackle as her fingers made their way to its hilt.

"You—" she hacked, "—you will need this."

Without another word, she yanked the blade from her body. The force of the wind tore her body apart, and blood splattered everywhere — on the ground, on Dante's clothes, and on his face.

What kind of cruel—

Dante turned over and retched. Bile escaped his throat and hit the dirt with a hiss. Catching his breath, he grasped his sword and wobbled onto his feet.

I have to get that mother… to safety.

When Dante looked up, a tall man on horseback thundered towards him, brandishing a broadsword. His black cloak whipped about.

There is something familiar about that blood orange hair.

Dante braced himself and lifted his blade.

But no, it couldn't be. That was centuries ago…

CHAPTER

9

Tugging at the reigns of his horse, Bence slowed to a stop. Two miles north of Deran Castle lay arid wasteland. Once lush and green, only shrubs and the occasional wild flower grew. While snakes slithered freely along the mile-wide patch, other animals, such as quail and rabbit, huddled at the eastern border, where the land met the Fuad River. Smiling to himself, he threw his kill over his shoulder.

A few rodents. Barely a full meal for a man, but not bad for a first hunting trip.

When he broke from this train of thought, he sighed. Bence's head throbbed at the looming task. Their mission should've ended by now. He dismounted, boots slamming against the parched earth. From afar, his home for centuries appeared as a crater in the ground, but he knew it stretched for miles beneath the surface. A weathered boulder in the shape of a tombstone stood beside the entrance. A large crack stretched down the length of the rock, but the engraving was still visible: *Cehennem. Prison of the Cursed Aeonians*.

Echidna managed to regain her talisman over the years, weakening the gates and allowing them to break out. Once his father obtains full control of the island's elements through the armlet, Cehennem would revert to its original form: Damian's amethyst.

Upon descent into the prison, hallways branched out like roots of a tree, winding around one another in a labyrinth of darkness. But he followed the center hallway that led to the belly of a lively metropolis. Even further below, where the damp earth smelled strongest, lay the fallen Princess of Deran.

A voice hissed from behind. "The monsters are outside. The monsters are outside waiting to kill you and your family."

Without hesitation, Bence clasped a dagger, turned, and hurled it at the wall. The tip of the blade struck at the heart of a shadow that wiggled and feigned injury.

"Shut up. Annoying ghoul," Bence barked.

It stomped its feet in place and howled. Bence ignored the shadow ghoul's hissy fit and continued to the end of the corridor.

I thought these things would shut up after the success of our invasion. The royal family's rule has been uprooted. How can they be a threat to my family now?

Jamming his hands into his pockets, Bence kicked the chamber door open where he found his mother and father. And their prisoner. The only sound came from mice scurrying about. The vermin scattered as his footsteps echoed off the walls. The room reeked of mold, and the metallic essence of fresh blood.

Isabel was caked in mud, lying motionless in the corner. Her ankles were chained, and her right arm bore the armlet; however, it did not shine. Dirt and blood filled the four holes where the talismans had been.

He still couldn't believe the talismans were gone.

Before he could open his mouth, Echidna clenched her bony fists at the sight of the lifeless body. "Useless," she scoffed. "We shouldn't have fired that last arrow."

A smile of satisfaction formed on Bence's face. Farid will pay for that.

"We needed her in case this happened. Now we are not sure if she will ever wake up. Without her, our mission will have been in vain!" Ebony strands fell over her eyes. Her angular body, framed by leather-like skin and bone, suggested a meek disposition, but her voice, high pitched and wavering like a flighty bird, betrayed her looks. She glared at her husband.

"I did not expect this to happen," Damian said, folding his arms. "I am sure this is only a minor inconvenience. With the country in chaos, it should be easy to retrieve them."

"You men and your pride," she said through gritted teeth. "Did you really think that when you touched the talismans, they would accept you as their new master? Only a fool would think it to be that easy—"

Bence cleared his throat. His mother welcomed him a curt nod, while Damian remained motionless. "I am here to report. It seems that the four stones returned to their home tribe. I have already taken the liberty to pay a visit to Buryan to confirm this. The attitude of their leader, Dante, the young brat—"

"Did you kill him? Make an example out of him?" Damian's hands balled into fists, squeezed, then released. Lips peeling back into a sneer, he breathed heavily through his mouth.

"I *would* have cut him down on the spot, but he informed me Tuuli's Opal is hidden in their house of worship, and has been enchanted so that only the Princess may enter... of her own will."

Puffing his chest, Damian squared his shoulders at him. "So? What does that have to do with Dante?"

"He is fond of Isabel," Bence replied rigidly, shooting a steely glare. "We could still use Dante as bait. She will run to him. She can retrieve the talisman, and then we can kill them both."

"You are wise and shrewd like your mother. You see, Damian?" Echidna turned to her husband with a grin. "It is more than the body count. You must be cunning. Then this might be just a 'minor inconvenience' after all."

Damian grunted and bowed his head.

"Bence. Do what you need to do with her to get Tuuli's Opal and more information about the other talismans. We will await your return and consider the situation. I want to know what challenges lie ahead of us. I am sure the tribes are on the alert, and I don't want to go charging into each city without a plan."

"How will you keep the talismans together after we retrieve them?"

When Echidna lifted her hand with the amethyst ring,

her green eyes darkened. Streaks of purple stretched into her irises like thirsty hands grasping for water. As soon as Bence blinked, the strange aura was gone. He placed his hand to his head and shook it. After all those years dealing with nightmares and shadow ghouls, nothing chilled him to the bone more than his mother's powers.

"I have been working on an incantation all night. When the talismans are in our possession once more, their powers will channel into my amethyst without even having to touch them. Come now, Damian."

Bence clamped his mouth shut and bowed his head as she glided out of the room with Damian.

Now alone, Bence took a deep breath, rubbing his hands together as he sat on the opposite end of the room where Isabel lay. He drew his broadsword and picked a pebble up from the ground. When Bence ran it down the edge of his blade, he let his imagination run wild.

Precious gems that allow supernatural power to manifest in those that possess it.

Isabel shifted her leg but made no sound. The high-pitched scraping between stone and metal hypnotized him. After running it up the other side, Bence brought the blade to his face. Blowing particles off into a cloud of dust, he stared into his reflection. The fuller running down the middle of the blade warped his face two ways.

I am unstoppable.

Bence shook his thoughts from his mind and turned his attention to the prisoner. The sight of the empty armlet infuriated him.

"My parents should be sitting atop the throne by now,"

Bence grunted. "Now I have to go treasure hunting. And I have no time for games."

Her body remained still. Only the subtle fluttering of her chest indicated that she was still alive. Gripping the hilt of his sword tighter, his thumb stroked the guard. Bence stood and approached her with steps so light, he barely made a sound. When he was inches away, he measured the precise area on her neck that would cause immediate death. He scraped the tip of his blade against her skin.

No. Not yet. I've got plans for you.

CHAPTER

10

The scales on the bluefish shimmered as it flopped in the air. Hakan opened his furred, wolf-like jaws and with a crunch, pierced its flesh. After a few chews, he swallowed it whole. He reached for another one in a golden bucket, ignoring the silverware that lay beside it.

Six pairs of eyes followed his movements. Hakan acknowledged his servants with a snuff.

I can feel judgment in their eyes. They are all descendants of Foti from the Volkwood.

He never had been to the larger of the two Fotian territories beyond this island. The majority of the Foti in Deran have lineage from Volkwood. And he couldn't help but feel prejudiced for being from "the Bridge."

After gulping down his third fish, images of his former home played before his eyes. It was never too hot, nor too cold. Multiple trees populated the land, and he had enjoyed playing hide and seek when he was a pup. His family lived a nomadic lifestyle, like all the Foti from the Bridge, and forged weapons for a living.

Hakan chuckled at the memory of everyone's faces when he took over when the Volkwood-born leader passed away. Since then, he demanded respect, and for the most part, that was what he got.

When he finished his meal, he patted his snout with a napkin. "Alright. Let's do our rounds."

The six servants swooped the bucket away and grabbed his cloak. Their claws scraped against the dirt as they weaved between the metal beams that supported the ceiling. Swords, spears, and axes hung on the walls. Hakan was proud of forging the blades of each one, although they served better as decorations than weapons these days.

"Please stop panting like that. You look like a common animal. We are trying to rise above that," Hakan barked.

The foremost servant whined and stared at him with doleful eyes. "Sorry, sir."

Judgement again. Eating without utensils doesn't make me uncivilized. But panting on the other hand—

"We are ready," the other five servants howled in unison.

"Let's go." Hakan ventured towards the exit. Once he opened the door, a wave of sulfur hit his nose. Even though the hot springs were a few miles away in the Fire Lands, he never got used to the rotten-egg smell that plagued every square inch of Ogonia. After sneezing a few times, Hakan pulled the hood over his head. He squinted his eyes as the sun's rays reflected off steel buildings. Each structure towered like a giant in the bustling metropolis, competing with the mountains that surrounded them. Rust-colored sand covered the roads. Foti strolled by him, carrying about their day.

"Okay. First, let's head to the Golden Falls."

As he strolled down the wide path, his servants wove left and right, inspecting each building.

"The framework to the blacksmith's is stable," said one.

"No complaints from the butcher's union," stated another.

"Good. Good." Hakan ticked his city's issues off his list. "Any reports from our guys at the royal trade posts?"

"They checked in an hour ago. Business is booming. I think we are about to take the majority as the supplier of fish and fur."

Hakan purred as he stroked his braided mane. "Perfect."

Roaring waters overpowered their discussion as he approached a large circular plaza. Two torches stood before Hakan. The flames stretched their fingers to the sky. He stepped onto a platform that opened its mouth to the fury of the Golden Falls.

When Hakan brushed his mane again, the rubies embedded in his fur glowed. His servants backed away, tails tucked in between their legs. After a pulse of energy caused the water break into chaotic waves, a fireball ignited in Hakan's paw. Without hesitation, he dipped the fire into the base of the waterfall. The reaction caused everything to bubble around him. He grunted in discomfort, but waited.

After a few seconds, he pulled his paw out, and instead of fire, sat an orb of solid gold. Hakan howled, his servants following his lead. Blood rushed in his veins. The thrill to create gold was like no other. And he had to thank their alliance to the Kai for this.

"To this day, I have no idea how Dover commanded the waterfall to do this. But as long as fire and water produce gold here, I will never forget our alliance."

After he tossed the gold orb to one of his servants, Hakan stared into the basin of water. Rivers branched from this reservoir and curled all around Ogonia. After a long journey, it would end up in Lake Hama or Pekas Bay — where the Kai would swim in its blessed waters. The only fresh water they could tolerate.

He continued to stare, as if daring to see the bottom, which stood hundreds of feet below the surface. But all he could see was a black abyss.

"The chambers remain secure?"

"Yes, sir."

Even he didn't know the horrors that lay down there. But the only order he received when he became leader was to ensure it remained hidden from the Foti. From the Deranians. From everyone.

"What's down there?"

Hakan furrowed his brow, upset for jinxing himself. "Onto the *Fire Lands*," he pressed, avoiding eye contact with his five attendants. The sixth bounded toward him from the other side of the plaza.

"Sir! I received another contract proposal from Dante."

Growling, Hakan reared his head and flicked his tail. "That *child* doesn't understand no means no. It's not my fault the Tuuli settled in the part of Deran with no fresh water. Why should we help them? They've done nothing for us." If Hakan could shave that pretty boy bald, he would.

A whistling noise interrupted his fantasy. Ears perked, he said, "Did you hear that?"

His servants surrounded him and searched the skies. A flash of red plummeted down Golden Falls, into the basin with a splash, and towards Foti's chamber. Hakan's heart pounded and his hind legs shook. Suddenly, his mane felt like weights pulling at his scalp.

"What was that?" the servant to his right yelped.

Hakan managed to loosen his tongue from the roof of his mouth.

"Foti's Ruby has returned to us."

CHAPTER
11

Isabel rotated slowly onto her back, wincing in agony. Pain gnawed at her insides so intensely, she could not produce a sound to match. Not sure whether she was lucky to be alive, she recalled her last moments of consciousness.

How long have I been here?

She felt along her arm to the armlet, and prodded the dirt from the empty slots.

The gems are gone. Where is my father? … Mother!

Her stomach soured. Tears wouldn't form, but waves of despair continued to crash against her. Images of her mother and father flashed before her eyes. Blood everywhere. Her whole world turned upside-down within hours, and here she was, captive in a dingy prison.

All she wanted to do was to curl into a ball and mourn. Mourn until her insides rotted. Her whole family was dead. First, her sister. Then, her parents.

No. It can't be. I refuse to believe it.

Isabel prayed that they somehow survived. She couldn't live without them. They were her rock, her pillar she could lean on. The thought of their bodies decaying crushed her soul.

I could've protected them.

The armlet pressed against her skin as she rolled over. The metal was cold. Lifeless. Pounding on the dirt with her fists, Isabel bit her lip until it bled.

I should've cared more. Taken interest in the armlet and gotten familiar with its powers. But, no. Never in my life would I think it would fall into my hands. And because of my incompetency, they're probably dead.

Moaning, Isabel pressed her fingers against her eyes and rubbed them. A throbbing pain came from her left shoulder. It radiated down her arm, which gave way and sent her crashing onto her chest. She broke into spastic coughs as she clenched her injured shoulder. After catching her breath, she peeled her garment back. A blood-soaked bandage covered her wound.

She rotated her arm carefully, gritting her teeth as her joints popped and tendons twisted. It was a wonder how it didn't pierce her heart. The Aeonians didn't seem like people who had bad aim.

The Aeonians. They have to pay!

With adrenaline rushing through her body, she pulled herself onto her knees with shaky hands and looked around. Only a pair of candles lit the room. A single door loomed before her. Where it led, she yearned to know. It took several painful minutes for Isabel to stand. Supporting herself against the wall, she limped towards the door. She moved faster, curious to see what the next room had in store.

The chain tugging at her feet allowed her no further. The sound of footsteps returned. Holding her breath, Isabel prayed that she was just imagining things. But the steps continued to echo in the hallway, increasing in sound until the door flew open and banged against the stone wall. A man strode in, her mind putting a name to his rage-filled face. *Bence.*

Her first instinct was to knock him off his feet. She swung an arm, but Bence ducked and snatched her wrist and twisted. When he released his hold, Isabel stumbled backward. His eyes pierced right through her with such intensity.

"What do you think you're doing?" Bence rumbled. "Stupid fool!"

He shoved her with his free hand, waving a satchel through the air with the other. The sensation of pins and needles prodded her limbs as she crashed onto the ground. She moved her lips but nothing came out, as if the wind was knocked out of her.

"And to think, I was going to feed you!" The veins in his neck bulged.

Angling her jaw up towards him, Isabel balled her hands into fists. The blood rushing to her head spawned a pounding headache. "I just want to know where I am."

"Welcome to hell," Bence said, throwing the bag onto the floor, spilling some fruit and chunks of stale bread. "You can eat it off the floor. Now, I am going to have fresh clothes brought to you. If you try to escape again, I will kill you myself!"

Isabel stared at the pitiful morsels. Powerless, and surely

outnumbered, she nodded to herself. Deep down, she knew she had no choice but to listen. She watched Bence leave the room.

Time passed painfully. She only took a few bites of a rotting apple before vomiting it back up. She left the rest of the food on the floor and waited. Her fingers roamed her pockets and found nothing but chalky crystals, the dream crystals that Dante had given her. Bursting into tears, she gripped them close to her heart as she rocked back and forth. She prayed for happy dreams to take her far away.

She could picture it now. Yes. She saw herself floating in the air. Her body tingling in anticipation of escaping. Floating higher and higher through muddy walls, she saw a glow in the distance.

The sky.

She extended her hand as her body continued to float closer. But just as she thought she was free, a chilly hand grasped her ankle, dragging her back to the pit of darkness.

Isabel kicked and screamed, jerking awake, just in time to see a shadow jumping from her side and into the wall. Her throat froze in terror. She couldn't believe the sight before her.

The shadow ghoul waggled its fingers, taunting the light from the dream crystals away. With a howl, the ghoul cartwheeled across the wall and slipped under the door. Isabel cast the lifeless crystals into the dirt. As her head fell into her hands, she squeezed her eyes shut. She hiccupped, lungs begging for fresh air. The room spun as her head pounded so loudly she thought it would explode from her skull.

The longer she sat there, doubt ballooned in her chest. Doubt she could get out alive. Doubt she could successfully seek revenge for her fallen family and kingdom.

Hopeless.

Footsteps sounded again. Isabel's mouth ran dry. When Bence opened the door, he grunted in silent approval and released her shackles. Isabel recoiled at his touch.

This is it. It's a trap.

A second set of footsteps pounded against the floor. A husky female appeared at the doorway. She tossed Isabel some rags before slouching against the wall and crossing her arms.

"I'll give you three minutes," Bence said as he walked out and slammed the door.

The female warrior stood guard. Her skin resembled mottled cheese and her posture was much like a troll's. Isabel frowned at the mop of ashy hair that covered the guard's eyes. Isabel hesitated, eyes darting between the warrior and her clothes.

"Hi. Um, any chance you can turn around while I undress?"

No answer. She didn't even budge.

"Okay," Isabel mumbled. She crouched and changed without taking her eyes off the woman. "So, you and Bence are siblings? You're… *all* siblings?"

The guard blinked at her incredulously. "Hurry up, you

spoiled brat!" She drew a dagger and pounced on Isabel. Her face was so close; Isabel could see the hairs on her chin.

"I can't finish changing with you staring at me," Isabel said.

The oneway conversation ended as she pulled a grimy tunic over her head. Its musty stench made Isabel gag. When she pressed her left arm through the sleeve, she shrieked at the explosive discomfort. Heat washed over her wound and it pulsed as if it had its own heartbeat.

After several minutes of awkward silence, Bence returned and dismissed his sister.

Isabel's heart sank with each fading echo of the guard's footsteps. When she finally glanced at Bence, he released a tight-lipped smile. Draped in a black cloak, every inch of his skin except his face was covered, from his leather boots to his gloves. He tilted his head, causing strands of his orange hair to fall over his eyes.

Strutting slowly towards her, he cleared his throat. "How badly do you wish to leave me? How much do you crave your freedom?" He sat on the floor, pulling Isabel closer to him.

She held her arms against her chest. The flimsy tunic draped over her like a sheet. Isabel smacked his hands away like flies. "Not as much as I wish for your death," Isabel spat, narrowing her eyes. "I also want answers. You have not told me what you want with me. You... you killed my parents. You destroyed my castle. The kingdom must be in chaos. How could you?" Isabel lunged forward, punching his chest.

Bence rolled his eyes and shoved her away. "Farid killed your parents. Not I."

"Oh, that makes me feel a *whole* lot better."

He pointed his index finger right between her eyes. "Do you know what it is like to live in a nightmare your entire life? *This* is Cehennem. This place, it molds you. It infects your mind like a parasite. It constantly punishes you even though you have done nothing wrong except for being *born* here. I was born because my parents needed me. They were stuck here for centuries, thanks to your ancestors! This country belonged to my parents, but no, they thought they could usurp the throne and be made into heroes…"

"My ancestors came here because of all the abuse and war your parents caused in Deran. They were subjugating the rights of all the other tribes that immigrated here to start a new life!"

"What a cute story. Now, I would be careful what words you choose. I am your only way of escape." His grip squeezed her arms, causing Isabel to wince.

"I can talk to you however… wait. Escape?" She bit her lip as she glanced at him suspiciously. "Do not take me for a fool. Why kidnap me in the first place?"

"You don't know when to shut up, do you?" Bence cleared his throat and drew his broadsword. Placing the blade close to her neck, he whispered. "Take it as a challenge. The gems, the four elemental talismans that you don't know how to control, are gone. Want to know what happened?"

The blade pressed against her, nicking her skin. "When my father tried to take the armlet off you, the gems glowed with a searing intensity and in a lightning flash, they shot out in all directions and disappeared. Where, oh, where did they go, I pondered. So, I took the liberty to speak with the

Tuuli, because, you know, you folk seem to have such a favorable relationship. Especially with Dante."

"I swear if you hurt him—"

"Ah, watch the blade. This is my favorite sword. I just washed off the blood of some foolish Tuuli. But don't worry, Dante is alive. He is very fond of you. He misses you, wants to see you." Bence's honeyed words slipped from his tongue one by one. "So, from the goodness of my heart, I am going to let you see him."

"The challenge?" Isabel bit her nails.

"I'm getting to that. Dante confirmed Tuuli's Opal is in their temple. Let's see who gets to it first. I will even give you a head start." His gaze remained fixated on her.

Heat rose in her cheeks as she squirmed in place. "There is no way you would be so stupid as to let me loose."

Breaking into a chuckle, Bence pressed at her with his sword. His laughter made her simmer with anger.

How I want to crush every bone in his body.

As if he read her mind, he said, "You think you are a threat? My parents are going to be the next rulers of this land. You are the least of their worries. Follow me."

He grabbed her by the elbow and shoved her towards the door, pointing the blade against her back. Then he shoved her forward. Isabel's heart raced, but she moved straight, no idea as to where the exit was.

The dirt path crunched beneath her feet. When Isabel tripped over a rock, Bence hooked his arm around her waist then shoved her forward. The scent of sweat and metal grazed her nostrils, making her sick. Isabel wobbled to the right wall and vomited.

"I don't have all day!"

She stumbled forward, tracing her fingertips against the lumpy stone walls to maintain her balance. She stared at her feet to avoid tripping again. Each step Isabel took was like walking on fire.

When a rat scurried in front of her, Isabel shrieked and hopped back. The tip of Bence's blade dug into her flesh. Laughter broke out around her. Turning her head from side to side, Isabel noticed eyes piercing the darkness. Fear slithered through her like a snake, wrapping around her neck to the point where she could barely breathe. Bence's siblings crowded around her, brandishing their weapons and licking their lips. She picked up her pace, closing her eyes this time.

Bence directed her around a corner and up the stairs. Each step creaked beneath their footsteps. After two flights, they reached a wide hall. Moving shadows populated the corridor, and it twisted and turned for what seemed to be an eternity.

Eventually, they arrived at the gates, where the sun glared into their eyes. Isabel welcomed the warmth. Bence shielded himself from the light.

"You have till sunset before I follow you to Buryan. You had best move quickly. If I get to the stone before you, it will not bode well. Go!" Isabel's mind raced, unsure of whether he would end her life or not. But here he was, brandishing his sword at her to move.

It's a hunting game to him.

Panic, despair, and confusion pulsed through her body. What was a Princess to do? Bence cried again for her to leave. She turned and ran as fast as her legs would allow and did not look back.

CHAPTER
12

Ignoring the pain in his knees, Dover hopped furiously through his main chamber. He kept brushing his ears aside every time they flopped over his eyes. He whizzed by the pearl studded walls that winked at him. The lamps that hung on the wall cast a shadow twice his size.

"Dover, where is your cane?" scolded a Kai.

Dover did not stop to answer. His hands were occupied with something other than his cane. He sped along the corridor and stopped at a pool of water — a connector between his domain and the bay. It stretched five hundred feet, and its reflection shimmered against the cave ceiling. He hopped into the pool that funneled downward until it split into a labyrinth of tunnels. The seawater cooled his fur.

He navigated through the network of passages without hesitation. He passed by the submerged homes of his people, all decorated with chunks of coral, scallop shells, and more pearls. It all told about Kai's history in Deran, and in their previous home. Dover had them all memorized.

And our history may be very well uprooted if I don't do something!

Dover darted past seaweed and startled fish. His arthritic knees were already feeling better. From the corner of his eye, he spotted a few elders following him. Dover swirled upwards, fins working gracefully. He broke the surface and swam to shore, where the gold-plated gates stood.

A few stone cottages dotted the beach. The walls were painted various colors, resembling the vibrant environment in the reefs below the ocean surface. The Kai that were inside poured out, twitching their whiskers in curiosity. Dover shook his body wildly, spraying water everywhere. When he had sufficiently dried himself off, he sized up the growing crowd.

"What is going on?" Bo cried, swishing his tail to keep his head above water.

"I am sorry that I did not seek your counsel." A woebegone expression formed on Dover's face. The Kai's eyes stretched wide and many jaws hung slightly open. "Well, everyone, let this speak for me."

As he revealed what was in his paws, a flash of brilliant blue glimmered over them. The Kai gasped in unison, then broke out in chaotic conversation.

"You know what this means, Bo?" Dover's voice wavered.

"Yes, I do," Bo replied.

"I must act. Quickly."

"Dover!" Calder shouted. He leapt from the water and towered over Dover. "What are you going to do with Kai's

Sapphire?"

"This talisman is not safe here. It found its way to Pekas Sanctuary. Calder, Bo, this talisman *belongs* in the armlet. If it is here, this can only mean one thing. Someone has put their hands on Isabel." Kai bobbed up and down with the momentum of the waves. He narrowed his hooded eyes at his people who continued to stare blankly at him. He bristled as he drew his next breath.

"We are in danger."

Calder's long ears folded back.

Bo balanced his pearl necklace in between his paws. Shuffling his hind legs, he gazed at Dover. "But we have had no reports of disturbances here, my lord."

"My aim is to act *before* danger arrives. It is not a matter of if, but when."

Calder and Bo bowed.

"What is your plan then," Calder asked, eyes fixated on the sand.

"I am going to bring it to Hakan—"

"What?" Everyone cried.

"—and swap the stones," Dover asserted. "I will return with Foti's Ruby. I am sure they are in possession of theirs. This will create a disturbance in nature, and we will repel the assailants from our demesne."

"That's ridiculous," Calder replied. His snout wrinkled as he let out a low hiss. "Bringing Foti's Ruby here certainly means destruction!"

"I know what I am doing. This is the only way to make the retrieval of the talismans impossible for those other than Isabel. I have faith that she will come in time before any permanent damage is done here."

"That girl is probably dead!" Calder turned to the rest of the Kai, extending his paws. "You all know she was only the substitute for her sister. She does not have what it takes to rule this country. Look! She cannot even keep the talismans inside her armlet! I would not be surprised if the stones took flight just because she is incompetent."

Bo flung his arm out. "That is enough!"

When Calder dodged him, he grabbed Bo's necklace and tugged. It snapped and pearls sprayed everywhere. They plopped into the sand in silence. One landed inches from Dover's feet.

"Of all ideas, really. Switching the talismans? Why not keep the sapphire and just defend ourselves? We have the advantage of living under water. Pekas Sanctuary is hidden deep in the ocean. Or we could just leave the island! Join our brethren back in the Pekering Islands—"

"*Quiet!*" The sapphire in Dover's paw flashed, sending a pulse of waves stretching ten feet high into the bay. The Kai swam under the disturbance and resurfaced, eager to observe the confrontation. As the sapphire continued to pulse with energy, Calder and Bo backed away, whiskers drooping.

Dover narrowed his eyes. "You shall keep watch while I am gone! I am leader of the Kai, and this is my decision. Don't forget, I was the one who led the migration of the Kai to safety here. I am the eldest and wisest, blessed by our god. I will swim upstream, be gone no more than a few days, and return with the ruby. Your job, with Bo, is to secure the area and raise defenses. Wait until I return before we make any further decisions."

Calder crossed his finned paws across his chest. Without a word, he bowed and hopped into the bay.

"He just hates the heat," Bo joked.

Shaking his head, Dover picked the lone pearl up that lay by his feet and rubbed the sand off. Its glossy surface remained unscratched. He continued to pick up the remaining pieces. Everyone watched in silence.

"Dover, you shouldn't need to bend and pick them up," Bo said.

"Each pearl is precious, like each and every one of you. Like each and every moment in history of the Kai."

Emotions washed over Dover, constricting his throat. The more he spoke, the closer he was to tears.

If only they understood the feeling of persecution like their ancestors did.

After swallowing a lump in his throat, Dover said, "Make sure everyone has a place to hide if any invaders come."

"I can send some scouts along the river and keep an eye on the area."

"Good. Please do so and report back." He dropped the pearls into Bo's paws.

"Dover... Do you know who they are?"

His stomach soured instantly. When he tried to respond, his lips clung to each other. "Hm?"

"The invaders," Bo answered cautiously.

"You would laugh, but I feel that Damian and Echidna are back." An icy chill crawled beneath his fur at the mention of their names.

Dover turned, waved to his people, and pushed the gates open. A wide plain and river greeted him. Without hesitation, he jumped into Fuad River. After a minute underwater, Dover's head spun. But he pressed forward, knowing his body was adjusting to the fresh water.

Many Kai still feared traveling through Fuad River, no matter how much Dover encouraged them that it was safe.

As long as the blessed water of Golden Falls fills this river, no Kai shall perish.

Pushing upstream, he swam northbound towards Ogonia.

CHAPTER

13

Isabel stumbled to the top of a hill. She sat down to catch her breath, taking her worn shoes off to rub the soles of her feet. Sweat dripped liberally down her forehead. Her mind reeled from lack of water, but one thought kept repeating itself.

I cannot stop.

The mantra nagged at her to continue. The District of Buryan expanded from the western shoreline to the fields of central Deran. The task seemed impossible on foot, but she had to try. The rolling grass turned into thick woods that seemed to stretch for miles with no end in sight. Isabel had to pass through Stopping Valley.

Her cooks had boasted about this place. They would travel in search of wild grains for bread that she took for granted, bread she would likely never taste again. They also spoke of a river that fed into the lush land. With a sigh, Isabel put her shoes back on and continued forward.

She had veered off the West Royal Trade route, fearing she would run into the Aeonains. But her stomach gurgled incessantly, and if she didn't eat something, she would faint. After scanning the perimeter, Isabel changed course towards the main road.

Loud clicking of cicadas echoed in the woods. It would be a matter of days before they migrate to Camilia, a country five times Deran's size, a couple hundred miles away. It created a strange sense of serenity as she navigated her way through heavy brush. Sticks crunched beneath her feet and the occasional leaf danced around her face.

The colors should change soon. The season is turning.

When she arrived at a clearing, Isabel ducked behind a boulder. She held her breath and peeked around the corner. The dirt road ahead, lined with foot-high iron fences, was empty. Emerging from the woods, she stepped onto the West Royal Trade Route. It spanned for miles, from Deran Castle all the way to the District of Buryan. Not a soul was in sight.

Isabel trudged along for a mile when she came upon a couple of wooden huts. She approached the nearest one and peeked her head through the open window. Everything inside was covered in a layer of dust. A sign that hung above a wooden counter said 'Foti artisan weaponry'. No one was inside. When Isabel tried to open the door, she found it locked. She rammed into it a few times, but it only led to her shoulder throbbing.

"Damn. I wonder if I could squeeze through the window."

Slowly contorting her body, Isabel slid her head and

torso through the open window. One leg got through. Then, the other. She fell onto the floor, hands first. After wiping the dirt from her slacks, she scanned the room. Weapons that once mounted the walls were gone. It seemed that all the merchandise was swept away to an unknown location. All that was left was a half-eaten cod. The fishy stench reeked as Isabel's hands instinctively flew to her nose.

As she left the hut, all she could think about was if the Foti left before the Aeonians got to them. There were no signs of struggle, so Isabel remained hopeful. The other two huts, one belonging to the Tuuli and the other also belonging to the Foti were abandoned. She recovered a stale loaf of bread and a jar of fruit preserves.

After she finished inspecting the area, Isabel plopped onto the ground and dipped a chunk of bread into the preserves. Her mouth watered as she shoved it into her mouth. With a loud crunch, Isabel took her first bite. Her gums ached at the hardened bread. It was hard as a rock and the preserves had soured. She groaned and spit it out.

Isabel tossed the loaf over her shoulder and dropped the jar of preserves. Frustration mounted and weighed on her like a bear sitting on her chest.

"Maybe there will be food at the next few shops. There's got to be more in a few miles," she croaked.

A twig snapped in the distance followed by dirt crunching underneath footsteps. Isabel scrambled to her feet and looked in both directions. When she couldn't spot anyone, she dove back into the woods and behind the same boulder. She chewed on her nails and breathed rapidly. The crunching stopped and started on and off for a few minutes. Isabel strained with all her might but couldn't determine where it was coming from.

She sat there for about fifteen minutes without hearing another sound. Fear crawled underneath her skin.

I have to get going, but I have to stay low. Looks like I should stay off the road.

Isabel wiped her sweaty palms against her tunic and wandered away from the road. She followed the sun west. Every time she stepped on something, she would freeze, always questioning if she made the noise.

After a few hours of trekking, the sound of running water trickled nearby. The army of maple trees thinned out. Peaks pierced the skyline, the rolling hills transformed into a deep evergreen, spackled with orange. She stumbled into a clearing at the center of the valley and found the river she was searching for, calm and clear.

Low hanging trees dipped their branches into the refreshing waters while the air was abuzz with bees and birds chirping. Though she could make out portions of hills sculpted out as farmland, not a single soul attended the fields.

After waiting behind some trees for any sign of disturbance, Isabel crept towards the riverside. Clusters of berries hung from a nearby bush. Nearly toppling over with joy, she grabbed them by the handful and gobbled them down. The berries provided a nice touch of sweetness, bursting into cool jelly in her mouth.

While far from the typical meal she was used to, Isabel closed her eyes and thanked the heavens. She then turned to the water and drank in hasty gulps. When she drank her fill, Isabel rolled onto her back, closed her eyes, and breathed slowly. She was more than half way there. Cries from the cicadas morphed into the humming of crickets. The soft grass called to her, lulling her to sleep.

Isabel awoke to the Adin, glowing high in the sky, as its sister moon Deva trailed behind. But her lethargy evaporated quickly. When she jostled her limbs, she couldn't move. Sucking in the cool air, she tried to yank her arms up, but they remained by her side. She swallowed a lump in her throat and looked down: her body was bound with dirty, worn ropes.

Yellow eyes glowed in her peripheral vision. Biting her lip, she turned towards her captors. Maybe it was Bence and his army. She had wasted her chance, and she had lost.

But, these yellow eyes were not human.

One creature stepped out into the moonlight, and she gasped. The creature was a Kana, one of two native species to Deran that inhabited the island before the tribes immigrated.

Her gaze traced its feline features, distorted with a razor-sharp beak and bat-like wings. They fed on prey as large as humans. In packs, they could take down even a large Dunya. As long as it was breathing and living, Kana would consider it food.

She hadn't seen a Kana in years. Uncontrollable tremors took hold of Isabel as her tongue struggled to form words.

"Tonight, we eat," the largest cried in it's heavily accented tongue. A dozen Kana stomped their feet in glee in response.

"You must be the leader. Pay some respect for the Princess. Set me free!"

"We serve no one!" The Kana flexed its muscular frame, causing its fur to puff out. Rearing its head, it lunged at her.

Isabel shrieked and struggled with her bindings. Twisting her right foot sideways, she managed to release one leg. As she swung her leg up, she landed a solid blow to its black furred jaw. It shook its head in its claws, emitting a guttural cry. The rest of the Kana howled and pawed at the ground.

One Kana struck a rock with its paw, igniting a spark. Another brought over some dry brush and nurtured a fire a few feet away from her. Isabel quivered as the yellow and orange flames licked higher. As black smoke billowed around her, she broke into spastic coughs. Her lungs burned every time she inhaled.

When they rebound her, Isabel wrestled until the rope burned her skin. Their claws scratched her, causing thin trails of blood to soak her garments. With each movement, panic seeped through her muscle fibers until she felt completely paralyzed. Tears blurred her vision.

When the leader cracked its jaw into place, he flapped his wings. "Roast her alive."

"No!" Isabel screamed. She tried kicking again. And again. A Kana grabbed the ropes with its beak and dragged her. She squirmed, but the ropes dug into her wrists and ankles. Isabel closed her eyes, trying to dim the pictures of death playing in her mind. Warmth touched her skin, and she knew the fire was close. Each crackle made her heart jump.

At that moment, shrieks erupted around her. Isabel was jerked, violently, in the other direction. Dust surrounded her as she was dragged away. She peeled her eyes open — the fire shrunk into the distance. Kana cries echoed into the open sky. Who was dragging her? The stranger pulling her stopped and bent over her.

"I am cutting you free. Run as soon as I cut the ropes." The familiar baritone voice shocked her senses as if ice water was dumped on her.

It's him!

Isabel leapt onto her feet with renewed vigor. As she sprinted, she turned around to confirm her fears. Brilliant orange hair colored the night.

She stumbled over a rock and tumbled down a little hill, smacking branches along the way. After coming to a stop, she brushed off the dirt and, despite herself, chortled at her own clumsiness.

After catching her breath, Isabel crawled behind a large tree and listened for the victor. Screeches died down. Smoke billowed into the sky. Three Kana flew off the hill, spiraling through the air and scattering in different directions. Isabel ducked as one of them dove over her head.

The Kana crashed into the ground, but got up quickly. It spat blood and hissed. Large gashes plagued its abdomen. When it caught her eye, it lunged. It only made a few feet before Isabel's savior jumped in between them. A sickening crunch hit her ears as the creature's head was ripped from its body. Silence.

It all happened so fast. She couldn't even make out the whites of his eyes. Her heart still pounded, blood rushing to her limbs, readying herself to run if need be. Balling her hands into fists and positioning them in front of her, Isabel commanded her voice not to waver.

"Bence?"

The figure turned towards her. He was the spitting image of her enemy, down to the scar by his square jaw and olive complexion. But the eyes under his thick brow... those eyes were not human eyes.

Isabel dropped her arms, breathing out a sigh of relief as if her lungs deflated. "You must be a Zingari."

Zingari were the other original species native to Deran. She recalled the fragments of information that she knew about these strange creatures. They, too, were an intelligent species, much more so than the Kana. Killing only when they needed to, Zingaris spent most of their time scavenging for food and entertaining one another with their unique trait.

The imposter barked in laughter. "Yes. How did you know?"

The large figure shrunk, sprouting fur while howling in delight. Its true form was canine-like with two tails. The slit eyes were the only thing that remained the same whenever a Zingari took another appearance. Isabel relaxed her shoulders and smiled.

"Your majesty." The Zingari bowed his muzzle. "I am Jabin, wandering entertainer."

"How did you know who I am?"

"Your barren armlet, my dear," he barked. "The Kana may be too blind to differentiate royalty over common folk like myself, but I am not."

"Jabin, thank you. I will make sure you will be rewarded

once my quest is complete."

Jabin nudged her forward with his muzzle. "Let us talk and walk. Where are you headed?"

"Buryan," Isabel replied.

"May I ask, why are the tribal talismans missing? My people are confused and frightened. I witnessed the attack on the castle yesterday. I was alone; I could not do anything. But I saw this brute, the one I took the form of, dragging you away. He seemed greatly feared. I believe he is the offspring of Damian and Echidna." Jabin paused to lick his fur. When he seemed satisfied, he set his slit eyes back on her.

"His name is Bence. He said he was the eldest. But if his parents were sealed away two hundred years ago, how is he not... old?" Isabel stared vacantly at his wagging tails.

He paused for a moment. "Well, I can only think he must have committed a great sin when he was at the age he appears now. If I am not mistaken, time only passes mercifully in Cehennem if you are innocent, correct? Damian and his wife remained ageless. So, one can only imagine Bence had done something horrible to stop his aging. This makes sense for them to have a large number of offspring at the prime age for warriors."

"I see," Isabel said. "Ah, I digress... I was kidnapped and yes, I was in Cehennem. I lost consciousness and woke up to find the talismans missing. Bence told me they took flight upon the touch of Damian's hand."

"They were not meant to serve evil. My, you do have your work cut out for you... Please, I would like to add one more burden, if you are so merciful."

"What is it?"

"Do not let them enslave my people." The moonlight washed over his face, exposing his wet eyes. He let out a whine as his tails fell between his legs. "Damian and Echidna tried to enslave our race once before. They took all we had... My ancestors were persecuted because they would not work for them."

Shock enveloped her. The Zingari were a species she had not interacted much with either. Only one or two would be in town at a time to entertain her family during special events, like her birthdays. Like wandering gypsies, she thought they embraced the outlaw lifestyle. Her heart grew heavy for this lonesome traveler. This left Isabel in deep thought, and after she nodded, the two moved forward into the night without another word.

Rain clouds formed as dawn broke. Isabel hunched forward as she dragged her feet; Jabin nudged her to move. She wobbled, trying to keep her foot steady. When Buryan came into view, she plopped down to the ground.

"No, my dear, you must keep going. You are so close!"

She bowed her head into her clammy hands, her whole body starting to shake. Isabel moaned. "Please. Just a minute."

"Very well, my Princess. Now, with all due respect, since the District of Buryan is in sight, I must take my leave. I am not allowed in the tribal cities without invitation. You should be safe now. I wish to inform my fellow wanderers that this threat is real. I hope you can forgive me."

"No, no," Isabel said. "You have done more than enough. You must go. I will try not to let you down."

Jabin's eyes softened and nudged her one more time.

"Please, look at me. I want to give you something."

She lifted her head and gazed at the little creature. He poked his snout into a satchel tied loosely at his waist. He pulled out a tiny whistle, a brilliant pearl color, on a worn string. Jabin whined, waiting for her to accept his gift.

"Do not lose this. I used this when I entertained, but you need it more than I!" He barked excitedly. "In your possession, it can alter your physical appearance to any person with whom you have been in contact. It is simply an instrument to us since we already have that ability. Blow it once, and think of the person you wish to become. Blow it again to revert back. Remember this, you can only change into a member of your own species. I know it will help you on your journey. If you need anything else, please ask for assistance from any of my brethren. If there is any doubt, you show them that whistle, as a proof of our friendship."

Isabel hugged the stranger. "I shall give your people your own land someday. Go, and be safe!"

As Jabin howled, he shifted shapes into a large soldier. With a wink of his eye, he trudged away in the opposite direction. Ready to move forward, she pocketed the whistle and marched towards the distant buildings.

Rain fell sparsely, keeping Isabel cool. The drops provided a tranquil tapping sound against the earth; she swore she could hear the whispers of her friends and family calling for her.

When she was about halfway there, the gentle tapping turned into a thunderous pounding. The ground shook, and Isabel froze. Flashbacks of the castle invasion flooded her mind. Her instinct was to fall to her knees and hide, but her eyes focused on a silhouette of a man on a stallion gaining distance. The land at the city's border was flat, and there was no place to hide. She had no choice but to cower there in fear or—

The whistle!

She grabbed the whistle and blew into it. It made no sound, but strong vibrations emitted from the device. A tingling sensation overcame her. It wasn't quite painful, but still uncomfortable. It felt like her limbs were stretched gently. Her hands shifted first, growing twice her size, bulging with veins, up her arms, and throughout her torso. As her clothing ripped, leather material formed underneath. Shoes grew into boots, gloves materialized over her fingertips. A soft black cloak wrapped around her, granting her the exact appearance of Bence the last she saw him.

"Hey, you," the silhouette exclaimed.

The figure was now only a few yards away. Whether the change was in enough time, she did not know.

"Brother?" This man bore a striking resemblance to Bence. His hair was also orange, though more crimson in tone, and he had a pallid complexion.

It's his twin!

"Bence! What are you looking at? Your face is like you saw a ghost!"

"Uh." Groping her face, she discovered her nose was pointy, jaw line squared… and she felt that signature scar.

It worked. I look like him!

"What… er… what do you want?" Isabel asked.

"What do you mean, 'what do I want?' Is that how you greet your brother? Where the hell is your sword?"

A tickle formed in her throat. "I was in battle shortly before you arrived. I no longer have it." Covered in cold sweat, her mind raced for words.

I wish I had one to slice your throat, murderer!

"Listen, I know you are on your way to Buryan, but maybe you should wait. I doubt that prissy little princess has come this far yet."

Isabel bristled at the remark. "I would watch out for her if I were you."

"*Excuse me?* She couldn't slice her way into a turkey feast—"

Isabel clenched her jaw.

"—she will be more useful as personal company once the mission is over. I'm sure she's got something going underneath that dress. And don't worry, I'll share if I'm in a good mood."

Farid's words scalded her skin as rage exploded in her skull. Every inch of her being wanted to leap out and strangle him. She wanted to bring the wrath of every element crashing on the unabashed warrior.

"What's wrong with your face?"

Her nostrils flared. She counted to ten before responding. "Nothing. Just stand down. I am planning to move forward. Watch for her closely. I do not want to underestimate anybody."

"We need her to retrieve Tuuli's Opal first. You cannot get into that temple. You know that. Clever, though. I did not think she would buy into your trick. She probably is racing there, panicking, totally unaware of the advantage she actually has. What an ignorant girl."

"Let her do all the dirty work..." Isabel muttered.

Farid narrowed his eyes. "Uh, yes. You know, I don't know why mother and father picked you to lead this army. You may be a big brute but sometimes, your pride makes you lose sight of the mission. If I were in your shoes, I would be sitting back at home drinking a lager. Let her fetch *all* the talismans."

"Tell mother and father that I have everything under control. The fact of the matter is, I *am* in charge," she said, baring her teeth.

His eye twitched. Lips pursed tight, he tossed Isabel his sword. "I hope you know our parents are awaiting the outcome of Isabel's success of obtaining Tuuli's Opal and information on whether the other cities have a similar protection mechanism. If not, they are going to want to divide our efforts to expedite the mission." Turning his horse around, he galloped towards Cehennem, his face as red as his hair.

She looked down at the sword and unsheathed it. At the hilt, it was engraved with the twin's name.

"*Farid...* You will pay for what you have done." Isabel looked up. He finally disappeared into the horizon. It took a few minutes for the anger that simmered beneath her skin to quell. Isabel redirected her focus on her task in hand. "So they really cannot get Tuuli's Opal. And to think I let myself be intimidated."

With that thought, Isabel blew Jabin's whistle once more, returning to her more delicate form. This time she ran, nonstop, to the white gates of Buryan.

CHAPTER

14

"Princess Isabel! You're safe!" Aysu gamboled in circles.

The passionate greeting from the Tuuli Isabel knew as Dante's trusted servant was a bit shrill for her taste. She had just crossed the heavily chained gates to the District of Buryan. Aysu had spotted her from a high tower and summoned the Tuuli to forgo their lockdown. She was short and pudgy, but Aysu sped about, pushing and shoving the watchmen to release the chains as quickly as their fingers could work.

"Are you alone? You are here not by force?"

"Even if I were, it would be too late. Please, focus." Isabel said with a wan smile. "I would love to rest. And speak with Dante."

"Dante will return shortly, and I will notify him of your arrival," she said. "You look weary. Let me get you a horse!" When Aysu sped down the narrow cobblestone street, Isabel trudged behind.

As she traveled deeper into the district, Isabel noticed something was off about the cottages that squeezed next to each other on both sides of the road. Their trademark white brick walls were coated in soot. Many of the thatched roofs were singed. Even the glass from lanterns that hung on ten foot poles were smashed.

"You probably want to know what happened. We were attacked by the Aeonians shortly after I surmise that you were."

Isabel nodded. The broken homes continued to line up and lasted for miles. She picked up a faint hint of smoke.

"And your parents—"

"What about my parents?" Isabel exclaimed. Her heart pounded ferociously as alarms sounded in her head.

Aysu stopped walking. Her lips pushed her chubby cheeks up. "Tuuli scouts have been searching the castle and have just sent word that they were found alive. The Aeonians are looting the palaces for any riches they can get their hands on. So, they must wait in hiding until it is clear."

As Isabel's hand flew to her mouth, tears formed in the corners of her eyes. She squeezed them out with each blink until Aysu became a blur. The news imbued her with new-found hope. The lancing pain in her shoulder, the aches in her feet, all seemed to dissipate as she developed a second wind.

"I—" she sobbed. "I am elated."

"And I am lucky to convey the news to you, Princess. We will bring them here as soon as we can and provide them with whatever care they need."

Aysu flagged down a man who gaped at Isabel from his

stable. Isabel wiped her eyes with her sleeve and waved.

Keep yourself together, Isabel.

"Hello, there," she said.

The gentleman approached the pair and silently handed Aysu the reins, still staring at Isabel. His unkempt hair pointed in various directions, and he slouched — unusual for a Tuuli.

"Your majesty," he muttered as he bowed his head and retreated into his cottage. Bright black ink in the form of wings shone through his worn tunic.

"Is he alright?" Isabel asked.

Standing on her tip-toes, Aysu whispered into her ear. "They are all spooked. While Dante was able to drive off the Aeonians, everyone is nervous that they will return once more. As long as the Opal is in our possession, they will be back."

Isabel hummed as she craned her neck. She could barely make out the temple north of the district. It stood tall on a cliff, but remained intact.

I wonder how Dante was able to protect the talisman.

After brief silence, Aysu instructed her to head to Dante's manor. She insisted on a bath and change of clothes. Isabel nodded, mounted the horse, and trotted away. She kept her head forward, avoiding the stares of the Tuuli that poked their heads from broken windows.

Thoughts swirled in her head like a hurricane. A surge of relief came first. Closing her eyes, she could picture her parents the night of the ceremony. Before the attack.

How I miss them terribly.

When images of her parents warped into Damian and

Echidna, a tirade of anxiety pricked her. She was in the middle of a cat and mouse game with their eldest son, and there was a chance she wouldn't survive her mission. The possibility of death nauseated Isabel. It was not a concept she had thought much about since her sister's death. Gripping herself tighter, she shifted her focus on the warmth of the sun on her back.

"Everything is going to be okay," she murmured as she reopened her eyes. When her sight landed on the broken buildings once more, Isabel's shoulders slumped.

The manor stood a hundred feet away, a contrast from the other homes. The bright four story building, blessed with many windows, bordered the coast. The sun broke through the gray clouds, allowing a rainbow to shine above the chateau that stretched over the ocean. Waves crashed against the jagged rocks, as if challenging the manor's strength.

Isabel dismounted her horse and tied it to a broken post. When she walked past the waist-high iron gates, she noticed the lawn was nothing but dirt and dead grass. No one attended to the gardens on either side of the front door. Tomato vines dried up, and the leaves of the pear trees flaked off one by one. Dante had promised to pick a basket of pears for her, and the barren fruit tree told her things weren't going to return to normal for a while.

A maid poked her head out the door. When she noticed Isabel, she beckoned her in.

"Hurry, hurry," she said, huffing with impatience.

As Isabel rushed indoors, the maid pulled her up the grand stair case without another word. She was directed to a room on the second floor, where a hot bath was drawn.

Slipping into the water, Isabel sighed deeply. She was grateful to be rid of the grimy tent-like tunic. Eucalyptus replaced the scent of decay. Her muscles immediately relaxed, and even her wound started to hurt a little less. Moments of peace were hard to come by, and Isabel had a lot to think about. She stretched her body as much as she could, then let her limbs hang limp over the edges of the porcelain tub.

Beige walls surrounded her, speckled with baby blue. Through the windows, she had a grand view of the city. Gulls cried overhead, and blue flags with a silver wing painted in the middle flickered over a market square. Some Tuuli still walked around, carrying on with their daily lives, although grimly, without joy.

Eventually, Bence will come, stalking her like a shadow. He needed her alive to retrieve Tuuli's Opal. He'd follow her, but he wouldn't hurt her. Not yet. The Tuuli, she concluded, won't be safe as long as she was here.

Isabel had barely finished bathing when Aysu rushed through the door with packages in her chubby hands. Aysu presented two new outfits. One was a stunning peach gown with a sweetheart neckline. The other was a warrior's garb.

Aysu pointed at the latter. "I know it is not very lady like, but Dante told me what you needed to do. These slacks are leather, which will provide you some protection. The tunic is form-fitting, made from the best cotton around. And this belt will tie it all together. You will need to carry a lot with you. Functional and yet feminine, I think!"

The sight of the outfit invigorated Isabel. She wanted to try it on and fantasize of defeating Bence, Farid, Damian, and Echidna. A desire for revenge burned for what they did to her parents. For killing all those innocent people.

"Isabel?"

"Oh, sorry. I just got lost in thought," she said, patting Aysu on the head, sending her servant into a tizzy. "The two outfits are lovely. Thank you."

"Never you mind. Please try the gown on. I anticipate Dante to arrive any minute."

The news filled Isabel with apprehension. When she last saw Dante, she had been revolving under the spotlight of hundreds of eyes. And all was well. Shuddering at the events that had transpired since then, Isabel looked ahead and wondered how he was going to greet her. Would he be happy to see her, or would he see her as incompetent? Twirling the fabric in her hands, she imagined the warm gaze in his eyes.

Filled with ebullience, Aysu giggled and disappeared as quickly as she had appeared.

Slipping the gown on, she focused on the silk gliding over her skin. Knots that twisted in her gut unraveled as she relished at the idea of reuniting with Dante. In minutes, Isabel glided down the stairs. The hairs on the back of her neck stood in anticipation. She beamed. With Dante by her side, they will be an unstoppable duo, and she wouldn't have to face this journey alone.

At the bottom of the steps, she found him pacing in front of a giant fireplace. Dante's shadow loomed over her. His movements were quick and erratic. As she twiddled her thumbs, Isabel cleared her throat. When their gaze met, his eyes softened.

"Isabel." Raising his arms, he beckoned for her embrace.

As if her breath was sucked from her lungs, Isabel scurried to him. When he wrapped his arms around her, he squeezed tightly. Her heart swelled as she nuzzled against his chest. The smell of musk and clean laundry filled her nose as tears fell liberally. Words failed to escape her lips. The elation that blossomed within her was ineffable.

Finally pulling away, she gazed at Dante. His face was a faint pink, and his hair hung over his misty eyes. New lines freshly etched into the sides of his mouth and the top of his brows as stubble formed at his chin. Relief washed over like she was wrapped in a giant safety net. Her desire to embrace him again tugged at her chest, but her trance was broken when he cleared his throat.

"I am sorry if I have worried you," Isabel blurted.

Dante's smile faded. "You shall apologize for nothing. Come now, let's eat. There's much to discuss."

He took her by the hand and led her into the dining room. Isabel's mind raced; the fugacious moment evaporated too quickly. Even though she knew it was an impossible time for a romance to develop, she couldn't help but swallow the lump of disappointment lingering in her throat.

The glass table stretched across the length of the room, and the windows towered from floor to ceiling. When Dante clapped his hands, petite maidens rushed into the room carrying plates of food. Fresh loaves of bread, steamed spinach, and sun-kissed turkey left an aroma that overwhelmed her senses. At ease for the first time in days, Isabel stuffed her face with food. Dante pecked at his as they exchanged sneaking glances.

"I know why you are here, Isabel. You need the Tuuli's Opal."

Isabel cast her eyes downward, hoping they would talk of anything but the talisman. She wished she had the courage just to ask how he had been — and if he missed her.

"Please pay attention. You cannot travel into that temple alone. In fact, I would rather have you stay here, and I retrieve it for you. But as we both know, only you can unlock the doors."

Isabel bit her lip. A pang of guilt crept up her spine.

Am I really that incompetent?

"The Aeonians were here once. They will be back, waiting for your exit from the temple. I can feel it," Dante said.

She winced. At least Dante was coming with her. After she finished her meal with little else said, Dante led her back into the study. He stopped in front of the fire, eyes fixated on the flames. Isabel focused on his back.

With a sigh, she plopped onto the couch. Tracing her fingers on the beige fabric, Isabel fought for words. All she wanted right now was for Dante to be affectionate. Tousle her hair. Kiss her cheek. Maybe because she wanted a distraction from the daunting task ahead. Her thoughts screamed at him, but Dante remained in his trance. She drummed her fingers to the ticking of a nearby clock.

"I should go to bed," she said.

As Isabel stood, Dante hooked his hand around her lower back. "No." His voice faltered. "You're good company. Stay."

Leaning back onto the couch, Isabel folded her arms and listened to the crackling of the fire. Dante didn't say anything as he kept staring forward. In the heated room, her eyelids felt heavy, and she closed them without hesitation.

Exhaustion caught up to her.

He's acting different, a little distant. This is the last thing I need.

The couch shifted, jolting her from her worries. She peeked up at him as he stretched back and leaned against her shoulder. As he stroked her hair, Isabel placed her hand on his chest and smiled. Dante turned his head towards hers, pulled her face close and kissed her.

His lips were soft, warm. Her heart fluttered.

Dante pulled back. "Sorry. I shouldn't be doing this, especially right now."

As soon as he stood, Isabel tugged at his sleeve, pulling him back down. "Please stay. I'm frightened."

Dante lay back down with her and wrapped his lanky arms around her waist. They melted into each other in front of the roaring fire.

"I'll protect you."

Isabel blinked repeatedly, her eyes still stinging from the fire's smoke. Fresh linen tucked her into a bed behind gossamer curtains. Her head spun, but she managed to rub the drowsiness from her eyes.

He must have carried me to bed.

The stars had faded, and the sun rose to another day. She hastened into her warrior outfit. Oddly enough, a rush of excitement coursed through her veins.

She grabbed Farid's sword and bound up the stairs to Dante's room. Isabel's mind wandered to what happened last night. Her emotions of fear and excitement volleyed back and forth. Perhaps Dante will reject her for her fragility. She continued down the corridor of the upper floor, her teeth chattering. She arrived at what she thought was his room — oak doors lined with silver plating and adorned with opals. Knocking on the door, Isabel listened for his voice.

"Come in. I'm finishing my meditation."

She entered to find Dante, facing the window, arms crossed. He wore no shirt, exposing his tattooed wings. The black ink nearly covered his entire back. Even the minute fibers of the wings were in the design. She wondered if he ever regretted the decision to remove them. Mesmerized, Isabel reached out.

"Please," Dante said, turning around. "Don't touch. I prefer you to not remind me of them."

"But the art work is so striking. It looks as if they could spring from your back any minute." When Dante didn't respond, she flushed. "I still don't understand why. You didn't have to continue Vindur's tradition."

Dante glowered at her.

"I mean, the Tuuli in your homeland don't do this—"

"We are different from the Tuuli in Waaken. Wings are obsolete. It's not worth it when people treat you differently."

The irony of life is to covet those that are different from you. I certainly would trade anything for wings!

Shaking her head, Isabel peeked out his window. A young family passed the manor's gate. The father and son, who was no older than nine, still had their wings; however, their mother did not. She dragged the child by his hand towards the front door.

"Are you ready to go?" Dante asked.

"Yes."

As Dante dressed, she tapped her foot, curious if he would mention about their time together last night. Isabel's heart skipped a beat when he walked towards her, but Dante stopped at his desk to reach for his sword. After checking the blade, he sheathed it and tossed it at her. She caught it clumsily, and he nodded in approval.

"I guess we aren't completely hopeless." Dante chuckled, and Isabel forced a smile.

"Um, I don't need it though." She tossed the sword back to him and brandished Farid's sword.

"Where did you get that?" Dante's eyebrows raised.

Isabel bit her cheek. "Found it."

Dante said nothing as he secured his and Isabel's armor. She desperately wanted him to talk. To say anything at this point. Last night ended so well, she feared she wouldn't find comfort in his arms for a long while. But each time their eyes met, Dante would avert his gaze.

I shouldn't have brought up the topic of wings.

As they walked down the steps slowly, Aysu bolted towards them.

"Excuse me, master Dante. We have another request."

"*Now?* Did they make an appointment?"

While Dante and Aysu spoke, Isabel spotted the family she saw outside Dante's window sitting on the couch in the study. The parents exhibited handsome features, from their chiseled jaws to their high cheek bones. The mother stood abruptly and veered towards them.

"Excuse me, master Dante. I know this is sudden, but I need to have my son's wings removed immediately."

"My dear, appointments must be made. I am in the middle of an important engagement."

The mother's eyes bulged when she connected eyes with Isabel. "Oh, my. Princess Isabel, I am so sorry to interrupt."

"It's fine. I actually would like to listen to your inquiry," she replied, sneaking a sideways glace to Dante.

"I don't think it's a good use of your time," he volleyed back.

Isabel was chagrined by his answer, but she continued to press. "It most certainly is."

"Alright, then." Dante marched towards the study, dismissing Aysu with a flick of his wrist. He avoided eye contact with anyone.

Isabel followed silently. The child fidgeted in the sofa, clinging to his father. They both beheld her with doleful gray eyes. Neither of them spoke. When Dante approached them, the boy withdrew his wings from sight.

"Please, don't take them away."

Drawing his sword, Dante studied his opal talisman. As he closed his eyes, he drew a deep breath. "Why has this become such an urgent issue?"

"He was attempting to fly off the cliff and into the horizon. He plummeted like a rock into the ocean!"

The child inverted his toes and dropped his head. His curly hair covered his eyes.

"We all know it takes years to develop flight, if we are lucky. I explained that it poses more of a danger to him this way. I can't have him jumping off of any more cliffs."

"Angelina!" The husband pounded his fist against the armrest. "I had enough. It's time for my say!"

"You will not. Your son almost *died*," she screeched.

The husband jumped up and puffed his chest. "If he wants to invest in the art of flying, then let him."

"The *art* of flying?" Angelina scoffed. She pursed her bright red lips and brought her face within inches of him. "It's a dead art. Obsolete!"

Obsolete. That must be the word Dante uses on everybody.

Her locks bounced around as she shook her head. "I'm embarrassed of my untoward behavior. We should not be acting this way in front of Master Dante. And the Princess, no doubt. But Marcus, honey, you finally agreed this morning. You cannot change your mind now in front of everyone."

Marcus turned to Isabel. His eyes appeared sunken, as if he hadn't slept all night. When he frowned, his mustache dropped. "Princess Isabel. I would simply ask for your opinion."

Everyone stared at her. Breaking into a cold sweat, she struggled to speak. She wanted to stand up for the child, who started trembling. Dante tapped his sword against the floor. Each *tap* bored into her thoughts. It would've been easier if she wasn't under such political scrutiny. She knew she had to start acting like a ruler.

After swallowing a lump in her throat, she said, "I, unfortunately, must defer the decision to Dante. This is a situation that falls under his jurisdiction. The Deranian royal family has pledged to remain neutral in every tribe's internal affairs."

Isabel hated that line. Her mother had drilled it into her and Victoria's head when she was younger. It was one of many lessons about ruling the country she never believed she would use. Of course, Victoria took that rule to heart. Maybe that was why she was a better fit to lead Deran.

"Isabel is correct," Dante interjected. "Marcus, don't forget. While this is voluntary now, my goal is to push for mandatory removal by next year.

Marcus' posture deflated. His face appeared gaunt. When he turned to his son, he broke into sobs. He kept brushing his son's hair back. "I am so sorry. Looks like mommy is right."

"No!" he screamed. The child vaulted off the couch and tugged at Isabel's tunic. "Please, please don't let them take my wings. I like them!" The child's face grew blotchy as snot ran from his nose.

"Don't bother the Princess like this." Angelina swooped in and picked him up.

The boy squirmed in her arms, kicking and screaming. Dante instructed her to turn her son around and remove his tunic.

"Stand still, son. This will only sting for a second."

"Why did you make up such a stupid rule?"

Aiming the sword in between his wings, Dante said, "Please, hold him a little tighter, Angelina."

As he navigated the point of the blade around the base of the left wing, the opal talisman flooded the room with light. Isabel covered her eyes as the boy squealed. A roaring wind filled the room, blowing her hair in all directions. She peeked one eye open and could barely make out the boy's wings shrinking in size.

The boy sounds like he is in agony. I need to stop this. Jurisdic-

tion or not.

Before Isabel could react, a booming erupted from the center of the room, knocking her off her feet. As she landed with a thud, the commotion in the room stopped. When the light subsided, the boy was on his hands and knees. His whole body shook and his back was raw. A tattoo replaced his wings, the black ink glistened as if it were painted on by a brush.

The boy immediately reached for his back. When he felt nothing, he wailed. Angelina picked him up and turned to Dante.

"Thank you for your time. Now he is safe from committing another stupid act."

He nodded. "I will have Aysu see you all out. Now, he may be drowsy for the next few days. Such a drastic change drains a lot of energy."

With a snap of his fingers, Aysu teetered in. Angelina bowed to him, then to Isabel. She followed Aysu out the door. Marcus trailed behind, silent. The boy looked up from his mother's shoulders and stared blankly at Isabel. Dried tears streaked his cheeks. His face was completely expressionless.

Anguish filled Isabel from the toes up. Her feet remained glued to the ground, but her heart wanted to reach out and hold the child.

I was too late.

As the front door closed, Angelina's voice was muffled.

"See, dear? That wasn't so bad. Now, you will fit in with everyone."

CHAPTER

15

The massive Dunyan king craned his head towards the entrance made of dried palm leaves and mud with a roof supported by wooden beams. Clay pots filled with herbs littered the floor, lining the walls and spilling across the center of the room. He inhaled the earthy scent.

"Adem." Broad as a boulder, Kaj blocked the sunlight from the entrance.

With a wave of his claw, Adem silenced his servants who were playing a lively tune. They all stood, tails still thumping against the floor.

"What brings you here, Kaj?" Adem shifted his golden brows in curiosity. "Or shall I use the expression, son-in law?"

Kaj bowed. His brightly polished scales were less tarnished than Adem's — a symbol of Dunyan youth. Adem flashed a wide-toothed grin. However, Kaj's blood-shot eyes glared in warning.

He studied Kaj for a moment. "Not more about the drought. The rains have not graced the east end of the island for weeks."

"If only I came to talk about the drought. The leaves are breaking apart, and the soil is splitting. Dust dances everywhere. But I bring grave news."

"More grave than the drought?" The sound of jingling filled the room as Adem's head shook dramatically.

"Scouts have reported attacks on Deran castle!" Kaj exclaimed.

Adem grunted. He grabbed a chalice of wine and slurped it down. When he was finished, he slammed it on the granite pillar that served as his table. "I do not believe you," he finally replied.

"I would not jest about this."

"We were just there the other day. All is well." Adem twirled his tail with a claw.

Kaj snapped his jaws, thrashing his tail around. "Avani, would you please come in here?"

When she waddled into the cavern, Kaj took her by the arm. Avani rubbed her swollen belly and sat on the ground. She groaned as she swayed back and forth.

"Do you need anything, dear?" Kaj whispered.

"I'm fine."

Adem rose up from his chair. "My daughter, you don't look well," he said.

"I'm okay. Just tired."

"Well, then what is this maddening news? There is no way Deran castle could be attacked without any of us knowing beforehand!"

Avani nuzzled her neck against Kaj. She gazed at him

with uncertainty, but he nodded. "Father. We suspect that it is the work of the Aeonians."

Adem erupted in laughter, causing the room to quake. His daughter shot him a hard look as the color drained from her face.

Without another word, Kaj stormed out.

"Look at what you've done," Avani scolded.

"He's a full grown Dunya. He can handle it. But you must understand how silly you both sound right now."

"Silly, huh?" Kaj's voice echoed outside.

All the Dunya in the room glanced at one another with a dumbfounded look on their faces. When they broke out into whispers, Adem slammed a claw against the table, splitting the granite down the middle. Cups and plates crashed onto the ground, spilling wine and dried fruits everywhere.

"This joke has gone on long enough—"

Kaj hurled a body into the cavern. After hitting with a thump, the whole room fell silent. Adem teetered towards the lump of flesh. Human. He was draped in dark clothing and blood stained armor. He turned the body over. A horizontal line striking four other vertical lines marked his right cheek.

Recoiling with a hiss, Adem fell onto his tail. "It cannot be. This man is too young to be Damian. And yet he bears their symbol. Who is he? What is going on?"

"This Aeonian was found lurking at our shrine. Our supposed safe house. He turned everything upside-down, like he was looking for something," Kaj said icily.

"But what could possibly be there he would want? A few statues of our gods?"

"The Dunyan Amber—"

"The amber that belongs to Isabel's armlet? That's impossible!"

"You also thought the return of the Aeonians was impossible. Now look at the dead man here. It must be related to the armlet. Something is going on. And it's not good."

Acid bubbled up Adem's throat. Fearing his lunch would come right back up, he plopped back into his chair. It groaned beneath his weight. Rubbing his temples with his claws, Adem muttered, "This can't possibly get any worse."

As Avani pushed onto her hind legs, she clung to Kaj for support. Her face was void of any emotion. After a few beats of silence, she said, "Kaj and I have decided to leave Deran. We fear it is not safe."

Roaring and kicking the dead body aside, Adem charged at the pair. The rest of the Dunya scattered clumsily out of the way. "What are you saying? You cannot desert your father! You are heir to the throne!"

Kaj nodded to Avani.

"Father, I am ready to lay my eggs."

The news struck Adem across the face. He gasped as if someone dunked his head into the ocean and held it there.

"Is this true?" His words seemed to fall off his tongue like bricks.

"Yes. And this environment is no longer suitable."

Adem's yellow eyes twitched as he mustered all of his strength to keep his disposition together. He couldn't bear any more surprises. "You know our ancestors had come here to escape persecution."

"Yes, father."

"Our ability to seek survival is keen. You hold the future within you." Adem's voice faltered. The large reptilian leader did not take his eyes off his daughter. Her scales had a scarlet hue, like her mother. Adem thought she would produce beautiful hatchlings. "Your survival sense tells you... to flee."

"Yes, father."

"Then go." He turned and stomped beyond his throne to his sleeping quarters down the hallway.

"Father," Avani cried.

"Do not be angry that I do not see you out. My old heart would not be able to take it."

Moments passed as Adem paced in his quarters. Prompted by guilt, he left his room and strode outside. If it was too difficult to say goodbye, he could at least watch them from afar.

It was bright outside. Dusty. Avani and Kaj hurried towards the coastline, located one mile past Maz Shrine, filled with jagged rocks and cliffs. Perilous to anyone who attempted, the couple climbed down Dunya's Point. At the bottom, bobbed a large wooden boat. They took nothing— their scales would provide enough protection for them.

Adem's heart ached as the couple pushed from shore and floated out to sea. Straining his slit eyes, he tried to cherish every last moment until they were a dot on the horizon.

Maz, you who watch over the earth, see to their safe journey as I cannot do so.

"I am sure I will live to see my daughter return," Adem said aloud, consoling himself in a forlorn tone before he returned to his quarters.

CHAPTER

16

Isabel crossed her arms at the sight before her. Buryan Temple sat on top of a hill on the north side of the city. Tufts of yellow grass dotted the area while dirt covered the bald patches. The sparse vegetation eventually disappeared at the temple's front door. From there, only rocky ground surrounded the perimeter, eventually dropping off into a precipice. There were no homes around it. Only a graveyard and a mill stood close by at the base of a bridge. The mill where had she had met Dante.

The motionless vertical wheel groaned as the breeze picked up. The planks of wood were chipped by the elements and chewed by termites.

"The mill has not been able to produce much lately," Dante said, as if reading her thoughts. "The current is weak. There are no rivers that run through western Deran. In fact, we are the only tribe without a direct source of fresh water. Our ancestors once found a way to siphon water from the ocean and the temple was originally meant to be a place for purification. Fresh water used to burst forth from it." He brushed past her shoulders to crouch down and run his hands through the stream.

She nodded, chin resting on her hand. Her gaze lifted back up to the temple. From a distance it seemed benign, crafted with white stone and hundreds of windows. A tall steeple extended from the center. Ivy wrapped around the walls, and upon closer inspection, some stones crumbled apart.

Following his lead, Isabel crossed the bridge. Each step resulted in an ear-piercing squeak. She shuddered and looked down. Isabel was no more than a few feet off the ground, which was hallowed out as if a small river once flowed through. The parched dirt exploded into a dust cloud at the slightest disturbance.

Must be where the purified water went.

As she stared at the back of Dante's head, she couldn't help but recall the events from this morning. Guilt still plagued her for letting him remove the child's wings.

He was too young. They should've waiting until he came of age.

She pictured the boy jumping off the cliff, believing he could fly into the horizon. The rush he must have felt as gravity stole his breath. The heartbreak when he plummeted into the ocean below.

A wave crashed into the distance. The end of the bridge was a few feet away.

And yet, terror swirled in that boy's eyes when Dante drew his sword. Isabel had never seen Dante so serious before. His narrowed brows and crooked frown seemed novel to her.

Cold.

Dante had acted like a coat of armor, tough on the outside and hollow within. Of course, maybe she was being too hard to judge him because that was his duty. Vindur passed down his only dream to Dante. He was only trying to honor his predecessor's wish.

But I don't think I could carry on any tradition I didn't agree with.

When Dante turned his head and met her eyes, Isabel nearly tripped on her own feet. "You okay?" he asked.

"Yes. I'm okay." Isabel played with her hands behind her back.

"I'm sure you are still shocked by what happened today."

Isabel chuckled nervously. "Me? Barely."

"Anyway, thank you for respecting my authority. I promised to remove the wings of whoever desires so."

"Of course," she replied, biting her lip. After crossing the bridge, Isabel gulped as the temple's shadow cast over her. Her goose bumps multiplied. A rustling noise surrounded her.

Dante waved his arm out to Isabel. "Careful. We set a lot of traps to prevent Tuuli's Opal from falling into the wrong hands. And remember, only you can open these gates. Lead the way. The ivy will come get you."

"The ivy?"

As if she had summoned them, tendrils of vines grew out from under the door and crept towards her. She stepped back in fear, ignoring the cries from Dante.

"Get up! Do not be afraid!"

The vines stopped short of Isabel's feet and shot upward. As the tendrils intertwined with one another, it formed a wall with an imprint of a hand. The leaves shuddered, then became still. She walked around the pillar of ivy, knotted so tightly that she could not see through it. When her gaze met the imprint of the hand once more, a chill ran up her spine.

"Put your hand in there," Dante said.

"No way." She took a few steps back.

"We cannot afford to be scared anymore," he shouted, turning as more vines circled his feet.

Isabel swallowed the lump in her throat and extended her left hand. The tendrils wrapped around each finger and snaked up to her arm, stopping over her armlet. The vines twitched like they might release her, but they clamped down.

"I think it's working," Isabel said, turning to face him. When the vines near Dante retreated, she sighed in relief.

The vines snaked around her ankles and yanked her off her feet. Lights exploded in her eyes as her back hit the ground. It dragged her towards the large rosewood doors that creaked open, just wide enough for her to fit. Twisting her body, she reached for anything to hang on to. Her nails scratched against the earth as dust danced around her, clouding Dante from view.

She squeezed her eyes shut. "Dante!"

The doors slammed shut as soon as she entered the temple, the floor ice cold beneath her. When she reopened her eyes, Isabel could barely see her own hands. The ivy released its hold on her, and she reached to rub her ankles. Her breath quickened, and her heart pounded so loudly she couldn't listen for the rustle of the vines. Isabel stood up and felt the wall. Shifting her hands slightly to the left, the doors greeted her with a splinter.

She shook her hands wildly, cursing. As she reached for the doors again, Isabel held her breath and listened for any signs of ambush. A water drop sounded in the distance. Reassured, she groped the handle and pushed against the door.

Light blinded her as she cried out to Dante. "Come in. Hurry!"

Dante slid past her and into the temple. There were no other signs of the ivy, and the great doors closed once more.

"How?"

"I honestly don't know," Isabel said. "When the doors closed, the vines let me go. It was as if they just wanted to secure me within the building. Nothing got in the way of me opening the door to let you enter."

She could barely make out Dante's silhouette as he strode towards the center of the room. Dante unsheathed his sword and whispered words Isabel didn't understand. Within moments, the giant opal on the hilt of Dante's sword glowed to life. She ogled at the priceless gem.

I wonder if I can perform such feats when I retrieve my stone!

The light exposed granite walls that stretched hundreds of feet high to a single window near the ceiling.

"This small altar helps modify the structure of the temple." Dante gestured to an obstructing object before him. "Give it a try," he said, imitating a swinging motion.

Isabel drew her sword. Wobbling awkwardly, she struck her blade against the rock. With a hum, the stone illuminated. Isabel stepped backwards as the room vibrated, eyes peeled wide. The floor sank slowly until a lower floor was revealed. Dante ran towards a newly exposed door.

"Follow me."

"Dante, how do you know what to do?"

As he struggled with the rusty door knob, he turned to her. "Lots of temple visits with Vindur. Before he passed, he showed me the ins and outs of this temple in the event something went wrong."

Isabel held up her sword as he yanked the door open. "What should I be expecting?"

"Just a few trials."

"Trials?" She blinked rapidly as her mouth went dry.

Without another word, Dante made his way through the next passage. Isabel followed behind, mustering all her strength to keep her sword steady. She prayed Dante couldn't hear her blade rattle within its guard, rusted to the point of disintegration.

Moss plastered the damp walls. Winding to and fro, the corridor led the pair to a locked door. Dante checked his tunic and sighed.

"Forgot the key." He struck at the knob with his sword, and when that failed, he kicked the door. Isabel peeked through the opening, resisting the pull of Dante's hand. The pitch-black room caused her to root her feet on the ground.

"Scared?"

Shaking her head, Isabel took a step forward. "Of course not."

With a whisk of his hand, Dante's sword illuminated once more with a deafening *woosh*. Wisps of light danced from it, twirling around Isabel and into the chamber. As soon as the light settled into lanterns, colors burst about from the multitude of stained glass windows that painted the story of the Tuuli people. Standing in the center of the room stood a statue of a male Tuuli, surrounded by three pillars.

"Are you going to have a statue erected here, too?" Isabel's lips twisted into a grin.

"This is the first Tuuli chief of Deran." Dante cleared his throat as Isabel circled the pillars. "And those are vital to our quest."

Isabel's gaze followed his direction towards the pillar tops; each held a small vial. Dante took a deep breath and moved his hands rhythmically, as if playing an invisible harp. With each stroke of his finger, wisps of air appeared from nowhere, and suspended the vials mid-air.

Mouth askew, Isabel glanced at her armlet, eager to obtain Tuuli's Opal so she could also do the same. The vials were carried by the invisible wind right into Dante's hands. She wondered what they were, but a rumble interrupted her musings. A pebble assaulted her head. Rubbing her scalp, Isabel looked up to see the pillars shuddering. Cracks formed at the base and stretched their fingers up. Dante's hand pushed her back as chunks of stone rained down on them. She shielded herself with her arms.

"Do not be afraid. There is always a reason for everything."

Dante stuffed the vials into his satchel then pointed at the rubble. It formed a rocky pile leading up to an opening in the middle of the wall, not accessible by ladder or steps.

Isabel shot him a steely glare. "We have to climb up that?"

Nodding, Dante rested his arms on his knees. He took a few gulps of air and blinked furiously.

"Are you alright?"

"Yes," he said as each word came in between breaths. Sweat beaded atop his forehead. "I haven't needed to utilize my powers as much before. From the unexpected wing removal this morning, to everything I have to do now. While the magic lies in the stone, it draws from your life-force."

When she rested her hand on his shoulder, Isabel said, "We can take a minute if you wish."

"No. I'd prefer to keep moving. Time is of the essence."

Without another word, Dante produced a bow and arrow. He found some rope and tied an arrow to it. Shutting one eye, he aimed for the opening. His hands shook and took a minute to settle.

"I can try," Isabel peeped.

The arrow soared past her and secured itself between two jagged rocks. After tugging the rope a few times Dante nodded in approval. "Don't worry. I got it."

He extended his hand and beckoned Isabel to go before him. She eagerly made her way up the rubble, desperate to prove herself.

I wish I could be more of use.

Blowing a strand of hair from her eyes, Isabel grabbed a rock with one hand and placed the other on the rope. As she slowly made her way up, her arms burned after only a few pulls. Ten feet. Twenty feet.

Halfway there.

Isabel's arms shook uncontrollably. The next rock loomed in front of her and she stretched her arm, but her foot slipped.

She fell backwards, aiming straight for the ground. She screamed soundlessly as her breath rushed out of her lungs. An airstream cocooned her body, but Isabel continued to plummet to the ground as its strength weakened by the second. Squeezing her eyes shut, she waited for what would come next.

Dante screamed somewhere below. She wondered if he already hit the ground, and she counted the seconds until she met the same fate.

Her back slammed into something soft as she bobbed up and down. She fluttered her eyes. Once, twice. Then opened them. Dante held her in his arms. His wings had ripped through his tunic, and they flickered vigorously, keeping them both safe from falling.

His wings were nonexistent. I saw it for myself this morning!

As she gripped his waist, Isabel couldn't stop staring at him. "How?"

He shushed her and flew upwards. The ascent was slow as Dante struggled to fly. They both clambered onto the ledge.

"Thank you." She panted, observing him tucking his wings beneath his torn shirt.

Dante appeared as stunned as she was. "All I remember was my strength failing me. I knew I didn't have enough power to command the wind to save us both. Then, I felt it. Like my back was thrown into a fire. My skin seemed to bubble then my flesh ripped."

Rushing to his back, Isabel peeked under his tunic. The skin where the tattoo touched was raw, but his wings remained opalescent. There was no trace of blood. It made no logical sense, puzzling her to the point of speechlessness.

"Th-that's incredible." She traced her fingers along the base of his wings.

When Isabel touched his shoulder blades, Dante flinched.

Dante's flushed face contorted. "It's quite painful," he said through grit teeth.

"I guess I need to lose some weight." Isabel jabbed him with her elbow. Dante raised an eyebrow.

"I was just kidding."

"Right. That's such a Victoria thing to say," he said. They both broke into laughter. "Now, get ready."

"All right. But you sure *you're* ready?"

Rubbing his shoulders, Dante nodded. His face pinched as he rotated his arms. "Just got to stretch it out first."

Isabel and Dante continued along the hallway and into a round room. Creaking followed their footsteps as they went. She glanced at the floor. It was made of glass. Staring at her reflection, she didn't realize how gaunt she looked. How dark the circles under her eyes were. She brushed her fingertips along her jawline; her porcelain skin cried for water. Her tongue that stuck to the roof of her mouth agreed.

Dante straightened his posture, glancing at the walls with hooded eyes. Isabel followed his line of sight. Tiny porous openings, as small as a grain of sand, lined the walls. Before Isabel opened her mouth, the creaking grew louder until harsh snaps filtered around the room.

With a high-pitched whistle, tiny needles rocketed from microscopic holes in the walls. Dante grabbed one vial from his satchel and tore the cork stopper off with his teeth. A roaring wind barreled from the miniscule opening and formed a barrier around them. The needles stopped mid-flight and fell to the ground when the wind dissipated. Isabel fell back onto Dante in amazement, but he pushed her forward.

"Hurry, there is no time to lose," Dante said.

Isabel stepped gingerly over the needles and followed him silently to yet another door ahead of them. She held her arms against her chest, bothered by his curtness as much as the eerie creaking that resumed.

After opening the door, Dante drew his sword. Isabel followed suit. This new path snaked into the bowels of the temple, forming a maze composed of the ivy she encountered at the entrance. Dante's strides were long and quick; Isabel had to jog in order to stay close. They followed the path, which had many twists and turns, until they arrived at a fork. He stopped, mumbling to himself, and looked to his left and then to his right.

"Are we lost?" Isabel asked.

Dante shushed her. Taken aback, she struck the sword into the ground. This wasn't turning out to be the epic team adventure she had imagined. Dante went left without a word. She stumbled quickly to keep up.

When she rounded the corner, her eyes fell upon a black mass. It contracted and expanded. Studying its shape, she realized it was a giant Kana, sleeping. Its body curled up, feathers rustling with every exhale. Craning her neck, Isabel estimated it to be at least three times her size.

"Dante, we should have taken a right," she said, swallowing the lump in her throat.

"No, this is the correct path."

The Kana grunted, and one of its eyes flickered open. The slit pupil roamed around the room lazily until it spied Isabel.

"Could not keep your mouth shut, could you?" Dante growled.

The creature stood and stretched its wings, cracking its dusty old bones. Isabel drew her sword, and the Kana reared its head at the glimmering metal. Its screeches were deafening, and the ground shook each time it stomped.

The gigantic Kana soared into the air and dove at them. Dante leaped out of the way. Isabel held out her sword, trying to deflect the Kana's claws, but instead was knocked down like a paper doll. She clutched her chest, gasping for the wind that was knocked out of her.

Dante flexed his wings and soared onto its back, slashing wildly with his sword. The Kana shook its head. He sheathed his sword and pulled out some rope. He lassoed the beast around its neck. Dante hung on, swinging his legs and flexing his wings to work his way back onto the beast. He pulled at the rope, strangling the Kana.

"Isabel!"

She rose from the ground and ran towards them, swinging her sword arbitrarily. She managed to slice one of the Kana's legs, causing hot blood to burn her face as it splattered over her body. The Kana's roar shook the whole arena, knocking Isabel off her feet.

"Keep it up! I cannot hold him much longer!"

Dante was tossed from the creature. On a wild idea, Isabel jumped for the rope. She swung around the creature's erratic movements, gritting her teeth as the twine burned her hands. When she came close enough to its chest, she thrust her blade into it.

"Yes!" Dante shouted behind her. "Let go. I'll catch you!"

Without hesitation, Isabel released her grip. The squeeze of her stomach nauseated her. After he caught Isabel and let her down, Dante drew an arrow and placed a final shot into the Kana's right eye. The creature fell backward and became still.

"I'm so proud of you," he exclaimed, huffing. "This is the warrior Princess I need! Come, let's go. There are more of them."

As she turned to gaze at the dead Kana, a twinge of guilt fluttered in her stomach. Her sword had cut into the Kana's heart. Never in her life has she witnessed blood spilt by her owns hands. She was responsible for its death. Numbness washed over her, but her mourning was interrupted by Dante, shaking her shoulders.

Isabel flinched. "Sorry."

Trailing behind Dante, she noticed the gash on his arm. His blood soaked his garments. He shook his head, and pointed at the exit. A high gate led into an opening. As they marched forward, Isabel noticed the pebbles on the walkway vibrated. The slight tremor magnified, sending Isabel's heart racing. When the flapping of wings became seemingly deafening, she turned her head. Hundreds of Kana flooded the maze and charged towards them.

CHAPTER

17

Isabel sprinted through the gate, fear dogging her steps. "What is going on?" she exclaimed as she caught up to Dante. "This temple is meant for *me* to come in and for *me* to retrieve the gem? Why are they attacking us?"

"The Kana are effective mercenaries, that is why we made them our guards here. I cannot account for their lust for blood. Just keep running!"

Arriving at the gate, Isabel jiggled the handle. Locked. Hot and cold flashed through her veins as she reached for her sword. Dante fended off the Kana behind her. His pained grunts urged her to hack the handle with all her might. His sword scraped against talons, with ear-piercing screeching. Black feathers littered the air and bodies covered the ground. She peered over her shoulder. Dante's body was consumed by an ocean of Kana.

A crack, following by the ringing of bolts and screws hitting the floor sounded heavenly to Isabel's ears. She hooked her arm around Dante and jerked him towards the door as she kicked it open.

"Ouch! Watch it."

"Sorry," she exclaimed, ignoring the burning in her lungs.

"Hold up!"

The echo of her footsteps magnified in the next room until she dug her heels, coming to an abrupt stop. The tips of her shoes hung over a dark abyss. Waving her arms, Isabel regained her balance. A gigantic pit loomed before her. A door stood on the other side, hundreds of feet away.

"I hate to say it but thanks for yelling at me. I would've not paid attention and fell." Gulping for air, she twisted her head to find the Kana closing in on them. "Shoot."

Dante took a deep breath and pushed Isabel off the ledge and he jumped after her. The Kana did not follow.

"Are you *crazy*?"

They fell several feet with no bottom in sight. However, long after Isabel finished screaming, Dante pulled out a second vial and released the cap. A thick fog escaped this vial and swirled into the form of a platform right below them, breaking their fall. Isabel felt like she fell onto a cloud. She remained straight on her back, hyperventilating until Dante pulled her up to her feet.

"Hurry!" he urged.

Isabel noticed a door with no platform at its entrance in the distance. Dante rushed her towards it. The mist began to dissipate as she trudged forward, struggling as if wading through mud. Clambering into the entranceway, she extended her hand to Dante. The mist vanished under him, leaving him to grab onto the ledge with his hands. Isabel pulled him up.

"Why not use the mist to reach the door above?" Isabel asked.

"That door is a decoy," Dante replied. "Anyone that goes to that room will meet certain doom."

She pressed her lips tightly together. Placing a hand to her forehead, she fluttered her eyes, trying to regain focus.

"This barely seems like a temple. It's more like a labyrinth."

"Who said it isn't one?"

Isabel rolled her eyes as she entered the next room. It was empty, except for a wall of glass dividing the room in half. Dante took the last vial and opened it.

"This one, we drink."

When she shared a sip with Dante, she gasped at the tingling sensations washing over her. Her skin turned blue and a violent chill coursed through her veins. Waggling her fingers in amazement, she turned to Dante, skin also blue. Without hesitation, he walked right through the glass. He held out his hand and Isabel approached him. She paused in front of the glass and held out her hand. Fingers inching closer, she held her breath.

Instead of feeling solid glass, a jelly consistency greeted her fingertips. The tingling intensified as she pushed her arm through the barrier and met Dante's fingers. Encouraged, she passed right through the glass. Within moments, the chill left her and they returned to their original state.

"Those were our three trials. We have one more," Dante said, grinning.

Isabel and Dante approached formidable double doors. She pushed them open, squeezing her eyes shut at the sound of rusty hinges rubbing against one another. This room was well lit, but she could barely make out the ceiling above her. Isabel jumped at the tapping on her shoulder. Turning her attention to what Dante was pointing at, her mouth ran dry.

There it was. Embedded in chains and floating in the middle of the room — Tuuli's Opal. She approached the shining stone, but Dante knocked her over and rolled them into the corner. Isabel shot him a confused look. She saw nothing in the room but metal chains and the stone they worked so hard to reach.

The walls of the room vibrated. Dust and fragments of stone rained from above. As soon as everything settled, the room shivered again. Feeling Dante's grip tighten on her arm, goose bumps formed all over Isabel. Hesitant, she glanced upwards. The glare of the sunlight blinded her, but there was no doubt that something dark was swinging from the ceiling.

In a large funnel of dust and air, yet another Kana, three times the size of their last giant foe, swooped down from its perch. Isabel burst into a fit of hysterics when its high-pitched roar echoed loudly in the arena. Windows shattered, raining glass on them.

Fumbling for her sword, she struggled to find words. "Where did it come from?" She stared in horror as the Kana stomped towards the stone and swallowed it in one gulp.

"What are you doing?" Dante shouted and waved his hands.

The Kana looked past him and right at Isabel. "I am *Mag*

Kana. Master from many years ago said to keep gem away from any one person. Or else he would destroy all my people. So I let no one pass," it roared in broken speech.

"*What?*" Isabel shouted up to the giant. "Who threatened your people? I can help—"

"It is nothing but a violent animal," Dante screamed.

Before she could react, he pushed her out of his way as the Mag Kana lunged at them. Leaping onto its beak, Dante plunged his sword into the beast's feathered head. Adrenaline pumped through Isabel's blood, snapping her out of her frozen state. Charging forward, she slashed at its stomach, blood spewing from its wounds. However, this giant did not fall as easily at its comrades. The monster raised its foot to step on Isabel when a blast of air formed a tornado and trapped the creature in place.

"Amazing," Isabel stammered, as she spied Dante orchestrating the gusty attack with his nimble fingers.

"You bought me enough time," he exclaimed, eyes straining. His whole body trembled. Isabel knew he couldn't hold it much longer.

The monster tumbled about and then flung high up into the air. It crashed to Isabel's left, throwing her off her feet. Before she could pull herself up, the Mag Kana turned and pinned her under its claws. She ground her teeth, holding in her tears. Pain stabbed at her ribs as if she lay under spokes of a wheel.

Dante veered towards Isabel. He tried with all his might but was unable to free her. Each time he pulled her arms, she screamed in agony. Dante released her and tried summoning a tornado of air, but not even a gust of wind budged the Mag Kana this time.

The gale turned into a whispered breeze. Groaning, Dante collapsed onto his knees. The Mag Kana flexed its claws, talons digging into the floor.

"You must unbuckle the belt to the sword. Go. *Now!*"

As Isabel released the belt, she was able to squeeze free before the sword splintered under the beast's weight. Free, she held her arm to her abdomen as she limped to the corner of the arena. Dante joined her, but his legs gave way, and he collapsed on the ground.

"Isabel, I don't have any more strength. We must reach that sword. The one I lodged near its beak."

There was no way she could physically retrieve it. She dug deep into her pocket and pulled out Jabin's whistle. A miniscule smile formed at the edge of her lips as a glimmer of hope threaded through her mind. Blowing into it, she turned herself into Bence. Dante cried out in shock as Isabel blinked with her now thick brow.

With her new physique: burly and possessed of seemingly limitless energy, Isabel lunged at the Mag Kana and latched onto its feathers. The pain in her ribs was non-existent. Scaling her way up the beast with an impossible amount of ease, Isabel was tickled with laughter. She ducked the creature's talons and continued to its head. With a quick yank, she ripped out Dante's sword.

She leapt off the beast and rushed towards Dante. He still was shaken, so she grabbed his bow and an arrow and what was left of his rope. Tying the rope to the arrow, she told herself to focus. She tuned out the deafening screeches and the uncomfortable trickle of sweat down the nape of her neck. Isabel took aim. When she exhaled, she released the arrow, sending it past the Mag Kana's head.

"What are you doing?" Dante cried.

The arrow turned and made its way back down on the other side of the monster's head. Isabel dodged the beast's latest attack and ran to where the arrow had fallen. She snatched the arrow with one hand, while the other held the start of the rope. She sprinted around the Kana's feet, intertwining the rope between each leg.

The Mag Kana began tripping over the ropes. As the beast tottered, Isabel's breathing quickened. When the monster finally crashed onto the floor, she slashed at it as furiously as she could. And within a few miraculous moments, the beast fell silent.

"Bravo!" Dante clapped rigidly, eyes stretched wide.

He stood beside Isabel, who was still sporting Bence's body. Dante put his arm around her, but twitched at the feel of the rippled muscles.

"That is a peculiar object you have there," he said, pointing at the whistle.

"A gift from a friend," she growled in a low tone.

"This body... This is the leader of Damian's army. Have you met him?"

"Yes."

After pocketing the whistle, Isabel ran toward the felled beast. She paced around its entire body, wondering how to best to perform the necessary surgery.

"It looks like it will be messy." She went over to the Mag Kana's sliced throat, blood still oozing out, causing her to gag. "Well, looks like I have no choice."

Isabel drew Dante's sword once again and cut the creature down to its bowels. Tears welled in her eyes. But she wanted that gem desperately. More importantly, she wanted to get out of here as soon as she could.

After two episodes of vomiting over the foul stench of the beast's entrails, her eye caught a sparkle. It called out to her: Tuuli's Opal, repelling the bile and blood that tried to cover it. She clawed at her prize, and upon her touch, the talisman erupted into the air and hovered over her. Dante's mouth grew slack as he called out to her to return to her original form.

She pulled Jabin's whistle close to her lips, blew into it, and shrank back into her delicate figure.

"That is much better!" Dante enthused as he caressed her cheek. "I am very proud. I will admit, I didn't think I would be walking out without dragging your dead carcass out."

Before she could react, Tuuli's Opal shot straight into Isabel's armlet, almost knocking her over. Hot energy surged up her arm. It filled her entire body as her exhaustion drained away.

"Time to try this out. Let's get out of here!"

Isabel raised her left arm and prayed for the talisman to shine. A blinding white light erupted from the opal and sent a rush of cool wind around her and Dante. They clung together tightly. The swirling gale engulfed them in a cocoon as they were lifted from the ground and carried towards the ceiling.

Her newfound confidence pushed them at a dizzying velocity as they crashed out of the temple and into the sky. The wind Isabel commanded pushed her feet forward.

Dante let go, spreading his wings so he could fly by her side. She laughed, and Dante winked at her. Joy inflated her chest as tears welled in her eyes.

Maybe I can do this after all.

They circled the temple a few times before heading to Dante's chateau.

The horizon darkened. The sun hid behind smoke, rising from various homes in Buryan. Isabel commanded gusts of wind to part the billowing ashes. Dante soared past her, dodging arrows shot from the ground. They landed in front of the mill which was engulfed in flames. Chaos raged everywhere: Tuuli Veijari galloped on dark horses, pursuing civilians. Houses were burning. Screams rang in the air. It seemed that Bence did not waste his time.

"Find Tuuli's Opal! Find the Princess! Orders are to take her alive!" shouted a nearby Veijari.

Dante pushed Isabel out of the path of a Veijari on horseback who was swinging a large battle axe. Dante leapt at him and used his bow to strangle the traitor.

"Two hundred years of working for the enemy, how dare you return thinking you can be victorious? Not while I am around!"

Dante twisted his opponent off his horse. He called for his sword. Isabel threw it to him, but it landed beyond his reach. The Veijari kicked Dante and scrambled towards the sword. He grabbed the Veijari's foot. Isabel ran to the axe the rogue dropped and charged at the pair. She lodged the axe into her enemy's back. He howled and fell onto the sword. Dante got up and grabbed a hold of Isabel. When her eyes fell on the Veijari, she gasped.

"Look!"

The fallen Tuuli Veijari's back was exposed. Beyond the blood, they could see his shoulder blades protruding. He was wingless. Nothing but infected scars remained. Dante covered his mouth and stumbled backwards. Isabel could hear him gagging, but all she could do was stare.

Light-headed, Isabel started seeing double. While the grotesque image of metal slicing through flesh nauseated her, she could not look away. Not even blink. This Veijari's blood had sprinkled over her, and Isabel could only think of the warm spots all over her garments. Senses overloading with despair to the point of feeling numb, she knew that these images would haunt her memories for the rest of her life, however long or short it might be.

"Here. Take his horse, transform into Bence or whatever you can to disguise yourself. You *must* get out of my city unnoticed. I will get my sword and defend my people." Dante's voice seemed like an otherworldly echo.

"Dante."

"Yes?"

"Why are his wings sawed off?" Isabel's voice was barely audible.

"My Princess, I must go protect my people. I beg you. Go. Please!"

He turned and mounted another stranded horse and galloped away into the cloud of dust and destruction. Isabel did not hesitate further. She blew Jabin's whistle once more, transformed into Bence, and fled towards the city gates. No one tried to stop her. Not even once.

CHAPTER
18

The sun glowed high in the sky. Isabel's blood boiled with anxiety, and while her dry eyes stared straight, she saw nothing. Images of death flooded her mind. The memory of hot blood spraying onto her made her skin crawl. Isabel kicked at the horse to gallop faster. She had never murdered anyone or anything before, and she feared for her sanity.

It almost would be easier to throw myself into the ocean and join my sister!

As she tugged at the reigns, the horse whinnied and slowed to a stop. Isabel hopped off. She brought her hands to her face, not recognizing any of the foreign features. From the corner of her eye, Isabel could see red hair. A scream lodged in her throat. She cried out and began tearing at her hair.

"I am going to kill that bastard!"

Her hands wandered to her belt. However, the sheath was barren. Isabel's mind cleared, and she remembered

Farid's sword had been destroyed.

She dropped to her knees and rocked back and forth. Her cries transformed into sobs as she pounded the earth with her fists.

"Who am I kidding." Isabel shuddered upon hearing Bence's voice leave her lips. "I cannot kill that man. I cannot kill anyone. Even if I could, he could easily get to me first."

As her hands grew clammy and tears cleared from her eyes, Isabel found the strength to collect herself. She sat on the ground in silence, and caressed the grass beneath her. Listening to the leaves rustling in the breeze, she focused on her breathing. Her heart pounded in her chest.

"Okay, focus on what you need to do. What do you need to do? Uh, supplies. I need supplies."

Her horse nudged her from behind. Isabel released a smile as she patted its nose. Massaging its mane, her thoughts that held her hostage loosened their binds. Images of Dante and her parents replaced the ones of blood and death.

With a deep breath, Isabel said, "I'm sorry, beast. I don't know what got a hold of me. I'm okay. I won't give up."

The horse snuffed, and warm air tickled her skin. With one final pat, she mounted the horse and continued her journey.

In the back of Isabel's mind, she ticked off the numbers of weapons on display in the castle. If they still were there, she could seize them and move onto the task of finding the next stone of power.

Who would be at the abandoned castle? Would my parents still be there with the rescue team? And the scavengers…

Trotting through Stopping Valley, her train of thought broke when she spotted a heap in the grass. Nudging her horse to speed up, she gasped when the heap turned out to be a body.

The figure lay motionless. Leaping off her horse, she approached it cautiously. Two arrows stuck out from his back. Isabel ripped them out, and with a grunt, she flipped the body over. He was draped in black and purple. Scars covered the man's pockmarked skin. His eyes stared blankly at the sky, and his chest remained still.

Shuddering, she brushed her fingers over his eyelids.

Dead bodies still discomfit me. Even an Aeonian's.

After a moment of silence, she searched his clothing for anything useful. Nothing. No shield. Not even a dagger. She cursed, wondering what had happened to him. Her hand ran over a lump in his cloak.

She pulled out a scroll of parchment. Pulling at the ribbon, the paper unfurled, revealing a poorly drawn map. Smudged ink outlined the island and x's marked the four tribal cities. Deranian Castle was situated in the center, crossed off in red ink. Or blood. Isabel gagged.

A dotted line connected Buryan, Cehennem in the northeast, and Pekas Bay down south. At the bottom the word 'surveillance' was scribbled. After giving the body a once over, she determined he was a scout.

"They must be as confused as I am. I'm sure they are curious how the other talismans are protected," she mumbled to herself.

A rustle in the distance stole her breath. Peeking up subtly, she spotted miniature figures atop a hill.

Wolves? No. They have two tails. They must be Zingari. Maybe Jabin is among them!

Sighing with relief, she dropped the map and waved. Instead of waving back, the Zingari appeared to quarrel amongst themselves. She made her way towards them as one drew an arrow. Isabel stopped in her tracks.

The rest of the Zingaris shadowed him, releasing arrows at her. As they whizzed over her head, Isabel ducked. She crawled up to her horse, struggling to mount it. Looking down at her hands, she realized she still looked like the enemy.

"No! No, I am—"

Three more arrows flew by. A fourth one hit her horse, who reared its head and knocked Isabel off. She yelled out in frustration and ran for cover. She scrambled for her whistle. But as soon as she found it, the Zingaris retreated. They yelped and pushed against each other as they vanished from sight. One dropped their bow.

Hyperventilating, she held a hand to her chest. Her life flashed before her eyes, leaving her stomach queasy. She had to rush to the castle as fast as she could. Isabel approached her fallen horse. Discovering it was dead, she brushed her hand through its mane in mourning. The river gurgled indifferently.

I've got to keep moving.

She turned towards the direction where the Zingari attacked her. The bow still lay in the grass. Scooping it up, she slung it around her shoulder. After a few minutes of scavenging, Isabel collected five arrows. Satisfied with her haul, she scanned the horizon. Rolling hills seemed to go on forever. Trees that dotted the area swayed in the wind. Not a creature was in sight. Even the birds had stopped singing. A shudder trickled down Isabel's back, but she pushed forward.

Isabel did not arrive at Deran castle until nightfall. Her shoulders tensed and a migraine tore through her skull. Taking care not to trip over rubble, she meandered up the marble stairway to the main entrance.

Cold air descended on her, causing goose bumps to crawl up her skin. As she wrapped her arms around one another, she stepped over a fallen column. Debris floated in the air in thick clouds of gray. The sound of cracking glass snapped from underneath her feet. Isabel's stomach sank as she surveyed the area.

This place is barely recognizable.

When she pushed the doors open, she retched at the smell of rotten flesh. Many purple cloaks were draped over scores of bodies. She tip-toed down the main corridor and into the first inner chamber. Isabel coughed. The only response was a rat scuttling into the shadows, startling her.

When Isabel determined that there was no other threat, she surrendered her guise with a gentle blow into Jabin's whistle. Isabel stretched comfortably in her own skin, and then continued exploring. Her heart welled with memories as she walked up the stairs and down the hallway. Each step echoed in the silence. Around every corner, her heart twisted in anticipation of possibly finding her parents. Or an enemy.

She headed to her chapel. The lanterns were extinguished, leaving Isabel to rely on the stone walls for guidance. While she traveled the familiar path, Isabel constantly checked behind her, swearing she heard a footstep or something dropping to the floor. Her mouth ran dry the further she walked. Even the sound of her own breath sent her on edge.

The chapel doors were indeterminable at the end of the dark hallway. Recalling her trip to Buryan Temple with Dante, Isabel summoned Tuuli's Opal, curious to see if she could procure some light. As she raised her arm, she closed her eyes and prayed for brightness. A slight breeze fluttered by her, but when she opened her eyes, the hallway remained dark.

How was Dante able to do that?

When Isabel squeezed her eyes shut once more, the sound of an object dropping somewhere from behind interrupted her thoughts. Her heart raced and caused the opal to flash brightly, emitting gusts of wind so strong that the doors to the chapel burst open. The light from the talisman vanished in mere seconds, leaving her in the dark once more.

I've got to get a hold of my powers.

Turning around, she checked for intruders. "Anyone there?"

Only silence greeted her. Inching closer to the chapel, she held her breath, waiting for anything to jump from the shadows. Her heel met the steps into the room, and Isabel released a sigh. As she wiped beads of sweat from her hairline, she scanned the inside of the chapel. It was dim; the only light seeped through the stained glass.

The room was charred to a crisp, but the stone altars remained. Amid the dust, Isabel found what she was looking for: her family's royal sai. This pair of silver weapons glimmered under the light from the hole in the ceiling. It was still encased in glass. Her fingertips grazed the surface, marveling at this rare three-pronged weapon. She looked up to see if there was anything she could use to smash the case. However, her attention was diverted to the historic scrolls, once tucked neatly in shelves, which were scattered on the floor. Most of them were open and unraveled, as if someone decided to do a little late night reading.

That's peculiar.

A hand hooked around her arms, locking her in place. As she struggled, a blade inched closer to her neck. The assailant's breath warmed the base of her neck. Fear stole her breath and paralyzed her limbs.

"I would hold still if I were you—"

Immediately recognizing his voice, Isabel stomped on the attacker's instep. His grip relaxed just enough for her to elbow his stomach and drop to the floor. She rolled forward, jumped up, and raised her fists.

A hooded figure stood opposite her, sword drawn and pointed at her chest.

"What? You're not happy to see me?"

The figure removed his hood and opened his arms in a mocking embrace. Isabel's fingers trembled. Her blood curdled. Her soul froze. And yet, an unbearable heat rose to her cheeks.

"Bence!"

"Go ahead. I'll even break the case for you. I'm not afraid of some oversized forks."

He peeled his upper lip back and smashed the glass with the hilt of his weapon. Isabel's heart thundered as she watched the glass fragments rain onto the floor.

How cocky can this man be?

"*Go on.* It makes no difference to me," he said in a blasé tone. He took a step back and gestured to her.

Her lips quivered, desperate to berate her enemy. Without taking her eyes off him, Isabel snatched the pair of sai. Bence studied her every move, but he remained as still as a statue. His lack of concern reignited her hatred for him and his family.

"You had better start taking me seriously," Isabel snapped.

She mumbled prayers, begging Tuuli's Opal to work. The stone glowed, stirring the air around her, sending debris off the ground.

"This is how you greet... an old *friend?*" His lips twisted into a smirk.

Her fingernails dug into the leather handles of the sai. They weighed heavy, but her arms remained raised. Anger boiled from the depths of her bowels, bubbling up to her throat. "Cut it out. Why are you here? I thought you were alongside your men attacking Buryan."

"I had better things to do," he said.

"Like snoop around?" Looking him up and down, she noticed a few scrolls tucked into a satchel that clung to his hip.

Bence's eyes flashed. "Why do my plans interest you?"

"Well, judging from what I see, you are looking for some answers. Maybe you Aeonians are just as clueless about the disappearance of the armlet's talismans as I am. And from what I know, your parent's talismans of power were transformed into the physical form of Cehennem. As long as that still stands, then they don't have their powers to make a dent in this war!"

The gale picked up, whipping Bence's hair around his face. Yet he made no expression. After he shielded himself from a broken tile that flew at him, he took steady steps towards her. His words fell from his lips each time his boot connected to the ground.

Isabel was strangely calm. "That is supposed to frighten me? A bunch of brutes broke through some metal bars and…"

Bence crossed his arms and barked in laughter. "It takes more than just strength to break out of an enchanted prison. You have no idea what we are capable of."

Get yourself together. It's a scare tactic.

"It doesn't matter. Let's focus on you for a minute. Last time we met, *you* threatened my life in the form of a game. But I figured out your tricks. Well, here I am. I got Tuuli's Opal for you. Come and get me!" The turbulence grew malevolent, like a pack of wolves racing around the room.

"It sounds harsh when you put it that way," Bence said as he paced around her.

"You manipulated me." Isabel clenched her jaw so tightly she swore she could've cracked her teeth.

Bence walked against the force of the wind, weakening with each step he took. Isabel followed his movements, refusing to expose her back. Panic seized her throat when she noticed her powers diminishing.

Come on!

As she shifted her weight, Isabel winced at the burn circulating in her shoulders. Her breathing grew labored. The pulsing energy from her armlet slowed to a stop.

I'm exhausted.

Bence smiled like a cat in play. "Or maybe you have some of the details mixed up. I was going to break in only after you *unlocked the entrance*. I didn't need you to bring the stone out of the temple. So, if that were the case, why would I let you actually reach it? You could *easily* crush me with that power of yours. Take some pride. You simply beat me."

"Oh?" Isabel sputtered.

After sucking in a deep breath, Bence exhaled slowly. "Relax. I'm not here to hurt you," he said, narrowing his eyes.

"Well, I-I am here to hurt you!" Isabel's voice wavered as he closed in on her.

When his body stood mere inches from her, Isabel shrunk back in disgust. Locking eyes, neither of them blinked. After a minute of silence, he sheathed his sword and pulled her into an embrace. Isabel gasped. Losing focus, the light from the opal flickered until it went dark, and the air finally came to a rest.

"Much better." He let her go and relaxed his shoulders.

Isabel gawked at his sudden switch in tone.

"We will get a lot more done if we talk like civilized adults."

"You're *joking*." Her jaw fell askew.

How can a murderer advise me to talk like a civilized adult?

"And as for being here… It's quite peaceful. A little light

reading. You know, I had to escape my father's wrath after he discovered you got Tuuli's Opal," Bence said with an exaggerated shrug of his shoulders.

"What? No, you are making this all up." Isabel pushed him away. "You seek to deceive me!"

"Farid was the one who ordered a score of soldiers to shake Buryan up to find you. He apparently has no patience for me to do *my* job," he sniped and rolled his eyes. After taking a deep breath, his eyes narrowed. "Anyway, I have a proposition."

Isabel could not figure out his intentions, and his fickle personality stumped her. She squeezed her eyes shut to break away from his hypnosis. But there was no escape from his chilling voice.

"My father and mother now think I am out 'mapping out the situation' and searching for you. But what a waste... to kill you for one stone? With all the time I spent with you back at Cehennem, I think I grew to like you," he said, sarcasm icing every word.

"What are you getting at? I can kill you in an instant now!" As she tightened her grip on the sai, she focused her attention on the armlet. The light from the opal flickered, but died out instantly.

"Oh really, you can?" Bence paused. "Know that Damian will rain hell upon you with or without me alive. Don't forget. Their mission is much bigger than me."

"No. You are their son!"

"I am a piece to their path to success. If they want me as a pawn, so be it. Now, listen to my proposition: word is, the Kai and Foti swapped stones. This created a great disruption in their lands, but this sacrifice made it impossible for my men to penetrate their temples. It seems like the Kai would rather boil in their own homes than let anyone else possess the stone!"

Isabel's heart skipped a beat. Images of Kai floating face down in Pekas Bay flooded her mind. She winced at the gory thought.

"Now, here is the problem," he continued in a sing-song voice. "No matter how you perceive it, Damian and Echidna want you dead, and they want the talismans. But from both what I have read and heard, only you would be able to retrieve them. So, what happens when you do? You would have them in your possession and also enough power to turn the tides of this war. Interesting, yes?"

There is no way such a man could speak with reason. This is just another game to him. And he will be waiting at the finish line with a knife to my throat.

Without another word, Isabel backed into the closest pew and sat down. She urged Bence on with a nod. He knelt to her eye level and brushed her stringy hair away from her face. Isabel dug her nails into her palm.

"My allegiance remains with my parents, but why don't you let me accompany you for now—"

Isabel interrupted with a snort. "You're insane to think I am this stupid."

"As I said, for *now*. I will help you retrieve the remaining talismans. It's what both you and I want. And when you finally do, we will have a proper show down. And who knows, maybe you will give yourself to me in the mean-time."

Once he broke into a snicker, Isabel's lips twisted in disgust. Bence pushed her playfully but she refused to budge. He got up, cleared his throat, and stretched out his hand.

"Your humor is disgusting."

"What have you got to lose?" he pressed. "With me, my men will not touch you. Not until you are ready for a fair fight."

"...And what if I refuse?" She eyed his lips, waiting for his words.

Bence tapped his index finger against his nose. "We could start with your parents."

"Wait, how do you know—"

"I caught wind that my twin apparently had less than perfect aim. But that is a mistake easily rectified if you don't go along with me. We have scouts all over the country, and they will hunt them down before you even had time to blink."

"You are despicable!" Tears formed at the brink of Isabel's eyes as white hot anger pricked her skin.

"Well, you could have said 'yes' to start, and I wouldn't have to make such a threat." Hands on his hips, Bence stared at the wall with a brightly painted mural. After studying it for a moment, his eyes bounced back to Isabel. The menacing grin he wore faded. "I'm cruel because I have to be."

Isabel heard his words but wasn't listening. Her brain was busy trying to reason with herself. Bence didn't seem to have a single ounce of integrity, but her gut wrenched at the realization that there was no other option.

Maybe he is bluffing, maybe he isn't. But I can't take that risk.

"You look like you need rest. Think it over and give me the answer in the morning," he said, interrupting her thoughts. His voice was cool, void of the malice that was laced in his previous words.

Isabel grit her teeth. "And have you slit my throat while I'm asleep?"

Holding his hands up, he backed away silently. He positioned himself by the entryway and said, "Well, I'm not letting you go anywhere, so you best take advantage of down time."

"I can't sleep with you watching me either."

As soon as he turned around, Isabel stretched onto the pew, sai in hand. The wooden seat was nothing like her bed that she missed so much. As she wiggled to find a better position, Isabel's muscles stung. Her eyes burned, but she was too scared to blink. Bence sat outside the door with his back against it.

"With me guarding the door, looks like you will be forced to sleep. Terrible, aren't I?"

She crossed her arms. Isabel was fighting a losing battle. "Fine. But do not even think of coming in while I am sleeping," she warned.

"As you can tell, I haven't moved."

"Because you know I'm still awake. I am fully armed."

"Congratulations. Be careful not to stab yourself when you roll over."

After a minute of silence, Isabel pushed the sai away from her. They made a faint clinking sound. Bence turned his head slightly at the noise. Her thoughts churned as the minutes slipped by. The chirping of crickets filled the air between them. Occasionally, she heard Bence's fingers drumming on the ground.

"You really should be sleeping," he said.

"Shut up."

Her guts were still turning, sending signals of doubt into her mind. Images of Farid shooting arrows into her mother and father flashed before her eyes. Isabel bit her lip, stifling a whimper.

"Are you okay?"

His voice sent her into a cold sweat. Though the tone was soft, it was still the voice of a ruthless warrior.

"F-fine," Isabel said with a stutter.

Curling into a ball, she commanded her heavy lids to close. She wished away Bence's haunting voice. And somehow, she eventually fell asleep.

The next morning, Isabel awoke with a start. Her hand flew to her neck instinctively but felt nothing. As she sat up, she found that she was unscathed, with Bence at the door as promised. She was so sure her throat was going to be slit in the night.

When Isabel stood up, she massaged the knots on her upper back. She welcomed the pain as a distraction from the mental agony caused by her situation. Bence cracked his neck and turned to face her. There were bags under his bloodshot eyes.

"Sleep well?" he asked.

"Better than you did it seems," she replied curtly. "Listen, I have a few… requests."

Blinking in shock, Bence looked around as if seeking an audience. "Like?"

"Let me walk behind or beside you. I am not comfortable if my back is to you."

"Seems fair. Tell you what. I'll throw in another deal. When I safely get you to the location of the last talisman, I will give you an hour head start. From there, all bets are off." Bence rocked on the balls of his feet.

When I get to the final destination, I will be powerful enough to end you.

Isabel reached out for Bence's hand and shook it. "Done."

"It's settled then," he sighed. "Our first stop, Pekas."

Calling for her to prep for their journey, Bence assembled his armor. Without taking her eyes off him, Isabel gathered her belongings with one hand, while keeping a sai in the other. He shook his head, now shuffling through his satchel. As he stood, the door handle snagged his bag, sending the contents within pouring out.

Food, scrolls, and various traveling supplies tumbled out. Bence's eyes bulged and darted between her and his satchel. His cheeks flushed beet red.

"What did you steal?" Isabel scrambled towards him and clasped her hand to her mouth. *"Where did you get that?"*

A peridot ring was among the mix of goods.

"Er, from a room down the hallway?"

Whacking his hand away, Isabel scooped the ring up. Stroking the gem, Isabel frowned. Heat rose to her cheeks as she formed a reply. "It belonged to my sister."

"Hell, really?" Bence exclaimed. "I cannot fathom dealing with two of you!"

"Well, you don't have to. She passed away. You would

have liked her, too."

"Why? Was she prettier?"

Growling, Isabel crossed her arms.

"She definitely must've been." Bence snickered.

"She was supposed to receive the armlet and inherit the crown."

"Wait. You weren't the chosen one?" Bence slapped his knee. He extended his hand, and she hesitated. "You unfortunate soul. Ready?"

"As I ever will be…"

CHAPTER

19

Isabel stood before the gilded walls that separated her from Pekas, headache thumping between her ears. The barrier stretched for miles and towered over palm trees. She and Bence traveled all day and night to the southernmost tip of Deran, which consisted of a vast bay and grassy beaches. Isabel reminisced about summertime vacations spent there with her family.

Her parents had always found a way to talk about the kingdom, so Isabel would slip away and explore Pekas. She had befriended many Kai, finding their playful spirits refreshing. They would let her grab onto their lengthy ears and jet out to the coral reefs where Isabel would poke her head into the sea and gaze at the explosion of colorful fish and underground buildings. She hoped the same city was still intact.

When she shouted at the gate tower, no one answered.

She pulled at the door handle, wooden and carved into the likeness of a Kai's head, but it didn't budge. Isabel glanced back at Bence, who hung behind her. She threw her pointer finger at him and waggled it.

"What did I say?"

Rolling his eyes, he walked up to her. "Better?"

"Yes. I always want you in my line of vision—"

"—so you won't expose your back to me in case I throw a knife in it. *I know.*"

Her face heated when he broke into the smirk he loved to wear. He had been teasing her mercilessly about her sister throughout their journey, and Isabel guessed he was replaying her reactions in his mind.

As she huffed, Isabel raised her left arm. When she centered her focus on the gates, a tingling sensation crept down her arms, gathering at her fingertips. Tuuli's Opal glowed weakly. Closing her eyes, she commanded its power.

Wisps of fog appeared around her armlet, and a gale erupted from the heart of the opal's core. The stone shone brightly as white hot power pumped through Isabel's veins. As she swung her arm, gusts of wind blew in all directions. The metal screeched under the oppressive gale as welts formed along the surface. The doors bent until an opening formed. Bence clapped in exaggerated amusement.

When Isabel stepped onto the grounds of the water metropolis, her heart skipped a beat. There was a faint splash of water as she stepped into a puddle. Clouds of mist, as if in a sauna, drifted about. The level of water had receded by an astonishing amount since her last visit. She tugged at her collar in the sweltering heat.

"Looks great?" Bence murmured, fingers drumming his lips.

Isabel continued down the slope, where many blue domes poked out from the water's surface and approached one completely exposed into the air. Cursing loudly, Bence stumbled as he tripped over a body. It was a Kai, lifeless, with a gash at its neck.

"Your people were already here," she said with a scowl.

Before Bence could respond, three Kai Veijari rounded the corner from behind the structure. Their unusually large foreheads bore the sign of the Aeonians.

"Why did you bring her here?" grunted one, pointing out the pair to his companions.

"Why do you question your commander?" Bence snarled, puffing his chest out. "If you say another word, I will slit your throats!"

Isabel recoiled from him, eyeing the monsters that roared and flailed their tails in defiance. One of the Veijari stepped towards Isabel and lowered his weapon before speaking.

"But master—"

Bence drew a dagger and threw it at the offender. The knife caught the creature in the neck, and he fell silent.

"Anyone else?"

The other two Veijari shook their heads, staring down at their paws.

"What have you useless carcasses been doing here? Killing for fun? That's not our mission!"

"We have been sending one Kai at a time to get into the sanctuary. None have survived the boiling temperature. There must be a way because the Kai leader cannot be found. We think he is hiding in there!"

"Well, I'm here now. Damian and Echidna have commanded me to detain this wench as my prisoner. I have decided to keep her alive and use her to retrieve the stones for us."

Isabel glared at Bence and bit her tongue. This man could betray her at any moment. She was counting the minutes until she could knock him off his feet, but knowing her parents' lives lay in the balance, she had to bide her time.

"Genius!" they cried.

Bence raised his brow. "Uh, yes. Now, be gone. Go guard the gates."

The two Veijari grumbled as they ambled over their dead partner. Bence waved them off and coaxed Isabel to keep moving. Though she made it to Pekas without Bence doing her any harm, she still held a lot of reservations about him. He killed without hesitation and with frightening precision. His eyes always remained alert and his body poised, ready to strike like a cobra.

Isabel particularly did not like his smile. It was wide and crooked, sending chills up her spine every time he curled those lips, as if taking pleasure in playing with his prey.

They waded as far as they could up to their thighs. The water here was warm, but not boiling. Not yet.

The sanctuary must be further out.

She took a breath and dove in with Bence.

CHAPTER

20

Once in the water, Bence opened his eyes. Sapphires and pearls of different shades embedded the walls with intricate designs of the history of the Kai: stories of great harvests, ceremonies, and folk lore about fairies. Clumps of seaweed floated past him. The filaments danced around his body and through his hair.

Fixated on the precious stones in the ocean wall, he swam closer for a better look. When a black pearl caught his eye, Bence pulled out a dagger and pried it free. As he kicked away, he noticed it belonged to a montage. The black pearl was the eye of a rabbit-like creature, much like a Kai. But there was something different about this one. It spanned from the seafloor to the surface and was depicted waving seven arms. Smaller Kai were illustrated swimming around the currents made by its movements. He shook his head, growing dizzy with the rising temperature. The seven arms looked like fourteen. He continued to float off, entranced by

Pekas' beauty.

It was then he realized he had lost track of Isabel.

Running out of air, he chose a tunnel that led upward. The water kept warming up by the second. Bence shed his armor piece by piece, fighting the dizziness that seeped into his mind. He broke the surface to catch a breath, observing the empty cavern in which he'd emerged. Debris floated on the surface around him and the aroma was musty.

As his thoughts became clearer, Bence hoisted himself from the water. He rotated on the spot and searched for an exit. An opening no more than a few feet high stood at the other end of the cavern. "I hate small places."

Bence rolled up his sleeves and crawled into the space. The tunnel twisted downward as he stepped waist deep in water. He explored the path and felt instantly grateful for the dropping temperature. Groping the mossy wall for direction, he cut his hand on a jagged rock.

"I really hate small places."

The tunnel took a dip. Taking a deep breath, he dove down and followed the path that twisted back up. When he resurfaced, Bence arrived in a large circular arena with a pointed ceiling. After wrapping his hand in a cloth he ripped from his tunic, he explored the room. Many miniature tables decorated the dining hall half immersed in water.

He climbed a tall statue nearby and leaped onto a chandelier for a better view. But his attention was drawn to the crystals that dangled from it. They glowed a soft yellow, inducing a green covetous feeling. Bence plucked a few and pocketed them.

The chandelier started to shake violently. The fastening

gave way, and he crashed onto the ground. He froze and listened for any noises. No one was within ear shot. After rubbing the pain out of his shoulder, Bence looked up, and to his surprise he made a hole in the ceiling. Ladder like indents suggested it was more like a doorway. Another small space. But curiosity nagged at him.

The stone!

Climbing the statue once more, Bence drew one of his daggers. He tested the walls; they were made of clay. So he pierced the wall with it, pulled out a second dagger, and slowly climbed his way to the top. His abdomen burned to keep his feet up and in place. But his tested strength prevailed, and a ledge at the entrance of the pathway gave him great relief. While tracing his fingers on the wall, Bence gripped the indentations. After climbing this pseudo-ladder, he surfaced in another rounded room. He fell to his side, exhausted.

"Dover?" a worried voice whispered.

Bence held his breath and squinted his eyes.

"No, it's not him. Stranger… a human." Another voice rang out.

As each word floated from the darkness, his fingers fidgeted against the handles of his daggers.

"It's not the princess. It's a man, but who?"

A wave of mumbling broke out. Then, a fire ignited, exposing a crowd of Kai.

So this is where they're hiding.

Standing slowly, he backed up a few steps. While small in stature, the Kai greatly outnumbered him. Bence calculated his immediate targets and steps required for a possible escape.

"It's a baddie, mommy! Look at his tattoo!" cried a juvenile Kai.

Bence covered his neck with his hand in unfamiliar shame. A full grown male Kai stepped towards him, spear in hand.

"Get out of here. And tell your wife to burn in hell."

Blinking repeatedly, Bence's blood boiled. "You mistake me for my father. And I do not care for how you insult the woman who bore me life."

"Calder, It's the son of Damian!" cried yet another Kai.

"*First* born son," Bence snarled in defiance. "And I command the army that destroyed the kingdom of Deran!"

"We must dispose of this filthy blood kin. Born in Cehennem. He is cursed!" Calder exclaimed.

In the blink of an eye, twelve additional spears surrounded him. Bence spat on the ground and raised his two muddy daggers before him.

CHAPTER

21

Isabel swam through the main channel, a tunnel half filled with water. Sapphires of varying size dotted the walls. Seaweed waved their slimy arms, tickling Isabel as she kept swimming. The channel opened up into Dover's residence, a wide chamber lit with a multitude of candles in oyster shells. Wax melted onto the floor and chairs were toppled over. She wondered when the last time a Kai was here.

She climbed onto the clay surface and waited for Bence. She waited for some time, but he did not appear. With a sigh, Isabel glanced behind her, where Dover's throne sat. A small child could probably fit into it, although it was far more ornate than the Deranian throne. Intricate designs were carved into the pearl setting. Sapphires lined the arm rests while rubies traced the legs. Isabel cocked her head to the side.

The rubies were probably a more recent addition. Hakan and Dover have become very chummy over the years.

A small smile escaped Isabel at the thought of the unusual pair walking towards her during her armlet ceremony. After staring at it for a few seconds, she realized a slight opening behind it didn't flow properly, a doorway discreetly painted to blend into the wall. A clicking noise was coming from the room. She approached it in curiosity and opened it. Isabel entered a room with aquamarine walls and white tiles. Wooden poles towered throughout the room, topped with crystals that emitted light, exposing various pipes, motionless cogs, and wheels all over the room.

"Pretty unproductive, huh?"

Hand flying to the hilt of her sai, Isabel spun around. Dover stood right behind her with dropped whiskers. As she relaxed her hands, Isabel bent over to hug him.

"Where is everyone?"

"The ones that survived?" He smoothed his ears behind his head as his eyes darkened.

Isabel squirmed in her skin, guilt consuming her. She hoped she wasn't too late.

"They are past this room in the ceremonial chamber. The only place that those savage warriors and rebels did not destroy yet." He struck the floor with his cane in frustration.

"Take me to your people so I may speak to them." Isabel fumbled for the right words. "I heard of the swap of stones. I plan to take the Foti's Ruby away from your city. I know why you did this, but I can't allow you to suffer any more for me. I'm here to resume responsibility as your leader."

"Bless you, my dear Princess. Or do I dare say, Queen?"

"My parents are alive. Dante is working on bringing them to Buryan," she said, choking on her words.

His black orbs widened. "Heavens above, that's a miracle!"

"Yes," Isabel said, nodding. "It truly is. I am counting down the minutes until I see them again. So, tell me what's going on?"

"I had brought the talisman into Pekas Sanctuary just beyond our city borders. In fact, as soon as I opened the doors, it flew from my hands into the depths of the sanctuary. I do not know where the volatile ruby has settled." Dover's dry lips quivered, as if ending some ghost tale. "Come this way."

Strolling past the hidden chamber, Dover and Isabel entered a mossy tunnel. The ground squished under each footstep. Wiggling her toes, Isabel grimaced at the sensation of her waterlogged boots. She reached her hands out, unable to see more than a few feet ahead of her.

After tripping on a rock, Dover grumbled and struck his cane. A sapphire dangling from his necklace glowed, filling the passage with cool light.

"That's better," he huffed, smoothing his fur with his paws.

Rounding a corner, Isabel stepped into a room with a pointed ceiling. The porcelain texture of the walls glimmered with blue light. As Dover withdrew his power, she scanned the room. To her right, a broken chandelier lay on the floor. Isabel scurried towards it. Dover whimpered behind her. When Isabel noticed an opening in the ceiling, she broke into a cold sweat.

Bence.

Isabel grabbed Dover's paw and propelled them upward

with a gentle gust of wind. She focused all of her attention to making sure he landed gently, but Dover whimpered again. Isabel gulped at the sight before her.

Calder stood on his hind legs, muzzle inches away from Bence's face. He snarled as Bence's fingers' twitched. Everyone had drawn their weapons. Children hid behind mothers. Any sudden movement would trigger bloodshed.

"Stop!" Isabel waved her arms to grab everyone's attention, while Dover looked around the room in consternation.

When Bence caught her eye, he released a nervous chuckle. "Thank goodness you're here. The Kai were about to execute me without trial!"

Isabel raised her left arm. "Leave him alone. He is not worthy of death... yet," she said, quelling the shakiness in her voice.

His smile faded.

"What is the meaning of this?" Calder did not take his eye off Bence.

Dover turned to her. "Is it true? You know this fiend? Are you friends with this man?"

Her lips twisted at his clipped tone. Taking a breath, a lump swelled in her throat. Bence stood at the corner of her vision, staring blankly at her.

Maybe this is my chance. I could have him killed now before he has any opportunities to betray me.

Stomach churning, her eyes darted between Dover and Bence. A Kai coughed in the background. The room was quiet; it seemed everyone held their breath as they waited for her answer. But her thoughts played tug-of-war in her mind.

He deserves to die.

The sensation of searing hot needles pricked Isabel's skin as images of her parents flickered in and out of her mind's eye. But as the feeling subsided, the daunting task ahead dulled her senses. She knew Bence's aid would shield her from the rest of the Aeonians.

"Well?" Dover's voice broke her train of thought.

I will never know for certain if Bence will keep his word or not. I guess that is the true definition of risk.

Isabel exhaled deeply. "He's here to help me retrieve the four stones of power," Isabel said. Her voice wavered as Dover's brow wrinkled.

"But what possibly made you think he is being truthful with you?"

When all the Kai laid their eyes on her, Isabel's jaw clenched. While her partnership made sense at the time, there was nothing she could say that didn't sound foolish. She glanced at Bence as doubt twisted her stomach into knots.

Bence stepped in front of her, lowering his daggers. "It's true. Yes, I *am* the commander of Damian's army. But I know that only Isabel can retrieve the stones my father and mother are desperately seeking. The gems are designed to only be in her possession. So I have chosen to help Isabel achieve her destiny. You cannot fight destiny…"

A sour taste crept up the back of her tongue as everyone's face remained blank.

"As soon as she reclaims four talismans, we shall have our fight. My loyalty will remain with my kin. And that is when fate will determine who the final carrier of the stones will be."

The Kai withdrew their spears but shook their heads. Dover, particularly, did not seem convinced.

"Once a heart is blackened, it will always be that way. Your nature, *sir*—"

"My name is Bence."

The tension thickened, nearly suffocating Isabel. Each drop of water falling from his tunic seemed to send her nerves on edge.

"Your nature, *Bence*, is to always betray, to spill blood, and only for the one purpose. So, you are essentially using the Princess to achieve your kin's ends."

Frustration mounted in Isabel's chest as her eyes expelled tears. "Dover, their army is too strong. They possess monsters, influence over the Kana, and dark powers supporting them. I cannot continue my journey without his help."

At least I hope I'm right. Too late to go back now.

Dover's sagging eyes turned back to her.

"A stalemate. So be it then. Two young humans who use one another for their own purposes. We shall see who prevails in the end." He turned to Bence. "But you must swear to be true to Isabel until all the stones are retrieved and she has a fighting chance. If you do not, I will not stop until I see the last breath leave your body."

Bence remained silent. Clearing his throat, he turned towards Isabel. He clasped her hand and bent on one knee. "I swear it."

There was a mix of shouts and cries at his pledge. Isabel flushed at his gesture as she fumbled for words.

"Bence."

Before she released his hand, a tremor threw her off balance. Bence pulled her towards him and wrapped his other arm around her shoulders. She winced at his touch. Dust from the ceiling shook as the tremors grew violent. Mothers took hold of their children.

Calder growled, pointing his spear at Bence. "You are a betrayer already."

"I did not send for anyone, I swear it," he exclaimed, waving his hands wildly. He scanned the room for the source of the quake.

Deafening explosions erupted to their left, then their right. One blast sent Dover flying, purple blood oozing from his head. A herd of Veijari charged into the room.

"Kidnap the Princess and kill the rest!" the foremost Viejari cried.

Drawing his sword, Bence pointed at them. "What are you doing? I demand you to tell me what is going on!"

"You are no longer in command. You are to report to Damian at once!"

Bence's lips thinned as Isabel glared at him. Drawing her sai, she sliced at the air. Tuuli's Opal, in full power, sent vicious bursts of air into the thick of her enemies. Many stood their ground and snarled in defiance, some were blown back by the onslaught. Isabel crossed her sai across her chest.

Let's try this.

She released another gale. A whistling sound erupted from the stone, a sound that only winds belonging to a tornado could make. As weapons flew out of her enemies' hands, Kai flung their spears towards their enemies. One Veijari fell, then another.

"Take Dover and get out of here," Isabel exclaimed.

She summoned one last blast of wind that swiftly howled around the room, picking up all the debris caused by the explosions. Rocks and hardened pieces of clay danced around the Veijari to the motion of her arms. An invisible pressure gripped her shoulders.

The pain increased exponentially. When her arms gave out, she collapsed to the floor, dropping the debris onto her enemies. Shrieks filled the air, her enemies crushed with nowhere to move. Bence ran to Isabel, but she shook him off.

"*Leave me alone*" she hissed. Her mind raced so quickly she couldn't think straight.

At that moment, one Veijari emerged from under a rock, drew back its bow, and sent an arrow her way. Bence shoved her out of the way and took the arrow to his thigh.

"Go!" He urged her towards the exit.

She sprinted towards the hole where the Kai escaped. She jumped through without a word. When she crawled through the space, something tugged at her chest.

He saved me?

Mixed with guilt and relief that Bence had not betrayed her, Isabel's head jerked towards the sound of his cries. After an impatient sigh, she turned around. She poked her head through the hole.

Before Bence could remove the arrow, the foremost Veijari pounded his fists against the floor. He kept pounding, the room shaking with each hit. The creature's power sent debris tumbling down towards him. As he turned to sprint towards the exit, Isabel heard a cry. A baby Kai was stranded in a corner, surrounded by hard clay.

Bence limped past the baby as it wailed louder. He

stopped. He blinked forcefully as his lips skewed into a frown. The cry was so piercing Isabel had to cover her ears. After a moment, Bence swiveled on the balls of his feet and reached for the baby. A chunk of the ceiling crashed inches away from them. With a free hand, he hurled a dagger that burrowed between the Veijari's eyes. Bence scooped the baby in his one arm and dove towards the tunnel. Isabel ducked.

As rocks rained behind him, Bence crashed into her. They both tumbled downwards and crashed onto the floor. The debris blocked the exit. He sighed and chuckled grimly, the baby Kai clinging to his tunic.

"Sasha's baby!"

Isabel looked up and saw a female Kai hop towards Bence. The mother eyed him and extended her paws out to her child slowly. When the baby reached out, she scooped her child into her arms and without breaking her gaze, backed into the crowd. Silence filled the air. The baby, before she disappeared into the mass, poked her fuzzy head out.

"Thanks, bad man!" she peeped with a shy little grin.

As she stood up, Isabel could not help but release a smile. Dusting the dirt from her tunic, she gazed upon Bence with a relaxed brow. He shrunk back, shoulders tense as she stroked the side of his face.

"You did a good deed. You do have a heart in there somewhere."

"N-no. The brat was in my way!" He crossed his arms and glared at her.

"Well, you saved my life, too."

"Because I need you to complete your mission."

Isabel bit her lip and giggled softly. Bence stalked to the corner of the room, hiding his face with his hand.

"Wait. That arrow needs to be removed," she said, scuttling after him.

"No. I got it," he barked.

Plopping onto the ground, Bence groaned. Wrapping his fingers around the shaft, he inhaled deeply. Isabel reached out, but he shook his head. When he yanked the arrow out, Bence shouted as blood oozed around the obsidian head, still lodged in his skin.

"Son of a bi—"

Isabel flew to his leg and observed the wound. "You should have listened to me!"

"Oh, as if you know how to fix a battle wound, *Princess*?"

Looking him square in the eye, she said, "I know a lot more than you think."

Without another word, she ripped part of her sleeve and pressed it against his thigh. When it soaked through, she asked for more linen. The head of the arrow was barely protruding from his flesh, and she wasn't sure if she could pry it out with her bare fingers.

"Bo. We are close to the dining hall. Can you possibly find tongs?"

"As you wish."

He hopped off and returned in minutes. She grabbed the metal and clipped it to the edges of the arrowhead. Breathing heavily, Isabel tried to steady her hands.

"Isabel, I also brought some towels," said Bo.

"Perfect. Keep them ready to apply when I pull it out."

Bence's eyes narrowed at her. "Maybe I should do it."

"One. Two."

Before she said three, she jerked her arm back and felt a *plop*. The arrowhead flew into the air and landed a foot away from her. Bo wrapped towels around Bence's thigh as he cried out.

"You best hold your hands here for a few minutes until the bleeding stops. It seems like a vein was punctured, not an artery. You are one lucky man. And I would also thank the Princess here. None of us would have done this for you," Bo spat.

As Bence opened his mouth, Isabel placed a hand on Bo's shoulder. "I don't need any thanks from the likes of him."

The Kai gathered around Isabel. Their doleful eyes were glued to her as if begging for help. Guilt re-emerged, tugging at her vocal cords. She knew the Aeonians would likely attack again. And with the rising temperatures, their homes were sure to reach boiling within days. Dover lay a few feet from her.

"How is he? Let me look at him. Maybe I can help him as well."

Dover's chest rose and fell, but blood covered most of his matted fur. Gashes plagued his body.

"He's alive, but without the rich waters we thrive in, death is sure to come," Bo said.

"No, that can't be. I'm sure I can help him." Her voice wavered. Anxiety buzzed in her chest like a swarm of angry bees. She crouched over him and observed every wound. Some cuts were extremely deep, draining any hope she had left.

"I think that we should travel to Ogonia where Kai's Sapphire resides. This may be Dover's only chance of survival. Any Kai's survival at this point. We need you to remove Foti's Ruby as soon as possible," he said.

Her knuckles whitened as they pressed against the ground. If Dover died, she would blame only herself. But Bo seemed confident in his answer. Nodding, Isabel rose to her feet.

"I believe you will do the right thing." Isabel said.

Calder brushed past Bo. "Wait just a second. Don't you all think it's about time we return to our homeland overseas? Cold water is plentiful there, and our own kind would be there to help us."

"What about loyalty to Deran," Sachiel said, raising his voice. Frowning he adjusted the coral bracelets on his wrist. "This represents wisdom and loyalty. You should embody those traits like Bo and I. You may be an elder, but both of us have been by Dover's side longer than you have been alive."

"I have the wits to distinguish life from death. Travel to Ogonia will kill us all. How can we be loyal to the country when we won't survive the war?"

"Kai's Sapphire is in Ogonia. Dover brought it there for a reason," Bo said with hooded eyes.

"Why did Dover and Hakan have to switch the stones? I knew this would happen!"

Sachiel stepped in between Calder and Isabel. He stood on his hind legs to be at eye level with him. "Kai's Sapphire and Foti's Ruby are safe, are they not? The Aeonians cannot get their hands on it. Even Damian's firstborn has the wits to know it was a foolproof plan. And if the talismans had not been switched, they would be in the Aeonian's possession by now, and we would have died by the sword!" He bent to cradle Dover in his arms. "Take your pick of which death you wish! At least here, we have one possible hope. I agree with Bo. Cease your despair and let us adapt. We must move quickly!"

Isabel cleared her throat. Bo, Sachiel, and Calder stepped back and observed her. "Let's take a vote. Regardless of what you decide, I will right the evil that has befallen us. I will make this place safe again."

"In your hands? But you are just a girl! We would've been safer if your parents were here," Calder barked back.

Her gaze fell as tears welled in her eyes. This same feeling of uselessness cast over her like a shadow.

Bence stomped towards her, and held her up by the shoulders.

"If anyone had spoken to me like that, I would've killed them for such defiance. And if you should know, if it weren't for her, I would've cut your throats by now!"

Calder growled, and some Kai drew their weapons. Bo raised his hands to try and calm everyone.

"This man is correct," Sachiel said. "The Princess has swayed this warrior to her aid for the moment. Let's not forget this. Also, let me remind you how Dover stood up for this young woman at the armlet ceremony. Dover has faith in her. Those who wish to stay in Deran and migrate to Ogonia, raise your hand! Those who wish to migrate out, keep your hands down."

Isabel's heart sank as a few paws were raised. A few more popped up. The ones that kept their paws down didn't look at her.

Don't you have faith in me?

When Bo tallied the votes, she clasped her hands tightly in prayer. It was split down the middle. None were willing to negotiate.

Isabel sniffed as she wiped away her tears. "So be it. The Kai must part ways. Say your good-byes."

After an hour passed, everyone made their way to the sandy shores of Pekas. The wind blew a lonely whistle as Sachiel and Bo flagged all the Kai that wished to migrate to Ogonia. Isabel tagged along, helping carry Dover. She laid him by the gate and sat by his side. Bence stood a few feet away from her, arms crossed and staring up at the sky. Stroking Dover's ear, Isabel wished that he could speak.

Calder hung by a brightly colored building to her left, lining up boats one by one. Each boat was six feet long and six feet wide. The Kai that trickled to Calder carried their satchels, made of fibrous seaweed, over their slumped shoulders. Nervous looks were exchanged; the Kai haven't seen their homeland in over two centuries.

"Light..."

The whisper came from the lump of fur beside Isabel. As if struck by lightning, Isabel jumped in place and fell back. Scrambling to her knees, she gazed at Dover intently.

"Dover. Dover!"

"Gleam of light," he wheezed, giving her a wan smile.

"I don't get it. Keep talking. Bo has to see this—"

"I see it. A gleam of light shrouded in darkness... Is still a light."

When he finished his last word, Dover closed his eyes. He still breathed, but was no longer responding.

"Bo!" Isabel shouted in place. As she heard his feet shuffling in the sand, she waved her arm. "He just spoke to me. He said something about a light or whatever."

"His heart is still beating, but he must be getting a fever. We have to speed things along."

"But—"

In a flash, he was gone. Isabel turned to Bence, who was still starting at the sky.

I wonder if that meant anything.

Snapping from her thoughts, the three elders locked eyes as cries of sadness and mourning surrounded them. Families were splitting. Friends embraced for the last time. Calder's group marched solemnly and gathered where the ocean water lapped at their feet.

"Board the boats. Sachiel, Bo, I pray that you are right and find salvation here." Calder turned to Isabel. He grunted and bowed his head. "Your forgiveness, my lady."

She nodded silently.

"Now, I will also get a boat for you. Pekas Sanctuary lies at base of the reef. With the water this hot, you will not get there by swimming."

By sunset, Sachiel, Bo, and a handful of the Kai, had gathered their rations. They placed Dover on a gurney, and marched away solemnly under the blood red sky. Calder loaded up a dozen boats that fit three, four at most, saving the last for Isabel and Bence. Before Calder took off, he gave her one lantern.

"A gift."

Lifting the lantern by the handle, she observed it solemnly. "Thank you."

"This is not just any lantern. It can light the pathways of the sanctuary, even underwater."

Isabel smiled. She pat Calder's arm. "Even better. Good luck. I wish you could've stayed. Be well. Stay safe."

She waved as the Kai paddled away, moving swiftly through the steaming waters. Stars poked out one by one, and the moons stretched across the sky, shining full and bright. The ocean blended into the horizon. A cool breeze dried Isabel's sweat. Fluffy sand stretched for miles. The moment was a brief respite of serenity.

"Well, there is no time like the present." Bence sighed, hands at his hips. He played with the hilt of his sword. "You ready?"

"I'm scared," she whispered. "Pekas is deserted. The Kai are divided. I was never a strong person before. How will I be sure I can be strong now?"

Isabel trembled as the burden of her journey pressed against her chest. Pekas Sanctuary was somewhere out there in the steaming waters waiting for her.

CHAPTER

22

Bence faced his sworn enemy. One he would never imagine looking like this. She was as pale as the purest silk. Her body, leaner and more fit than he expected for royal women, was shaking. He sensed vulnerability, which normally induced a lust for violence. But this time, all he could do was brush Isabel's hair from her eyes. Her cool features contrasted his greatly from his dark skin and fiercely orange hair. He did not know how to comfort her. He had never known it for himself. Yet he felt a tug in his chest, almost moving his whole being.

"Princess…"

"What do you want?" Isabel placed her chin on her hand.

He held his breath a moment. Exhaling, he shook his head and smirked. "My *princess*, someday you will find your own strength. I can't tell you how, nor can I show you the way. But here you are, not your sister, about to sail and plunge into a dark ocean with the man who attacked your people and kidnapped you. You're stronger than you know. What may seem like a weakness is only wisdom and power disguised."

When he received no response, Bence cleared his throat and boarded the boat. Isabel lingered behind, still rooted in the spot where he left her.

"Let's go! Procrastination is an intolerable thing," he said. Tugging at his collar, he avoided her gaze.

Isabel twisted the hair he had touched, shrugged, and followed him. After everything was packed and set, they departed from shore and made their way to the coral reefs that safely buffered Pekas from the greater ocean. The trip would be an hour or so. Isabel napped and Bence rowed.

The objective of his mission repeated in Bence's head. It had been embedded into his subconscious for so long, he could think of nothing else. As a gull cried in the distance, he squeezed his eyes shut. The gentle lapping of the waves failed to distract him.

Opening his eyes, his gaze migrated to his sword, then to Isabel's neck. It was instinct to calculate the best way to slit her throat with optimal precision. Jerking his head away, he silently scolded himself for his murderous thoughts. It started to sicken him.

Or maybe it's just seasickness.

And yet, with every rock of the boat, one word ebbed in and out of his mind.

Kill.

Even when it is all over, Isabel doesn't need to die.

Kill.

In fact, we may still need her alive when we collect all the stones.

Kill.

Bence spotted the rowdy surf ahead. His fingers grazed the hilt of his sword. As he swallowed the lump in his throat, he reached for her.

CHAPTER

23

A hand gripped Isabel's shoulder. Her eyelids fluttered and focused on a blurry figure. As the hand shook her, she jumped awake.

"What? What happened?" Isabel's hands gripped the sides of the boat as she flinched.

Bence loomed over her. "We arrived, I believe," Bence murmured.

"Don't scare me like that!"

Shrugging, he reached for the Calder's lamp and lit it. The flame within glowed fiercely, emitting a bluish light. "How did you sleep?"

"I could've used a few more hours. Are you okay? You look pale." Isabel yawned.

"I'm fine."

She bit her lip as they studied one another for a silent moment. When Isabel finally rose, she peered into the ocean. It was pitch black and the steam tired her eyes. There was a whole world beneath the surface, one that remained a mystery to her. Until now. Once her fingertips grazed the water, she drew her hand back and sucked on her fingers.

"We can't even get in. It'll burn our skin!" After a moment, she gasped. "I could use Tuuli's Opal to open a path downward. But that would require a lot of power. I would need to know where the entrance to Pekas Sanctuary is—"

"Let's lower a rope with the lamp, and we'll see if we are near it."

"Brilliant!" She reached for the lamp, but Bence swung it out of her reach.

"Wait a second there. I think that is a job for me. I'll be able to tie a reliable knot."

Swatting at Bence, Isabel grazed the metal handle and missed. Irritation mounted each time she tried to snatch the lamp away from him. "And I spent years learning to sew. I know a thing or two—"

"But this is not sewing class! This is life or death!" he exclaimed.

The boat rocked violently, splashing hot water on the both of them. The lantern flung from Bence's hand and plopped into the water.

Pulling her hair, Isabel kicked at him. "You idiot, what have you done?"

"What do you mean, me? What have *you* done, thrashing around like a clown in a tiny boat? You should've known the boat would rock!" He puffed his chest out.

"I ought to push you into the water right now!"

A bright glow stopped their arguing. Isabel leaned over the side of the boat. Hundreds of feet below the surface, she could spot the lantern's light. Starting as a pea-sized blip, like a lone star in the night sky, its reach expanded until it illuminated the broad landscape of the ocean floor. She squealed in delight and shook Bence's arm. He nodded in approval as he scoured for some sort of entrance. Isabel moved to check the opposite side of the boat while he gingerly moved between the bow and stern.

Isabel spied what seemed to be white smoke coming from one bundle of coral, like some sort of hydrothermal vent. The smoke was shooting out at a great speed.

"It must be somewhere there," Isabel said. "If Foti's Ruby was placed in Pekas Sanctuary, would it not be the source of all this hot water?"

"Makes sense," Bence muttered under his breath.

Rolling her sleeves back, she raised her left hand. Tuuli's Opal proudly glowed once more. She twirled her arms in a circular fashion. At first the water did not stir, but when she looked upward, clouds twirled above them. Rumbling and whistling sounded. Then, like a rocket, a water spout appeared and a tunnel of wind blasted downward, tearing a hole through the ocean's surface. This funnel of air crept down into the ocean floor. When the sands were exposed into the open, Isabel waved to Bence.

"Now, let's jump in!"

Her enthusiasm dissipated when she stepped on the edge of the boat, now rocking violently. The distance from the ocean surface to floor made her dizzy, and the world around her spun.

I forgot that I hate heights.

"What's the hold up?" Bence called from behind.

When Isabel turned her head, she lost her balance and fell backward into the eye of the magical tornado. Air rushed from her lungs as she plummeted further. As her hair whipped around her face, she barely spotted Bence diving in. He shouted something, but she couldn't make out what he said.

Twisting her body, she faced the ocean floor.

Fifty feet. Twenty.

Focusing her energy once more, she commanded a gust of wind to slow her fall.

Ten feet. Five.

She stretched her hands outward. Upon impact, she curled her arms, leaned forward, and rolled a few times until she slammed onto her back. Gasping for air, she pushed herself onto her knees. Her arms wobbled like jelly. All the energy it took for her to conjure this vortex as well as support her fall made it seem like she ran around the circumference of Deran, twice over.

I don't have much time.

Lifting her head, she commanded one last gust to buffer Bence's fall. When he landed on the ocean floor, Isabel ran to him. His eyes were open wide, staring up where the boat stood as a mere dot in the distance.

"That was madness. I thought I was going to die," Bence exclaimed as he panted, tongue hanging from the side of his mouth.

"How's your leg? Can you walk?"

"I'm fine."

Isabel chuckled, taking in the salty air that saturated her lungs. Luminescent patterns from hundreds of jellyfish whirled around her, competing with the light of the lantern. Ribbon-like seaweed weaved in between blowfish that puffed in alarm. Yellow brain-shaped coral littered the rocky ocean bottom with anemones that flickered their tentacles. Right in front of her eyes stood the mighty reefs of Pekas Bay, glowing in a myriad of colors: pink, orange, scarlet, and blue.

She focused on carving a pathway to the lantern with her wind vortex. "I can't keep this tunnel going. The water will begin to re-seal itself. I must unlock the doors to the temple. Run, hurry to the lantern and bring it to be me before the storm abates!"

When she finished her last word, the surface to the ocean closed up. Seawater rushed downward in a roar. Isabel sprinted towards the reef where she spotted an entrance: two tiny doors made of coral. She grasped the handle where hand prints were painted on in bright aqua blue. She whispered the prayers of her ancestors. The doors blasted open, releasing the boiling but sparse water from within. She turned and saw Bence running towards her with the lantern, water rushing in from behind and above him.

She reached out her hand. "Hurry!"

The ocean licked at his heels. Turning his head at the danger all around him, he threw the lantern to Isabel first. She caught it and began pulling the doors closed. Bence dove in, sliding just in time as the hot ocean water crashed against the coral. He wasted no time getting up to seal the doors shut. The pressure of the sea overhead was relentless. Isabel heard a click, signaling the hatch was sealed. She collapsed on the floor beside Bence, gasping for breath.

Bence huffed. "We're trapped in here. We have no choice but to succeed."

Isabel got up. The thrill of tearing a path down to the ocean floor with the power of the wind sent adrenaline rushing through her limbs. Isabel's chest swelled at her accomplishment. She glanced at the opal. Its light flickered and faded, seeming to suck away her energy with it. But Isabel pushed past the growing fatigue, confident in her abilities for the first time.

Armed with the lantern, the two set forth. The room was simple, angular and blue. In the center stood an altar, much like the one in Buryan Temple, empty without any sacrifice. There was no doorway to be seen, but Isabel played with the possibility that this room was originally submerged, so she scanned the ceiling and walls. There it was, an arched doorway that sat on a ledge ten feet above the floor. She pondered how to reach it. Meanwhile, Bence circled the altar.

"There's an arrow painted here, pointing in that direction."

Before she could react, he pushed the top of the altar off.

"Imbecile! What are you doing? This place is sacred to the Kai—"

The granite fell onto the floor with a loud thud. Bence beckoned to her proudly. After throwing him a nasty look, she ran over and looked inside. She found a small cannon with a hook and rope loaded into it. With a devilish grin, he took the lantern to the fuse and pushed Isabel down behind the stone altar.

The cannon boomed like thunder and sent the hook right up to the room she had spotted. The hook struck something with a clanging noise, and the line stayed. Without another word, Isabel attached the lantern to her hip as Bence grasped the line with his hands and legs and climbed up towards the room, she immediately followed. Isabel's arms burned, but she kept climbing with Bence leading the way.

Once they reached the doorway, Isabel found the door locked. She drew her sai and broke the lock with a few swings. The hallway within was littered with puddles of water. Steam tired her eyes. Yawning, she nodded for Bence to go ahead of her.

As they advanced, the hall narrowed to the point where the walls glanced her shoulders. Bence slumped ahead of her, mumbling. "What is up with these small places?"

"Well, this is the Kai's place of worship. I don't expect it to accommodate lumbering behemoths such as yourself."

"*Lumbering?*"

She bit her lip to forbid a laugh from escaping. With each moment Isabel spent with her captor, the more she found herself comfortable with him. But she didn't want to admit it.

Don't forget. This man is dangerous.

A sharp pain shot up her nose. Her eyes watered. Bence had stopped abruptly and Isabel walked right into him.

Rubbing the bridge of her nose, Isabel scowled. "What the hell?"

Bence's eyes were fixated on a row of black pearls that lined the wall around the bend. Isabel pushed him, and he stumbled forward, still eyeing the precious gems.

"Let me pry a few of them out. They would fetch a pretty price," he said, mouth growing slack.

"No. This is a sacred place! Shut up and keep moving."

"They would look pretty on you."

As he continued forward, Isabel gawked at him.

"Everything you say has such lewd undertones," she said, storming past him. She wondered what Dante's reaction would be if he heard Bence's remark.

After exploring for about a half hour, Isabel grumbled, scratching her head. The hallways were now a much more comfortable height but still adorned with black pearls. Her eyes flashed to Bence, who shook his head and blinked. It seemed his lust for the pearls disappeared.

"With the direction and distance we've traveled, we got to be past Pekas Bay and beneath the deep ocean," he said.

Isabel shuddered at the thought of walking under tons of seawater. "Do you think the ocean has been affected by Foti's Ruby yet?"

"Let's hope not."

After winding around numerous pearl-studded twists and turns, they arrived at a fork, split into two possible paths. The left corridor glowed with a cerulean light and the right emitted a crimson hue. The hairs on the back of her neck stood as an eerie chill ran up her spine. Biting her nails, Isabel debated with herself. Right seemed like the obvious choice.

"We could split up. Cover more ground that way." Isabel stroked her chin and glanced at Bence.

Flicking hair from his eyes, he scoffed. "You think I'm stupid? You're sticking with me so you don't pull any vanishing acts."

Damn.

"Besides, if all hell breaks loose, I will have you to save my life. Fair exchange, right? I protect you from my men, and you protect me from the elements," he continued.

"Fair? Forcing me into this 'partnership' wasn't exactly fair. And please remind me what happened a few hours ago, when your 'men' defied your orders?" Her tone grew more sarcastic with each word. She flashed him a sardonic smile before heading towards the right corridor.

Bence raised his eyebrows. Imitating a curtsey, he walked alongside Isabel. She arched her shoulders, fuming in silence. All she could hope for was that Foti's Ruby was around the next corner. After walking a few feet, the steam in the air turned into smoke, a black smoke.

"Fire!" Bence's arm shot in front of Isabel.

Towering coral branches in the room were aflame, casting a smoke into the air. He pushed her to the ground, and they crawled closer to investigate.

Craning her neck, Isabel tried to discern the source of the fire, but couldn't find one. She crawled into the room, gritting her teeth at the rough terrain scraping her forearms.

"Isabel. Stop! This is too dangerous," Bence shouted from behind her.

She turned and gave him a hard stare. Bence followed her reluctantly, drawing his hand over his nose.

I have to see if the stone is here.

As she continued to scan the room, Isabel's eyes started to burn. Her nostrils stung and her mind grew foggy. With no other entrance in sight, and the ceiling too high and clouded with smoke to check there, she signaled to Bence to return back to the hallway. He nodded, rubbing his eyes incessantly.

A loud crack sounded above them. A chunk of smolder-ing coral crashed beside Isabel, separating her from Bence. Another crack. More coral tumbled down in a rain of fire. She coughed wildly and looked for a way to reach him.

Standing on the tip of her toes, Isabel spotted Bence writhing in pain. A massive chunk of coral blocked the en-tryway, leaving an opening of only a few feet at the top.

Isabel tried to blow out the fire with gusts of wind. But the flames roared as it stretched higher. She cursed as the glow of Tuuli's Opal faded. A ring of fire surrounded her and crept even closer.

Stupid move.

"Isabel!"

"Bence?" She jumped at the sound of his voice.

"Listen to me very closely. I have some dynamite in my pack. If I were to ignite it in these flames, can you send a gust of wind to direct the explosion skyward? Hopefully, the ocean is sitting directly above this room."

"Where did you get the dynamite?"

"It's best not to ask."

"Did you swipe it? Bence—" Barely able to finish her sen-tence, Isabel's throat burned as her parched tongue grew swollen. She wobbled on her feet. Everything grew dizzy.

"*Can you do it?*" he shouted, demanding an answer.

"Yes!"

A bundle of red sticks flew into the air, fuse lit. She flung her arm in its direction, sending a stream of wind that caused it to defy gravity and fly up into the smoky cloud.

Boom!

Cold water poured into the chamber with an incalculable wrath, extinguishing the flames. The current ripped Isabel from her feet as bits of coral pummeled her. Opening her eyes, she lodged one of her sai into the wall. She looked around the flooded room and spotted Bence, flung in the opposite direction. She tried calling out to him. Only air bubbles came out.

She conjured a bubble of air from her fingertips and squeezed her head through it. Now breathing and in control, she turned her attention back to him.

I can be free from my captor once and for all.

As the room settled, Isabel swam towards the entryway. The opening was large enough for her to squeeze through. Her heart fluttered at the newfound freedom that was within her grasp. As Isabel latched onto the coral boulder, she turned and found Bence floating nearby. His limp body re-sembled a rag doll. For some reason, her muscles froze. Leaving this room meant she was letting Bence die.

He deserves it.

But Isabel never wanted anyone's blood on her hands unless it was in self-defense. And while Bence was her cap-tor, he had not betrayed her. Yet. And she knew she would never rid herself of the guilt by letting him die this way. Cursing to herself, she commanded Tuuli's Opal to flash a brilliant white.

Isabel tightened her core. A pressure erupted within her, radiating down her arm to her finger tips where she sent a stream of air bubbles in his direction and lassoed it around his middle. She flicked her hand back, generating the same motion with the air bubbles. Bence's body approached her quickly.

I hope I don't regret this.

When he was inches away, she reached out to grab him. Once he was secured, she conjured another air bubble and prayed he was still breathing. After commanding the air to fill his lungs, Bence gagged and spit up seawater. Her heart settled. Bence blinked weakly.

The room was now filled with ice cold ocean water. Isabel sighed with relief, the ocean beyond Pekas was still unaffected by Foti's Ruby. She pointed back to the hallway they entered from, and they swam through the other turn. When entering this room, Isabel noticed that the blue light came from lanterns similar to the one that they had lost in the coral avalanche. Within minutes exploring, she felt the temperature rising.

Isabel swam to the floor of the room and found tiny streams of hot bubbles escaping from cracks.

Is Pekas Sanctuary sitting over a volcano?

She clawed at loose rock, pawing out any mud. When a crimson light greeted her, she dug deeper.

"Bence, come see! I think it's here!" Her words only bounced back at her.

Jets of hot water erupted and popped her air bubble. Flung back a few feet, she conjured another one. As she swam back, Isabel panted. Her lips were cracked dry and it was difficult to swallow. Fighting through the heat and exhaustion, she extended her fingertips, barely grazing the opening.

Almost there!

When she made contact, a flash of red blinded her. Isabel

raised her arms as rocks and shells blasted upwards, exposing a gigantic volcanic fault. There shone a bright red glow
of a ruby.

"Foti's Ruby!" She gasped.

The gem was embedded in a claw-shaped setting composed of black obsidian and solidified magma. It glowed
fiercely as if feeding energy into the monstrous submarine
volcano that had been dormant until now. The volcano was
awake.

"It almost seems like this was its home before it was harvested," she muttered, swimming towards it.

As she approached Foti's Ruby, blasts of heated water
and clouds of minerals kept pushing her back. However, Isabel had to keep going. She couldn't stop. Her fingertips
barely grazed the searing-hot talisman when a swarm of fish
flooded the room. She flicked her hands everywhere to dispel them, wondering as to why they would swim into a
heated pool of water. These fish must have come from the
opening Bence had made with the explosive.

A shadow loomed over them both. Lanterns went out
one by one as a gargantuan body wrapped itself around the
entire circumference of the chamber. Throat too paralyzed
to speak, Isabel's gaze met Bence's. His eyes were peeled
back as his mouth fell agape.

Isabel's hands shook as the creature turned. She grasped
her sai. Massive in size, the fish-like creature stared blankly
back at her. A thin film of muck covered its lackluster scales.
Its lower lip jutted out, exposing thick, tapered fangs. The
creature groaned, causing the whole room to vibrate, and
charged at them.

Bence's grip failed him as he grasped at its slimy skin. Tuuli's Opal glowed instinctively. She didn't even have to think. Air bubbles formed at her feet, propelling her away from the monster. Missing her by inches, it crashed into the wall and sank to the floor.

It rolled its clouded eyes, and its hair-like fins swayed in the water. A peculiar aura surrounded the monster. The eyes too, glowed purple. As the hue grew brighter, the creature thrashed around, gnashing its jaws. Isabel could not locate the source of this power, and she had no more time to think. With a roar, arms sprouted from its body.

Isabel drew her sai, but they moved clumsily in the water. The grotesque transformation was something she only saw in nightmares. Her mind raced. If she didn't come up with a plan, she would die. Images of her parents and Dante flashed before her eyes, allowing her memories to invigorate every muscle fiber in her body.

I want to live to see them again.

Ignoring the fleeing fish, the creature headed straight towards Isabel. As its jaws opened wide, she hunched into a ball.

This is it. Steady, steady…

When the creature was about to swallow her whole, she stretched, sai outward, and stabbed the roof of its mouth. The monster shook its head, spitting her out.

In the corner of her eye, Bence pointed towards Foti's Ruby. Isabel nodded. He swam towards the monster, drew his sword and dug a place right into its back. It shook violently, but he held on. With one free hand, he took out a smaller dagger and slashed at it. The monster tried to use its arms to reach his foe. It missed Bence by bare inches.

Isabel turned her focus to the talisman. She used her sai to pry it from its setting. Once freed, the stone shot into her armlet like iron to a magnet. A very familiar warmth surged down her arm. As she faced the creature, Bence was flung off of it. When his air bubble burst, he flailed his limbs as he tried to catch one last breath. Isabel kicked her feet as she swam up to him. Grabbing him by the arm, she formed an air bubble large enough to secure their entire bodies.

"Foti's Ruby. Hear your master's command! Burn these waters! Boil this monster fish to the core!"

The talisman glowed obediently. Within moments, the water around them came alive with heat. The creature charged at them. The ocean waters began to boil, but the creature kept swimming. It opened its jaws once more and began to envelop them in its massive maw. Sweat dripped down her forehead and neck as Isabel took aim.

It all happened in an instant. She slashed up and down, cutting the teeth clean off. The couple fell into its large gullet unscathed. It was dark. Oily. The pounding of its heart jostled them, and the bubble popped. The air inside the creature was rank but somehow breathable. Isabel tried to awaken her fallen partner. Bence's breath was shallow and rattled.

"Come on. You can't quit now. We have the second stone, and I couldn't have done it without you."

The monster's innards vibrated as it let out a screech. A thud knocked her off her feet. After holding her breath, Isabel listened for the beast's heartbeat. The rhythmic thudding ceased.

She readied her sai and slashed through its flesh and emerged from the creature, dead on the ground. The water had evaporated, and the ocean's urge to refill the cavern was blocked by fallen rocks clogging the hallway. Isabel sighed and tumbled out of the monster's innards, covered in jelly and bile. The smell was earthy and salty. Bence stirred and groaned. She got back up and shook him. After slamming his back with her fists, he coughed up jelly. He blinked up at her in amazement.

His emerald eyes stared blankly at her. "What happened?"

"I think a thank you is in order."

Scowling, Bence crossed his arms and looked away. Isabel cleared her throat. As the seconds ticked by, disappointment filled her spirit. After risking her neck to save him, twice, even a brute like him should be thankful. She used to believe there was good in everyone. In the advent of the Aeonian invasion, she wasn't so sure any more.

Isabel stood up and twisted the slime from her hair. Her eyes fixated on the exit. It was a long journey back to Pekas Bay.

Bence coughed. "Thanks... I guess."

CHAPTER

24

Isabel did not know how long they were in the sanctuary. When they resurfaced to friendlier temperatures, the sky was still dark, but the stars were slowly disappearing. The pair sailed back to Pekas to gather their belongings. Bence had not said a word since Isabel obtained Foti's Ruby. Each time she looked at him, he averted his eyes. Right when she thought Bence could be trusted, doubt snaked its way into her mind. There was a twinge in her heart, secretly hoping he was true to his word.

"So," Isabel finally said.

"So, we are approaching the gates of the city," Bence mumbled, crossing his arms. "I am concerned."

"About what?" Isabel swallowed a dry lump in her throat. She instinctively reached for her sai.

Bence eyed her hands and grunted. "My mother and father expect me to report for my lengthy absence," he said, wringing his sleeves dry. Drops of water plopped onto the parched soil, filling the silence between words.

Isabel released her grip on her weapon and looked down at her soaked garments. She wrapped her arms around herself as a breeze picked up. "I thought you promised to help—"

"And I thought you viewed yourself as a prisoner." Bence locked eyes with her.

"Like I had a choice?" Isabel screeched.

His brows furrowed. "You cannot come to Cehennem, so here's your chance to be rid of me. Are you no longer suspicious of my plans?"

When the breeze picked up, Isabel's teeth chattered. "Oh. So you were planning to betray me in the end?" She asked as her shoulders slumped.

When they reached his horse, Bence rummaged through a satchel attached to the saddle. He pulled out a black cloak and tossed it to Isabel.

"I'll leave that for you to decide."

That wicked smile.

As Isabel draped the cloak around her, she shook her head. The wool made her arms itchy. "I cannot figure you out. All I know is that you haven't betrayed me yet. I couldn't have obtained Foti's Ruby without you." Her lips twisted downward as she put a hand to her forehead. "You *promised* to help me—"

"I didn't promise to help you. I forced you to help me. Don't confuse the two."

"You made a proposition, and it's double-sided. Honor it." Isabel lifted her head high while her heart raced. Her jaw tightened as she waited for his response.

I cannot believe I just said that. It seemed like a lose-lose situation either way. If he leaves, I would be free of him. But at the same time, I wouldn't be able to keep an eye on his actions, opening a chapter of uncertainty. And while it would benefit me in some ways to work by his side, I am sure Bence could turn on me any minute.

"I must report back to Cehennem. But if that is what you want." Bence paused, running a hand through his hair. "How about Zeyland? We will meet at the Dunyan city in five days' time."

"Why can't I just come with you now? If I use this whistle I have—" Isabel searched through her rucksack for Jabin's gift. "Then I can transform into a soldier. I can follow you. I will say nothing and wait there with you."

"You think you can fool my parents?" He flicked his bangs back with a sneer. "Do not patronize me. I am not to be supervised by anyone other than them. And do not doubt their ability to seek you out. They *will* know it is you."

Isabel cast her eyes downward. She put the whistle back and stared at Bence who kicked at the city gates and sighed.

"Well, I am glad we settled the trust issue. You have my word. I will help you seek the talismans. But do not forget what happened earlier today with the Veijari. My parents are suspicious. If I do not go, I will be ostracized from my family and my own army will hunt me down like they would you. That takes away the need for me, does it not? And besides," he pulled out his sword and observed it, "I need to clean off the slime from the monster we had slain. It is not coming off easily."

"Very well."

As Bence mounted his horse, he nodded, stone faced.

"Bence?" Isabel rocked on the balls of her feet, losing her words when he looked at her.

"Hm?"

Isabel removed the cloak and tossed it up to him. "You will be cold while you ride."

"Remember," he said. "Five days' time."

The sound of hooves filled the air. Without another word, he galloped away, leaving only a trail of dirt behind.

"I do not understand you, Bence. *Bence...*" She kept repeating his name, drawing out the one syllable.

She swallowed her words and explored the city gates. Grassy dunes rolled for miles both ways. A cluster of coconut trees stood a hundred feet away. Brown orbs peeked out at her. She licked her lips.

I could use a snack.

Trudging through the sand, Isabel wound her arm. She sent a stream of air right at a cluster of coconuts. They plopped onto the ground one by one. As she ran to her snack, a horse neighed in the distance. A brown and white spotted mare was tied to a tree. Its skin clung to its ribcage. Grabbing an armful of coconuts, Isabel snuck up to it and patted its nose. "Where is your master? Want to come with me?"

She split one coconut and held half of it in front of the mare's nose. After a snuff, it bit through the brown fibers and into the white meat. It devoured the whole thing and whinnied for another piece. When they had eaten through half a dozen coconuts, Isabel loosened the rope and rubbed the creature's mane. Its head bobbed up and down and allowed her to hop onto its back.

As she rode, her mind raced. It was time for her to gather her thoughts, plan her next move. Perhaps she could see Dante. Maybe her parents would be with him. Taking the route along the beach-filled coastline, thoughts ebbed in and out of her mind like ocean waves. She had spent so much time with the man who kidnapped her.

Was I right to trust Bence? What would Dante think of such an alliance? Should I even tell him? Most importantly, was everyone in Buryan safe?

Last time she was there, the city was under siege. All those questions rode alongside her the whole way.

Isabel arrived at Buryan as the sun melted into the horizon in shades of purple and pink. She fought to keep her eyelids open, yearning for rest. Her thoughts, once occupied with Bence, were now filled with anticipation of reuniting with Dante. She had two of the four talismans. Pausing to glance at her armlet, Isabel smiled at the glistening ruby and opal.

"Half way there." She sighed. "Maybe I will survive after all."

Isabel waved her arms and the ivory gates parted. The air was free from smoke. Riding through the empty streets, she noticed many of the buildings were damaged. Roofs were caved in and windows were shattered.

She did not stop until she reached Dante's manor, which was surprisingly still intact. Dismounting her horse, Isabel ran towards the door, but discovered it was locked. She knocked, then banged. No one answered. She called out Dante's name, but all was silent. Isabel bit her lip and turned away, sulking, with no clue what to do next.

Alarmed, Isabel's gaze fell to the ground. Fresh flowers were strewn over the cobble stone streets. Someone had to be here. Creaking echoed from all directions. Heads poked out of broken homes. They turned to each other, whispering. When a creak sounded behind her, Isabel whipped around and saw Aysu.

Large sunken bags circled Aysu's eyes. Her pale skin made it seem like she saw a ghost. Her hands trembled against the door, her ring creating rapid tapping sounds. Aysu smiled faintly but did not come forward. Isabel waved, but she still did not move.

"Are you okay?" Isabel asked.

Aysu's eyes darted around as she beckoned Isabel inside without a word. Isabel joined her, then peered back out at the broken homes. The few Tuuli that were peeping at her retreated back indoors.

"What's wrong?"

"My dear," she trembled and attempted a hug. "How are you still alive? I am so happy. The Tuuli have suffered great losses during the attack. Many were killed. But, we finally fended them off."

"Dante, where is Dante?"

Aysu's eyes welled up. Isabel's jaw clenched. Her intuition had warned her not to ask this question.

"Captured!" She wailed. "He commanded a great defense, and he drove the enemy beyond the gates. But within a blink of an eye, he—" Aysu choked. "H-he, some youth named Farid, rode past his retreating army and stormed at Dante. Dante held his ground, drew his sword, but Farid struck him, fast as lightning, and took flight with him in a tornado of purple haze. Witchcraft! I am ashamed! I stayed behind the gates when I should have run out to help him!"

"You cannot be too hard on yourself," Isabel said. "They would have cut you to pieces." She held Aysu, biting her tongue. "But if they took him, he must be alive. If they wanted him dead, they would have killed him on the spot."

"What would they want with Dante?"

"I don't know."

Aysu pulled back and rubbed her eyes. "Look at me. I should be preparing your room," she bustled around, grabbing towels. Isabel rolled her eyes and smiled as she waited for Aysu to set up her bath.

Isabel washed up and planned her next step. The Tuuli looked lost without Dante, and she needed to figure out how to get him back.

As she dressed for bed, faint voices echoed down the hallway. Squinting her eyes, she spotted a soft glow of light. Two Tuuli men, elders by the looks of their long white robes, were walking down the main stairwell from the level above. One of them stretched his wings.

That must be Lief!

They paused at her floor when they spotted her. The pair bowed slightly at her and continued down to the ground floor. Itching with curiosity, she tip-toed towards the stairwell. The elders continued to talk in hushed voices. When they stopped at the bottom of the stairwell, one of them cleared his throat. Isabel peeked down at them.

"We need to select a new leader, Lief." This elder's gruff voice cut sharply in the air. He flicked his wrists and tightened the cord around his waist.

"I know. Dante is as good as dead. But—"

"He never was a strong one."

Isabel scrunched her brow. When Lief opened his mouth, the other elder cut him off.

"I do not trust him. Even if he does return alive. I said it before, and I will say it now, putting a nobody into power was a foolish thing. He does not know how to handle responsibility!"

"Efrain!" Lief thundered. After pausing, he lowered his voice. "This was Vindur's decision. If he thought Dante was capable, then maybe you should forget those blasphemous thoughts."

"I stand by my opinion. It may have been Vindur's choice, but it was also his biggest mistake. Letting that peasant in. Some even suspect Dante had something to do with his passing!"

"You know that is a falsehood! How dare you even consider such a conspiracy?" Lief pulled his shoulders back and shoved his face forward. "We elders maintain balance of power between the tribal chief and the people. We voice the people's concerns, not meet in secret to plan a revolution!"

"He is not sophisticated," Efrain pressed. "And there is a darkness to him. A darkness that doesn't belong in a true Tuuli."

Isabel swallowed a hard lump in her throat. Her grip on the balusters tightened until she heard a *crack*. The wood splintered as she bit her lip, hoping they didn't hear.

"My dear?"

Isabel yelped and turned to see Aysu.

"I thought I told you to rest," she whispered.

"I could not sleep," Aysu said. Her chin quivered and Isabel sighed.

"I could not sleep either, so I decided to take a walk," Isabel trailed off, eyes wandering down to see if the two elders heard her.

"Princess?" Lief's voice confirmed her fears.

As Isabel shot up, her head banged against the handrail. Laughing nervously, she bowed hastily and scurried down the hallway. Her heart pounded so loud that she could hear nothing else, and when she reached her bed, she flopped onto the mattress. She could not believe what she had heard. Isabel kept shaking her head; she had never heard anyone talk about Dante like that.

Efrain is just jealous and aloof. They all are! For them to judge him because he had no royal background — absurd! They are just mad that they were not chosen by Vindur. Dante is a strong man, and he is more elegant than anyone else I know!

Picking her nails, Isabel sat on her bed. She had to be right. But her thoughts kept drifting back to Efrain's words.

'I do not trust him.'

With a huff, Isabel yanked the sheets over her head and squeezed her eyes shut.

CHAPTER

25

As Bence galloped towards Cehennem, his jaw tightened. His breathing grew rapid when he stopped short of his home. His horse reared its head. His surroundings were quiet. An occasional voice echoed from the gaping hole in the earth. The voices amplified as he neared the entrance.

My allegiance to my parents is strong, but would they believe me? Would they see my youth as a sign of weakness in front of a beautiful Princess?

Bence dismounted and nodded to the guards.

"Bence, reporting to Damian and Echidna."

"They have been wondering about your absence."

Bence pushed the guard out of his way and stomped down the spiral staircase, ignoring his brothers and sisters gawking at him.

"My son."

At the bottom of the stairwell, his mother stood clad in armor. Bence rushed down the stairs and kneeled.

"I apologize for my absence," Bence said mechanically. "I have been pursuing an unplanned mission that I felt necessary to our success."

She stroked her cheek with her long, yellow nails. Her features remained neutral. "Damian and I would like a report. Clean up. Tonight we rest. We have a small victory we would like to share with you. We captured the Tuuli lord, Dante, and plan on executing him as an example." Echidna paused. "But first, we wish to make him squeal!"

A toothless grin formed, and her brows narrowed under her ebony hair. It was a look Bence's mother wore often, one of devilish delight. She instructed Bence to dine with them within the hour. Then she departed towards the prisoner's chamber, whip in hand. Craning his neck, he wondered if what she said was true. Dante's death would make things a hell of a lot easier for him. But harder on Isabel.

Shaking his thoughts away, Bence ambled towards his bedchamber. It had been long since he slept in his own bed, not that he ever had a peaceful night's rest. He drew a bath — a tub of ice cold water and soap made from lard. Plunging his bare body into the water, he slowly sank his entire head underneath the surface, allowing the icy shock to jolt him awake. Even though his body was at its prime, his muscles ached for the first time.

The monsters are outside. The monsters are outside waiting to kill you and your family.

His fingers curled around the bar of soap as the petulant chant buzzed in and out of his ears like an angry hornet.

The monsters are outside. The monsters—

Bence hurled the soap at the wall. It collided with a surprisingly loud thud. Two shadow ghouls *whooped* and flew underneath the door and out of his room. Combing his hands through his hair, he released a growl.

After re-emerging from the bath, a newfound weakness lingered within him. Bence wondered if it was Isabel. She was completely innocent. So naïve. Far from a "monster." And it was beginning to make him vulnerable. She was laying him low with no sword, no bow, no weapon of any kind.

"A ridiculous woman," he muttered.

After he dressed, he promptly left his room. The shadows danced on the wall, taunting him. They hooted and screeched, but he did not flinch. As he continued nonchalantly, the shadows flailed their arms impatiently and sulked away.

He entered the dining hall, dark and drab, like everywhere else in Cehennem. A few torches kept the room lighted sufficiently for Bence to greet his mother and father, already seated and ordering their servants about. Damian was the first to notice his son, but he did not get up.

"Where have you been? Your men have been running about wild and unattended. Your brother and sisters listen well, but the Veijari are running amok, and it is not effective for my mission." Damian pounded his fist on the table. Plates and chalices jumped, while Echidna sat there sipping tea. "Farid felt you had been gone too long and led a troop to Buryan. What have you accomplished exactly? What do you know?"

"Damian, it was wrong of me for not informing you of the turn of events. But I was on a hot lead and did not wish to lose it."

"And that lead was to run around, consorting with the enemy?"

Bence raised a brow. So, they knew. "With all due respect, you both supported this idea in the first place! After seeing how easily she trusted me, I made the decision to continue manipulating her into retrieving all the talismans for us. Thus far, she has succeeded in two: the opal and the ruby. Those Veijari that you spoke of tried to interfere with my mission. They wanted to kill her, and what would happen if they were successful? We would have been out of luck!"

They paused as meat arrived at the table, steaming... except Damian's. He liked his meat raw. Damian and Bence ripped into their own plates, tearing off the meat from the bones. Echidna sat in between them, still sipping her tea, watching them with a feline silence.

"Father, our opinions may differ but I know what I am doing. I am keeping the princess under close watch while she does all the work for us. When the time is right, we will kill her. As long as she does not possess all four talismans, she should not be a challenge. She is still very childish and naïve. She is weak and would not be alive without me. Let me return to her and resume my mission."

Damian kept chewing, red blood dripping from his cracked lips.

Echidna put down her tea. "So, you chose to continue to work close to her. It is a shrewd plan, my son. But there is much room for error. Can you continue this mission, unaffected by her?"

"What are you implying?" Bence asked defiantly.

"You are a man, and she is a woman." Echidna picked at her dish with her bony hands. "Your father and I spent years and years forging an army that is iron strong. Unbendable to emotion: the worst of all human weaknesses."

Bence bowed his head, eyes fixated on the wooden table. He kept staring as if he wanted to burn a hole through it. "I understand, mother, but I am not compromised." When he glanced up, Damian and Echidna exchanged glances and continued to eat.

"Bence. You will escort Farid to Buryan while he scouts the area. You are to keep a look out for threats. And that's it," Damian said in a clipped tone.

"Finish up. We will head to the prison chambers next." Echidna patted her lips with a lipstick-stained cloth.

A piece of fat clung to Damian's teeth. Picking at it, he nodded. "We will pay a visit to Dante. Then start planning our next attack. Two talismans are in Isabel's possession, and there are two more to go. And again, *without* consorting with the enemy."

Bence swallowed his final bites, washing it down with a goblet of wine. He hoped it would dull the razor-sharp anger within. Suddenly, he felt he lost his place as top commander. Playing with the rim of the cup, Bence flinched at a splinter. "I'm ready." He stood up and followed his parents down to the prisoner's chamber.

When he opened the door, Bence hung his lamp on a hook on the wall, exposing a broken body on the floor. Dante's back was encrusted with blood around his shoulder blades. He blinked in horror. Turning to his parents, Echidna smiled. He sucked in a lungful of air and approached him, staring at where his wings should be.

"He doesn't need them," Echidna said, tapping her fingertips together.

The clicking of her nails felt like a hammer to his skull. Bence had seen many things throughout the years, but never had he experienced a loss of words. He knelt and shook Dante gently. A whip clacked on the ground, landing beside them.

"Mother?"

Echidna giggled in response. Damian kicked Dante onto his back, who gasped in pain. His hands trembled, and when they opened, they released what looked like fragments of crystal. Bence snatched them up and inspected them.

"You. *You killed her!*" Dante glared directly at Bence.

"What are you raving on about?"

"You!" Dante howled, eyes wild with delirium. "*You* killed Isabel! I saw it with my own eyes!"

Dante pulled and swatted at his hair, as if being attacked by bees. Bence glanced at his father who watched with amusement.

"He had a nightmare," Damian said.

"Oh." Bence crossed his arms and frowned at the pathetic being before him.

Someone who did not grow up in Cehennem would not be used to the demons that pollute dreams.

"Isabel is alive. I did not kill her."

Damian coughed.

"Yet," Bence added.

Dante became still but did not look up.

"She is alive," he repeated, studying Dante. Dirt smeared

all over his face, and his hair was tangled into knots. The usual shine that the Tuuli boasted had faded. He slapped Dante until the Tuuli's crazed look faded from his eyes. "Listen to me! You are close to Isabel. Tell us, what do you know about her plans, and what do you know of the Dunya?"

"Isabel?" he coughed. "I would rather die than betray her trust."

Bence wrinkled his nose and turned away. He locked eyes with his mother for a moment, then spun back around.

"The Dunya." He pressed, teeth clenching. "Where are they hiding the amber talisman?"

"Adem will only open up the city gates to Isabel. I will never tell you where in Zeyland it is."

"Ha!" Damian exclaimed. "They have no true defense for the stone. The Kai and Foti may have swapped stones and Buryan Temple may have been bewitched, but the Dunya have nothing! It is so then! Bence, we will proceed with the plans I had laid out."

"They had immigrated here to escape slavery from you," Dante interjected.

"Such a valiant story according to the history books, but do not forget the Tuuli, *your* tribe, came here not so self-lessly. The Tuuli sought out the powerful gems word had spread about. Your ancestors were just as greedy as we were. Well, it only makes sense..." Damian's lip curled "... as I *was* one of your people... a Tuuli with wings sliced off in exile, just as you are now!" He tore off his tunic and turned around. Huge crosses of hardened flesh marked his back.

Shock slapped Bence's face with an invisible force. Air was sucked from his lungs as he lurched forward, but he quickly bit his lip and froze. He felt his actions fell under scrutiny as his mother's eyes fell on him. Silent. Observant. Echidna nodded solemnly. Bence's mind raced. He had never learned of his ancestry, what his parents did or where they lived before Deran. Bence had never known that he was half Tuuli, half human.

Dante gagged nearby, but every sound came as an echo. Damian's voice rolled in one ear and out the other, rumbling like thunder.

"I was once a Tuuli citizen back in Waaken. I had started a political movement. The elders called me radical," Damian paused to take a breath. "The Tuuli government blamed it on my human wife."

"Not just any human. An *Irellian*," Dante spat, nodding at her lion paw tattoo. "Excuse me, an Irellian slave whore—"

Stomping towards Dante, Bence slapped him. Blood rushed to his head as he cocked his arm back to land another blow. "Watch your mouth," he thundered. "You shall not speak to my mother that way!"

"Let me guess, you didn't know that either? Must be awful to discover your legacy was based in filth."

His fist connected to Dante's jaw. Pain exploded in his knuckles, but Bence kept pounding him until all he could hear were groans.

"Rumor has it, you weren't born into anything special yourself, spoiled brat," Bence hissed, grabbing Dante's hair and shaking his head.

When Bence released him, Dante's body flopped to the ground and curled into a ball. As an emotional typhoon ripped through his chest, Bence's vision blurred. He could barely make out his parents standing before him.

"What a good son," Echidna's voice slithered into his ear.

"You never told us, your own children, that we were part Tuuli. Father, go on. I want to know."

Playing with her hemp bracelets, his mother rolled her eyes and gave a dismissive laugh. "Darling, why would you be interested in *that*? You never asked before. Why does it matter now?"

"*I want to know more.*" His hands balled into fists. His fingernails sliced into his palms.

Damian snickered. "The Tuuli elders in Waaken had said my ideals were too imperialist. I believed in expanding our powers and partnering with humans to seize control of the known world. The Tuuli and humans could be super-beings. However, I could not convince the elders that we had to prove our superiority over others like the Kai, Foti, and Dunya. For this, I was sent into exile.

"That is when fate blessed me. My wife and I sailed away and discovered this island, just as we were on the brink of starvation. With the aid of natives, we not only survived, but also discovered the precious stones which held an invaluable power. The Tuuli could truly become the superior beings I knew we were for the first time! We could only control one stone each at the time, so Echidna and I sailed home with two of our own. However, even with this great news, we were not welcome. So my wife and I swore that we would return to Deran and establish our own government. With those gems of power, we could grow stronger, bigger. Then, everyone would be dying to saw their wings off! But, oh, the irony. The Tuuli exiled me for my supposed power-hunger and greed, and yet I found them sailing to my island to harvest *my* precious gems. Hypocrites!"

Bence's lids felt heavy as he shifted his gaze to Dante, who shook his head.

"No, no," he mumbled weakly.

"Oh yes. But no matter," Damian cleared his throat. "Echidna and I chose to use this to our advantage. We let the Tuuli colonize the west while I sowed rumors of the precious stones to the Foti. Knowing their thirst to prove themselves, they too would try to colonize Deran.

"As for the Kai, my wife instigated persecution for their odd rituals and religion to the humans they lived amongst, pushing them to escape to the island, rumored to be free of terror. And finally, I hunted the Dunya. I rounded up the beasts because their strong backs would make them the best slaves. The foolish reptiles thought to escape by sailing right to the island I drove them to. All unknowingly, the four colonies arrived at Deran, believing they found what they were looking for."

"—when they were all just puppets acting by our invisible strings." Echidna squealed in delight.

"Yes, such easy manipulation. To put all the pieces in place. Now all I needed to do was to sit back—"

His father continued to rant, but Bence slipped in and out of focus. All this information overwhelmed him, as if consumed by a tidal wave. His vacant stare bounced from his parents to Dante.

"I had thought you were just opportunists, but no, you both are more conniving that I gave you credit for." Dante snarled. He shook violently as he supported himself on his elbows.

"Story time has ended. You have until dawn," Damian said as he pulled the tunic over his head. "…Till dawn to aid us, or face execution!" He stormed out.

Before he could sigh, Bence locked eyes with his mother. He dropped his gaze. Heat rose from his collar. "Till dawn," his father's words seemed to echo quietly. He clenched his fists and bid his mother good night, stomping off in a way much like his father. Before the door closed behind him, Bence glanced back. Echidna kneeled over Dante, and a shade of violet glowed around her. Walking faster, he did not break his stride until he reached the bedchamber. Bence released the crystals he found onto his nightstand and flopped into bed. Blowing strands of hair from his eyes, he tried to silence his thoughts. But there were too many questions.

Why did they withhold their ancestry from us all? What purpose did that serve? Why did I never ask?

Bence jumped back out of bed. He needed a mirror, but there were none in Cehennem. He ran to fill his bath once more and lit multiple lanterns to flood his room with light. He ripped off his tunic and tried to position his back towards the reflection, craning his neck in thirsty curiosity. Then, he caught a glimpse of his back. Blended in with lashes from whips, there were two huge scars in the form of crosses on his shoulder blades.

Losing his balance, he gasped in silence and whipped his head back around. One misplaced hand turned the whole wooden tub over and cold water washed over his floors, soaking his hands and knees. His eyes focused on his reflection in the muddy puddles on the floor. Bits of his mother, bits of his father, Bence could not tell who he really was. The question had never occurred to him.

He shuffled to bed and shed his clothing. The buzz of his thoughts transformed into white noise. To distract himself, he organized his daggers on his bed stand so that they lay perfectly parallel to one another. As his fingers trembled, he tapped at the handle of one, spinning it forty degrees.

The room spun as he laid back in bed. He closed his eyes, but the nagging thoughts didn't go away. Tossing and turning, he rolled over and corrected the one crooked dagger. With a sigh, Bence let his exhaustion take over.

When all the lanterns went out, he noticed the glow of the broken dream crystals through his eyelids, piercing into the darkness. Images crept into his consciousness. And then Bence felt as if he were floating away.

The darkness of his mind wrapped around him like a soft cloak. When his ears picked up the sound of a wailing infant, his muscles froze. The singular cry transformed into multiple shrieks from the far corners of his mind.

In an instant, the veil of darkness tore off, exposing a light. Bence covered his eyes until they adjusted to it. He found himself at the entrance to a room in Cehennem. Stone archways stretched above him and a lantern hung at each column. A dozen bassinets lay on the dirt floor. Pudgy fingers poked from each opening as if begging for something.

Anything.

Bence's heart twisted in a way he never experienced before. The longer the infants cried, the louder they became.
Their pitches wavered up and down, only pausing to sniffle.
As he lifted his left leg, blood rushed to his feet, slowing him
down. Each step seemed as if he were stepping through
quicksand, but he wanted to push forward and quiet the infants.

When he crouched over the first bassinet, the first thing
he noticed was the sheet lining, soaked in blood. This baby
looked a few months old, face pinched and purple. Her
limbs flopped around, brushing against the stained bassinet,
and the blood, still fresh, blotted her skin.

Fury burned his fingers and surged up his arms. He
scooped one hand beneath her fragile neck and the other
underneath her soiled cloth diaper. Her large eyes blinked
through the tears. Flecks of gold swirled in her irises. When
he lifted her up and against his chest, he peeked at her back.
Two incisions that marked her shoulder blades were poorly
sutured. Every time she squirmed, bone peeked through her
flesh and she cried louder. He almost dropped her as his
arms grew numb. A pin-pricking sensation poured into his
torso and up his neck, choking him from any words.

Someone. Someone needs to help her. She's going to die!

As if reading his mind, a figure materialized across the
room. First in the form of a shadow, the lighting revealed
Echidna scanning the room. Her eyes passed him without
any facial expression.

My siblings. These are my brothers and sisters!

Rushing to her, Bence clung to his sister as she pounded

his shoulders with her little fists. Tears welled in his eyes.

"Mother! What happened? Please. She will die—"

Echinda didn't budge. She peeked into a bassinet next to her, also stained in blood. This newborn's umbilical cord stump flopped around as he squirmed in place. He whimpered, stretching his arms out towards his mother. She crouched down and pulled him upright. After inspecting his back, also cut the same way as the babe in Bence's arms, she released him. The newborn fell onto his back and he screamed.

"What are you doing?" Bence swung one free arm, but it cut right through his mother as if she were an apparition. His vision clouded as the wailing of the babies around him grew so loud he couldn't hear himself think.

"Mommy!"

A youthful voice cut clear through the noise. He swung around and saw a little boy standing by the doorway. His shoes were nothing but cloth tied at his ankles. His fist clung onto a brown blanket covered in stains. His eyes were emerald green and hair was blood orange.

That's me!

Echinda walked through Bence, towards the boy.

"What's the matter, my son?"

The boy leaned past her, craning his neck to get a peek at all the bassinets.

"Why are they crying?"

Bence's heart froze. Even the infant in his arms became still.

"Never you mind. What's wrong?"

"Farid and I were wrestling. He fell against the sword

rack and he's bleeding," he said, tracing the ground with his toe. "I hurt him."

Without a word, Echinda grabbed little Bence's hand, and they walked down the corridor.

I have to follow them. But what about my other siblings?

Before he could react, the room spun. The walls melted to the ground, and the bassinets evaporated into thin air. The cries fell silent, and for a moment, Bence was shrouded in darkness once more. His sister disappeared from his arms. Whipping his head around, he called for her. The sour sensation of dread sloshed around his stomach, and he could bear it no more. Bence darted in one direction and kept running. The darkness seemed to stretch on forever, but he kept running until he heard a faint cry. He turned towards it and sprinted. His lungs burned. His heart pounded.

As the sound stretched over his head, Bence stopped. The darkness shifted once more, but this time into a drafty room lined with every weapon imaginable. He could vaguely recall his memories of the Veijari hunched over the fires, pounding away at every sword and spear. His mother and his youthful self, huddling in the corner, materialized. Approaching them with caution, he held his breath.

"Mommy. Did I do that?"

Déjà vu crept up his spine as a nine-year-old Farid curled into the fetal position, exposing his back. Tunic ripped to shreds, two large scars marked his shoulder blades. The thick collagen shined compared to the rest of his skin, which was torn and bleeding.

Placing a hand on little Bence, she whispered, "No. It wasn't you."

"Is this what all my brothers and sisters have? Do I have that?"

"Listen closely." Echinda pulled Bence's younger self close, her tapered nose inches from his. "Do you remember the nightmares you told mommy about?"

Little Bence shrunk back and nodded as she continued.

"The monsters that live out in the world did this to Daddy. They disgraced us and threw us in here. Now, it is a rite of passage because you are Damian's son. And now it has become a part of our identity. Remember what I told you?"

The boy remained silent. He shifted his eyes over to watch his brother, who was shivering. Echidna gripped him harder.

"Ouch!"

"Do you remember?" she insisted.

When Bence observed them, he noticed the ring on his mother's finger seemed naked. Upon closer inspection, he saw only fragments of amethyst. He remembered it took years for his mother to regain her full power. Little Bence also noticed it. His eyes were glued to the ring. When it glowed, the child whimpered.

"We must grow big and strong to avenge Daddy. And Mommy. From the bad men," he peeped.

Her ring glowed brighter. "That's right. The monsters outside—"

"Please stop! The shadows tell me this every day. It scares me! Stop it!" Little Bence shrieked and pushed away. He dropped to his knees and covered his ears. "You said you'd make it stop!"

Bence's legs grew weak, but he approached his youthful self, as if drawn by an invisible force. His heart ached, the pain from his childhood flooding back into his mind. Memories he thought he had forgotten were flooding back at the sound of the child's cries.

I remember being scared. Always scared but never sure why.

"Hey there. It's okay. It's going to be okay."

When his fingers grazed the child's shoulders, the boy glared right at him. His eyes shined like glass, filling with tears.

The child opened his mouth. "The monsters are outside. The monsters are outside waiting to kill you and your family."

Black. Little Bence was gone. So was his mother and brother. The draft disappeared, and Bence found himself floating in darkness once more.

"Take our home back, son. Lead your family home."

He turned his head to the sound of his mother's voice, but her words disappeared as quickly as they arrived. When he looked down, he noticed a rusted knife by his feet. The tip of the blade was stained with blood.

As he bent and clasped the handle, a figure appeared before him. He peeked up and saw Isabel. She looked the same as the last time he saw her, except her face was shrouded in darkness. His eyes darted between the knife and her neck. Even though he didn't command it, his arm pointed the knife at her. He ordered his body to put it down, but nothing happened.

"Isabel—"

She opened her mouth and released an ear-piercing

screech. Tornado-strength winds erupted in all directions, sending Bence flying backward. When his back connected with the ground, his hand released the knife into the air. It twirled and twisted until the tip of the blade pointed down. Before Bence could react, the knife plunged into his chest, causing an explosion of pain. When he ripped it out, a ray of light shot into the air from his wound. It stretched into the infinite darkness.

Light-headedness overpowered him as his fingers grew numb. While he couldn't feel it, Bence knew he was losing blood at an alarming rate. Death would arrive in seconds. As he lay there, he set his focus on the ray of light. He grasped for any solace and found himself fading away.

Bence awoke, covered in sweat. He panted, mouth dry as if it had been agape all night. He ran his hand through his hair and blinked in the darkness. "Isabel..." he whispered.

The crystals were void of their light. He fell back into his bed. Holding his hands before him, he could barely make out the silhouette.

These hands. Washed with blood since I turned thirty-two. When I stopped aging.

On that birthday, his parents had organized a combat tournament. In hind sight, it was probably to weed out the weaklings, especially since he was growing older. Maybe too old. But at the time, he was desperate to prove himself the leader over his competitive twin. The stakes grew during the semi-finals.

He remembered his sister well. Yana was tall, lean, and quick. Even though she was almost ten years younger than Bence, she was the closest thing he had to a friend. They trained together and took comfort when the ghouls harassed them at night. And yet she stood there before him, fists up and knuckles bandaged.

'Let the battle to the death begin!'

Echidna's gleeful tone echoed in between Bence's eardrums. Images of Yana flashed before his eyes. She ducked, rolled, and leapt in for the first punch. She had connected with his jaw. When Bence closed his eyes, he swore he could still feel the pain radiating down his neck.

The battle took a turn when Yana hooked her leg around his neck, yanking him down to the floor. By that time, he was bleeding profusely. She broke two of his ribs and had said nothing the entire battle. As a metallic taste filled his mouth, Bence knew he had to make a decision.

He had managed to flip over and pry her leg off him. As soon as he was free, he cupped his hands against her ears. In a moment of shock, Yana scuffled backwards on her elbows. He caught her foot, dragged her towards him and wrapped one arm around her head. Before he twisted, Yana opened her eyes and stared at him with her large eyes, speckled with gold.

A crunching sound snapped Bence from his memory. It sounded too real. He shuddered.

From the moment Yana stopped breathing Bence stopped aging, and his father ordered half of his brothers and sisters to slaughter the weaker half. Once the mortal sin was committed, they were reborn as Aeonians, just like his mother and father.

I am an Aeonian. Maybe that is why my past doesn't matter.

Bence awoke the next morning and suited up with fresh clothes. His senses were blurred, as if he had spent the whole night drinking ale. When he opened the door, the stale air climbed into his nostrils. After a deep breath, one thought dominated his mind: Dante's death sentence was today. He picked up his daggers one by one. The first had to go into his boot. The second tucked in a leather band around his thigh. Working his way up, he shined and hooked each blade into its rightful place on his body. Finally, he scrutinized his broadsword multiple times before placing it into its sheath.

It would break Isabel's heart for sure. But it could not be helped, and she would move on. He finally gathered his weapons and walked down to the prison cell. He ran into his mother and father, who were locking up the door.

"Did I miss the execution?"

"My dear son, he has escaped," she answered, smiling.

"This is not the time for jest. Where is his body?" Bence demanded.

"Do I joke? Perhaps your father, but not I." Echidna's smile turned into a sneer. "When I said he escaped, he *escaped.*"

"But how? I do not understand. There should be no way for anyone to escape from Cehennem," Bence said, stuttering. He cracked his knuckles in frustration.

"Since we broke through it, Cehennem is an open realm. Anyone can walk in and out. And speak for yourself, captain of the army. If you let a prisoner escape, how can we expect you to lead a good offense and defense?"

"What? You surely cannot blame this on me—"

"Son!" Damian barked. "I put you in charge of my army. And if *your* men let our prisoner slip by, then it speaks to your reputation!"

Bence bowed his head in silence. He could not argue with his superiors. Before he opened his mouth, Echidna grazed her fingertips on his arm.

"Maybe it was the power of love that got him through. He loves that little girl, what is her name? *Isabel...*" Her grip tightened. "I would not be surprised if the humans and the Tuuli unite once more. And what would not boost morale more than the two great leaders... you know, getting together?"

"They have no time to get married," Bence said through clenched teeth.

"Oh? I just meant uniting their efforts. I did not mention anything of that sort. Come now, Damian, let us send our other son, Farid, off. He prepares to invade Zeyland. We must make haste and strike without warning."

Bence was left alone, already planning his next step.

CHAPTER

26

Isabel ran as quickly as she could. Her hair whipped around her face as the salty air filled her lungs.

Could the rumors be true?

When the streets narrowed downtown, Isabel slowed so she wouldn't bump into the other hundreds of Tuuli milling towards the district gates. Even though it was still early in the day, all the shops displayed 'closed' signs. Everyone was chattering around her, creating a buzz in the air.

Isabel was now only a few hundred feet from the gates. The Tuuli guards shouted from the towers and waved their hands at Aysu, who led the crowd.

"Open them immediately!" she cried.

Heat erupted at the base of her neck. Finding an opening in the crowd, Isabel zipped her way closer to Aysu. Her heart fluttered with each step. As the gates cranked open at a snail's pace, she craned her neck at what it would reveal. A speck of white appeared in the fields of Deran.

"Is it him?" She broke into a pant as her hands fell onto her knees.

"That's what the guards are saying!" Aysu replied, hopping in place. "Oh, if I had my wings, I would simply soar over the walls to catch a glimpse and confirm for myself!"

"I would need a strong explanation for this." A frosty tone chilled Isabel to the bone.

She turned her head towards the speaker. Efrain walked in between the two and slid his hands into his sleeves. He kept his steel gray eyes forward, buried beneath caterpillar eyebrows.

The gates creaked to a halt. A tall figure limped towards the entrance of Buryan.

"Dante!" Isabel cried.

Forgetting about Efrain's words, Isabel broke into a sprint. As she pushed past the crowd, his face became clearer. His eyes shined when they locked eyes.

I can't believe it. He's alive! Alive!

She stretched out her arms and crashed into Dante. Breaking into sobs, Isabel pulled back and observed his face. Although his hair was tangled, it still glistened under the sun. His cheeks were scratched but otherwise unharmed. Even though she was dying to ask him questions, the words wouldn't come.

After a brief moment of silence, Dante broke into a smile. "Nothing could stop me from returning to you and my people."

"What happened?"

Before he could respond, Aysu arrived and fussed over him. Tugging at his sleeve, she insisted that he travel home to rest.

Isabel continued to observe Dante while he spoke with Aysu. The tunic he wore was nothing she recognized, and he seemed to be in fair condition. No major wounds. Curiosity blossomed.

How did he escape unscathed?

Dante mounted a horse his people brought him. Turning to Isabel he said, "Come with me."

She gasped. His eyes seemed different. They *were* different. All her life, she fell in love with the icy blue color, but now, his irises were darker. Almost violet. Dante shook his hand, dispelling her thoughts. Isabel mechanically took his hand and wrapped her arms around his waist. She blushed; hundreds of eyes were on them. In her periphery, Efrain stood in the same spot. His facial expression remained the same, only to shift when Lief approached him. When Efrain moved his lips, Lief whipped his head to face him.

Maybe I am just inventing things in my head.

"I've missed you," Dante whispered.

She turned her focus away from the elders. "And I have never stopped thinking of you."

As he flicked the reigns, he turned to Aysu and said, "You have done everything I instructed?"

Aysu blinked and stared at Isabel. Her lips trembled as if she wanted to tell Isabel something. But she nodded and instructed the Tuuli to return home.

"What's going on?" Isabel asked.

Turning his head slightly, Dante said, "Not to worry."

The horse broke into a gallop, passing the crowd of Tuuli who clapped and cheered. Shrugging off the questions she had, Isabel nuzzled into Dante's back. His tunic smelled earthy. Almost metallic. Looking up, she saw blotches of dried blood near his shoulders. His upper torso was completely bandaged.

I wonder if anything happened to his wings.

Her mind raced once more as the buildings blurred past her. The clang of the horses' hooves jolted her in and out of her pensive state.

"Alright. We're here. Please get comfortable. I'm going to clean up and have dinner prepared. I'm starving," he said, back still facing her.

She gently shook his shoulder to get him to turn around, but he flicked his arm to release her grip. Jumping off the horse, he finally made eye contact. His eyes were still an odd violet.

"I'm sorry, but I have sustained an injury and it hurt when you touched me. I know you have a lot of questions. But let's not dally. Please go on ahead."

Isabel flinched at his unblinking stare. She bit her lip and dismounted. Patting the fur absentmindedly, she searched for a response.

"Of course. Go ahead. I'll tie up the horse."

Isabel's stomach churned as she secured the animal. Peeking past the fence, the Tuuli swarmed on the sidewalks. Some chattered with excitement, others whispered with stoic expressions. Dante never had so much attention, it was as if he were announced King of Deran. When some men pointed at Isabel, she scuttled to the manor and closed the door behind her.

Releasing a breath, she scanned the foyer. A ray of light

from the second-floor window warmed the stone floor. A rumble erupted from her stomach.

Maybe a little snack before dinner would suffice.

Isabel strolled across the main hallway. Her eyes glazed over the paintings mounted on the walls until she reached the entrance to the dining room. The painting that towered over the table was of Vindur. She could tell by his pinched features. Snow white hair framed his face, from his eyebrows to his jaw. His eyes were the darkest she had ever seen. Vindur's slender fingers wrapped around each arm, and judging by the creases in his robe, he was gripping himself tightly. Cocking her head, Isabel shuddered. When Dante passes away, his portrait will be hung in its place.

A pot clanged in the next room, reminding Isabel of her mission. She veered right and pushed the swing door open. Two maids, who were chopping vegetables and dropping them into pots, stopped.

"Don't mind me. I just wanted something to nibble on while I wait for dinner."

"Princess Isabel! You shouldn't step foot in here! This is a place for servants!" squeaked one.

Isabel held her hand up. "Please, don't worry about it. Just show me what I can munch on."

The same maid hopped off the stool she was standing on and opened one of the pantries. Isabel spotted some dried berries, reminding her of Stopping Valley.

"That might hit the spot." She pointed at one bag.

"Is that all? Surely you would like something more fine, like wine and cheese. Caviar?"

"No, thank you. That's too rich. It will spoil my dinner.

Wow. I am starting to sound like my mother."

"But you may have whatever you wish. Someone of your stature should be above wild berries. We only use them as garnish or for flavor—"

"I'm fine with these. Thank you."

Before the maid could open her mouth again, Isabel curtsied and left the kitchen. The Tuuli always favored wine, cheese, and caviar because they did not have such things in Waaken. In fact, one of her fondest memories was sitting with Dante as a teenager and munching on blocks of cheese. When she tossed a handful of dried berries into her mouth, thoughts of her mother and father surfaced.

Dante may know where they are!

Her heart fluttered as she made her way to the stairs. Grasping the handrail, she swung herself up the first few steps and trotted up the rest. She fought her breathlessness, willing herself to keep going.

I'm going to find him now. I can't wait for the answer.

Isabel reached Dante's door, tossed the rest of the berries into her mouth, and chewed. It was silent. She knocked. The door creaked open slightly, but there was no answer.

"Dante?"

Isabel squinted her eyes to adjust to the dim lighting. Poking her head into the room, she discovered that it was vacant.

"Where the hell is he?" Isabel crossed her arms.

"Isabel?" A shrill sing-song voice floated through the air.

"H-here!" she jumped up. Isabel turned and spotted Aysu. "I was eager to find Dante."

She fidgeted. "Ah, Princess. He is waiting for you in another room."

It figures.

Aysu led Isabel to a hallway she had never been to before. They arrived at a door made of heavy oak, and Aysu pushed with all her might. It creaked open.

On the other side stood Dante, who finished pulling it open. Aysu thanked her master endlessly, and he shushed her away. Dante was dressed in his best silver tunic and smelled of musk. He smiled at her, the edge of his lips twitching. Isabel's chest tightened.

Something just seems off.

Dante cleared his throat, startling Isabel back to the present. Clenching her fist to her breast, Isabel curtsied and pressed her lips together.

"Isabel. I am here to bring you great news. I am sorry I was not here to present them to you earlier. They were not ready. Behold, your mother and father!"

Isabel gasped as he moved to the side. Febe and Hadi lay in beds next to each other. Their eyes were slightly open. She ran towards them, swallowing a lump that stuck in her throat like a jagged rock.

"My child," Febe whispered. She strained to reach out to Isabel, but recoiled in pain.

Isabel beheld scars on her mother's arms and neck. A wheeze escaped each time Hadi exhaled. He gazed upon his daughter, his eyes welling with tears, which fell liberally. Isabel reached to brush aside his thin hair.

"Oh mother, father. How grateful I am to see you breathing and alive! How I wished to have seen you earlier."

Dante appeared by her side. Her muscles tightened.

"How long have they been here?"

"I am sorry I didn't let you visit them earlier. Your parents were brought here shortly before my capture. The rescue mission was successful. They were, and still are, in a critical state. I wished for them to have time and peace to recover first before you laid eyes on them."

"I wish you would've at least told me," she said in a clipped tone. "But my mind can be at peace knowing that they are on the road to recovery."

She immediately thought of Bence and if he knew where her parents were. "Dante. Are we sure no one has followed them here? We need to make sure no one knows of their whereabouts—"

"They are safe here."

"Are you *sure?*" she pressed. "The leader of the Aeonians threatened their lives if…" Isabel paused. Words hung at the tip of her tongue as Dante's face flushed beet red.

He grasped her arm. "Bence. I heard about him. Trying to pass off like he is working with you—"

"How do you know about that?" she exclaimed, yanking her arm away.

Releasing a sigh, he jerked his head to the right. His eyes flickered as if recalling a memory. "I just heard things during my imprisonment."

A faint gurgle sounded in the air. Hadi struggled to lift his head, while Febe tried to reach for him.

This is not the time nor the place.

She mustered a smile and hugged him. "Thank you for taking care of my parents. I think I will spend the rest of the evening with them if you don't mind." She took his hands and bowed, they were strangely clammy.

"Well, there was one more surprise I had. And I also wished for your parents to bear witness too."

Dante genuflected. Isabel instinctively tried to jerk her hands away, but Dante did not let them go. Her eyes widened as his lips parted.

"Isabel, would you marry me?"

Isabel's mouth dropped open. Her first instinct was to turn to her mother and father. Febe wept in joy, but Hadi was motionless and silent. His face did not move.

Oh, father. If only you could speak!

Turning back to Dante who was still on bended knee, Isabel shook her head. Her heart raced faster than her mind could make any sense.

The day I've been dreaming of, and yet it was nothing I expected. I feel so sick.

"Dante. Why? Why now?" She tried to exercise as much control as possible to not reveal her shock.

"I have always wanted you, since the day I laid eyes on you. I always thought you were a strong woman. I never had the courage to properly court you, and with recent events, I feel like I cannot waste any more time… I wish to wed as soon as possible."

Isabel bit hard on her lip at his last words. She tasted blood. "Dante, do not take my hesitation so heavily." She frantically searched for something to say. The urgency shook her system, leaving her light-headed. Thoughts stormed into her head with hundreds of questions. She once was concerned Victoria would steal his heart, and now she was concerned over his motive to marry her in the blink of an eye. "I just feel like this is such an inappropriate time to be marrying. Every day, people are dying. Our country's freedom is at stake."

Dante's face fell, but his chin held strong. "Isabel. You've seen my people. They look so broken. Even though we have been fighting since day one, they are losing sight of hope by the second. The assaults on our city... it left scars on those who survived. So much blood was spilled. And this is just the beginning. Deran is still very much in danger. And I thought, how can we win this war?"

By marrying me as if I am some secret weapon?

"Our swords and shields may be intact, but we are nothing with broken spirits. My people do not have faith in the servant boy turned leader!" He sputtered bitterly. "*Our* alliance can bring your humans and the Tuuli together."

Alliance. How about love?

"Together we can give our people the strength to ensure our success."

Her head throbbed in pain as she debated with herself. She had to make a decision, but couldn't decide if her heart or her mind would speak up first. It would not be the first time in history a couple wed to further their political power. Maybe it was silly for her to think she deserved love.

"Okay," Isabel blurted in a broken voice.

"You will?" Dante relaxed his grip on her hands.

My people need this. Everyone always told me marrying for love was a silly concept.

"I will," she said, folding her arms into her chest.

"It is settled then!" Dante clapped his hands, turning to Hadi and Febe. "Of course, I wanted to do this in your presence, to promise that I will take care of your daughter. Most of all, I wanted to seek your permission to allow a member of the Tuuli to wed the Princess of Deran."

Febe turned to her husband. Hadi only blinked. A thin trail of drool dribbled from his cracked lips. Febe then gazed at her daughter.

"As long as you wish for it." Febe paused to draw a rattled breath, "My little Isabel." She broke into spastic coughs.

Cradling Febe's head until her coughing ceased, Isabel prayed feverishly for things to return to the way they were. To the era of Hadi and Febe, where peace reigned, and her biggest threat was being upstaged by her sister. To when she foolishly thought Dante fancied Victoria. Isabel kissed her mother's forehead and felt beads of sweat. She turned to her father and held his hand. Isabel felt a faint squeeze, even though his face remained vacant. She couldn't bear it any more. She turned away and ran out of the chamber.

Running. Running.

Isabel could not stop until she reached the cliffs at the edge of the city. Gasping for breath, Isabel screamed her tears out.

CHAPTER

27

As blood trickled down his knuckles, Bence stared forward. He couldn't detect any pain. In fact, his whole hand was numb. Fragments of slate peeled off the wall one by one. A chuckle followed a deep breath. He was so sure he got rid of the petulant ghouls this time. "Thirty-two years, and I am still plagued by haunting chants. Not anymore."

"Bence?"

He whipped around and found Farid at the far end of the dining hall.

"What do you want?" Bence growled as he brought his injured hand to his face. A rusty taste filled his mouth as he licked his cuts.

"You ready? Or were you so obsessed with your reflection you forgot?"

"Heh. Escorting my brother? Why would I forget to do that? Someone needs to protect you."

Farid sneered and flicked his cape. "I need no protection.

But it seems you need protection from yourself."

"Shut up, fool." Bence reached for a napkin and wrapped it around his hand.

In a few steps, he caught up with Farid, and they both exited the room.

"You know, I never like to wear cloaks."

Farid shook his head. "Indulge me. Why?"

Reaching his left leg out, Bence stomped on the edge of his twin's cloak. Farid jerked back by the neck and gagged.

Twisting and turning, Farid pulled himself free and glared at him. Massaging his neck, he said, "You could've just told me."

As Bence released a devilish grin, he wrapped his arm around his brother neck, squeezed, and let go. "Come on, now. Time to go."

Farid punched his back and picked up his cloak. Instead of putting it on, he simply hooked it over his arm. They made their way up and out of Cehennem, occasionally punching one another.

When they reached the surface, Bence blinked his eyes. He was starting to adjust to the sunlight much better now. His twin cursed in the background and shielded his eyes.

The air had a slight bite to it, even though there was not a cloud in the sky. The parched dirt crunched underneath his boots as Bence searched for his stallion. It stood beneath a twisted oak tree that looked like it was inches away from rotting into ash. The leaves already turned and broke into the wind.

Everything in a mile radius of here seems dead or dying.

"Where is my *damn* horse?"

Bence rolled his eyes at his brother's screechy voice. "You sound hysterical when you are upset. It's very… unbecoming."

"Unbecoming? *Unbecoming?* You care whether or not my voice is becoming?"

"I believe you lose credibility, crying out like that over something so small. I'm sure Rek was borrowing her."

Waving his arms, Farid raised his tone even further. "There are plenty of wild horses she could've used."

"Let's ride together, then." Turning away from his twin, Bence grasped the reigns of his stallion.

Once the twins hopped on, Bence nudged the beast, and they darted eastward. Hoofs pounded against the earth and the scenery rushed past them in a blur. After almost an hour of riding, they came upon Fuad River.

Bence tugged at the reigns, and the horse stopped short of the shore. Hopping of, he knelt over the river and scooped up a handful of water. He slurped the cold liquid and relished the feeling as it rushed down his throat. The next few handfuls were splashed onto his face and over his hair.

"Ugh. I'm never riding with you again."

Ignoring his twin, Bence unraveled his bandaged hand and washed it in the river. The numbness disappeared and waves of pain radiated from his cuts.

"Seriously, a horse is meant for one traveler—"

The pain from his wound traveled to his head, taking the form of a headache. Every word Farid spoke was like a hammer to his skull.

"Could you please stop whining?"

From the corner of his eye, Farid plopped down next to

him. Bence only fumed more.

"I still don't understand why you're in charge."

Here we go again.

"For the last week you've almost gone rogue, disappearing, then you were found running around with the Princess—"

"The talismans departed upon our father's touch. I was charged with finding a way to bring them back and fulfill our parents' mission. And I will do whatever that takes. I don't need step by step instructions. Just as long as I achieve the desired results. You, on the other hand, require so much instruction."

"Excuse me? I don't need instruction. I just follow our parents' commands without making any personal tweaks to the plan."

"Well, then that explains why I'm in charge, not you. Our parents don't need a follower. They need results. And a direct siege upon a city is one way, but not the only way."

"I *will* get them results," Farid thundered. He pounded his fist into his other hand. "I guess we just have different methods."

"I guess we do."

A rumble in the distance interrupted them. As Bence looked up, a rain drop splashed on the bridge of his nose.

The rains sure roll in fast.

When he stood, he checked the direction of Cehennem. Even though clouds shrouded the entire east coast, a tiny gap spanned the field where his home was. It seemed even the rain did not want to touch the land they lived under.

"Do you take back your statement about cloaks?" Farid

pulled his over his head and covered his face with the hood.

A few drops turned into a sheet of rain.

Bence looked up at the sky and allowed the rain to cascade down his face. "No. I like the feeling of it against my skin."

Bence beckoned his twin to hop on his stallion, and they continued along the riverside. They rode in silence until they reached a bridge.

Slowing to another stop, he held a finger to his lips and gestured to Farid. He nodded and hopped off the stallion, disappearing into a cluster of huts to the right. From there, Bence scanned the area and strained his ears. Not a creature was in sight.

Looks like the Aeonians did a good job clearing up the path for us.

His thoughts were confirmed when he laid his eyes on a crooked sign. It creaked on one hinge. Blood was spattered across its face, but Bence could still make out the writing — ROYAL TRADE ROUTE: EAST.

A splash caught Bence's attention. His senses heightened as he scoped for the source. The frigid air pricked his skin as he inhaled a mix of soil and smoke. He didn't see his twin, so he jumped onto cobblestoned path and drew his sword. In between the pitter-patter of the rain, another splash sounded to his right.

Avoiding the puddles, he wove his way towards the abandoned huts, all once had been stores that sold foods and other various goods. He peeked into the first window, completely broken in. The room was no more than six feet both ways. Rain poured in through the partially disintegrated roof. The harder the rain fell, the more the burnt remains bent underneath the pressure.

A shadow swept by the far window on the other side of the hut. Bence ducked and wiped hair from his eyes. It clung to his forehead like a wet mop. After taking a few breaths, he sheathed his sword and produced a dagger. Twirling the blade in between his fingers, he crept around the perimeter.

Another splash, louder. He sensed the presence of another body nearby in the form of quick, light breaths. A life he was soon to take.

Gripping the blade end of the dagger, Bence leapt forward and cocked his arm. Before he released his grip, he faltered.

A creature no higher than his knee peered up at him. Its slit eyes stared at Bence as its two tails drooped in between its legs. It cradled an armful of dried meat, but it did not mask its emaciated abdomen.

"Zingari," Bence said.

Its legs shook.

"Your kind saved my parents when they first came to this island. Before they discovered the stones of power." He sized up the creature and its vital areas. He couldn't imagine such primitive and fragile creatures were the reason for his parents' survival during their first visit to Deran. Of course, they were the same creatures to warn them about taking the stones of power for their own use.

And we all know how that went.

With a flick of his wrist, he sent the dagger towards the Zingari. The blade dug into one of its paws. He released a yelp and dropped the meat. Whimpering, he tried to wiggle free, but the dagger pierced through his flesh completely and pinned him to the ground.

"Try to transform now and you'll run the risk of mortal injury."

Bence bent and collected the dried meat. After nodding in approval, he tucked all but one slice into a satchel attached to his belt.

Stifling a whimper, the Zingari closed its eyes. "Just kill me, already."

"You're not one for many words. No 'you'll rue the day you've harmed me' or 'the Princess will slay you?'"

Sharp claws exposed themselves and scratched the dirt. Taking a mouthful of dried meat, Bence chewed thoughtfully.

I could kill this pathetic creature. But it has no will to put up a fight.

"Bence?" Farid's voice echoed in the mist behind him.

"Oye!" He waved one arm in the air. After taking another bite, Bence leaned into the Zingari and whispered. "My twin. He is more blood-thirsty than I am, you know. Want to meet him? He might be able to grant you your death wish."

The Zingari's breathing picked up. Farid stomped closer. He was about one hundred feet away. Bence swallowed his snack and stared at the Zingari intently. It another minute, he would witness a bloody scene, and yet his stomach grew sour at the thought.

On the other hand, more good will come of sparing his life. My idiot twin would not understand.

After a split second, Bence ripped his dagger from the

Zingari's paw and grabbed the scruff of his neck. Bringing his snout close to his face, he said, "You better run. You better run fast and true. Tell your people to stay out of this war. If I so much as see your kind fighting by the Princess' side, I'll personally make sure your whole race is extinct."

He hurled the creature into the air. Crashing a few feet from him, the Zingari shook the mud that coated his fur and bounded in the other direction. He did not look back.

Standing up, Bence observed his dagger. Thick blood oozed from the tip, slowly covering the faint reflection of Farid approaching him.

"No threats. The place is clear. Not a single soul, or a snack to be found," his twin quipped.

He turned and glanced at his twin who puffed his chest and rested his hands on his hips. "Oh yeah? Come here."

Shrugging his shoulders, Farid approached him. When he was within arm's length, Bence reached for his twin's cloak. He folded his dagger in between the folds and wiped the blood off.

"You missed one," Bence grumbled. He observed his blade. There was still a smudge. He let a few rain drops fall on it and wiped it against his twin's cloak once more.

Farid furrowed his brow. After clearing his throat, he said, "I don't know why you bother cleaning your weapons so meticulously."

When he was satisfied, he tucked his dagger away and pulled out another strip of dried meat. He tossed it towards Farid, who caught it with one hand.

"I like to keep them bloodied," Farid continued. "It keeps my motivation fresh."

"I believe one should not carry bad blood with them at any time. Besides, Echidna's wrath keeps *my* motivation fresh."

Farid broke into a snicker as Bence cracked a smile. They proceeded back to his stallion. It pawed the ground impatiently.

As they continued over the bridge and into Dunyan territory, Bence's thoughts swirled like the tempest above them. His statement wasn't exactly false. Goosebumps erupted beneath his flesh and his hairs stood on end as memories of purple fog clouded his mind. The color represented an insidious power, an unspoken threat that played a major role in his training. As one of the eldest, he experienced Echidna's returning and ever growing powers, even more so than Farid, although he was not sure why.

Maybe he was more malleable.

And while it terrorized his entire childhood, he never questioned her methods, succumbing to the full authority of his mother... and father.

Jagged rocks loomed in the distance. Farid pointed in their direction, so Bence tugged at the reins. They darted towards the towering formations and took cover from the rain. As they unpacked, Bence peeked further east. He barely made out the shape of the gates, but he knew Zeyland was a few more miles away. Despite the rain, the surrounding area seemed like a desert wasteland. Almost like home. Cracks infiltrated the ground, like the veins of a human. The droplets disappeared when they made contact, but the earth remained thirsty. Brown leaves crumpled into dust particles as they tumbled about.

"Thank you for seeing me off."

Bence shrugged. "Hm? It's no problem. Anything for my kin."

Appearing by his side, Farid said, "I'll have a full 24 hours to scope out the territory before our men join me. Then we wage hell over the city."

"Your best bet is Maz Shrine. I hear it is their 'holy place.' I would bet all the riches in the world that the talisman is there."

"Makes sense."

"Hate to admit it, but this is a pretty smart idea."

"Echidna recommended it," Farid replied in a matter-of-fact tone.

"Of course she did. Mama's boy."

Farid's elbow dug into his ribcage. Coughing, Bence shoved back.

"When you were growing up, were you ever haunted by... voices?" Bence's words tumbled from his lips before his brain could process what he said.

Their eyes connected, but his twin did not make a face. "What sort of question is that?"

"The shadow ghouls. Everyone knows about them. But sometimes, I feel that they get into my head. And lately, they have been louder."

"I think," Farid paused and drummed his fingers against his lips. "I think you are overtired and it's time for me to step in and take over."

"I'm serious." Bence balled his hands into fists.

"What's next? You going to tell me that you regret murdering our sister?"

A tremble formed at his finger tip, and spread up his hands. He swung his arms behind his back and shook his head.

"You've never reflected about the day you stopped aging?"

Farid shifted his weight and huffed. "I barely bat an eye at the memory of taking a sibling's life."

"Of course. The Aeonians have no remorse," Bence replied robotically.

"Lately, I haven't been convinced you still felt that way."

Bence turned away and tended to his stallion. He took a few rattled breaths as images of Yana flashed before his eyes. Waves of nausea rolled back and forth within his chest. Recently, his memories had rattled him to the core more than he cared to allow.

Five days' time.

Isabel's voice. He swore he heard it. It had already been three.

"By the way. You never returned my sword, ass."

Snapping from his reverie, Bence glared at his twin. "What are you talking about?"

"A few weeks ago, I spoke with you when you followed Isabel to Buryan. You said you lost your sword in battle or something?"

As he raised his brow, Bence pulled his sword from its sheath. He grunted as the scabs that formed from his wound stretched with movement. The metal blade gleamed even though the sun hid behind a curtain of clouds. At the base, his name was engraved: *Bence Brechenhad.*

"No way, liar! You stole my sword then out of spite!"

Farid rushed towards him and grabbed the sword from his hand and examined it. "You know how difficult it was to obtain another decent sword?"

Bence rolled his eyes.

I have no idea what this idiot is babbling about. Maybe he is the one hearing things.

He tuned out the nasal sound of his twin's voice and shifted his attention back to Isabel.

CHAPTER

28

Isabel sat on a stool, pulling the flap of her tent slightly open. Dawn had broken, painting the sky a brilliant pink. The Tuuli stood outside of their homes bright and early. The air was abuzz with gossip and excitement.

"Can you believe how fast Dante arranged this wedding?"

"Clearly a power move! Send a message to Damian. Why else?"

"Of course, I always thought he was better fit for Victoria."

Flushing at comments, Isabel strained to listen for more.

"Well, it's not like he has a choice now."

Isabel bit her nail. She was on her eighth finger. Blood oozed from the corner of her cuticle. Sucking on her index finger, she released the tent flap. Simply hearing the name of her sister boiled her blood in humiliation. She moved onto her thumb and chewed.

Over the last night, she had tossed and turned in bed, debating if she should even go through with it all. Traditionally, there would be a weeklong betrothal celebration, but Isabel was faced with a twenty-four-hour wedding. Deep down, she could have fished for a "no," but the word never escaped her lips. The hopelessness in her people's eyes screamed for something. Anything. And if her marriage to Dante offered any chance of getting out of this war with the Aeonians alive, so be it.

As her emotions continued to simmer, Isabel turned her attention outside the tent once more. There were humans among the mix of Tuuli, refugees from their former kingdom, helping with the decorations. They worked swiftly and quietly, smiling nervously at one another.

A mass of gold and white populated the seaside. Women and children were clad in their best garments. They all wore flowers in their hair or pinned on their tunics. Primarily a Tuuli custom, everyone chose a flower based on a wish because weddings were considered lucky.

A hurried feast has been prepared with freshly caught fish and wild ducks. Carrots and potatoes from the Tuuli's gardens were plucked from the soil and broiled in large quantities. It was a simple layout, but everyone still ran about, worrying over the smallest details. Bales of hay for guests to sit on were laid out last. The betrothed's table, made up of a glass top and supported by carefully placed rocks, stood north by the cliffs. The guest seats were arranged in a horseshoe around it.

When she spotted it, Isabel released the cloth, shutting the tent entrance. Rocking back and forth, she clutched her elbows. "It's really happening. I said yes." Her muscles tensed, causing her fingers and eyes to twitch.

Trumpets sounded.

Isabel hung her head. "I practiced saying yes all these years. But I've never felt so unprepared."

"My dear," Aysu sang as she poked her head into the tent. "Are you ready? The crowd is growing restless. They are babbling nonsense, asking absurd questions—"

Isabel turned to her as tears squeezed from her eyes.

"Are you ok?" Aysu exclaimed, scurrying to her with a handkerchief.

"I don't know what to do. I had loved Dante for the longest time. Even as a little girl, I would imagine him as my prince who would sweep me off my feet. Never did I think that our wedding day would be filled with fear." She cast her eyes downward, finger twirling the hem of her cream-colored taffeta dress.

Aysu cocked her head to the side. "I do not understand the fear."

"It's the rush. I never imagined getting married so suddenly. If it were not for this war, I fear that Dante would have taken his time. He has been so driven lately—"

"It's a sign maturity and knowing what he wants!"

"Driven mad!" Isabel blurted.

The little servant remained in place, blinking in confusion.

"Ever since his return from capture, he seems different. Look at his eyes! He is acting like the leader that you all *think* he should be, but it's not like him. He paces a lot. He gets lost in thought. He makes abrupt decisions… like mar-

278 · J.E. KLIMOV

rying me in the midst of war. I just think that is such an anti-quated tactic. I don't think Damian is going to give a damn about our wedding."

"Well, dear, I think it is unifying the people and giving them the morale they need."

Isabel chewed on her fingers once more. "Is that the only way?" Grabbing a brush, Isabel combed a stray hair in place. But the hair remained stuck out of her bun defiantly. "I just feel Dante hasn't been the same since his return and uneasy how it may have influenced his hasty decision." As Isabel's head plopped into her hands, she sighed. "I have no clue what I am doing. I should have been the one that died, not Victoria. I should not be here. I don't deserve the arm-let."

"Keep yourself together!" The maid wrapped her arms in a hug. "I pledged my life to Master Dante. But it breaks my heart to see you so upset. What does *Isabel* want? Everyone wants to know. And everyone is waiting. In the end, we all will support you, follow you, no matter what. You are our Princess." When she finished her sentence, Aysu reached over and placed a bouquet of calla lilies in her hands.

"Let's go," Isabel said. With her free hand, she grabbed a handkerchief, Isabel blotted her forehead. Beads of sweat formed quickly. She ran a comb through her hair once more and followed Aysu out.

The sound of flutes filled the air. Everyone scrambled to their seats. Families herded their children and friends shook hands. When the flutes fell silent, everyone cast their eyes towards Isabel.

The music picked up again as Aysu bowed and stepped

away, leaving Isabel at a narrow walkway. The melody was gentle as the breeze, lifting her spirits. Taking a deep breath, Isabel took her first step forward. Everyone stood and faced her. Smiles. Frowns. Some with no expression. The bouquet weighed heavy in her hands. With each step, Tuuli and Deranians tossed wild flowers at her feet and bowed their heads. The sweet fragrance filled her lungs.

Tears choked her. She could just sense the anxiety from her subjects in the air, so thick she could pierce it with her sai. Everyone hoping this would work. Isabel hoped along with them. Taking a deep breath, she finally looked at her future husband. Dante stood mere feet away, eyes fixated on her. A crooked smile adorned his face, leaving her feeling more unsettled. Isabel smiled in return as she finally arrived at his side.

When Dante grasped her hand, she shivered at his clammy grasp. Adorned in silver, Dante grinned from ear to ear and waved to the crowd. Isabel looked down at her gown. Purple ribbons tied her hair back, and two pearl studs, borrowed from her mother, weighed heavily on her earlobes. The flutes faded as violins sang into the crisp air.

Her thoughts floated up towards the chamber where her mother and father remained. She grimaced at the memory of her mother trying to stand up last night, insisting she be present at the ceremony. But she hobbled and fell onto her knees. A fever that flared this morning secured her spot back in her bed. Her father, remained still as a stone.

Her mother and father were lucky in their marriage. She happened to fall in love with a man who belonged to nobility in Noreland. Their union had further established Deran's relationship to the humans in the northern mainland. Febe required no coercion, no second thoughts. Marriage for love was a novel concept, and it usually required at least some positive political side effect.

"What a grand sight." People murmured in the sea of heads.

They turned to the glass table where Lief stood. The ocean crashed into the rocks below, spraying flecks of sea water into the air. The sun reflected off each drop, creating an explosion of color. Lief smiled warmly and bowed, extending his wings outward.

"You alright? You had us waiting. Worried," Dante whispered.

"It's not about me." Isabel bowed. "It is about our people."

Lief didn't seem to notice their little conversation. "My friends. We gather at this troubled time to remind ourselves what is most important: love and togetherness. Many of us forget what trials we endured, and not just those of the Tuuli and humans, but also the Kai, the Foti, and the Dunya. We all came to this country and made a living here. We were refugees. Pioneers. Dante and Isabel represent the union of cultures. May they grow to love and cherish each other like we all cherish one another. It is for this reason we must remember why we fight."

Her heart fluttered. She still loved him, but couldn't shake off the sense of foreboding.

There's nothing I can do about it now. Maybe I am just being overly paranoid.

"Now, recite your vows to one another!" Lief exclaimed.

Dante tightened his grip. "I defer to your culture's custom; the woman goes first."

"I, Isabel Deran, take my one and only beloved and welcome you into my ever-open heart. The heart where you will make your home. The heart where our love will blossom for years to come. The promise I make to you is that I will always support you, care for you, and love you like a wife should." Her lips quivered. She blinked rapidly. Her heat skipped a beat.

"I, Dante Roril, take my one and only beloved and welcome you into my ever-open heart. The heart where you will make your home. The heart where our love will blossom for years to come. The promise I make to you is… is…"

Peeking to the side, Isabel saw her subjects squirm in their seats.

Why is he struggling for words?

Dante pressed a hand to his head. His brows scrunched as if in pain.

"Are you okay?" she whispered.

Nodding, Dante blinked rapidly. Isabel couldn't quite make out if he was tearing up, but his eyes seemed cloudy.

"The promise I make to you is to protect you from the evils of this world. I will not allow any harm to come to you, and I will ensure our success as a couple ruling Deran lasts for as many years as the heavens allow."

Without a beat, someone in the background struck a gong. Lief raised his hands in applause. Tracing his fingers along her jaw line, Dante pulled Isabel into a kiss. His lips enveloped hers. A hint of muscat danced on the tip of his tongue.

So, that's it. We're married.

A sense of disappointment tugged at her shoulders. It seemed so anti-climactic. The vows were said and done as quickly as the wedding planning itself. Peeking back at Dante, her heart softened. She desperately wanted to let go of her securities and enjoy him for who he was to her. Lief's hand met the small of her back. He locked eyes with her and nodded.

"I have faith in you, Isabel," he said before he left the pair.

After the applause died down, Dante and Isabel sat down at the glass table, and everyone else followed suit. Dante raised his glass and a cheer erupted. Oddly, the noise jarred on her ears. Then, as the noise settled, Dante stood up to speak. His voice cut clear into the air. But Isabel was not listening to him. Her stomach had been turning for hours. She had barely slept, and her eyes were sunken in from the tears.

"With this marriage, we will show our enemies that we remain united and strong. We will not budge, and we will defeat them!" Dante exclaimed.

Another round of applause ensued. Isabel sighed and gazed into the sea. Restless as ever, the white foam sprayed everywhere without direction. Dante pulled her arm, startling Isabel. It was time for her to speak.

She froze, as a lump formed in her throat. When she stood, she scanned the crowd. There were some familiar faces from the castle. They looked at her with such intensity, evoking an emotion within Isabel that even she could not describe. A turbulent storm of pain and hope were playing in everyone's eyes.

I must put my people's needs before my own.

"My people, I know you have seen some horrible things over the past few weeks. Fate has forced our hand. Our long -time enemy has returned, and they think they can break us. Our union will show how much stronger we have gotten during a time of trial. Our love..." she choked, falling silent. The only sound she heard was the gentle flapping of her gown billowing in the breeze.

Isabel kept failing to maintain eye contact. She was finding it harder and harder to enunciate. Everything around her seemed to blur together in a collage of color and sound. Consumed with vertigo, Isabel swayed in place. The world seemed to twirl beneath her feet, and she grasped the table to keep balance. Mustering as much strength as she could, Isabel held up her hand, her ring finger now bearing a large diamond that glimmered in the sun's rays.

"Ou-our love... we will show everyone that our enemy—"

When Isabel's gaze finally made its way to the Buryan Temple, her words locked in her throat. A dark figure stood on the roof. It was not clear, but she was certain of one thing, a pair of green eyes pierced her gaze. Her words evaporated into thin air as her eyes grew wide.

Her senses came alive. The pungent smell from the hay filled her nostrils. The salty air stung her eyes. Cool air dried the beads of sweat that clung to her. Colors suddenly became intensely vivid- from the cobalt sea to the marigold leaves dancing on the heads of her guests. But most of all, the emerald shimmer of those eyes.

His eyes.

"Bence?" she whispered.

How many days has it been? Is he here alone?

The crowd broke into mumbling.

Am I imagining things?

As soon as the figure vanished, a rush of energy invigorated her. She couldn't identify the emotion: joy or fear? Whatever it was, her senses remained heightened and her muscles itched. Her eyes darted between Dante and her guests, examining their reaction.

Had they witnessed what I saw?

"My wife is just overwhelmed," Dante shouted over the crowd, laughing nervously. "Everyone, let's cut our speeches short so we may feast!"

He clapped his hands and food appeared on polished trays carried by his servants. They huffed about, extending a rolled napkin with each serving. The busy atmosphere fed into the anxiety that bubbled in her gut. Her hands grasped her thighs as her legs rapidly tapped against the ground.

If he's here, there could be an army of Aeonians waiting outside to slaughter us.

"Are there guards in the watch tower?" Isabel whispered to her husband.

Dante chuckled. "Are you serious right now? Of course. You think I would put my people in a vulnerable position even during our wedding?"

The trembling in her legs grew stronger.

Well, they clearly missed someone.

"What's wrong? You look like you are about to launch from out of your seat into the sky!"

Grabbing her by the shoulders, Dante twisted her so that she faced him. Beneath his stare, shadows colored the bags under his eyes. His lips held a firm frown. His hair glistened in the sun's rays. The color of his hair seemed lighter today. It was no longer dirty-blonde and more platinum.

"What happened to your hair?" she blurted.

"Oh. This? You like it?"

Twisting her lips, Isabel nodded slowly. Even though her thoughts slowed down at the sight of his hair, her mind started to race again.

"I cleaned myself up last night and wanted to look... more the part," he said.

"More like the other Tuuli's hair color?"

Dante flinched and sat back. His mouth fell agape but made no sound. Fumbling with his words, Isabel turned her head back to Buryan Temple.

"Well, I mean. The pure color of the Tuuli hair has a certain regal connotation to it. And if I am going to be taken seriously, I should *look* the part—"

His words faded into the background.

Could he be here to see me? No. Not likely. What about my parents! Has he figured out their whereabouts?

"Excuse me, Dante."

Unable to contain herself, Isabel leapt up and ran towards the temple. Dust swirled around her feet in little puffs. Guests stood as she approached them. Weaving through the crowd, she ignored their comments and focused on the step ahead of her. Heads turned as she passed them, feeling the heat of their stares at her back.

Should I tell them?

Two children chasing one another stumbled in front of her. Swinging her arms to catch her balance, Isabel side stepped as they continued down one of the guest's rows.

No. I don't want to raise a panic yet.

She craned her neck upwards. The only movement came from falcons scanning the ground for a meal. The stone temple loomed over her as she crossed the bridge. Isabel held her breath and listened for any noise. She was certain that she had spotted Bence. When she heard nothing but the caws of seagulls, Isabel tip-toed around the perimeter of the temple.

"Bence," she whispered. "I know you're here. Give it up!"

There was no answer. After traveling a few feet, Isabel glanced back at Dante's manor where her parents were. The building stood peacefully; all the movement was concentrated by the cliffs. The crowd resembled insects buzzing in confused circles.

She continued around the building, occasionally stealing glances at the manor until it disappeared around the corner. Isabel lifted her gown up from the ground as she stepped over a patch of mud. One misstep landed her left foot into the soggy earth, as she wobbled to and fro. Once she regained her balance, Isabel pulled her leg free with a *plop*. After stumbling a few steps, her back hit a wall. Feeling the cool stone at her back, Isabel lifted her gaze at the towering structure.

Tall, bright, and wrapped in ivy, the Buryan Temple stood proudly behind her. Isabel shuddered at the memories she held within those walls, which seemed so serene from the outside. But the terrors within caused Isabel's hair to stand on end. Shaking her thoughts from her mind, Isabel kicked off loose mud from her heels and walked the perimeter of the temple. Isabel bit her lip each time she rounded a corner, but she was only greeted with an invisible breeze.

Where is that bastard? I swear if he finds my parents and harms them...

After a fruitless search, Isabel wound her way back to the bridge. Resting her elbows on the handrail, Isabel stared at Dante's manor. She hummed to herself as the crowd erupted into song in the distance. When she shifted her weight, a splinter pricked her elbow. Grumbling, she picked at it.

When she flicked the splinter off the bridge, something caught her eye. A set of foot prints flattened the grass in the graveyard, disappearing at the cobblestone entrance. Her heart pounded in her chest. She turned and sprinted from the bridge and past the mill.

"My lady?"

Isabel dug her heels into the ground and spotted Aysu.

"You startled me," Isabel said, suppressing a nervous laugh.

"What are you looking for, my lady?" Aysu asked.

Clasping her hands behind her back, she said "I, uh, just wanted to remove myself from the crowd for a moment. I was starting to feel overwhelmed. But I'm fine now."

Aysu stood on her tip toes and extended her arm. With a smile, Isabel reached down and held her hand.

"If I may ask," Aysu said as they walked down the street, "what were you looking at? Everyone is talking about it. You stared off into the distance in the middle of your speech and suddenly became still as a statue."

"You didn't see it? Nobody saw anything?"

"Saw what?"

After smoothing her gown, Isabel crossed her arms. "Never mind. I want to see my parents."

"Is something wrong?" Aysu's pitch wavered higher and higher.

"No. Fine. I'm fine. I just want to check in on them to make sure they are okay."

When they reached a fork in the path, Isabel curtsied, avoiding eye contact.

"Tell Dante I will return to the party shortly."

"Yes. And, Princess?"

"Yes?"

"You have made master Dante very happy. He walks with a spring in his step and seems to carry the confidence of our old chiefs. You have inspired him so!" Aysu nodded vigorously, eyes glued on her.

"Inspired?"

Knowing Dante since they were children, doubt polluted Isabel's thoughts. He certainly had big dreams to make a name for himself, but she couldn't imagine that she moved him in such a way that he would change his appearance or act as callous as he had in the last twenty-four hours.

If that's what Aysu calls inspired.

"Thank you," she finally replied.

Aysu scuttled to the right and Isabel veered left. As she walked, she inspected the shrubbery for anything out of place. The cobblestone path was clear and there were no disturbances on the grassy areas on either side. Nausea sloshed within her body and refused to drain. Isabel wouldn't feel comfortable until she saw her parents safe and alone.

Pushing the fenced gate open, her walk turned into a jog. The clicking of her heels echoed in the air. Isabel reached for the door knob and found it locked. She pounded at the door. When she heard a shuffle from behind the door, she took deep breaths to calm her nerves. The door swung upon, revealing the maid from the kitchen with shock slapped across her face.

"What are you doing here, Princess?"

"I want to see my mother and father."

"Of course. I have been looking after them, and I assure you that they are well—"

"I am sure you are doing your job wonderfully. I just want to see them." She continued taking deep breaths in between sentences.

The pounding in her chest subsided as the maid led her up the stairs.

"I was about to bring them lunch," the maid said, turning the corner.

"Mmhm." Isabel chewed her fingers as they approached her parents' room.

The maid opened the door. A sour aroma oozed from the room. Pulling an arm to her nose, Isabel glared at the maid.

"What is that smell?"

"I'm afraid King Hadi has contracted an infection in a bed sore. We have been draining it as often as we can, but it's hard to keep the infection from spreading."

Turning her attention back to her parents, Isabel made a silent prayer of thanks. Her mother and father lay in bed, unscathed. No Bence.

Her mother moved her elbows back to prop herself up.

"My, what a beautiful bride my daughter has turned out to be. What are you doing here, honey?"

Isabel moved to her bedside and kissed her forehead. Febe's forehead burned her lips and her complexion was paler than the twin moons.

"Oh mother, you look worse." Isabel waved to the maid. "Please, grab a rag and soak it in ice cold water. Immediately!"

Dropping her head, Isabel squeezed out tears.

"Isabel. What's wrong?"

"I'm sorry, mother. I didn't want to disturb you. I was just… Just so worried about you and father."

Febe's hand rested on top of her head. "We are fine. We could be in better shape, but my spirits are high. Today you are the bride on your wedding day!"

"How is father? Is he really that bad?"

As if her legs were weighed down by anchors, Isabel's body wouldn't budge. She so desperately wanted to look at her father, but was afraid of what she would see.

Or what I wouldn't…

"Your father has been quite dull company. Oh well, he was never the talker." Febe managed a slight giggle.

"Mother, you shouldn't joke at a time like this."

Febe traced her index finger on Isabel's jawline and stopped at her chin, using it to lift her head. Isabel stared into her mother's eyes. Even the color seemed to fade into a cloudy gray.

"I don't know how much time your father and I have left on this earth. One must find the light in even the worst situations. And you must learn to find your own way to cope."

Isabel forced a smile. "Yes, mother."

"And I mean cope in any scenario."

As she leaned in to hug her mother, thoughts of Dante flooded her mind. Squeezing tightly, Isabel closed her eyes. She didn't want to let go. But now that she knew her parents were safe, it was time to return to her celebration.

I cannot escape reality. But I guess I can cope.

The ground beneath her vibrated. Opening her eyes, Isabel noticed the tremor intensified, as if the earth was shuddering. Running to the other side of the room, Isabel threw the window open. Guests were grasping onto one another as plates and glasses fell off tables, and those who had drank too much wine were tossed from their feet. Dante ran towards the district gates.

A loud crack rang into the air. Isabel turned her focus towards the Buryan's gates where she heard an isolated scream.

"Mother, I have to find out what's going on."

Before leaving, she gave her mother a swift kiss on the cheek. Turning to her father, Isabel grabbed his hand and squeezed. As she let go, Hadi squeezed back.

Isabel sprinted down the stairs and out of the manor as fast as her legs could carry her. She grabbed the hem of her gown to avoid tripping as she turned towards the city center where everyone was gathering.

In the distance, Aysu leapt towards the gates. She snapped her fingers and the gates blew open from a strong gust of wind. At the entrance stood a Tuuli scout, huffing. His clothes were tattered, and he was covered in grime.

Isabel fought her way to the front, huffing. Her lungs burned.

"What is it? Look at you!" Aysu tried to support the

scout as he fell to his knees.

The scout grabbed onto Aysu, now hyperventilating and whipping his head around with wild eyes. His body trembled so violently, his wings ripped through his tunic without warning. Aysu fell back and cried out.

"The Aeonians! They've attacked Zeyland! We're next! No prisoners… No prisoners!"

"When do they plan to attack?" Isabel asked, running towards him.

"I do not know for sure, but—"

In the blink of an eye, he was thrown forward. An arrow protruded from his back. Isolated screams rang into the air as Isabel gasped. Terror gripped her throat, paralyzing her body down to her toes. Lief appeared by his side, put his fingers to the scout's neck, and shook his head.

Finally releasing herself from the mental bind, Isabel ran past everyone and beyond the gates to scour for the culprit. Her heart pounded hard and fast, to the point where she could not hear her own words.

"Show yourself!"

However, there was no sign of her red headed foe, nor any other Aeonian. It seemed as if death itself swooped in and took the scout's life. The only sound came from a cold breeze setting in as the wind changed direction.

"My people," Isabel shouted. "The wedding has ended." She turned to face everyone. "We are not safe. No one is safe. We should seek refuge at Lea Island until all has settled. Dante and I will lead troops to Zeyland to try and stop them. It would seem, and I had a feeling about this," she glared at Dante, "that the Aeonians have moved forward despite our union. They fear nothing."

PART II

CHAPTER

29

"Do not despair, my people! This is not a permanent flight, but a temporary maneuver that we must make to survive. We have endured enough bloodshed. When we arrive at Lea Island, Princess Isabel, our army made of every able-bodied man, and myself will continue on and stop the rain of fire that Damian wishes to pour over us. Do not be afraid!" Dante roared and raised his sword high into the air. Applause spread through the ranks slowly but steadily.

When Isabel met his gaze, she forced a nod. Memories flooded her mind. Her parents had taken her and Victoria to Lea Island so they could dance along the beach and collect shells. Lea Island was off the coast of Deran between Buryan and Pekas. The weather always idyllic, and the setting of many weddings, funerals, and festivals. She never thought she would have to evacuate people there.

"Now, onward. We board our ships and sail south until we reach Lea. Avoiding the fields of Deran should secure our safety." He lowered his gaze at the women and children who were cowering, comforting one another. "I may be *young*, but I stand before you, stronger than ever before. I am confident in our survival."

Dante looped his other arm around Isabel's waist. He leaned in to kiss her. His lips felt cool. Pulling away, she gestured to the women and children.

"You shall go first. Please start boarding this vessel."

Herds of Tuuli and Deranians pulled away from the crowd, shuffling slowly as if in a funeral march towards the first boat. Isabel ushered them in as quickly as she could, coaxing in the little children that were tugging at their mothers' hands.

Dante was still rallying the men. Their armor was polished to perfection, according to his wishes. The Deranian were indistinguishable from the Tuuli. Turning to her husband, Isabel noticed that he was finishing his speech and leading the last of his men on the other ship. When everyone had boarded, Dante approached Isabel. He took her by the waist and touched his forehead to hers.

"Would you join me on my ship? Keep a lonely man company?"

Isabel studied his smirk as she shook her head. It did not fit him well. She missed the sense of humility that no longer was there.

They had not consummated their marriage like they were supposed to. Both Isabel and Dante hadn't slept in the wake of the Tuuli's scout's death. From his burial to preparing everyone for evacuation, neither of them slept a wink, let alone spent time together. No doubt this was on his mind now, but Isabel couldn't bear to separate herself from her parents. Once they arrived at Lea Island, Isabel would have to leave them, and she wasn't sure if it was the last time she would see them alive.

"I would love to join you," Isabel replied. "But I must look after the women... and my parents. They are both on my ship. I do not wish to leave their side before we begin our long journey."

She turned away and scampered towards her vessel, trying to escape guilt that dogged her steps. When she reached the bow, Isabel found a handful of Tuuli soldiers staring at her. Taking a deep breath, she waved to them.

"Alright. Let's set sail now."

One soldier glanced at another, but no one moved.

"Dante and I are ready to proceed. Please release the sails."

"As you wish!" shouted one that was nearest to the mast.

As he climbed, Isabel noticed there was minimal wind. "We won't get very far in good time."

When Isabel squinted her eyes, she noticed Dante's ship was sailing off at a faster pace. She bit her cheek and wrapped her arms around her. As her fingers graced the armlet, Isabel said, "Of course. The power of wind."

Raising her arms up, Isabel closed her eyes and imagined the Tuuli's Opal. She coaxed the power of air to come forth, and a surge of warmth flowed through both her arms. As she opened her eyes a gale erupted from her armlet and pushed her ship along. Men behind her clapped, and Isabel smiled to herself.

The two ships coasted along the rocky shoreline. As they

moved along, the coastline gradually softened. Isabel gazed upon the sandy beaches and patches of long pale green grass. Even the ocean water grew lighter by the time she could spot Lea Island. Isabel tugged at her collar; the humidity wrapped around her in a thick blanket.

Once things seemed settled, Isabel rushed to find her parents. They were tucked away in the bowels of the ship. There was no answer when she knocked. Isabel twisted the doorknob and tensed when the door squeaked. A foul stench greeted her, burning her lungs. A sour smell.

"Mother? Father?"

A resonating snore answered her. She sighed. At least they were still alive. Isabel tip toed to their cots, with father on the lower one.

Sweat beaded on Hadi's forehead, dripping into his beard. When Isabel placed her hand on it, she recoiled. He was burning up.

Invisible strings tugged from within her chest. Isabel was grimly reminded that her fears of her father's passing might soon come to fruition.

I can't let this happen.

She dug into her satchel and pulled out a handful of herbs and wild flowers. The earthy fragrance dulled the odor that plagued the room. Turning, Isabel found a mortar and pestle on the table. The Tuuli woman who had given her the herbs when she disembarked the ship told her to grind them together to form a salve. So, she scattered the ingredients in the stone bowl. With each twist of her wrist, the green leaves and maroon petals muddled into brush mush. Oils released and moistened the concoction, giving it a sticky consistency.

The smell started to make her feel lightheaded. She knew the women was no healer, but she swore it kept her newborn alive through a fever.

There used to be a score of healers throughout the land. Until they started utilizing their stones of power to bring people back from the dead. Which at first, people found to be a joyous miracle. And how Isabel wish she had the ability to do so, and never worry about losing her loved ones again.

Grind. Grind.

But the resurrected were troubled. Troubled at the memories of their death. Some didn't want to be 're-born' as the Deranians called it. Some healers manipulated them for their own purposes. Other re-borns turned to isolation in the Chailara Hills. For years, they attacked merchants and pillaged them for their goods. Though from what Isabel was taught growing up, the last of the re-borns had died out, and healers were stripped of their ability to utilize stones of power.

Grind. Grind.

The herbs and flowers reduced to a muddy pulp. Wiping the pestle clean of every drop, Isabel carefully balanced the mortar and approached her father. His head was surrounded by a halo of sweat on the pillow. Her grip tightened to steady her shaking hands.

"Isabel?"

Febe's wispy voice floated down to her from the cot above her father's.

"Yes, mother?"

"I'm so nauseous."

Scooping up some salve with two fingers, Isabel smeared

it onto her father's forehead. He didn't move.

"We have set sail, that's probably why," she responded. Her lips trembled. It took every ounce of energy not to break into tears.

"Ha. I never used to get sea sick. Oh, to be young again and travel the wide ocean. See Noreland. The Pekering Islands. Even Camilia."

"I would love to see all those places," Isabel mused. She continued to paint her father's face until it was completely covered in pulp.

"What's that smell?"

"Just some herbs. From a Tuuli woman who thinks it will help father."

"My, it's strong. But I like it. May I have some?"

A pale hand flopped over the cot.

Twisting her lips, Isabel said, "Maybe I should put it on you." She reached for a footstool and made herself level with Febe. Her mother's face had thinned out, skin as fragile as rice paper. Dipping her fingers into the mortar, Isabel applied a thin film beneath her mother's nose.

Febe took a deep breath. "Ah. The smell. It makes the room stop spinning."

"At least it's working on someone."

Propping herself onto her elbows, Febe frowned. "How's your father?"

"Well, we definitely need to hydrate him. He is losing liquid because he sweats so much. His fever won't break. I just hope he isn't in the throes of sepsis."

When she finished speaking, Isabel blinked and tears plopped onto the sheets.

"He's held on this long. He's fighting for you, dear. So be strong."

"You both shouldn't be in this position. It should be me, fighting for my life in this room."

Isabel's whole body felt weighed down by a boulder. If she let go of the cot, she might as well fall through the floor and sink into the ocean.

You had the stones in your possession. You could have protected them.

"Isabel. You need to learn to forgive yourself. What could you have done? You didn't have enough experience with the stones, and the Aeonians were preparing for this battle for years, it seems." Flopping back in bed, Febe sighed.

"Victoria would've been able to save you…"

"Isabel Deran!"

Febe's head shot up. She grimaced and held a hand to her stomach before she continued. "You need to stop this self-pitying! For years, you have lived in the shadow of your sister. Not because your sister's shadow was too big to escape, but because you put yourself there!"

Isabel's eyes flicked up. She wiped them so she could see her mother more clearly.

"You are here now. In a position more dangerous that I have ever experienced. Deran has lived in peace for years. Just have the confidence to know no one could possibly do a better job than you now, because no one has lived this before. You're a smart girl. Stop following and start leading."

Her mother's words bounced between her ears. Speechless, she placed the mortar by Febe's side and kissed her forehead. Before stepping down, Febe touched her cheek.

"Thanks, mother. I hear you."

"Good," she whispered and closed her eyes.

Isabel back tracked until she was at the door. The snoring wavered in and out. At least the sour smell was gone. Now it was time to lead the ship.

Lead.

Gripping the sai tucked by her side, Isabel nodded and left the room.

CHAPTER
30

The moon sailed across the sky with peaceful silence. Many soldiers had lain their heads down to rest, while Isabel remained awake. She nodded off from time to time, but there was always a knot of anxiety embedded in her muscles that prevented her from peace.

Isabel hadn't even set foot on Lea Island. She recalled watching Tuuli and Deranian citizens disembarking in a confused herd, carrying what they could. Her parents were brought ashore last. And just like that, she had to sail away with Dante and her men. No proper good-bye. Isabel rubbed her eyes from the strain. She stared at her parents and her people as they vanished into a dot in the distance. That was hours ago, and the vision still haunted her.

Dante's back was to her the entire time. As she rested her chin on her hand, Isabel tried to muster courage to approach him. She repeated one thought in her mind: this was her husband, someone she could confide in, find comfort in. But her legs remained frozen in place, refusing to budge. The thrill of her quest and her partnership should excite her, but only dread tugged at her insides.

As dawn approached, Isabel extinguished the mini-fire she created and tip-toed towards two soldiers.

"Gentlemen?"

The pair scrambled to salute her, but Isabel only waved them off in fatigue.

"At ease. What are your names?"

"Ethen, your highness," said one. His lips held up his full cheeks. His long hair was tied tightly into braid. The deep creases across his forehead gave off a somber look, even when he smiled.

The other Tuuli's cheeks and his prominent brow gave this soldier a gorilla-like appearance. Running his callused hand through his closely shaven hair, he finally spoke. "And I am Harmon. What's wrong, Princess?" Harmon asked.

"Nothing," Isabel sighed. "Idling has made me anxious."

"There's no need. You are the mistress of the talismans of power."

"You clearly haven't met my sister…" Isabel bit her lip. She imagined her mother scowling at her.

"Ah, but I have," Harmon interjected.

Isabel shot him an incredulous look.

"I recall many times you and your sister visiting our city with the King and Queen. These old watchful eyes have seen a lot. I've seen you practice archery with the Deranian guards. And Benjamin spoke highly of you."

"I'm sorry for not recognizing you," Isabel said sheepishly.

"I do not expect you to distinguish one armor clad soldier over another. All I say is I have witnessed your insecurity stem from your sister's large, aggressive shadow." Harmon gazed at the black horizon, in deep thought. "Victoria seemed like an obvious choice as the future bearer of the armlet, but we soldiers always liked you better."

Isabel stared at him.

"What I mean is… Well, you were not a brat."

She smiled to herself.

"I know you probably would prefer the approval of tribal leaders and those of status, but my men and I hold you in high regard. You have integrity and modesty, and you studied arms and armor when you could have been knitting. The lowly soldier will always support you." Harmon bowed.

"Thank you. You and your men… Your support is valued equally as anyone else's in this kingdom."

Harmon grunted as he stretched. His joints cracked, but the silhouette of his broad shoulders exposed no sign of weakness. Isabel played with the rim of her hood, feeling a swell of hope in her chest.

"Anyway, we will see some action soon so don't you worry, miss," Ethen said. "I heard rumors that Damian built his army by reproducing with his witch of a wife. Is it true that they let them grow to a ripe, strong age, then have them commit some atrocity to keep them young? Their eldest son. I believe, is said to be only in his early thirties and the commander of the whole army."

"That is disgusting. Such manipulation of innocent life." Harmon growled.

Isabel instantly thought of Bence. With a frown, she nodded. "Yes. That is true. Makes you wonder. When we face them in battle, will we be looking at enemies or abused victims?"

"I am sure they will have no problem cutting us down," Ethen exclaimed with a grim smile.

"Then surely you will be there to save me!" Harmon responded.

"I will be there, my friend, always." Ethen struck his spear on the deck and turned to patrol the port side. He stopped suddenly to shield his eyes at the sun piercing the horizon. "Look. We have arrived."

Isabel removed her hood and ruffled her hair. Rubbing her eyes, she gazed to the east. Her nostrils scrunched at the dust that swirled about. Peering past plateaus and rock formations, Isabel barely made out Dunya's Point. The Maz Shrine was somewhere over there as well. Rays of light peered from behind the peaks were blurred by dust... and smoke.

"Dante." Isabel raised her voice. "Something is wrong."

"Smoke?" Dante mumbled as he approached her side. He cursed and roused the soldiers. "Everyone, suit up. We dock our vessel here and begin our march. We must hurry. There's trouble!"

"It may be too late," Isabel sighed.

Five days.

The anchor dropped into the Fuad River, and within an hour, the army suited up and marched towards the city. Dante and Isabel led the way. The clouds of smoke billowed high above them. The closer they got, the darker the clouds of dust.

"Ash?" Isabel asked him. "Maybe they had a huge bonfire. You know how much Adem likes a good party." Isabel exaggerated her gestures.

Dante stared blankly back at her.

"Come on. I just wanted to lighten the mood. We can't assume the worst until we really see what's going on."

Isabel peeked behind her. The ship shrunk in the distance. Hundreds of soldiers followed in a perfect line behind them, clad in metal armor. A Tuuli flag flickered on one end, while the Deranian flag flickered on the other. The first few rows of Tuuli carried spears. They bobbed up and down as they marched. Leaves crunched beneath their feet. There was a squeaky wheel from a supply cart. No one spoke. Everyone kept their eyes forward. Some brows were furrowed. Isabel wished she could reassure them.

Harmon caught her eyes. He summoned a paternal smile, but it faded quickly. His eyes strayed upwards, widening in horror.

The quiet morning air was broken by an arrow of fire that flew into Dante's army, striking someone's shield with a clang. Isabel looked around wildly and saw no visible archer.

"Isabel!"

A roar filled the air from behind the wooden walls of Zeyland. A shower of arrows, also set aflame, rose up from right behind the barrier, covering the sun for a brief moment. The deadly hail began to rain on her troops. Men shouted and dove for cover. Isabel took a step back and tripped. She landed on her back and gazed upon the hundreds of arrows. Extending her hands, she tried to command the wind to slow the assault. No matter how much the wind howled, the arrows continued to pick up momentum.

Am I not strong enough?

Energy drained from her fingertips to the point where she couldn't even move.

"Reporting for duty!" Harmon shouted, sliding besides her, throwing his shield above them. "Pardon my reach."

Isabel sucked in a breath of air. Tuuli's Opal stopped glowing as her strength picked back up.

Now I know why Dante and I can't just use our powers alone. I'm already drained!

Arrows struck the shield. They pierced the ground. Some of her men that did not react in time shouted in pain. One arrow that hit Harmon's shield splintered and showered wooden fragments around them. Fire consumed the fragments; however, there was a purple tinge to the glow.

"What about Dante?"

"No worry, Ethen has him."

The metal shields of the Tuuli fared well under the first wave of arrows. When the field fell silent, Isabel rose from Harmon's arms and waved to her men.

"The Aeonian's have already made their home in Zeyland! Shall we see to it that they leave? Charge!"

Despite her unwavering voice, terror nipped at Isabel's heels like a pack of wolves in a ravenous pursuit. She had never witnessed a war, let alone stood in the midst of a battlefield. The pounding of boots rattled the ground like thunder, and the sun reflected on everyone's swords like flashes of lightning.

Images of Benjamin, his men, and her parents attacked

underneath a stormy sky flashed before her eyes. Her knees buckled. As she hit the ground, he mustered all her strength to stop trembling. Fumbling for her sai, she fought back the urge to gag from her tunnel vision.

An arm hooked beneath her armpit and dragged her up. "You alright?"

Dante's voice echoed by her side. Nodding her head, she finally released one of her sai from its leather holsters. Uncertainty sloshed around her stomach, but Isabel steadied herself as Dante released his hold on her. One foot in front of the other. The battle cries from the Zeyland walls intensified. Harmon and Ethen cried to their brethren to hurry forward before the archers could launch their next assault.

Lifting her head, she shouted, "Let's go!"

As her army approached, the massive doors of oak and steel swung open, exposing a line of Damian's archers, arrows at the ready. Isabel squinted her eyes to see past them. Fire ravaged the already dry land and there were no Dunya in sight. Only the mutated Kai Veijari.

Chaos ensued after the next volleys of arrows, slaying a dozen of Isabel's men. But everyone forged ahead towards the gates, keeping their wedge formation tight. Isabel scooped a shield from a fallen soldier. The shield weighed her down, but Isabel's adrenaline lent her an unusual strength. When the Aeonians charged towards them, she signaled to Dante who swirled his sword in the air.

"Brace yourselves, men!"

Heart racing, Isabel sized up the Aeonian in front of her. The man was tall and lean, eyes peering through matted black hair. A spitting image of Echidna.

Enemies or victims?

When she blinked back into focus, he was about two hundred feet away from her. In seconds, he and hundreds of his brethren will clash with her army. A hundred feet. The Aeonian lowered his sword in front of him, aiming straight for Isabel's heart. The rest of the front line mimicked him, forming a line of blades. Fifty feet. Hoisting the shield in front of her, Isabel braced for impact.

The blow struck Isabel's shield, sending her flying backwards. Hitting the earth with a thud, Isabel's back burned with pain. Screeching metal erupted around her as the two armies clashed. As she scrambled to her feet, the Aeonian raced towards her, blade thrashing about.

When his sword made a downward stroke, Isabel lifted the shield once more. He swung to the right. Shifting her weight, she met his blade with her barrier once more. Each clang resonated in her bones, weakening her knees. Before he wound up for the next swing, Isabel ducked and swung a sai upwards toward his abdomen. His weapon met hers, locking it in between the prongs of the sai.

Her muscles burned as she tried to wiggle free. The Aeonian's biceps flexed and powered through her attempts to unlock herself. The tip of his sword inched towards her face. Sweat dripped from every inch of her body. Even her hands were losing grip of the sai and shield.

"I'm going to take my time with you, Princess," he hissed and licked his lips.

Before she could react, his other arm swung around. Stars exploded in her eyes as his fist slammed against her cheek. Isabel crumpled to the ground like a paper doll and lay still. Her arms burned like fire and legs weighed like lead. Heat rushed to her face as she chocked up the dust that filled her nostrils. The sounds from the melee around her grew muffled.

You got to get up!

When she rolled over, the Aeonian's blade sliced into the ground one inch away from her ear.

"Stay still!"

The Aeonian fell onto his knees and pinned her arms and legs. No matter how much she twisted and turned, she couldn't free herself. Her fingertips grazed the sai she had dropped.

An arrow zipped in the air and struck the Aeonian's shoulder. He jerked back, giving Isabel enough time to grab her sai. Clenching her teeth, she rammed it into the man's boot. As he howled in pain, she sprung to her feet to look for her savior. Everything around her was a mesh of flesh, metal, and blood.

Appearing through the blur was another Aeonian male holding a Tuuli soldier by his neck. Beneath the Tuuli's feet was a bow. He cycled his feet, gagging for air. Before she could react, an arm wrapped around her neck and dragged her down.

"You can't escape so easily."

As he locked her arms behind her back, the other Aeonian snapped the Tuuli's neck whose arms fell limp instantly. Isabel's heart plummeted along with the dead body. He was now just a heap on the ground.

"You see that? You're next. Oy! Brother, help me put a sword in her heart. Let's carve it out for mother!"

"With pleasure."

The Aeonian pushed his jet-black hair from his eyes as he pulled his brother's sword from the ground and pointed it skyward. Isabel squeezed her eyes shut.

This is it.

All she heard was a gurgle. The man who held her back released his grip. Without hesitation, she swung her legs around and knocked the Aeonian off his feet. Isabel got up, locked her foot against his neck, and raised her weapon. For a brief moment, her eyes softened at the struggling figure. His fingers clasped her boot as he panted. When she lowered her sai, the Aeonian twisted her leg and wrestled her to the ground. He reached for his sword, fingertips grazing the handle. Isabel slashed her blade against his neck. With a gurgle, the man's movements slowed to a halt.

Shock pricked her like a thousand needles. Even in self-defense, killing another being, another human, shook her in ways not even an earthquake could have.

But I had to. He would've… would've…

She couldn't hold it in anymore. Contents her breakfast spilled from her gut. The hot soupy liquid burned her throat as she hacked. The bile-colored vomit mixed in with the spilled blood, swirling around like some sick piece of art.

Got to get moving. Move!

Crawling on her hands and knees, she found her sai and shield beneath her captor. A spear protruded from his back and another Tuuli soldier lay on his stomach a few feet away. His head was crushed. Isabel was unsure from what.

Breathing hard, Isabel jumped up. The battle broke into

pockets. Some fought one to one, but many were clumped off ganging up on one another.

Side-stepping a dueling pair of soldiers, Isabel counted a hundred feet from the sculpture of Adem where she could take cover. When she took another step, a careening body shoved her a few feet to the left. Regaining her balance, she hid behind the shield. When there was no attack, she peeked over the bent metal. A Tuuli soldier had been backed into the wall with four swords pointed at his chest. His hands were bare. No sword, no shield. His grey eyes shined, blinking out tears. One of the Aeonians laughed.

Isabel had to do something. But could she take on a handful of fully armed men twice her size? Foti's Ruby glowed obediently.

Fire!

As heat pricked her skin, Isabel tiptoed to the cluster of hunched backs. The prongs of her sai glowed an angry red. The Tuuli soldier caught her eye. He shook his head.

"This fool is so scared, he's having a fit!" barked an Aeonian in the center.

Taking his eyes off Isabel, the Tuuli mouthed, "Don't do it."

But her head was filled with emotions that exploded with red rage. She leapt in the air and drove her sai into the largest Aeonian's back. The horseshoe formation broke apart as the Aeonian shouted. He swatted his back as Isabel ducked each blow.

"Run!" she screamed.

Arms ripped her off the Aeonian's back. Her shield fell to the ground. She kicked her legs and landed a blow on his jaw.

"You think you can take all of us down just by yourself?"

The man loomed a good foot taller than her, cracking his knuckles, adorned with steel. Isabel swallowed the lump in her throat. His pockmarked face flushed as he snapped his fingers.

How could they come across so many weapons?

The Tuuli soldier, who had crawled his way to this man, drew a dagger. But what stood out to Isabel was his bloody, mangled foot.

"Watch out, brother!" shouted the Aeonian woman who restrained her.

Without hesitation, the man swirled around and drove his meaty fist into the Tuuli's skull. The crunching sound on impact felt like a kick to her stomach. Blood stained the Tuuli's hair, and he lay still. Another one dead. A person she intended to save.

She dug an elbow into her captor's ribcage. The Aeonian woman shrieked, but Isabel was tackled by the pockmarked soldier. Blood still dripped from the fist he formed. The hot liquid sizzled onto her skin. Her chest welled like a balloon. She couldn't restrain herself anymore. Wiggling her arms free, she pulled out both sai and aimed them at his neck.

Arrows pointed at Isabel's left and right.

"I wouldn't do that if I were you."

The Aeonians circled around her. They laughed.

"Poor. Helpless. Princess."

Emitting a piercing cry, Isabel chucked one sai into the chest of the opponent in front of her. Arrows whizzed by as she fell onto her knees, rolled over and dug the other sai into the pock-faced Aeonian's foot. Another arrow grazed her thigh. An iron-like smell stung her nostrils as she ripped her weapon free. Specks of red painted her sai.

Light gleamed above her.

The sun reflected against a rusted sword. As the wounded Aeonian wobbled to maintain balance, he swung the blade down, aiming for her head.

Before she could react, a forceful gale rushed in, sending him onto his back. Hair whipping around her, Isabel could barely make out all of her other attackers hitting the ground with a thud. Sand pelted her, like a swarm of angry bees.

Amidst the howling wind, she could barely make out a voice.

"What are you doing? Get out of here!" Dante cried.

Holding one hand over her nose, Isabel fought her way to her feet. She blinked the gritty feeling from her eyes, but the sand storm didn't cease. One foot in front of the other. She made her way to the female Aeonian, where one of her sai stuck out from her abdomen.

"I'm not helpless," she growled. Ripping the sai from the motionless Aeonian, Isabel sprinted towards the large rock sculpture of Adem.

Once she was out of sight, Isabel's hands fell to her knees. She hunched over, wheezing and shaking. An uncontrollable tremor took hold of her as images of the Tuuli soldier's skull being crushed replayed over and over again.

I failed to save him. I couldn't even save myself.

All she could hear was scraping of metal. All she could smell was blood-stained earth. Everything was a blur. All she could see were clouds of sand dancing around dead bodies. All she could taste was the bile bubbling up her throat.

Waggling her fingers to rid them of the pins and needles feeling, for a brief moment, she feared she couldn't feel anything either.

Once her vision focused past her hands, she noticed silver blood pooled at her feet.

Dunyan blood. These men didn't bring me here so I could fight. They are fighting so I can live. I've got to find Adem and the Dunyan Amber. Fast.

Isabel checked her thigh. The arrow ripped through her pants, but the scratch was superficial. Blood trickled in a steady stream. She ripped one of her sleeves and tied it around the wound. Pressing against it, Isabel glanced around. Every grunt, every scream sent her on edge.

Taking a few more breaths, Isabel peeked around the statue. The visibility was so poor, she could barely see further than a few feet. Past a heap of bodies, she spotted a shield. She couldn't tell if the bodies were friend or foe.

Okay. Grab it and go.

She contemplated using Tuuli's Opal to clear the path for her. But she figured it was best to go unnoticed. She ripped her other sleeve and wrapped it over her nose. Ducking low to hide within the sand storm, she scuttled to the shield. Each grain of sand that assaulted her eye stung. Even with one hand on her brow, she couldn't stop the burning.

Hoisting the shield onto her back, Isabel scanned for the statue. Her head spun. There were two large projections, either one could've been the statue. As the sand whipped around her, Isabel grew more disoriented.

I have to dispel Dante's storm.

When she pushed her arms outward in opposite directions, she drew as much energy from her core and exhaled. Out came a guttural cry Isabel wasn't even aware she was capable of. But as soon as the last breath escaped her lips, the wind died and sand flurried to the ground like a tamed beast. Blurred shadows became more defined. They took the form of Tuuli soldiers and Aeonian warriors. Still fighting tirelessly.

Isabel spotted the statue of Adem. And past that, a narrow pathway leading deep into Zeyland.

"Argh!"

A soldier's cry rose, then was drowned by clashing swords.

Isabel spotted Harmon amidst the chaos, struggling under the blade of an Aeonian. This warrior was sleek and swift. Her hair wrapped tightly at the base of her neck.

A knot formed in Isabel's chest. Her eyes bounced between Harmon and the statue.

Last time you tried to help, the Tuuli still died. And you almost did too!

Harmon's sword was knocked from his hand. His forehead shined with blood and sweat. But his brows remained furrowed as he stared defiantly at his attacker.

Even though Dante's warning rang in her head, Isabel's feet remained glued to the ground. She knew what she had to do. Without another thought, she raised one arm, sai in hand.

Aiming with one eye closed, Isabel generated a blast of fire in her direction.

"Rek!" cried a scruff voice in the crowd.

The Aeonian halted the stroke of her sword at what must have been her name in time to avoid Isabel's attack. Rek rolled out of the flame's path, leaving Harmon in harm's way.

"Watch out!" Isabel screamed.

Flames engulfed the seasoned Tuuli warrior. He collapsed, but rolled back and forth. Before Isabel could run to him, Rek leapt in front of her, dual swords drawn. She smiled, exposing teeth that seemed to have been filed down to resemble fangs.

"Princess! Your head is mine!"

Rek charged towards Isabel, the tips of her dual blades causing a trail of dust. Her movements were so swift; Isabel couldn't bring her shield forward in time. The Aeonian knocked the shield from her hand and laughed.

Rek swung her left arm horizontally. Isabel reacted and brought her right arm down, meeting metal with metal. The Aeonian woman swung her other sword in a downward stroke as she shrieked at the top of her lungs. Catching the blade between the teeth of her other sai, Isabel's biceps burned. Her legs shook as Rek pressed down. Isabel pushed, and Rek shoved. The thigh where the arrow grazed her throbbed intensely. Blood rushed to her wound the more pressure it took on.

Knees buckling under the pressure, Isabel landed on her back. Rek's swords however, were still locked in the teeth of the sai. Twisting the handles ninety degrees, Isabel was able to lock her attacker's arms. She kicked her legs up and dug her heels into Rek's abdomen.

When Rek stumbled back, Isabel scrambled to her feet.

She held her sai up as Rek charged again. The Aeonian swung both swords simultaneously. Isabel ducked and held her ground as Rek crashed into her. When they made contact, Isabel stood once more, using her opponent's momentum against her. Rek flew a couple feet and crashed onto the ground.

Wiping sweat from her brow, Isabel took deep breaths. And Rek gnashed her jaws, still eager for blood.

Rek swiped again. And again. Each time Isabel met a sword with a sai, the more her arms felt like jelly. She tried to side-step when Rek stabbed both blades forward, but fell victim to an elbow in the solar plexus. As if her breath was sucked from her lungs, she gasped for air.

She swayed back and forth, trying to shake the vertigo washing over her. Through her double vision, Rek wound up for what would be the final blow. Isabel caught her swords on the down stroke, twisting once more to lock Rek's arms. But she had no strength left. As Isabel's legs gave way, she swung her foot behind one of Rek's knees. In one sweeping motion, she took the Aeonian down with her.

Rek landed with a thud besides her. They both panted for air. Peeking over to her left, Isabel spotted her opponent reaching for one of her swords.

You must stay alive.

Isabel rolled onto Rek and swat the sword so it slid out of reach. She dug a sai into the Aeonian's ribcage. Hissing, she writhed in place. Isabel flinched. Harmon cried in the distance.

Isabel held her gaze, and then slowly backed away to find Harmon, who had managed to extinguish the flames. A bright red sheen covered half his face.

"I will be fine," he urged, pushing her off him. Harmon grit his teeth as he took up his sword with his blistered hand. "But you... your leg is bleeding! Here."

Pulling a handkerchief from beneath his breastplate, he replaced the blood-soaked sleeve with it. He tied it as tightly as it could. When he was finished, she scrambled for her shield.

An arrow darted past her hand. Looking up, Isabel saw a dozen Aeonians had jumped to Rek's aid. One held a bow in his hand. However, when he reached for the quiver, he cursed to find no more arrows.

"Where is your leader?" Isabel demanded. "And where is Bence?"

They all smiled at one another.

"Well?"

With a sneer and a cackle, one by one, the Aeonians charged at Isabel. Harmon maneuvered at lightning speed, knocking every soldier down before they reached her.

"Isabel, you have to press ahead!" he shouted.

She knew Harmon was right. But every time she tried to move forward, she was either ambushed or someone else was in danger. Her conscience wouldn't allow her to leave someone like Harmon so close to death.

The crushed skull of the dead Tuuli soldier flashed before her eyes again.

I've got to do something once and for all.

Peeling in the opposite direction, Isabel charged into the fray in search for Dante. She shook her arms, trying to rid herself of the cramping in her muscles. She had to recuperate some strength. Arrows zipped by. Axes were lodged into the ground. Parts of armor scattered about, stained with blood.

She reached Dante, who seemed to slay his enemies with ease.

"Looks like you do not need my help," Isabel barked. "But I have a better idea. Have your men round the enemy up all in one place."

Dante waved his sword which started to glow pearl white. The light soared into the sky, signaling his men towards him. Isabel calculated her mode of attack and the soldiers formed a ring, pushing the Aeonians into a sloppy circle. She was not confident in what she was doing, but her anger and adrenaline collided within her like ocean waves in a storm. The energy seemed to guide her every step.

"Watch this," Isabel exclaimed to Harmon as she eyed Rek among the herd. "Heads up!"

Isabel broke into a dash, dragging her sai into the dirt, drawing a circle around the cornered enemy. She circled faster and faster in fervor, everyone peeking over at her in nervous anticipation.

"Now!" Isabel yelled, and as soon as she did her blade left the dirt. When her men backed away, Foti's ruby glowed fiercely, and a ring of fire ignited around the Aeonians. Isabel twirled in place, faster and faster, drawing up dust around her. The ring of fire rose, climbing higher than the tallest creature.

Isabel punched the air. All the Aeonians were successfully trapped in a cell of fire. But her smile faltered at her energy that was sapped at an alarming rate. As her focused wavered, so did the flames. They flickered lower and lower. Isabel's extremities grew numb. As did her mind. Fighting to keep somnolence from taking over, Isabel's thoughts raced for a solution.

"You can't keep this up. You have to finish them." Dante's voice wavered in and out of her consciousness.

Blinking rapidly, Isabel fought just to maintain her balance. "But," she said. "There are hordes of men and women in there—"

"Men and women who are our enemies. Who have killed our men. And want to kill the rest of us!"

"I can't just kill hundreds of people just like that!"

"Then what are you doing wasting your energy?"

His voice jarred her ears. She fought for words, but they only manifested in her mind.

I was hoping to contain them. Give us a chance to defend ourselves. I-I didn't really think what I would do next.

Before another thought could cross her mind, a hurricane like wind rushed towards the ring of fire, knocking her over. Screams erupted. Lifting her head, Isabel witnessed the gale feeding the flames. It warped from a hollow cylinder to an oblong ball of fire, engulfing the entire army of Aeonians.

How is this possible? I did not command it!

Foti's Ruby flickered back to its lifeless state, while Tuuli's Opal remained void of light. And yet, the flames soared high into the sky, burning through the clouds. When, the pillar of fire subsided, scorched bodies could be seen. Indistinguishable from one another.

Her jaw dropped. Her only other guess would be…

"Now, we call all move onward," Dante shouted. His

palm was outward facing. Facing the horde of Aeonian bodies. And the opal at the hilt of his sword glowed faintly.

"What have you done?" She gagged at the scent of burnt flesh.

Even the sound of cheers from Tuuli soldiers muted as the stench rolled through the breeze.

Crossing his arms, Dante bowed his head and shook it. When he peered up at her, his blue eyes shined like ice.

"I did what you couldn't do."

Words clogged Isabel's throat. Her mind still whirled from conjuring the ring of fire.

"But—"

"It's okay. You're not used to war. Battles. Violence. That's why I'm here. To help in any way. Even if it means for me to act at the grim reaper."

When Dante scooped her up by her shoulder, Isabel was still searching for words. The burden of those deaths had been taken from her. For that, she was grateful. And yet, a sour sensation in her gut sloshed around as if she were still imbalanced. She wanted to be angry with Dante for killing them. But could she?

"You know if we didn't defeat them one way or another, the Aeonians would stop at nothing to kill us. You do know that, right?"

Isabel nodded. She turned her head to wipe a lone tear from her eye, hoping no one had noticed.

The occasional clank and clink of armor echoed in the vacant city as everyone marched. As the pounding in her heart subsided, Isabel found herself in awe over what had transpired. Ignoring the silence of the army before her, she wiggled her fingers on the handle of her sai. Her armlet still felt warm. Whether it was the rush of adrenaline or Foti's Ruby, she felt a second wind. Even the pain in her thigh seemed numbed.

"I would take care not to anger her, Dante."

Isabel's head lifted at the sound of Harmon's voice.

Dante barked a quick laugh. "Maybe I should re-think what I have gotten myself into."

Lips twisting into a frown, Isabel sped up her pace to remove herself from earshot. After passing one stone building after another, she made out a gorge in the distance. A rancid stench filled the air. She couldn't imagine how the smell followed them from the city entrance. She broke into a jog, covering her face with her arm. Slowing down as she reached the edge, the smell intensified. Isabel's gaze inched over the chasm and gasped.

CHAPTER
31

Charred bodies of Dunya filled the gorge. Limbs were scattered among the torsos. Entrails poured from stomachs. The sound of Dante's steps grew louder. All Isabel could do was hold her hand up for him to slow down. Panic bubbled in her chest. She wasn't sure she could forgive herself if they were too late.

Coming to a halt, Dante gagged. "Adem, where is Adem?"

"We have to go to Maz Shrine now," Isabel ordered. Her voice wavered as she continued to stare at the mountain of corpses. She searched for any recognizable signs of the Dunyan king. A cold sweat formed on the nape of her neck. "Come with me. Your men should remain here to secure the area."

Dante nodded. "Give me a moment. I will meet you up ahead."

Isabel ignored her cracking knees as she got up. Each step

she took through the winding natural bridge that spanned the chasm felt like moving with iron blocks. As the wind whistled in her ear, Isabel ordered herself not to look down. When she reached the end, she turned to the right. A massive mountain loomed before her.

Shriveled trees extended their fruitless arms into the sky. Large columns were carved from the rocky surface and the vines that once wrapped around them broke off into the wind. Dunyan statues sat atop each column with blank eyes staring down at Isabel. The shrine seemed untouched, except for the door that was broken in.

A snap sounded behind her, like someone stepping on a convenient twig. She turned around but saw no one.

"Dante?"

Silence. Isabel's lip quivered.

"Bence?"

Her mind reeled to Bence's promise. He was supposed to meet her here. To help her continue her search for the next talisman. Until chaos at the wedding dragged the Tuuli into a senseless battle.

Only the sound of Dante's boots answered her. Isabel bit her lip and waved him over, hoping he didn't hear her. Joining Isabel, he gave her a grim smile and gestured to the shrine's entrance.

"Ready?" Dante asked in a monotone voice.

Isabel couldn't make anything of his stoic face. "Ready."

Stepping gingerly over the splintered wood, Isabel entered a room with a high ceiling. All four walls were made of dark wood paneling, giving it a simple look. At the far left was a trinket box in a pool of silver blood. But no body. Isabel tip-toed towards it, extending her arm. As soon as she touched the box, a surge of warmth crept up her arm.

"This held the Dunyan Amber," Isabel said.

"It cannot be this easy to find."

"Because..." The box opened with a creek. "It's not inside." Isabel cast the empty trinket away with a growl. It almost seemed too artificial, like some gruesome presentation. "I thought we beat them to it."

"Let's explore the shrine. Although I'm afraid to find out whose blood has been spilled." Dante's words cut right through Isabel's train of thought.

An icy chill crept up her spine. Turning her attention to a door to the right, she nodded. When the pair entered the second room, she sighed. Another empty room with nothing but piles of sand.

So bizarre to find sand in the shrine. In Zeyland.

"Have you ever explored Maz Shrine?" Isabel asked.

"Never. You?"

"No. I wonder why I never did. I should have, shouldn't I?"

Dante cast a gust of wind to blow the sand from the floor. He pointed out a wooden trap door at the center of the room. "I never visited because the Dunya never drew maps for it. And from what I hear, it is confusing to navigate for anyone without reptilian senses." Gently pressing down, Dante triggered a contraption that popped the door open slightly. Isabel nervously peered down at the dark hole. The walls were of jagged rocks, and torches were strewn down the pathway.

"Looks like we will be trekking into the bowels of

Dunya's Point," she said.

"Let's hope we find clues," Dante replied in a hushed voice.

Dante's breath tickled the back of Isabel's neck, making her hairs standing on end. He gestured her down the stairs as he broke a torch from the wall.

The steep steps twisted downwards. Eventually, the man-made steps were replaced by randomly set rocks. Isabel hobbled clumsily one step and a time. The walls narrowed, as if closing in on her.

This is suffocating.

Isabel's heel slipped, sending her tumbling into Dante. The walls tore her hands as she grasped for anything. With a thud, Isabel landed on top of him. Her head whipped back and struck the ground.

There was a splash.

Pain gripped her skull as thin fingers of lightning flashed lights in the back of her eyes. Dante pulled her up and shook her gently. Isabel reluctantly opened her eyes, nauseated by her double vision.

"I'm okay." Isabel kept blinking.

Her vision slowly cleared, adjusting to the dim cavern before her. Isabel jumped when she felt a trickle of liquid down the nape of her neck. Isabel patted her wet hair in panic. Instead of red, the liquid was a murky brown. She sighed with relief.

"It looks like this place used to be filled to the brim," Dante commented at the dark waterline in the wall. "Let's keep going."

Isabel and Dante traveled deep into the cavern, filled

with ankle-deep water. The pair did not stray far from one another. Only the splashes from their footsteps echoed. It made Isabel's stomach turn. Her heart beat harder until it was so loud that she could hear it synchronize with each splash and splash. Water dripped from the stalactites in the ceiling. Bats fluttered from one end of the cavern to the other. Isabel shrieked and grabbed Dante's arm.

"Do not be so afraid of everything."

Before Isabel could respond, Dante yelped and leapt into the air. He sent the torch flying. Isabel dove to catch the precious flame before it could be extinguished. Isabel motioned Dante to remain still as she searched for the offender.

Plip.

Isabel looked up. The light from the flame did not reach as high as she wished. So, Isabel whispered to the torch.

"*Flame.* Dance higher for me."

Foti's ruby glowed with approval. The flames licked higher into the air until it reached the ceiling.

"Dante?"

"Yes?"

"You were frightened by a drop of water?"

"Of course not," he huffed.

"Look up." Isabel stifled her laughter.

Dante stormed off. "Stop fooling around and move on!"

Isabel took another minute to indulge in the humor of the murderous stalactite and its water attack. Before Dante disappeared from sight, she trotted after him. He took the torch back without a word. The eerie silence nestled itself into the atmosphere once more, and Isabel's anxiety returned.

He doesn't take a joke like he used to. Either that or my sense of humor has warped.

They arrived at a corner where Isabel was now waist-deep in water. Feeling around for a crevice, she was praying for a quick and easy escape. All Isabel found was a crawl-space, large enough to fit one full sized adult. Isabel gulped.

"I'll go first to make sure this leads us somewhere," Dante said.

Isabel's shoulders slumped, relieved in thankful silence.

"Just let me know when you can barely see the light from the torch. Then, I think you should start behind me." Dante turned, gripped the torch in between his teeth and began crawling.

Grunting and swearing liberally, Dante contorted his body cautiously as he entered the opening. Isabel crouched to watch him. Her stomach twisted as his breathing grew more laborious. Each rock that tumbled down caused her heart to skip a beat.

Isabel picked up another noise from behind. Her blood curdled as she held her breath to listen more closely. There was a scratch and splash. More scratching. Churning of water.

Dante yelped.

Her attention was directed forward once more.

"Dante?" Panic rose from her gut and paralyzed her throat. There was no response for a solid minute, which felt like an eternity.

A cough echoed. "Isabel?"

Relief washed over her, though fear still restricted her vocal chords.

"Isabel, can you still see the torch?"

"Uh, uh-huh," she stammered. "Are you alright?"

"Yes," he answered. "There is a dip in the cavity, and I gashed my arm pretty badly. Listen, maybe you should start heading up now."

Isabel reached into the cavity. Her hands shook uncontrollably, but she kept crawling. Just as she got her whole body in, Isabel felt something snag her leg.

"Isabel?"

"Sorry, my leg. Must be caught on a rock."

Twisting and turning with all her might, Isabel could not move forward. It seemed odd; however, a rock with a grip…

Isabel was yanked back into the cave before she could scream. Her arms scraped against the jagged surface until she plopped into the water. Whatever held her leapt onto her back and pressed her head under water. Thrashing around unsuccessfully, Isabel concentrated on the opal in her armlet. With a jolt of adrenaline, she conjured an air bubble. Gasping for air, she hoisted herself upright, throwing the offender off. It landed with a splash.

Her foe was more comfortable in the water than she hoped. It swam with great agility as Isabel splashed around clumsily. She snapped her fingers to generate a ball of fire, hoping to get a better idea of who or what she was up against. For a fleeting moment, everything remained still.

"Isabel? Isabel!"

Her head jerked towards Dante's voice. Jumping at the opportunity, the creature latched onto her leg. Losing balance, Isabel fell backward and hit the surface of the water, reawakening the pain from earlier. The creature crawled up her abdomen and wrapped its webbed paws on her neck. A

Kai.

"Bo? Calder?" Isabel's vision grew fuzzy.

No. They could not be here.

Isabel's fingertips grazed her hips as her strength sapped away. When she reached the hilt of one sai, the cold steel sent a surge of warmth up her arm. In a quick stroke, she landed a blow right into the assailant's neck. He screeched as steam emitted from her weapon. He leaped off Isabel immediately.

Oxygen rushed into Isabel's lungs. Clarity flooded her brain. Isabel scrambled back on her feet. Her armlet was pulsing to the beat of her heart. Unsheathing her other sai, she froze, poised and vigilant. The water was tinted with blood. Kai blood. In the corner of her eye, Isabel saw a stirring on the surface, and she reacted without hesitation. Plunging her sai into the water, Isabel felt it connect to flesh. With a yelp, the Kai leapt from the water and scampered towards the opening of the crawl space.

Blood oozed over its patchy fur. The Kai's ears were filled with holes from where earrings used to be, and its emaciated frame was defiled by the mark of the Aeonians. He hissed at Isabel.

"Veijari! Why do you betray your kind?" Isabel demanded. "Do you not know that Dover is fighting to his last breath because of traitors like you?"

The Veijari only glared at her in silence. And yet, it did not attack.

"Listen—"

"Isabel, answer me!"

Dante's voice echoed faintly from the other end of the

crawlspace. The Kai Veijari growled and clambered towards the source of the noise.

"Dante! A Veijari is coming for you! Are you out of the tunnel?"

"Almost!"

"Get out of there!" Isabel screamed. Scratching from its claws echoed into the cave.

She gave Dante three seconds. Isabel wound her arm and launched a fireball up the tunnel. The heat emitted from her hands burned. There was a brief squeal and a thud.

In a panic, Isabel crawled through the opening. Repeating prayers in her head, she squeezed her way through as quickly as she could, gritting her teeth when the rocky walls scraped her body. Isabel lost her footing when her left arm did not connect with a solid surface. Her weight shifted forward as her palms halted her from hitting her head.

"This must be the dip Dante warned about," she murmured, massaging her hands.

As Isabel pulled her body through the dip she spotted a glow in the distance. Disoriented and unsure if she was climbing up, down, or sideways, Isabel grasped at any protruding rock. Blinking through beads of sweat, she tried to ignore the dizzying sensation of claustrophobia. As soon as her eyes began seeing double, Isabel shut them and pushed herself through until she felt a tug.

Gasping for breath, Isabel was plopped from the tunnel with the help of Dante. He cradled her in his arms, but she punched him weakly.

"Put me down," she panted. "I need some space."

"You and I made it through. You know, the Veijari was

almost out of the tunnel, but your fireball caught it in time. I'm okay. Thanks to you."

Isabel's eyes fell on the smoldering body. The scent of burnt flesh overwhelmed her, and Isabel doubled over to vomit.

"I was a little singed as well." Dante chuckled, patting her back. "Now, you have to help me seal up my wound before we move on. I'm sure you do not want to remain in these caves for much longer."

Wiping her mouth with the back of her hand, Isabel nodded and attended to his burn. Amidst his red skin, she found a puncture wound. Isabel hiccupped, disrupting the pressure she was trying to apply. Dante kept a vigilant eye on their new surroundings: another cavern, but bone dry in comparison. Many passageways beckoned the adventurers.

"Where should we go," Dante mused out loud.

Isabel dressed the wound in silence, not ready to answer his question. When she finished, Dante stood up, but he quickly stumbled back onto his knees.

"Damn." He squeezed his eyes shut.

"You will not be able to focus on your powers," Isabel said with conviction. "Your body is exhausted."

"But you still can. Harness the wind. You can use it like how a bat finds its way out. It will take quite a bit of strength and concentration, but if you let me help you, we can probably find a way out. Close your eyes."

Isabel enveloped herself in darkness, letting her other senses take over. Dripping water in the distance. Dante's tight grip. The musty smell, a hint of sulfur. A slight pulsing sensation washed over her. Whether it was the surge of wind her body was emitting, or the intensity of her heartbeat, Isabel focused her thoughts on the singular feeling.

"Command the air to extend its fingers and explore the cavern." He let his hands go.

The pulsing slowed back down.

"Focus, Isabel."

Instinctively, Isabel squeezed her eyes tighter. She did not want to lose momentum of what Dante started. Searching for strength in Tuuli's Opal, Isabel imagined herself soaring through the various arms of the space around her. Her body, made translucent like a summer breeze, bounced from one tunnel to another, all of which had a dead end. Her consciousness tumbled about and blew towards a nook in the west end. Isabel dipped, turned, and twisted. Suddenly, she felt her body expand freely.

Isabel's eyes opened. Before her, Dante blinked in amazement. Looking down, Isabel gasped. The glow of Tuuli's Opal shone so brightly, it shrouded her whole body, elevating her a few inches off the ground. Her hair fluttered radiantly every which way. Isabel's shock caused her power to fade, gently placing her back on the floor of the cave.

"I found the right path." Isabel rubbed the armlet. "I saw it. I *felt* it."

She helped Dante up, and they trekked to the far west end where the opening Isabel discovered was located. This path dipped downwards, inviting them with flecks of green light, suggesting a plethora of emeralds embedded in its walls.

"Are you sure?" Dante asked.

"What do you mean, am I sure?" Isabel recoiled in offense. "Of course! Well, I think."

She huffed and crawled in first with a hasty determination. Isabel heard Dante's struggled grunts, but something within her grew agitated. Dipping, turning, and twisting. Isabel recognized every inch. Her breathing was more controlled and her claustrophobia dissipated. Before she knew it, she reached the final corner where a light flickered a hundred feet away. Crawling faster, she held her breath in anticipation.

I cannot believe it. It actually worked. I did it!

Pride swelled in her chest as she pulled up from the tunnel and into a manmade room.

"You proud of me?" Isabel asked as she helped Dante up.

"Not really. Then you will have no need of me someday!" Dante shook her shoulder. "I'm *kidding*."

Isabel allowed a polite chuckle to escape and resumed exploring the room. The rocky walls were chiseled and polished to a smooth consistency. Two statues of Dunya stood at opposite ends of the room.

"The Dunya love their precious metals," Isabel exclaimed. One statue was of copper and the other a white gold.

"And yet no doors?" Dante tugged at the copper statue. Unsuccessful, Dante kicked at it, but the blank eyes only stared back at him.

"One thing is for sure, I am *not* going back down into that cave." Isabel crossed her arms.

"We may have no choice," he blurted.

"There should be a way."

"Maybe you missed something," Dante ran his hand through his hair, pulling at loose strands.

As he stalked towards the tunnel entrance, Isabel frowned. She turned to the white gold Dunyan statue. Plopping onto the floor, she held her hand to her chin. Isabel tuned out the shuffling of Dante's feet.

Maybe I can make it work a second time.

Closing her eyes, Isabel focused her thoughts once more on Tuuli's Opal. The sensation of flight seized her quicker than last time. Her fingers acted like wisps of the ocean breeze as she felt her way around the statue, sensing the possibility of an opening behind it as the air escaped.

She broke off from her meditative state and latched onto the statue. Retiring Tuuli's Opal, Isabel focused the power of fire to her hands. The nerves at her fingertips tingled like pins and needles. The sensation changed from warm to searing hot within seconds. Wincing in pain, she pressed her fingertips into the metal that begrudgingly gave way. As the temperature climbed higher, the statue warped.

"Isabel!" Dante cried. "You need an extraordinary amount of heat to melt it. You will hurt yourself!"

"Shut up," Isabel growled. "I can do this!"

Isabel continued to transmit waves of heat, allowing her body to act as a conductor from the ruby of fire to the statue. Shaking off beads of sweat that poured down the nape of her neck, Isabel knew she needed only another moment. Encouraged by the growing puddle, she mustered the rest of her strength to blast one last wave of heat.

The statue gave way. Half melted, the head toppled to the floor. Confidence grew and the statue shrank. She embraced the inhuman heat as she melted enough of the statue to expose a pathway, protected by iron bars. Isabel beckoned Dante with her hands.

"Maybe you can help me pull the bars apart as I weaken them," she said, swallowing the awkward silence. "Come on. One thing we both agree on is an exit."

Dante wrapped his hands in cloth and pulled at the bars as she weakened them. The iron gave way like butter, and the pair squeezed through.

"Good job," he said as they broke into a jog.

"I accept your apology." Isabel reached for his hand. A forlorn look washed over her face as she held Dante's gaze. Her emotions still raged like scattered bulls every time she looked at her husband. Isabel realized she may never get over what he had done.

"Let's keep going." Dante flushed, breaking eye contact.

They continued to explore the innards of the Shrine. Each room was different: wet, dry, small, large. All were empty, not even an enemy to fend off. Isabel and Dante wound through passages that seemed to take hours. But after each frustrating turn, they ended up back in the same wooden entrance. Isabel cried out in desperation.

A cool breeze brushed past her, and she sighed.

Wait, where is the breeze coming from?

Sand blew into the room from the entrance. At first, sand entered in tiny wisps, but then poured in at an alarming rate. A pillar of sand accumulated and took the shape of a human. Dante cast his arm in front of her.

The figure of sand cracked and split in two. Out emerged a man… Tall, strong, orange hair.

"Bence?" Isabel whispered.

The figure before them growled and ruffled sand from his

hair. "You mistake me for my twin. I am Farid."

Isabel's hand flew to her mouth as memories of her first trip to Buryan returned.

"Have we met before?" He mused.

"He must have the Dunyan Amber. How?" Dante interjected.

The lean figure hooted. His laughter shook the entire room. "You remember Adem?"

Isabel and Dante exchanged glances.

"That is his blood over there. He tried to fight me and protect it. Such a fool." He breathed deeply, stroking his armor. "This is just the beginning. This stone will surely help me beat you to Kai's Sapphire. And Dover *and* Hakan are in Ogonia together, right?"

"Haven't you had enough bloodshed?" Dante shouted. "We will not let you touch the Kai and the Foti."

"You can never have enough!" Farid roared. His baritone voice caused the floor to tremble, knocking Isabel off balance. When she looked up, she also noticed that the ceiling seemed to lower a few feet. Shaking her head, she checked again. No doubt he made the ceiling drop.

Once he regained his composure, Farid caressed his armor again. Dark and rough, made of scales. It reeked of rotting flesh. It glimmered, it shined.

It was once the hide of King Adem.

When Isabel noticed, she gagged and Dante followed suit. Farid laughed once more, hands holding his belly, almost keeling over with madness. Dante wiped his mouth and lunged at him. The earth quaked as the two bodies fell to the ground. Wresting one another, their grunts and cries echoed in Isabel's ears.

Isabel summoned her focus and clapped her hands together in a prayer-like position. Focusing intensely, she threw her hands apart, creating a wind current strong enough to pull the two men apart. Dante flew to the left wall and landed softly. He collected himself and moved back towards Farid, who Isabel had slammed into the right wall.

Farid pounded the wall in anger with his fist, causing the ceiling to crack and drop another few feet. Dust and chunks of rock fell. Isabel did not hesitate. She charged at him. Her hands met his in a deadlock. He bore down on her, and she dug her heels into the dirt and her nails into his flesh in response. Inch by inch, Farid overpowered her, but just as Isabel's knees were about to collapse, He doubled over. Dante had thrust his sword into Farid's abdomen. Isabel broke free of Farid's grip and turned around to his exposed head. She unsheathed a sai and struck the back of his skull. As Farid hit the floor, the ceiling now fell so low that it grazed Dante's hair. The pair jumped back and waited a moment. The body appeared lifeless.

"We have to get out," Dante said. "This place is going to collapse any minute. We can search his body for the talisman once we know it's safe."

Isabel sprinted through the entrance with Dante following behind her. When she stumbled into the open, she turned to find Dante nowhere in sight.

A shuffle escaped from the Shrine's entrance. Isabel perked her head up, heart leaping into her throat.

"Dante?"

Farid appeared before her. Her heart plummeted. "What did you do to him?"

"I have wasted enough time on your pathetic souls. I

have one more stone to gather. Once I retrieve it, I will come back to claim your life." He snapped his fingers.

Isabel lunged at him, but she was blown away by a swirl of sand. When she rubbed the grittiness from her eyes, Farid was gone.

"Dante. No. Dante!" Anxiety flooded her thoughts.

As Isabel fought her way towards the door, she heard rumbling. The foundation of Maz Shrine shook. She feared that the ceiling would come crashing down on him. She stumbled into the entrance but saw no one, except the empty box... and a pile of sand. The ceiling was now so low, Isabel had to crouch to move around the room. She cursed aloud and called out for Dante. When she heard no answer, she called upon the power of air once more, and uncovered the suspicious pile of sand.

And there he lay. Dante. He coughed wildly and blinked at her. She took his hand and they scrambled for the door. The ceiling continued to shake. Then, it made its final drop.

"Roll!"

Isabel and Dante dove out the door. Her shoulder crashed against stone. Her knees. The world flipped around her as she tumbled down the steps. When Isabel landed at the bottom, she found Dante. Dirt caked his face, but he gave her a thumbs up.

A deafening roar erupted behind them. Pillars toppled, and the mighty Maz Shrine collapsed like a sinkhole into the mountain. Isabel's mouth fell agape in astonishment. The shrine was gone, just like the Dunya.

She sniffed, trying to hold back tears. "These were the last of the Dunya." Isabel's head fell into her hands. "I can't believe it. I let them down. They are gone because of me.

Silly, stupid, young, ignorant me!"

Dante sat beside her, drumming his fingers. He opened his mouth, but said nothing.

"Hallo!"

Isabel twisted and saw a figure waving his arms in the distance. "Harmon?"

"My Princess. More enemies came, but we fought with great honor. We lost about a score of men. But at the turn of battle, they retreated and disappeared into a great storm of sand! It was an amazing sight that I would only think that someone who possessed the power of the Earth..."

Her gaze fell to the ground. "Are all bodies accounted for?"

"Just about. Though we could not recover the bodies of Avani and Kaj," Harmon said, cradling his bandaged hand.

"Avani. That is Adem's daughter, correct?"

"Correct," nodded Harmon. "She was married to Kaj. Bodies are nowhere to be found. Granted, many corpses were quite hard to identify."

Isabel found herself lost in thought but was quickly interrupted.

"...Well, erm, where to ma'am?"

"There is little time left. We prepare for the final battle in Ogonia."

She heard Dante shift his body away from them. Harmon bowed and hurried to rejoin his troops.

"I hope we are wrong and that you are out there, Avani. I cannot accept the extinction of the Dunya people on my behalf." Isabel bowed her head in a quick prayer before leaving as quickly as Harmon.

CHAPTER

32

Dante's sculpted shoulders hunched over as he hugged the pillow. The scent of sweat lingered in the sheets. He had tried. But he wasn't able to complete his part. Dread filled Isabel's mind.

Am I not pretty enough? Did I not do enough?

Isabel nudged him awake and gave him a half smile.

"Good morning," she said.

He flushed and averted her eyes.

"Hey. I love you," she said. She mustered all of her strength to prevent her voice from faltering. The world was falling apart, and she still struggled to connect with Dante.

He craned his neck and kissed her cheek. Before she could return the kiss, he sprung out of bed and dressed. An awkward silence pervaded.

It was time to plan next steps.

After she got ready, Isabel followed Dante to the main cabin where Harmon and Ethen stood, bent over a map.

Their fingers traced the matted paper as if they were creating an abstract work of art. They grumbled in low tones until they noticed her.

The pair stood straight and saluted Isabel and Dante. Dark circles clung to their eyes.

"Thirty men are in the infirmary below. And the rest and mending their weapons. We anticipate full recovery before we reach Ogonia," Ethen reported robotically.

Dante said, "Good. There is no time to waste. So, tell me what you have."

"I think we should backtrack a little, then sail around Deran. Hit the Aeonians on the Ogonian oceanfront," Ethen said as he jammed his finger against the map.

Dante peered over his shoulder as he twisted his opal ring. "I think that's a great idea. They don't have a fleet. Let's do this."

"Ethen, timing is critical. I think we should continue on the Fuad River. It's much faster. We may not have the luxury of taking the long route for an advantage we aren't sure is worth it," Harmon interjected.

The two bickered as Isabel studied the map. Ethen's recommendation would take them an extra two days. Maybe a day and a half. And the flashbacks of scorched Dunyan bodies told her Harmon may be right.

"I vote for Harmon's approach," she blurted. "They expect our approach. There is no more element of surprise. The river is quicker."

Dante, who had been pacing back and forth, stopped. He was still twisting his opal ring. "Why are you trying to contradict my wishes?"

"Uh, that wasn't my intention. I was just throwing my opinion into the mix." Isabel paused. All three men stared at her. Clearing her throat, she continued, "I hold just as much power and you do."

I don't get why he's acting like he's on edge.

When she finished her thought, she caught Dante rolling his eyes as he stormed out of the main cabin. Ethen and Harmon followed him out. The creaking of the wooden walls emphasized her solitude. She sat down, sighing. She looked down at her ring. They seemed to grow farther apart with each passing hour. Isabel wasn't sure if he still felt bad about last night, or if something else bothered him.

At least our union brought about some coherence to our people.

Isabel walked out to the deck. The sun stretched its way into the sky, and the breeze mild. Dante commanded his men to raise the sails. Harmon and Ethen alternated watches, admiring the changing landscape. The rolling fields of the northeast were still a golden color, untouched by the flames of war. Birds flew between the sparse trees while deer nestled with their young in the brush, unaware of the turmoil that was slowly engulfing the island. The soldiers were restless, but Dante forbade Isabel to 'distract' them.

The day passed by uneventfully, and Isabel decided to retire to her room.

"Dante?"

"I will take the night watch as well." Dante's voice faltered.

"You need rest for tomorrow," Isabel pleaded. "And... I am trying okay? I am trying to be a good wife to you. Spend some time with me. I have been distracted."

Harmon approached Dante and patted his back, encouraging his leader to get some rest. Dante thanked his friend and left for his chambers with her. Isabel took his hand and kissed him.

"You must have been under so much pressure, I should not have taken it so personally," Isabel murmured. "I feared something had happened during your imprisonment. I thought you had changed. Perhaps it is just the emotional scars, the pressure. Or maybe it's all me."

"My insecurities are coming out," Dante blurted. "I saw Echidna. They had decided to execute me. I was not supposed to live, and yet she let me go. To this day it bothers me that Echidna chose to let me live, like I am in her debt." He shook his head and sat at the end of the bed. "She scrutinized my past like some otherworldly witch doctor. She exposed my needs, my fears to prove myself. And most of all, she manipulated my fear of losing you."

Guilt stirred within Isabel. Maybe she was too quick to judge Dante's behavior. She sat by his side. "All I ask is that you do not change. People look up to you more now. But people are fickle. Minds and opinions change with the times, but one sure thing that will break trust permanently is trying to fool them," she said, pointing at his chest. Dante's eyes flickered at Isabel's words. She remained still as he got up to prepare for bed.

Was he even listening?

Biting her lip, she hoped that his lack of response was due to his stubborn male ego.

But there should be no walls when united through marriage.

Dante removed his garments, and Isabel slid beneath the

blankets. Holding her breath in anticipation, she welcomed him beside her. Even though his skin felt warm, goose bumps spread all over her body. Running her fingers in his hair, Isabel kissed him. She pulled his hands around her, praying tonight would go more smoothly.

He sighed. She gasped.

This is really happening!

A deafening explosion rocked the boat violently. Dante flew off the bed. Isabel slammed her head against the bedpost. Stars exploded in her eyes as screaming erupted on the deck above her.

CHAPTER

33

Harmon banged on the door. "Sir. We are under attack!"

"Is it the Aeonians?" Dante asked.

Isabel swiftly moved about the room. Her hands shook as she lit a match and brought it to a lamp.

"Kana! There are hundreds attacking us! We were hit be a boulder launched by catapult."

Dante scrambled for his clothes. "But how are they organized in such large numbers to attack us?"

"Damian wants to slow us down. We will not let that happen!" Isabel exclaimed.

Isabel commanded Harmon to summon the soldiers to their battle stations. She tossed on her tunic and slacks, equipped her weapons and ran out with Dante. Kana swarmed like angry bees, diving at the ship. Feathers rained everywhere. She immediately grabbed her bow. The number of arrows was limited, so she summoned the power of wind to bolster their killing power.

The first arrow grazed a Kana. It snapped its beak and dove at her. It knocked the bow her from hands and scratched the length of her right arm. Screaming in pain, Isabel checked for bleeding. The cut wasn't deep, but she had no time to attend to it. The Kana swooped around and dove again.

She fumbled for her sai but wasn't fast enough. It extended its claws. Isabel shielded her face with her forearm. When the Kana made contact, Isabel grabbed its feathers and took it down with her.

She gasped for breath and the creature wrestled in her arms. Isabel rolled to one side, grabbed one sai, and stabbed it in the neck. The three-pronged blade slowly sank into its leather-like flesh. Blood spurted out as the Kana screeched.

Isabel shoved the monster away and hobbled to her bow. When she reached for it, another Kana crashed into her. She tumbled a few feet. Isabel ached everywhere.

"Shit!"

This Kana flapped its wings, lifting itself higher into the air. By the time Isabel steadied herself on her elbows, it dove at her.

She drove the same sai up and into its chest. The Kana's body slammed against hers but didn't move. Its vacant eyes stared at her. Shouting erupted everywhere. The faint scent of burning wood filled her nose.

Another Kana landed with a thud beside her. It scrambled onto its claws and screeched.

I got to get to my bow!

Tucking her head close to her chest, she hid under the carcass. The Kana she killed was fairly large and covered most of her body. Even if the other Kana saw her, maybe she could trick it into thinking she was dead. She held her breath and laid still. Her muscles burned trying to balance the dead Kana over her.

With a flutter of its wings, the nearby Kana took flight. Releasing a sigh, Isabel threw the body off of herself and rolled onto her stomach. Soldiers stormed by her. Some were plucked off the deck by Kana and dropped into the river.

Isabel grunted as she got onto her feet. Her surroundings seemed to whirl around her as she sprinted to her bow. She shot at every Kana that flew by her. Even though the pain in her arm drained her energy, she charged the tips of the arrows with fire, and shot down one Kana at a time. After a few minutes, she managed to take down half a dozen of them. But the searing pain burned to the point where she had to stop. Isabel ducked and took cover behind some wooden barrels.

When she took a moment to scan the premises, Isabel noticed the Kana that mobilized on shore. A mammoth-sized Kana prepared a catapult.

"Ethen! Rally some men and take down those Kana on land!"

Two smaller Kana were setting a boulder in place. Before they launched it, they set it ablaze. Ethen's arrow took one. Isabel drew her bow and aimed at the larger creature. She released the arrow, which zipped through the air and lodged in its eye. As the creature stumbled and screeched, it flailed it claws and released the trigger before it fell. The flaming rock hurled at the ship. Towards Isabel.

Panic erupted beneath her skin. She looked to her left, then her right. Everyone dove for cover. Twenty feet. As the boulder approached, Isabel set her bow aside and pointed at the target with one of her sai. Ten feet. Her hands trembled. Despite the torrential flood of fear drowning her, Isabel summoned a blast of wind from the tip of her sai. The force wrapped itself around the boulder, suspending it in place.

The tremble spread up her arms as the energy drained from her veins. The gash on her arm felt as if someone pressed a branding iron against her flesh. Before her legs gave out, Isabel swung her arms, batting that boulder back at her opponents. The impact shook the ground and mowed over scores of Kana.

"Come on, men! We've almost got them!" Isabel shouted from the deck.

Dante arrived by her side and helped her up. She wobbled on her feet.

"You alright?" he asked.

"I think so."

"You're wound doesn't look too bad. We will get that fixed as soon as we can. Stay strong. I'm going to get a better view of what we are up against," Dante said, squeezing her shoulder. He took off and scaled the mast.

"Isabel! There are more Kana approaching!" he shouted from above.

She cursed beneath her breath. "Ethen, station your men on the stern side. Harmon, take the bow. Dante and I will cover the middle of the ship!" Waving her arms, she positioned herself behind a cannon.

"Load the cannons and fire at will!" she cried. As Isabel

covered her ears, booms erupted everywhere, rocking the vessel back and forth. The stench of sulfur wafted through the air.

"Isabel, watch out!" Dante yelled through the haze of smoke. His voice cut short. There was a thud.

When she lifted her gaze to the sky, her heart plummeted. The moon, once full and bright, was shrouded by dense clouds. The dark mass broke apart into hundreds of smaller pieces. It was a legion of Kana, screeching at the top of their lungs. Isabel cupped her hands over her ears. When they neared the ship, the Kana dove one by one.

Some Kana crashed through the blood-stained deck, wreaking havoc in the cabins below. Others swooped soldiers up and dropped them from hundreds of feet in the air.

"Take cover! Abandon ship if you have to!" Isabel's orders were drowned by the shrill sounds of the Kana and howls of soldiers.

Bodies littered the ship and shoreline. Isabel wasn't sure she would have an army left by the time they reached Ogonia.

An idea struck her like a slap to the face. Isabel flexed her arm, commanded the power of Foti's Ruby. With a loud roar, fire combusted from the highest point of the ship, wrapping itself around the hull, encapsulating the ship in its entirety. The release of power winded Isabel, but she kept her focus strong.

Kana crashed into the fiery barrier, emitting piercing cries. Their scorched bodies landed on the deck. The flames that consumed their feathers licked at the wooden floor.

The rest of the Kana flew back, roaring in anger. Isabel's

smile faded when she observed the scene around her. The ship was catching fire from the burning bodies. The temperature skyrocketed. Sweat poured down her face and neck.

"We need to put these fires out. If we can do this, I won't have to release the barrier, and we can be safe from the rest of the horde," Isabel shouted to whoever was listening.

It was chaos. Men ran maneuvered around smoldering heaps towards the nearest flame. But when one fiery corpse was extinguished, another fire spread elsewhere. Black smoke accumulated, stinging Isabel's eyes. As she kept rubbing them, she grew disoriented.

"Princess!" Harmon screamed. "We must abandon ship. Please, remove the fire barrier. We will take our chances with the remaining Kana!"

Her heart thumped steadily. Isabel closed her eyes and released the fire barrier. As soon as it vanished, a loud buzz filled the air.

"Abandon ship!" she exclaimed.

Everyone leapt into the river. Isabel scanned the area for Dante. She spotted him leaning on the ship's helm, his left leg bloodied.

Something must have knocked him from the mast.

Mustering all of her remaining strength, Isabel sprinted to Dante and pulled his arm over her shoulder. He tried to walk, but his leg failed him each time. His weight taxed Isabel's body, but she pushed forward, past dead bodies and burning barrels. They shuffled towards the edge of the ship.

Kana crowded the deck, tearing out anyone who was still left. Isabel aimed fireballs from the tip of her sai at any enemy that came near. But with each shot her attack grew weaker. Stopping at the railing, she wavered. Everything seemed be in double vision. After taking a deep breath, Isabel pushed Dante off and dove in after.

The impact of the water stung. Sounds of splashing water surrounded her. People shouted. She rubbed her eyes and searched for Dante. When she didn't spot him, she dove below the surface. All she could see was black. Isabel conjured an air bubble around her body and lit a flame at her fingertips.

Dante floated a few feet below her. Even though he tried to swim up, his lame leg was dead weight. Breaking her air bubble, she reached for his sleeve and dragged him to shore. Even though her muscles burned, the ice-cold water refreshed her.

Don't give up on me, Dante. I need you.

When Isabel heaved Dante onto the riverbank, she screamed for help. Harmon slid towards them and helped carry Dante, who coughed incessantly.

"Don't worry, Isabel," Harmon said. "He's breathing. He'll be fine."

She nodded, teeth chattering. Her tunic clung to her skin, and the breeze turned what was a refreshing coolness into an icy death sentence. A patch of spindly trees and brush stood a few feet away. The trio took refuge there, Harmon laying Dante against the trunk of a willow.

"Hang in there," Harmon whispered to Isabel before he charged at Kana who landed nearby.

Shivering uncontrollably, Isabel held Dante close. His whole body shook as well. The clashing of Harmon's sword against the claws of Kana echoed loudly. Turning her head, Isabel saw Harmon backing up. He swiped to the left and missed. One Kana flapped its wings, scattering its black feathers about, and lashed out. It bit his sword hand. Harmon yelped and tried to rip the creature off.

Ethen slid into view and drove his sword through the Kana. Blood leaked from Harmon's hand as he released his hold on his sword. Without a word, Ethen took out a handkerchief and tied it around his comrade's hand. When Ethen reached for Harmon's sword, a rumble shook the earth. Both soldiers looked beyond Isabel, who also turned and gazed beyond the row of trees.

Like an ocean of darkness, thousands of Kana charged on foot, consuming any soldier that came in their way. Their claws tore up the fields of Deran as they approached her. Harmon and Ethen whizzed by Isabel, swords drawn. They stopped after a few feet and squared their shoulders, bracing for impact.

Five hundred feet.

Harmon shouted something to Ethen.

Three hundred feet.

Nothing Isabel did could summon the power of air or fire. Her body was exhausted.

Two hundred feet.

Dante squeezed her. She gazed into his eyes.

This may be the end.

Then, a blinding flash consumed the battlefield.

CHAPTER

34

Peering through the gaps between her fingers, Isabel saw a cavalry of white horses infiltrate the wave of Kana. Harmon and Ethen clashed with the front line, but chaos dispersed the Kana's formation. Isabel stood, breathless.

An army of Zingaris mounted on wild horses came charging in, shooting arrows, waving chains, and whistling loudly. They washed over their enemy like ocean waves over rocks. Even when the Kana snapped at the heels of the horses, the Zingari leapt to the ground, many armed with weapons in their hands and both tails. Some transformed into human soldiers or mountain lions and proceeded to tear Kana to shreds. This was the first time Isabel could recall the two outcast natives of Deran fighting one another in a pitched battle.

"What an amazing sight!" exhaled Isabel as her heart swelled.

Amidst the bedlam, Ethen peered back at her behind his hawkish nose. Isabel gave a thumbs up. He nodded and stayed near them to fend off any Kana that manage to squeeze by.

Within the hour, the Kana fell silent.

The crowd erupted in cheers as Harmon and Ethen approached Isabel with raised swords. Hundreds of Zingaris trotted beside the surviving soldiers. A few leapt to embrace Harmon and Ethen.

"What may your name be, little warrior?" Harmon asked the Zingari that hung by his side.

"I am far from a warrior," he chirped. "The name is Jabin, wandering entertainer."

Isabel's heart leapt at the sound of his voice.

"Jabin?" she whispered.

"It was a brave thing to aid us in battle. You should hold no love for humans, we drove your people to become nomads," Harmon said.

"The Kana are not a compassionate kind. And my easy answer is that nomadic or not, Deran is home to the both of us. All Zingaris want is peace. And as long as Damian and Echidna are around, there is no such thing. And war does not discriminate."

He ceased marching, knelt down and pat Jabin's shoulder, who extended his paw-like hand.

"May a great alliance grow from the fires of this war. I apologize on behalf of the Tuuli for any wrong we have done to your kind in the past," Harmon said, grasping Jabin's paw.

"Peace to all in Deran," Jabin closed his eyes in prayer.

"Jabin!" Isabel shouted. Tears welled in her eyes as she pounced on her long-lost friend.

"You know this fella?"

"I sure do," she said.

"I am sorry for your loss... Many losses. We came as soon as we could." His tails wagged.

"Thank you... but... I'm sorry... where were all of you until now?"

"My lady, I recruited all my friends to prepare for such a battle. But this did not happen for some time. Then word came that Pekas was abandoned. My people started to occupy homes that were above water. It was during this time that one night, someone spotted this ship as it passed. My people debated for a long time whether to help the humans, or their brethren, the Tuuli. In the end, we chose to all follow, and all fight. This is our land, too, and we are happy to share and protect it."

Isabel looked past Jabin, at his people, who genuflected before her. She bowed in return. Jabin announced his allegiance to the Tuuli and everyone cheered. He leapt on Isabel and licked her face. She released a giggle and patted his nose. When everything fell silent, her gaze fell on Harmon who approached her.

"Is that your new best friend?" Ethen jogged over with a smirk. He held his hands to his cheeks in exaggeration. "Have I been replaced?"

"Of course not, Eth—"

A whirring sound met with a thud.

Ethen suddenly fell forward, exposing an arrow lodged in the back of his skull. Harmon turned and spotted a fallen Kana with a bow in its claws. Harmon howled and sprinted towards it, hacking the head off in one stroke. The creature lay still, but the damage was done. Ethen was dead, blood trickling from the wound. Harmon cried and cradled his best friend's head in his arms.

CHAPTER

35

The burials were unnervingly swift. Isabel mourned silently over the dirt mounds that lined the riverbank. Her ship sat half submerged in the blood-stained Fuad River, still smoldering. The skeleton of their vessel creaked in front of her, a ghost of a reminder of the night's battle. The rhythmic chanting of prayers rose and fell behind her.

Isabel clutched the blanket wrapped around her shoulders tightly. Even though she had dried off, shivers still wracked her spine. They only had twenty-four hours to spare before they had to move on. After Jabin attended to her cut, she had spent until sunrise cleansing the bodies with river water. Normally, Deranian custom would be to fully wash the deceased and apply jasmine-infused ointment. It felt like bad luck to rush the process, but even Harmon gruffly told her to hurry.

The sun hung in the middle of the sky, playing peek-and-boo behind the occasional cloud. Isabel mumbled her own prayer, her breath curling into the air.

Harmon produced Jabin's whistle which he used during the wedding and began a similar ritual. Jabin pointed out his whistle with his muzzle in glee. Isabel smiled and scratched Jabin's neck. Each minute Harmon played was spent in the form of a fallen soldier. Mesmerized, Isabel wondered about the life of each man. The soldier was a son, possibly a husband and father. She wished there was something more she could do.

Afterwards, it was a short night's sleep. She returned to the tree where Dante rested. Carefully maneuvering around him, she draped her cloak over his torso and kissed his forehead. A lot weighed on her. She only had two stones. Farid had one. The Dunya were extinct. Half of her army lay buried in the earth.

I want to make things right. It was silly of me to assume Bence would keep his promise to help me. The Aeonians have brought nothing but death since their return, and I must rise to the occasion for my people.

The sun returned promptly. It was time to mobilize.

Isabel isolated herself from the pack of soldiers. She laid her weapons on the grass and examined her uniform. Much of her clothing was ripped, stained, and singed.

"My lady," Jabin cleared his throat timidly.

"I am not changing. Come," Isabel replied, peeking over at him.

"I have something for you." He bowed.

After he tossed over an item that hung in his jaw, he barked in excitement. Isabel fondled the lumpy gift. Tearing the package open, Isabel's guess was confirmed. The smell of fresh leather filled her nostrils. She excitedly tore off her worn vest and slid the replacement over her tunic. She used the laces on the new vest to adjust the fitting. Isabel admired the intricate detail and quality.

"There is more, you know," Jabin said, tongue hanging from his jaw. A drop of drool hung from it.

Stifling a giggle, Isabel turned her attention to elbow length leather gloves and new slacks.

"Jabin, this is too much!"

"I had a feeling we would meet again, and given your challenging journey, I guessed this would come in handy. Maybe boost your spirits, even."

Isabel held her gifts to her chest and squealed with delight.

"You know, I have seen you from afar when I used to entertain the royal family. You and your sister. It was easy for me to recognize you the first night we met. You stood with the same easy grace that you had as a child. However, from then until now, I have witnessed an extraordinary change within you. You grew from a timid girl into a strong Princess!" Jabin concluded with conviction.

"You are too liberal with your words," Isabel said.

"And you are too modest."

"Well." Isabel swallowed the lump in her throat. "Thank you."

"Here." Jabin gestured his paw to Isabel's heart. "I can sense it. Your heart is stronger. It has summoned my people to your aid."

Jabin's cryptic words resonated in her chest, which grew increasingly heavy. It was only moments before her knees pulled her down, and she embraced her friend.

After Isabel suited up, they checked on Dante. Jabin dressed Dante's wounds and sprinkled some herbal elixir on them. Within hours, Dante had recovered enough to walk alone. Jabin instructed him to not over exert himself, to use one of the surviving horses to allow time to heal. Isabel refused a horse, and insisted the handful to be given to injured men.

Harmon led the army, solemn and silent, speechless since Ethen's burial. Still, it was a grand sight, an ensemble of men, Tuuli, and Zingaris, marching now through Foti's Pass.

Pin-point slate rocks stretched towards the sky like fingernails. Trees and grass thinned out, and the trail transformed into a dusty road. Footsteps and clanging of armor echoed between the towering stone formations. The temperature dropped several degrees in their shadows.

Isabel led the troop, weaving to and fro. She held her breath every time she rounded a corner. Foti's Pass was quiet. Only an occasional fly buzzed by, dancing around the exhausted bodies.

The Golden Falls were a scant few miles away.

CHAPTER

36

Jabin's voiced rolled past Isabel's ears. "The Faud River wraps around most of Deran. It is a branch that flows from a waterfall that marks the line to the Ogonia. Just before the Golden Falls, large stone walls were built to surround the entire northern tip of Deran, stretching for miles. The part of the river that feeds into the Falls is not obstructed by stone, but protected by iron gates below it."

Young soldiers had walked alongside Jabin, listening to his stories the whole trek. He had relayed the history of Deran. He reached the chapter of Ogonia, which was fitting. They were very close.

When Isabel's army spied the walls intact from a distance, she sighed in relief. Ogonia had not been compromised. "And I used to make fun of their paranoia," she laughed nervously.

"Yes, I guess it finally served a purpose..." Dante appeared by her side on his horse. He kept his eyes forward.

Isabel pat his leg and looked up at him. "Man, I wish I had a horse." But Dante didn't laugh. Gritting her teeth, she tried not to get discouraged.

Maybe he is just irritated because of his injuries. I won't give up.

"Look!" Jabin yelped. He pointed at a smattering of tents and bonfires at the base of the wall.

Isabel squinted her eyes. Aeonians sharpened their swords while the Veijari warmed themselves by the fire.

"Why aren't they even trying, the brutes? They probably still have Dunyan Veijari that can smash these walls." Isabel tapped her index finger against her head.

"We now know there is a reason for everything the Aeonians do," Dante answered. "They are waiting for something."

"Should we take cover?" Jabin peeped.

Isabel and Dante hesitated, then glanced at one another.

"No," Isabel answered with conviction. "We take them now because if they *are* waiting for something, then they are not yet ready for battle."

"Agreed," Dante said. "Harmon, are you ready for battle? If you wish to refrain from this engagement…"

"I am well, sir. In fact, I shall fight stronger than ever."

"Prep the troops and await our signal."

"May I join you on your horse?" Isabel asked.

Dante nodded. Clearing her throat, Isabel clumsily mounted the horse and grabbed onto his torso. When she placed her cheek against his neck, she felt a cold sweat. His muscles tightened. Words tried to escape Isabel. Words seeking affirmation that Dante still loved her. But now wasn't the time.

When Dante nudged at his steed, they galloped down the line of men and Zingari. The thunderous pounding of hooves sped Isabel's heart rate. Jabin followed behind, panting loudly.

Turning her gaze towards her men, Isabel pulled out a sai and flashed it in the air. "We strike quickly. We strike hard. We strike now!" After waving her arm, she swung it down and pointed it towards the Aeonians.

With a loud roar, everyone poured down to the encampment in waves. The Zingaris sped past her men and infiltrated the camp like a swarm of bees. They transformed into soldiers, bearing the Aeonian mark, some taking the likeness of Edchina with ebony hair and sharp features, while others taking the likeness of Damian with a stocky build and blood-red hair. They looked indistinguishable from their foes.

"Careful not to slay our own people!" Isabel cried. "Remember to look into your enemies' eyes first before you swing your sword."

The horse swerved to the left, then the right to avoid falling bodies. Isabel clung tightly as she jostled around the saddle. Brilliant white swords clashed with the Aeonian's dark blades all around her. Scanning the area, many Aeonians had already fallen, but there was no sign of Damian or Echidna.

Something whirred by, missing her cheek by inches. Whipping her head around, she spotted a knot of Aeonians aiming their spears at her.

"That's her! Get her!"

Isabel reached for her bow and drew an arrow. She bit her tongue in frustration as she tried to steady her aim.

She'd drilled archery before and knew how to ride a horse, but she had never done them at the same time. Taking a deep breath, she released an arrow.

It zipped through the air and planted into the dirt in front of an Aeonian who released his spear. It whistled at high speeds and struck the horse. Isabel flew off the beast and landed on her back. Dante tugged the reigns, but the horse teetered back and forth until another spear lodged into its skull.

Gasping for breath, Isabel rolled onto her stomach. The horse's shadow loomed above her. In a split second, the creature and Dante collapsed on her.

She couldn't even scream. Her lungs burned as the weight of the horse crushed her ribcage. Clawing at the dirt, she tried focusing on her powers, but every time she thought of Tuuli's Opal, her mind grew fuzzy.

Muffled screams flowed in between her ears. Blood rained on her face.

If I die here… so close to my goal…

Someone tugged at her legs. The nails were sharp and tore her pants. Isabel couldn't feel anything but pressure. With each tug, pressure rose up her neck and face. She was sure she was purple.

The tugging stopped. The horse's body shuddered, releasing the pressure on her body. The corpse levitated a foot in the air and hovered. Isabel coughed incessantly as blood rushed throughout her limbs.

Another muffled voice shouted over the background noise. It repeated itself.

Grunting, Isabel got on all fours and shook her head.

"Move, Isabel. Quick! I can't hold it any longer!" Dante's voice doused over her like ice water.

She tucked her head and rolled forward as the carcass crashed onto the ground. Spears landed around her one by one.

Thump. Thump. Thump.

"Move!" Dante shouted. He drew his sword and drove it into the skull of the Aeonian that had attacked her moments ago.

Sharp pain radiated around her sides as she stood. Losing balance, she steadied herself on a wooden spear. Isabel took a few labored breaths and wiped her brow. The stabbing sensation undulated, returning each time with more intensity.

I got to keep moving.

Her thoughts were interrupted with a whirring sound. Isabel ducked. A hooked blade grazed the crown of her head and snapped off the top of the spear.

Dropping to the ground, she swung her legs around and swept the offender off his feet. It was a young man with a prominent scar across his nose. For the first time, she saw fear in an Aeonian's eyes. She hoisted the spear and aimed at his chest, but the soldier grabbed the pointed end and pushed back. Blood leaked from his hands as he squeezed the blade.

Isabel's heels dug against the dirt. He overpowered her easily, and she still felt too weak to summon any powers.

The Aeonian's hand shot to her neck and squeezed. Gagging, Isabel tried her best to drive the spear into his abdomen, but her attacker deflected her efforts with ease. All Isabel could do was stare at the shiny red scar on his face.

"Some say you are a warrior princess. I guess that was a rumor! Ha!" The Aeonian's rancid breath rolled by her.

Isabel lost her grip on the spear, and the Aeonian twirled it around, pointing the bloodied tip at her. He rolled his shoulder back, eyes ablaze with joy. She grappled with him as the spear inched closer and closer to her face.

From the corner of her eye, she spotted a Veijari drawing an arrow in her direction. Mustering every last fiber of her strength, she twisted herself around, positioning the Aeonian's back at the Veijari.

After a loud thud, the arrow tip poked through from the Aeonian's sternum. Rusty red liquid pulsated from the wound. Life flickered from his eyes, and his smile faded. His grip loosened and he dropped the spear. Isabel grasped his tunic and peeked around him. More Veijari spotted her and drew arrows. She crouched and let the rain of arrows shower over her. Some landed in the grass, while others struck the dead Aeonian's back. As soon as the fusillade subsided, Isabel released the body and rolled a few feet to her left towards a tent. Isabel drew an arrow and began to fire at the offenders. The Veijari fell one by one. Relief flowed through Isabel's airways. Aiming was much easier when on her own two feet.

Once Isabel got the attention away from herself, she ducked into the empty tent. Her knees buckled. Pain plagued her everywhere as she sucked in each breath.

"Hang in there, girl," she whispered to herself.

A barrel sat in the corner. Limping towards it, Isabel grinned at her discovery. A roll of bandages, a jar of opaque ointment, and a quiver of arrows. She popped the lid of the jar off. A menthol scent tickled her nose. Scooping a handful, Isabel shoved the goo beneath her tunic and massaged her sides. Her ribs cracked as she stretched from one side to the other. The ointment cooled her skin, numbing the pain. Wiping the leftovers on her pants, Isabel grabbed the cotton bandage and wrapped it around her torso. It clung to the ointment and created a snug barrier. A dull ache resonated with each sudden movement, but Isabel knew it helped. The two stones in her armlet glowed to life.

"Nice."

With a deep breath, Isabel seized the arrows, bolted out of the tent, and hid behind a stack of crates.

"Time to take out some more of these bastards," she hissed.

Squinting with one eye closed, she scanned the battlefield. Isabel fired arrows sped by wind and kissed with fire left and right, slaying larger opponents, freeing her soldiers to cut at their feet. Large Dunyan Veijari fell quickly under her deadly precision.

Isabel was in mid aim when someone grabbed her by the ankle and threw her on her face. Turning her head, Isabel located her assailant. A flea-bitten Foti Veijari, also on the ground, snarled at her. Isabel reached for an arrow to send a fatal blow in between his eyes, but an object collided into her. Stars twinkled before her eyes as she struggled to focus her vision. She turned blindly to a pained cry in the distance.

"Jabin?"

Isabel barely made out his silhouette, transformed back to his original form, writhing on his back. Panic crept up her spine as she wondered who had the strength to hurl Jabin with such force? Isabel turned her attention back to the Foti Veijari gnashing his jaws inches away from her flesh. With her free hand, she swung her sai and thrust it through the roof of his mouth. A scream escaped her lungs.

Her eyes squeezed shut. And she did not wish to open them. All she could feel was a sharp pain in her wrist...

"Isabel!"

Isabel opened her eyes to see her hand halfway in the Veijari's jaw. The long middle prong of her sai poked through his snout. The searing pain she felt was from a fang rubbing against her wrist, struggling to pierce her new leather gloves. However, this carcass was not what the voice had warned Isabel about. A shadow towered over her, expanding quickly. Isabel kicked the dead body off her and she rolled away from a gigantic claw that came stomping down.

Isabel's heart beat wildly at the abnormally large Dunyan Veijari before her. It was already injured, but blinded with a lust to kill. The few talons that remained attached to its claws wriggled freely. The other appendages, bloody stumps, swung back and forth, mesmerizing her into paralysis. Isabel tore her eyes away, and her line of sight landed on Jabin, struggling to get up. His lips were soaked with silver blood. Ears behind his head, Jabin snarled and spit out one of the Veijari's fingers.

The monster huffed until smoke curled from its nostrils. Isabel sprung in front of Jabin, who was ready to leap.

"Let me at him!"

Purple flames erupted from the Veijari's jaws as soon as Jabin spoke his last word. The purple assault met Isabel's flames that blasted from the tip of her sai. The two jets of fire created a kaleidoscope of color and smoke.

"The Dunya breathe fire?" Jabin quivered behind Isabel.

"No. Who knows what the Aeonians did to the Veijari."

It was not long before Isabel's arms grew numb. The Dunyan Veijari had not stopped for a single breath. Isabel's eyes widened in horror as she witnessed her flames slowly falling back.

"Jabin!" cried Isabel, "You must run to safety! Jabin?"

There was no answer. It was now or never. Isabel counted down the seconds before her fiery attack would give out.

"Come on, you dirty beast!" Isabel exclaimed.

She abruptly retreated her sai and leapt into the air, summoning the wind to push her feet. Rocketing skyward with the force of a tornado, Isabel narrowly avoided the blast of fire that connected to the very spot she had just occupied. The burst of energy exhausted her right away. Tuuli's Opal flickered. The gale dissipated, and Isabel's stomach lurched as gravity took a hold of her. Shifting her weight head-first, she dove towards the Veijari, who was greeting her with a smoke-filled smile.

The smoke stung her eyes. Isabel shielded her eyes and held her breath.

As the monster opened its jaws, she anticipated purple flames to end it's life, but out came a shriek instead. The creature fell onto all fours, allowing Isabel to land on his back. She locked onto the body by digging her nails into the scaly hide.

"Jabin?" Isabel gasped as she spotted her friend, whose teeth sunk into the Veijari's ankle. "Brilliant!" She cheered.

Isabel grabbed her sai and sank them into the Veijari's flesh. The reptile swung itself upright, but Isabel held on. Then, using sai like picks, Isabel scaled its back. Gaining height quickly, Isabel was inches from the base of his skull. She was one strike away from the fatal blow. And yet, this beast was relentless. It kicked Jabin off, sending him flying into the distance.

As soon as Isabel took her eye off the beast, she was flung off its back. Landing with a violent thud, she struggled to gain the wind that was knocked out of her.

"My sai... My sai," Isabel gasped.

"Fool." That was the only word that escaped the Veijari's mouth.

"Hey! Hey! Over here!" Jabin shouted from the battling crowd.

It growled in irritation. Before the Veijari even glanced back at Isabel, she had an arrow drawn. She sent it flying into the monster's throat. The next two arrows lodged into each eye.

The Dunyan Veijari crashed unceremoniously onto the ground.

Running up to the reptile, Isabel scouted for her sai. After ripping them from his flesh, she shouted at the top of her lungs. Her heart still pounded with adrenaline. A sudden crunching sound snapped Isabel out of her trance. She swung her body around and aimed her bloody sai at the next assailant. The weapon halted just short of the figure's nose when Isabel saw its eyes.

"Jabin?"

The newly transformed warrior nodded.

"Thank you," she blurted.

"And thank *you*." He swiftly bowed before he took off into the thick of battle. Isabel, too, charged into the chaos.

With each step she took, the dull aches in her body reminded her of her injuries. But she refused to let herself rest or retreat. Gritting her teeth, Isabel painstakingly cut down one Aeonian at a time. Thoughts of her mother, father, Dante, and even Jabin kept her momentum going.

A flash of silver caught her eye. Dante danced around an Aeonian, meeting each stroke of a sword with his own. She ran towards him.

But as if she jinxed herself, the ground rumbled. Crevasses opened wide and swallowed soldiers whole. Soil and rocks spouted upward. Isabel was knocked off her feet. She turned and spied a figure at the top of the hill, the Dunyan Amber hanging brightly from his neck.

"Farid!" she growled.

He was moving his hands as if directing an orchestra. Isabel's soldiers fell one by one, like puppets cut from their strings. But Farid seem to bore of this wholesale carnage quickly and turned to his main objective. He summoned huge boulders and rocks from the damage he created and hurled them at the Ogonia's fortress. He commanded vast holes to open at the base of the stone wall.

"No! The wall, the wall!" Dante screamed at Harmon.

Harmon zipped past Isabel. "Dante," she cried. "Wait!"

Dante mounted his horse and charged towards Farid. The two met, swords clashing. This diversion stopped the crevasses from tearing at the foundation of the walls. Dante was knocked off his horse. When he landed, he rolled away from Farid and waved for reinforcements.

"He has brought more men!" Dante screamed as he crawled towards Isabel, but Farid leapt on him, and the two wrestled. "Isabel! You must—"

The two combatants grunted and shouted. Some Zingaris came to Dante's aid in the form of Aeonians, which allowed them to approach closely and swiftly. They tackled Farid, but he pounded the ground, sending tremors and shockwaves severe enough to throw them off their feet. Harmon tugged at Isabel's arms.

"You must advance! All they want is the final stone. No matter how we fight this battle, we cannot let them get it."

Isabel turned to Dante, but Harmon shook her.

"I have some dynamite. I will run to the river and blow the iron gates open. You must jump in the river and swim under the stone gates and—"

"Down the waterfall?" She gulped.

"Yes."

Isabel hesitated. She wasn't confident that she had enough energy to summon a wind strong enough to buffer her decent. "Okay."

Arrows zoomed by Harmon's face. Farid's reinforcements had arrived. A line of a hundred or so archers that lined the horizon had fired their first round and were preparing for their second.

"We will go with your plan." Isabel winced. She looked at the archers. Harmon pushed her along, yelling for her to hurry, but a figure caught her eye. She lurched forward and tripped over her feet.

Her blood ran cold. Bence had arrived with the archers.

Standing by his brother's side, Bence knocked all the Zingaris off their feet with one stroke of his sword. Dante tried to fend both off with superb swordplay, but it was clear that his strength was failing. Isabel took out her bow and drew one arrow. She summoned the power of fire to ignite the tip, and sent it zipping through the war-torn air.

It pierced Bence's shoulder. Stumbling backwards, he glared around for his assailant. His emerald eyes pierced her gaze. Dante retreated to safety as he mounted his horse and charged at Isabel.

She waved her arms, pushing against Harmon. "Come and get me!"

Isabel sprinted towards the river gate. Harmon held his hands over his ears as he set the dynamite off nearby. Chunks of debris shot into the air. Pressing her sleeve against her nose, she pushed through the smoke and haze. The explosion created a gap sufficient for her to swim through. She saluted Harmon and dove into the water.

Ice cold water shocked her system. Flexing her arms, she broke the surface and gasped for air. Her waterlogged clothes weighed her down as she fought to stay afloat. The sound of rushing water drowned out the sound of battle.

As the current dragged her closer to the gates, she turned her head to find Bence clashing swords with Harmon. He glared over Harmon's shoulder at her.

Before she could fathom another thought, Isabel was sucked past the gate and flung down the waterfall.

CHAPTER

37

Bence brandished his sword at the Tuuli before him.

"I don't have time for you," he snarled. "I *need* the Princess."

"I will die to defend her from the likes of you!"

As Harmon charged, Bence flicked his sword up in agitation. He parried all of Harmon's blows with ease.

"You fight well, old man, but give up!" Swinging his leg, he knocked Harmon off his feet. Dusting himself off, Bence dug the tip of the blade into the leather cuirass. "Don't move."

"You're not going to kill me?" The Tuuli held his hands up and bared his teeth.

With a sneer, Bence bent over him. "I have higher priorities than you." Thoughts of Isabel peering at him before she disappeared down Golden Falls flashed before his eyes. His heart pounded harder. *Those eyes.* Bence didn't know how he would react when he saw her again.

Sheathing his sword, Bence bounded towards the broken iron gates. The river roared and sloshed around, creating white foam. He removed his outer armor and took a deep breath. Before he dove in, he heard footsteps pound behind him. He calculated the timing of the steps with his breathing.

Old fool.

Bence twirled to the side and kicked Harmon into the river. Jumping in, he swam past Harmon, heading straight for the waterfall. He held his breath as he swam underneath the broken iron gates. When he re-surfaced, the roar of the water greeted his ears. His arms burned, trying to keep his head above the surface. As he took another breath, he focused on his mission.

Isabel.

He was flung into the air.

As he fell, he could see the bottom of the falls.

CHAPTER

38

Isabel coughed violently. Her skin burned from impact. After she swam to the edge of the basin, her muscles gave out. The tumble down the Golden Falls should have meant death, if it were not for the little bit of wind she could muster to break her fall. Turning over, Isabel lurched and vomited the water she swallowed.

After gaining her composure, Isabel surveyed her surroundings. Her fears were confirmed. Ogonia was flooded. Opaque puddles littered even the driest spots. The Golden Falls however, still remained beautiful, reflecting the ceremonial torches.

Ogonia was an enclosed city, the shoreline blocked by a dense population of skyscrapers. She called Hakan's name, but no one answered. Drawing both sai, Isabel approached the two ceremonial torches at the center of the city. The whole city seemed deserted. The flickering of the torch to her left drew her attention. The flame was dying. But the torch to her right was extinguished. As far as she knew, the Foti always kept these lit.

"Here you go," Isabel said half-heartedly as she conjured a fire to light the bare torch.

A tremor shook the earth. Isabel staggered forward as she flailed her arms to remain balanced. The roar of the waterfall was drowned out by the din erupting from the basin. Gaining her composure, she gaped in amazement at the site before her. As if a giant removed an invisible plug, the Golden Falls drained from the basin, exposing a spiral staircase.

"Who goes there?" demanded a tense voice.

"Hakan?" Isabel rotated full circle. She spotted his rusty-red braid at the corner of the water fall.

He appeared from an opening behind the waterfall. He did not move from his exposed spot. Isabel looked for a way to get to his side, but he barked in warning.

"The Foti and Kai have taken refuge behind Golden Falls. There may be those following you, and I cannot jeopardize their lives. Proceed to the chambers below. You will find what you are seeking. Quickly!" He directed his muzzle to the pit below.

"Hakan!"

The mighty beast disappeared behind the falls, leaving Isabel with no choice but to rush down the staircase. The waterfall poured its contents into the center of the seemingly bottomless pit. To keep her balance, she kept a hand on the smooth stone wall. Every few steps, she stumbled on the slick surface. Vertigo plagued her each time she peered down the abyss. The smell of rust intensified her nausea.

Swallowing the acid that crept up her throat, she kept running.

One step in front of the other.

Isabel's heart stopped as she came to a grinding halt. The stairwell ended. Her toes extended past the edge, knocking pebbles into the abyss. She clawed at the wall but slipped as she turned. Her head slammed against the ground. Everything around her spun. Losing her grip, Isabel slipped and slid off the ledge.

A pipe protruded from the wall. Extending her reach, Isabel managed to grab onto it by the tips of her fingers. Her feet dangled like dead weight. Straining her ears, Isabel tried to measure how deep the fall was. All she could make out was deafening cacophony.

She closed her eyes and took deep breaths. As her spinning mind came to a halt, she focused on the ledge. It was only a foot above her. Swinging her body, Isabel gained momentum and strained her left arm. She missed.

Swinging harder, she reached for the ledge once more. Simultaneously, her right hand lost its grip on the pipe. Everything occurred in slow motion. Isabel's heart plummeted. She lost her breath. Her fingertips barely grazed the ledge.

Gravity pulled her down like toxic sludge.

When she made contact with water, her body was already numb. She swam around blindly. The turbulent water sent her in random directions. Isabel didn't know how large the area was. It was darker than the midnight sky. The only sign of day was the opening above, now the size of the head of a needle.

Her back slammed against a formation. Wrapping her

arms around the cylindrical form, Isabel cried out. Heaving, she mustered all her strength to awaken Foti's Ruby. It glowed weakly.

A platform extended from the wall a few feet away. Isabel pushed against the formation with her legs and launched towards the stone slate. Her muscles burned as if Foti's Ruby set a fire beneath her skin, but she grasped onto the platform and pulled herself from the whirlpool.

She stood and leaned against the wall. Her clothes clung to her. Water dripped from her sopping hair, getting into her eyes and mouth. A metallic taste filled her taste buds. Water lapped at her feet. The water level was rising, inching up to her ankles.

After catching her breath, Isabel felt the wall as she inched farther from the edge until she came across a knob. She twisted it, and a lock clicked. What seemed like a hidden door slid open sideways. Sighing gratefully, Isabel stepped through and slid the door shut behind her.

It was quiet — the roar of the waterfall muffled by the walls of the circular room. An uncontrollable shiver took hold of Isabel, so she wrapped her arms around herself. Only now did she become aware of how ice cold the water was. She took one step at a time, ducking her head to accommodate the low ceiling. Torches fixed in metal casings were ignited, exposing smudged paintings that looked like they were worn down by time. Red blobs with tails holding whips. Black formations kneeling in submission. Taking her attention from the artwork, she noticed a short pillar in the center of the room. Upon closer inspection, a gold-plated handle stuck out from the side.

Looking to the left, then the right. There was no other door than the one she entered in.

"There has to be a way to continue," she murmured.

She eyed the handle. A miniscule red arrow painted on it pointed to her right. Taking a deep breath, Isabel pushed the pillar clockwise. The stone groaned but moved steadily.

When the room vibrated in response, she clutched the pillar. The walls stretched, revealing more primal paintings. A tingling sensation filled her stomach as they lowered by one floor. When the room shuddered to a standstill, Isabel spotted two hallways. She approached one cautiously, sai and shield at the ready. The length of the corridor was dark, but a dim light flickered at the end. Water dripped from an unknown source.

"What is this place?" she muttered to herself. "How could Hakan conceal such a place from us? What could they be hiding here?"

Left foot. Right foot. Pause. Isabel swiveled around, but no one was behind her. Multiple drops of water echoed now, sending a shudder up her spine.

"I swear it was footsteps." Her breath rattled.

Without hesitation, Isabel scampered to the end of the corridor where a rickety door stood. Grabbing the steel handle, she pressed it open. She commanded a flame with Foti's Ruby and ignited a torch that sat against the wall.

The light illuminated a simple room. A bookcase and desk hugged a corner. Papers were scattered around the room, and a melted candle stood in the middle of the desk. A wooden chest below it caught Isabel's eye. She opened it and saw a whip. The base of the whip was engraved with the

Foti emblem. It grew warm at her touch. The power of fire surged through her body, energizing Isabel.

"Never used one of these before, but who knows if I'll need it." She hooked the whip to her belt and headed towards another door to her left.

This room was also pitch black. Isabel retrieved the torch and peeked in. The walls were made of stone and stretched farther than she could make out.

"I wonder if there is a door at the end of this room." She squinted her eyes and still could not see the other side.

As she crept forward, Isabel held her breath, listening for any unusual sounds. Sharp creaking replaced the pitter patter of water. She clung to the wall, until she bumped into a wooden beam. Jumping back, Isabel observed the sight before her. It wasn't just a beam; it was a statue. As Isabel walked around the object, her heart raced.

The stature resembled a Foti, completely carved from wood. It towered over Isabel, fangs baring down at her. With a gulp, her gaze fell to its caved chest. A rusted latch loosely held a compartment shut. Her hands trembled as she used the tip of her sai to open it. A rancid odor poured out.

A man curled in a fetal position was strapped within. Flesh peeled off the skull and maggots poured out of the socket. The Aeonian marking was sewn on the tunic that hung loosely over his emaciated frame. Isabel's hand flew to her mouth. Averting her eyes, she stumbled to the right. Beside the statue stood two poles crossed in the shape of an X. The creature attached to it wasn't as decayed. Its paws were stretched outwards, and its wings were broken.

A Kana.

Its innards hung loosely from its open gut. Releasing a

screech, Isabel scampered backwards. Chains of all sorts hung from the wooden, porous ceiling.

Why are there holes in the ceiling?

Her head spun and her stomach soured. As she steadied herself, the cobblestone beneath her foot shifted. The creaking noise amplified. Eyes widening in horror, Isabel scanned the room. The chains shook. A draft came from the ceiling.

Isabel crouched and lifted her shield over her. As soon as she secured herself safely underneath, needles darted against the ground. The ones that struck her shield clanged loudly.

"Poisoned probably..."

When the hail of needles stopped, she stood and looked around, keeping the shield poised above her head. Needles covered the floor. Afraid of using wind to blow them out of control, she decided to utilize her new weapon. Securing her shield, Isabel pulled out the whip.

She spotted a bar hanging from the ceiling. It required a few clumsy tries, but Isabel got the whip to catch. She held her breath and climbed a few feet. Abdomen burning, she swung herself back and forth. A door stood at the other side of the room. When she gained enough momentum, released her grip and landed inches away from the door, where the ground was free of needles. After regaining her composure, Isabel used a gentle breeze to gently retrieve the whip. Tuuli's Opal glowed weakly as the whip floated into her hands.

Leaning against the wall, Isabel took a deep breath. Then another. Her blood still rushed through her veins, leaving her lightheaded.

So this is how they got around our laws about torture.

Images of the bodies flashed through her mind, and she jumped in place.

I can't allow this kind of torture. To anyone. If I ever make it out alive, that is one of the first things I am going to do.

Her hands trembled as she reached for the doorknob. Isabel couldn't shake the images from her head. Instead of the faceless man, she pictured Bence within the torture statue. She ripped the door open and rushed into the next room.

It was another hallway. Holding her breath with each step, Isabel tip-toed through the twisted corridor. Every time she tripped over a loose cobblestone, she collapsed on the ground, shield flung over her. Nothing happened.

I have to get out of here. I don't have a map. For all I know, I could be walking in circles.

As soon as she finished her thought, Isabel stepped out of the hallway and into the room she started in. Shaking her head, she pounded the wall in frustration.

A trickle of water landed on her head. Looking up, water seeped down the walls from the floor above.

"The water level is rising."

Dusting cobwebs she picked up from her slacks, Isabel considered the stone pillar once more. She pushed the handle again. The walls vibrated. As the room sank, so did her stomach.

The deeper I go in this chamber, the farther underwater I go.

After dropping another level, she spotted two doors. They stood opposite of one another. Isabel figured one would eventually lead to the other, so she turned to the one closest to her. She reached out towards the knob. When she twisted the knob, a scratching noise echoed behind her. Paralyzed, Isabel stood still. Twisting her hear ever so slightly, she realized the scratching was coming from behind the other door.

CHAPTER
39

Whatever was behind the door continued to scratch. When Isabel took a few steps toward it, the scratching intensified. Hypnotized by the noise, Isabel wondered who or what could be making such a noise. She had to know. Extending her left arm, she balled her fist. Tuuli's Opal glowed. The door rattled. The scratching transformed into pounding. Spreading her fingers, a blast of wind ripped the door open.

Three large disfigured... masses rolled onto the floor. Isabel fell back onto the floor, mouth agape in horror. Their rotten flesh nauseated Isabel. She could barely make out their appearance, but they resembled the Foti. However, they stood on all fours and were twice their size. Their skulls were exposed through patches of fur, and their eyes blazed with malice. Yet they made no sound.

"What the *hell?*" Isabel cursed.

She first tried her arrows. She shot her darts into the creatures' flesh, but they only jerked back a few steps and continued to creep towards her. She tried to blow them back into their rooms with the power of Tuuli's Opal. But they only crouched and held their ground. Isabel shouted in frustration as she ran at the leading monster with one sai. She stuck it straight into the creature's chest. It opened its jaws to scream, but no sound came forth.

Her muscles tensed, and she froze, terrified by the beast's empty eye sockets. She tried to free herself from the fearful bind, but the monster bit into her torso. Isabel finally released a scream, but her limbs remained paralyzed. The monster's jaw tightened its grip, and Isabel's breaths grew labored. The monster then tossed her into the air.

Isabel crashed into the opposite wall. She shook herself, trying to get her limbs to move again, and slowly stood to see the three monsters gaining up on her. Her weapons failed her, although she could try the whip.

She grasped the handle and lashed out towards the fore-leg of the monster in the center, but it didn't catch. Winding her arm back, she cracked the whip once more. It struck the beasts' foot. It didn't budge. A taunting rumble escaped its throat. Isabel tilted to the other side, and cracked the whip once more. With a snap, it snared its leg. Giving it a few tugs, Isabel was confident she had it. Pulling with all her might, she tried to knock the beast onto the floor. The sludge-like flesh only absorbed her efforts, and the creature took another step.

Isabel's frustration surged within her, taking the form of heat from Foti's Ruby. The whip sizzled. It grew hot, burning the monster's flesh. "Yes," Isabel seethed, putting her focus back on the monster. Then, a thin line of blue flame charged from the base of the whip and towards the tip. The whip burned hotly, enough to sever the limb entirely.

Isabel did not waste time. She whipped the other two undead monsters, only successful after the second or third attempt, but she managed to eventually snag a limb. She used her powers to burn away their flesh until they lay on their torsos, unable to move. Isabel walked up to the monster in the center. It flexed its jaws, but nothing came out. Tears ran from the open sockets. She kicked it and ripped her sai from its torso.

"Thanks. I need that back."

After securing her whip, Isabel took a deep breath to calm her racing heart. She walked over to the opposing door. She paused at the handle. Hearing no scratching, she opened it. The room was similar to the previous, simple and round. Instead of a pillar in the center, there was a statue of an ape holding the Kai's Sapphire.

As she stepped into the room, she heard a splash. The room was filled with puddles. But that did not stop her. Isabel ran towards the statue and found that its golden fingers were intertwined. There was no way for her to snatch the gem. Isabel placed both hands on top of the ape statues and focused, eyes closed. As heat surged down her fingertips, she pried the gold fingers apart, and reached for Kai's Sapphire.

"Hey!"

Isabel turned. Her blood curdled. Her heart thundered in her chest. "Bence!"

His face was covered by shadow, but it was definitely his voice. He drew his sword but looked up past her.

A stomp shook the room, and Isabel screamed. The

statue creaked on its own accord. Its eyes glowed a dark blue as it emitted a metallic screech and dropped her. Isabel scrambled backwards in terror. The ape slammed its melted hands on the ground until the fingers cracked and separated. It roared and flung Kai's sapphire behind it.

"Woah, there," Isabel exclaimed.

"I do not think it will listen." Bence appeared at her side, brows furrowed.

Her eyes met his for a split second. "And why have you not killed me yet?" Isabel spat.

"You *see* this thing? It can wait." He chuckled at Isabel, who fumed. "Hey, I say it is a fair race to get to the other side. I do not think this thing cares who it kills."

So, that is how it is going to be.

As soon as Isabel finished her thought, the ape clubbed its hands at her and Bence. They jumped in opposite directions. She rolled to its right and studied the statue. It was made of pure gold, with no cracks or any signs of weakness. Arrows and blades were useless. She sped towards Kai's Sapphire, but was pummeled by the large range of the ape's arm. Bence slid beneath its legs, but the statue swatted him backwards.

"Well," Isabel muttered to herself. "Might as well stick to what has been working."

Isabel took out the Foti's whip. She waved to the ape to grab its attention. When its arm swung towards her, she tried to grab hold with the whip, but missed. She dove and rolled, barely missing the heavy blow. While the golden ape screeched and wound up for another punch, Isabel snatched a leg with the whip. She wished the whip aflame and the temperature rose. She needed to hold on until the whip reached the gold's melting point...

The ape swung its arm at Isabel again. But just as it made contact, the ape lost its leg and fell. Isabel struggled to free herself from beneath its arm, but she cringed from the pressure. She wrapped her whip on the arm that held her down as the ape was trying to get up. She severed the arm and gasped for air as it fell away. This now only left the left arm and left leg. Maybe that was enough. The large statue groaned and teetered from side to side. As Isabel hoped, it crashed on the ground, pounding its only hand.

Isabel caught Bence's eye. They both sprinted towards the stone, but Isabel fell back, leg snatched by the ape's only hand. It lifted her up to its face. She gazed upon its empty features. It shifted its sculpted lips into an evil grin. It lifted her high, ready to slam her down, but Isabel wriggled her arm free and sent the whip around the ape's neck. In an instant, the ape released a metallic screech and released her. Isabel clung to the base of the whip with both hands. Foti's Ruby shined so brightly, it blinded her. She grit her teeth, sending pulses of heat until its neck was completely severed. She cut through an entire foot of gold. The head rolled away in silence.

"Bence!" Isabel summoned as she put her whip away.

In a flash, he rushed past her, a glimmer of blue shining through his fingertips.

"Give it to me!" Isabel pounced on Bence.

She grappled with the Aeonian, the man destined to be her sworn enemy. And yet, as she pried his fingers loose to release the Kai Sapphire, tears welled in her eyes.

390 • J.E. KLIMOV

"Why did you break your promise?" Isabel yelled, blinking through her falling tears.

Bence winced as the wet droplets landed on his cheeks.

"I trusted you!"

"What did you expect?" He exclaimed as he kicked her.

Isabel landed on her back, shrieking in pain. He faltered, looking back at her. As she got up, he ran. Bence only made it a few feet before he tripped over the remains of the golden ape. When he crashed onto the ground, Isabel's tackled him, digging her nails into his shoulders. He kicked back. They both crawled towards the precious stone, elbowing each other.

"Bence." Isabel panted. "I just want to know why—"

"Will you quit it? It doesn't matter. I must—" He huffed to push past her. "I must complete the mission I was created to complete." His trembling fingers grazed the stone. "What did you expect? To fall in love?"

Hearing this, a surge of anger tightened in Isabel's chest. She flung her hand onto the sapphire. As both hands wrapped their fingers around Kai's Sapphire, a flash of blue blinded her.

They were hurtled through the door. Water tumbled down from the top of the entrance, now three stories away. The room flooded in seconds, trapping the two in a watery grave. Waves washed over Isabel as she tried to stay afloat. The current dragged her upwards as the room continued to flood. She tumbled in circles, unaware of what was up or down.

The pressure sent her back first against a wall. Bence was flushed through the opening beside her. Inching to her right,

Isabel found the opening and pushed herself through. The vortex of water spouted Isabel up the main entrance and out of Foti's Chamber.

Gasping for air, Isabel grasped the muddy earth. She clung for life as the chamber overflowed. Waves of water swept over the land, washing over everything.

Isabel and Bence lay by the basin. Kai's Sapphire lodged itself into the mud a few feet away. Its glow faded. Isabel stirred and noticed Bence reaching for the stone. She tried to summon the wind, but a pathetic breeze escaped her. Bence got onto his knees and fell again. But his hand was finally in reach of the coveted sapphire. Upon touching it, he jolted up. Filled with energy, he sprinted up the long pathway to the city gates.

"No," Isabel whimpered.

"Isabel!" Hakan bounded towards her and looked up at Bence. "You must go and not let him leave with Kai's Sapphire. Go!"

Hakan pulled a cork from a bottle he held and gave it to Isabel. She downed the drink in one swallow. She could feel a fiery warmth flow through her veins. Her body pumped with adrenaline, and she shot off after Bence.

"We will wait for your victory, Princess!" Hakan howled behind her.

Isabel raced up the winding pathway. It was a steep incline, and the mud slowed them both down. Isabel had to catch up. When he reached the gates, he turned around and pointed Kai's Sapphire in Isabel's direction. It glowed again and water spouted forth onto the already muddy road. Isabel slipped, desperately trying to get a grip as Bence searched for his exit. As Isabel began to slide backwards, she unsheathed her sai and stabbed them into the earth, pulling herself up with her arms one by one. She finally reached the top, only to see a stone entrance collapsing and Bence running out. She stood up and continued to pursue him.

Isabel flew by bodies, left and right, some standing and others dead. The sun's rays assaulted her vision. Isabel clambered up the rising hill, slowly gaining on her target.

"Bence!" she cried. "Why are you doing this?"

He turned his head and tripped over a rock, sending him crashing into the dirt.

Isabel approached him, and she grabbed his collar, lifting him with almost inhuman strength. "Why did you not meet me at the Zeyland? Why did you betray me?"

"My lady," his deep voice cracked.

A shadow cast over the two, and Isabel lifted her heavy head. Damian stood a few feet away from her, his sword drawn. But before she could react, he slammed the tip of his sword into the ground, and the chain reaction of energy threw Isabel backwards. When she opened her eyes, she saw a body float over hers and towards Damian. It was the broken body of Farid.

"I stayed alive and fought well, my father, to honor you and—" Farid coughed up blood. "a-and I preserved the Dunyan Amber for you."

"My son, we shall nourish you and make sure you will live. Come, you and your brother."

With once last glance at Isabel, Damian sneered and pulled his sword out of the earth. He conjured a gigantic sand storm before her eyes.

"No!" Isabel ran towards them.

She covered her eyes and ran furiously, but when she arrived where she thought they were, the sand storm settled. Damian, Farid, and Bence were gone.

Isabel fell to her knees and wrung her hands. Harmon approached her from behind, his footsteps heavy.

"Ma'am? What shall we do? The rest of Damian's army has disappeared. We had slain most, but now they are gone."

"Ask Dante," Isabel sighed, defeated.

"He... is unconscious. He *is* a-alive, miss—"

"What?"

Isabel had Harmon escort her to Dante's body, which was lain under a tree. He shooed some soldiers away. She knelt by his side, and let her tears fall.

"I am sorry, Dante," she whimpered.

"Miss?" Harmon interjected.

"Harmon, please order the soldiers to take refuge in Ogonia. The waters should have subsided by now. Bring Dante to Hakan. Watch Dante and protect this place. Buryan and Pekas are abandoned. The Dunya have been destroyed. A small population of people are hiding on Lea Island. Oh, what has become of my country?" Isabel bemoaned. "Harmon..."

"Yes, Princess?"

"The Tuuli needs a representative, and until Dante wakes up, I want you to lead them."

"But, My Princess—"

"Please, Harmon. I know it bears a big burden. But if I have learned anything throughout this journey, it is that you must do what you have to do. And you will be shocked at what you can achieve in the face of necessity."

"And you? Will not you come with us and rest for a little while?"

"Rest is one luxury I do not have," demurred Isabel. "Right now, Damian has two stones, and I have the other two. I know for a fact he will move swiftly and will show no mercy with the powers he now has. The more he has, the more he craves. Every wasted breath I take, the more people he hurts." Isabel turned her gaze towards Dante.

"As you wish," Harmon said, bowing.

At that moment, all of her army surrounded them. All mimicked Harmon's bow. Isabel nodded in approval and raised one sai.

"I promise I will do everything I can to protect the lives of all here."

The men rose, some approaching her to exchange hand-shakes. One gave her all his arrows. Another gave her his shield, taking her worn one. Jabin, too, approached her and gave her a bottle full of elixir.

"To heal your wounds. Use it when the time gets dire…"

She bent down to hug her little friend. When she stood back up, Harmon already had a horse saddled and ready for her.

CHAPTER
40

Rays of sunlight retreated behind the Chailara Hills, outlining it with blood red. Red mixed with orange, which in turn faded into lavender purple. Hooves thundered across the field. Isabel nudged her horse to go faster. She made a steady pace southward, but worried she wasn't fast enough. Her throat ran dry. A cold sweat formed at every crevice of her body.

I could be riding into the very last night of my life.

Isabel's heart continued to pound, she gripped the reigns tightly until her knuckles turned as white as the sister moons that inched into the sky. Isabel gazed at Adin and Deva, both shining in completeness. Although well equipped with sai, bow, Foti's whip, shield, and her two elemental stones, her soul felt vulnerable.

As Isabel rode past the fields of Deran, she fought with a constant nagging thought about Bence. For a weak moment, she believed she could trust him. He really had her convinced that they could be temporary allies. This foolishness only intensified Bence's betrayal and her pain for Dante. Such thoughts spun around her head as she swat at the invisible flies that plagued her.

Isabel's distraction was broken when her horse reared and kicked its front legs up. Hugging the reigns to her chest and tightening her grip, she cried out.

"Woah, there!"

It reared again, knocking Isabel off. When she landed, sharp pain pricked all over her torso. Isabel groaned. Her wounds from earlier were far from healed. Standing slowly, she focused her attention to what spooked her horse. A gaping pit fifty feet away indicated she had reached her destination. The pit of darkness. Cehennem.

Isabel crouched and walked slowly and silently towards the prison, noticing a faint purple haze rising from the depths. It stung her eyes, and the smell reminded her of stale perfume.

I've seen this purple aura before. But what is it?

"Greetings, Princess Isabel!"

Isabel squinted and picked out a dark silhouette standing at the edge of the other side of Cehennem. The figured dissolved into the earth, and a rumble erupted behind her. Weeds, soil, and rocks swirled upwards and took a human form.

Without hesitation, Isabel drew her sai and swiped at the growing figure. Her blade struck against a forearm blocking its face. A resounding crack echoed in the air. Chunks of earth fell from point of impact, revealing a heavily armored arm. She swung her other arm and was met with equal force. Arms locked, Isabel stared at the blank face made of dirt and stone.

"Be afraid," it hissed.

Shoving the figure, she squat and slammed a round-house kick to its skull, the most powerful kick Benjamin ever taught her, and one she had never landed so firmly. The figure crashed against the ground, shattering the earthy encasement. Clumps of dirt abandoned its face, revealing orange hair and beady eyes.

"Farid! Last I saw you, your body was close to death!" Isabel snarled.

"It's the beauty of magic." Farid leered. "Our power is multiplying exponentially, so of course the new head of Damian's army would be looked after with utmost priority."

Isabel's stomach lurched.

"And the best part? My mother and father let me keep Dunyan's Amber until the mission is complete."

"They only let you keep it because all four stones cannot be together in the wrong hands or else they will split again. Do not think so highly of yourself!" she spat.

"That's what you think," Farid said. Smiling, he reached to the back of his skull and plucked an earthworm from his hair. It writhed in between his fingertips. He bit into the creature and ripped the body in half. When he threw the other half away, he stepped aside to reveal a large ball and chain.

Isabel took a few steps back. Her horse was nowhere in sight. He picked up the chain and twirled the spiked metal ball around his head with inhuman strength. He hurled it at Isabel, and she leaped out of the way easily, but the aftermath was what shocked her. The impact ejected waves of dirt and rocks in its proximity. Isabel huddled on the ground, hands over her head until the first attack ended. Farid dragged the ball and chain back and swung the weapon again. Isabel's mind raced. She quickly drew an arrow and released it towards Farid's abdomen. He doubled over and dropped the ball, sending tremors that made Farid's gait unsteady. Isabel charged at Farid and knocked him off his feet. She drew her sai and sliced into his abdomen. However, no blood spat forth from the wound, and Farid shoved her away from him. His hands were ice cold against her flesh. Farid began swinging his ball and chain once more, Dunyan's Amber glowing somewhere from beneath his armor. He launched the weapon. The metal grazed her scalp as she ducked. She rolled towards Cehennem, blinded by the dirt in her eyes. She knew Farid was going to attack again. Isabel drew her shield, which crumbled like tinfoil under the impact. Rubbing the crud from her eyes, Isabel arose, shaken but unharmed. She cast the shield aside and drew another arrow. But Farid's assaults only intensified. Every time she took aim, he tossed the huge spiked ball at her.

"Have you had enough, Princess?"

Breathing heavily, Isabel tried to maintain her balance. Her whole body ached, as if she could collapse any minute. Instead of firing back a witty response, she filled her mind with pictures of her parents and Dante. Tuuli's Opal and Foti's Ruby glowed, surging energy up her veins.

She unleashed Foti's whip and aimed it right at the chain as she dove away from the ball's path once more. Missed.

This isn't my best weapon choice, but I can't give up.

She ducked another attack and cracked the whip once more. This time it snagged and held, and she sent fiery fury down the leather, melting the chain apart. The spiked ball rolled to a halt. Farid growled, casting the useless weapon aside. Dunyan's Amber shined with blinding intensity from beneath his armor. He drew his sword and charged. Isabel met his sword with her sai to a deafening clang. Isabel fell backward from the force of the blow. Farid pressed at her with a wide grin. His power was superhuman.

"Bence?" Isabel blurted.

Farid blinked. "You're a fool. You cannot even tell the superior brother over the other—"

A crack rattled the area, and Farid crumbled like a doll. Behind him stood Bence. Darkness shrouded his features, but Isabel could make out a scowl from his long lips.

"Brother," Farid choked, facing his brother. "What are you doing here?"

Bence pulled Farid by his hair and growled, "You are not my brother anymore!" Bence drew his sword, and after a slight pause, drove it into his twin brother's chest.

Isabel leapt to her feet and waved her sai wildly. The scene didn't make any scene to her, but she had no time to analyze the situation. She was feet away from her nemesis. "Stop! Throw down your weapon, traitor!" Isabel cried.

Bence stepped over Farid's still body and approached her.

"Why did you kill your brother?" Isabel demanded. Her hands were shaking, but she stood her ground.

"Makes no sense, he is already dead," Bence spat.

Isabel looked past him. Farid's body twitched.

"And if you had *let* me finish," growled Bence, "I would have removed Dunyan's Amber—"

Farid's body flung itself into the air. His eyes were rolled to the back of his head. His body was limp and seemed to be suspended by the force under his armor that was ripped back by Bence: Dunyan's Amber embedded itself into Farid's flesh by his clavicle. Isabel rushed forward, but Bence flung his arm in front of her.

The body settled on its knees. Its lifeless arms pounded the ground. Left arm. Right arm. Within moments, pillars of earth erupted from the ground. Bence pushed Isabel one way, and he ran the other way.

"Hold him down somehow so I can get near him!" Bence shouted.

Isabel nodded and cracked her whip at her foe. She caught his leg and pulled. The body slipped, but the fists kept pounding.

"The arms!"

"Shut up, I get it, I get it!"

Isabel pulled out her bow once more. She aimed for one hand, shot at it, pinning it to the ground. Before she could draw another, a dirt pillar tossed her up into the air. However, she did not fall downwards. She felt a cool force surrounding her waist. Bence had invoked the sapphire and summoned a branch of water to snatch her and let her down gently. Isabel drew another arrow and pinned Farid's other hand. As Farid emitted a piercing cry, Bence charged towards him. Sheathing his sword, he pulled out a tiny dagger. He attempted to pry the Dunyan's Amber out, sending Farid into a frenzy. Bence cried out. Clouds appeared above his head, and in a flash of blue, it down-poured. The soggy soil sucked them down like quicksand.

"You really going to destroy yourself with me, brother?" mocked Farid's empty shell.

"You, my *brother*, have been brainwashed, abused, and used by Damian and Echidna. They have betrayed you. You shall thank me in the heavens for putting you at rest!"

The two men were waist deep in a mud hole. Isabel ran, slipping and skidding, towards them. She reached for Bence's arm.

"I have you!" Isabel exclaimed. She pulled and pulled, harder with each try as the earth engulfed Farid's head.

The downpour turned into a drizzle. The top half of Bence's torso was still above ground. Isabel started tugging at both his arms. With just a little push from a gust of wind, she plucked him out from the earth.

She could hear him panting beside her. Everything about this was so backwards. Bence was a traitor, her enemy. He broke his promise to help her collect the stones. He stole Kai's Sapphire from her reach. He should have killed her, and now she saved his life.

So backwards.

"Here. Dunyan's Amber. And Kai's Sapphire. They belong to you."

Sitting up, Bence grabbed her hand and dropped the two precious stones. He stared at the stones as if the lust for power tempted him once more. Isabel inched her other hand to her sai and gripped the handle. His head jerked away as she made contact with his palm, but he closed her hand into a fist and released her.

The Dunyan Amber and Kai's Sapphire vibrated in her palm. Taking a step back, Isabel released her fingers and the two stones rocketed into the night sky, blending in with the stars. A heavenly breeze surrounded Isabel, lifting her feet.

"Wha... what's going on?" she asked.

She kicked her legs, but the wind took her higher and higher. Bence shrunk to the size of an ant. When all movement ceased, Isabel tilted her head back. Adin and Deva were superimposed, creating a mirage of a single, massive moon.

A whirring sound snapped Isabel from her wonder. The pair of stones circled her in a clockwise fashion. They spun faster and faster until they looked like two streaks of light. Then, Tuuli's Opal and Foti's Ruby shined from her armlet, sending pulses of energy into the air. Before Isabel could blink, the Dunyan Amber and Kai's Sapphire shot into her armlet, causing an explosion of energy, throwing Isabel back down to earth.

Beams of silver, blue, amber, and red streaked from her fingertips as Isabel extended her hands to the heavens. The ribbons of color flickered and danced around her until she slammed into the ground. A deafening explosion burned her ears, but there was no pain. Turning her neck, she was embedded a good five feet into the earth. Even her injured ribcage felt untouched.

As Isabel pulled herself up, her muscles and bones felt invigorated. Nothing stung. Nothing ached. Gazing at her hands, she let her jaw hang open. "Amazing..."

"Why?" Isabel turned her head, facing him. As the four

stones faded into their original state, fear drained away with it. Now she wanted answers.

Bence crossed his arms, but no words escaped. Isabel cleared her throat. Bence could only open and close his jaws like a mute.

"*Why?*" Isabel pressed.

"Why, what?" Bence arched his back and towered over her. She did not flinch like she usually would. "You have the stones now," he continued. "You earned them. Fair and—"

"No," Isabel interrupted as she got on her tip-toes and pressed her index finger to his lips. "You know I could not have done this without you. And yet you betrayed me at the last second. Tell me. What motivates you, Bence Brechenhad?"

A slight twinge in her stomach stopped her words. Isabel hung onto Bence's silence, as if she were expecting something. Anything. Bence squirmed, seemingly uncomfortable in his own skin.

"I…" Bence struggled as Isabel dropped her hand.

"Yes?"

"I have been battling with myself. This journey has tested my true intentions. To serve my parent's purpose, which involves genocide and usurping power… or to take the time to look at the whole picture."

"And the whole picture?" Isabel twisted her lips into a scowl. She didn't buy his lies for a second.

"Because… you. Of you, my lady."

"Excuse me?"

He ran a hand through his hair. "Everything was a lie!"

Isabel stepped back and grabbed her sai.

"I don't have time to explain this. Time is ticking. Damian and Echinda are below, ready to consume this island for good. Soon they will know you have all four stones and attack with their full wrath. You might think you're indestructible with your armlet, but don't forget, they too have stones of power. They've had them for centuries. They will obliterate you knowing their backs are against the wall. The games are over. They want Deran. They want it now and are tired of you getting in the way." He peered into her eyes. Darkness circled his emerald eyes. "You don't seem convinced of anything?"

"I know what I must do," Isabel replied, jerking her head towards Cehennem. "Aren't you going to stop me?"

Bence fell onto one knee. "You may not accept any explanation now, nor is there time for me to give it even if I thought you might, but I pledge to aid in your mission."

"You do understand that mission is to exterminate the threat to Deran: your parents and your siblings."

Bence's head fell. His breathing, labored. "Yes. I understand—"

"You, even," she hissed. For the first time, she had the upper hand over the head of the Aeonian army. Her shoulders weighed heavy with indecision. If she didn't end him now, what other consequences would follow? Images from her parents to the Dunyan corpses flashed through her mind. Her armlet vibrated as it absorbed the anger bubbling within. "I couldn't overpower you when we first worked together. You foolishly surrender the last two stones, and now I have all of them. What makes you think I won't finish you off?"

"You can, if you want. But if you do, you eliminate a possible advantage."

He locked his feral eyes with hers. "If you keep me alive, I can lead you down Cehennem and offer protection along the way. Kill me now, or kill me later — but it would be wise to let me breathe a little longer."

Drawing her sai, Isabel tapped the pointed tips on Bence's shoulder. As he stood, she pointed at Cehennem. "We shall make our decent together, then." Her jaw tensed. She mustered all her might to hide her trembling. She was not confident in her decision, but Bence offered an invaluable option.

I can deal with him at the end.

After drawing in a deep breath, Isabel approached the gaping chasm. She wove around various bits of debris and the skeletons of slaughtered animals. Maggots rolled through holes in their flesh. Flies danced from mound to mound, circling around Isabel before moving on. The rancid haze assaulted her nostrils, but it didn't sting. It was as if she was getting used to the scent of decay.

The crunch of rocks beneath her feet caught Isabel's attention. She stood at the first step into Cehennem. Chunks of the stair broke off. The darkness absorbed them in an eerie silence. She waved for Bence to lead.

He snaked past her, brushing his arm against hers. Isabel retracted and gripped the sai tightly. Bence tread the stairs with a feline grace. He kept one hand on the hilt of his sword to prevent it from clanging with each step. The purple haze swirled around his body before rising to meet hers.

Frozen in her tracks, Isabel held her breath. "What is

this?" she muttered through her teeth.

"You know, I'm not one-hundred percent sure."

"That's inspires confidence." Her head spun from a lack of oxygen.

"It won't kill you. That I can say. Echidna has the full power of her amethyst while Damian is slowly regaining command of his stone. The haze is more prevalent now, likely due to their growing power. Or confidence."

Releasing her breath, Isabel balanced herself against the stone wall and continued down the stairs.

"I hate purple," Bence grunted.

Termite infested wooden-frames hung every few feet. Each one Isabel peered into contained a gray slate. Occasionally, she would see a shadow slide across it. But when she turned around, she couldn't find the source.

The shadow ghouls.

The spiraling staircase narrowed to the point where Isabel felt she was circling in place.

Bence stopped and held his hand up. A melody of groans rose and fell. "The layout of this place changed."

"First of all, what was that noise? Second, what do you mean? You were just down here, weren't you?"

His fingertips grazed the walls, feeling every crevice. He closed his eyes. "Those are just the ghouls. Probably here to warn everyone the monster has arrived," he said in a trance-like state.

"Monster?" Looking to her left and right, Isabel scratched her head with the base of her sai. "What are you talking about? Bence?"

Green eyes snapping open, Bence shook his head. A hint

of lavender swirled in his irises.

"Hey, are you okay? You sure this purple smoke is safe?"

"Yeah, I'm fine," he said, rubbing his eyes. "Just stings a little. Gives me a headache." Clearing his throat, he pushed in two granite blocks. A portion of the wall sank, exposing a six-foot wooden door. It was splintered everywhere. A tarnished door-knob hung loosely from its spot. Bence turned the knob and used his shoulder to push the door open.

She entered a simple room with an opening to a walkway on the other side. Its smooth charcoal walls contrasted the decrepit exterior. When she took her next step, goosebumps erupted down her arms. There were no foes. Only shadows cast by ghastly gargoyles.

"What?" Isabel whispered as she approached the next set of stairs.

"It is pleasing to see you more confident than ever. It's quite attractive."

"Everything you say is perverted."

They continued down the walkway made of earth and clay rocks. Lanterns aflame showed them the path, which was worn down by hundreds, if not thousands, of footsteps. A worm fell onto Isabel's shoulder, causing her to flinch.

"Oh, it's just you." She sighed. Isabel plucked it from its place and returned it to the dirt floor.

A whirring sound zoomed up and down the hall. Each time it passed her, it sent her hair whipping around her face. Isabel fell back against Bence. He hooked his arm around her torso and caught her. The rushing wind turned into a wailing. Isabel's knees buckled and she cupped her ears. Bence stepped in front of her and in a steady stroke, lodged his sword into the clay wall. A high-pitched scream emitted from the point of contact.

"Is Cehennem alive?" Isabel asked as she stood up.

"No," Bence replied curtly.

A shadow ghoul writhed in place. "Monsters gonna kill you! Monsters gonna get you! You're gonna die, traitor!" As it uttered the final syllable, the ghoul shrieked once more and faded into the wall.

"Is it dead?"

"Those damn things never die." His voice was a little shaky, but he just stared straight and avoided her gaze. Pulling his sword out, he turned his back to Isabel and said, "Let's go. Looks like our cover is blown."

A knot formed in her stomach. If the ghoul called him a traitor, they both very well may be in danger. Not just her. The sense of foreboding haunted Isabel until they reached the next room. Small and square.

She scanned it from top to bottom, but Bence's gasp cut her observation short. On the ground lay piles of corpses in armor, decorated with the image of a Phoenix.

"Are those..." Isabel paused to swallow the vomit that surged up her throat.

"Your Deranian knights."

"Why would you steal dead bodies?" Isabel recoiled with a hand over her nose.

At that moment, the glow of the torches pulsed, absorbing all the purple haze in the room, casting a violet light onto Isabel's former guardians. An ear-splitting creak hissed from the pile. A crack... then groans. The broken bodies, with scraps of flesh stretching over rotting muscle and bone, were vibrating. A forceful wind suddenly sucked everything towards the center of the room.

Bence shot a look at Isabel, but she shook her head. Tuuli's Opal was not glowing.

"It's not me!"

Isabel grabbed ahold of the door handle. Bence lost footing and threw his arms around her waist. The gust was short lived, as the ghoulish flames left the torches and lit up ribcages of the dead. With a flash of light, the dead rose, their congealed blood glowing purple, and limped towards Isabel and Bence.

"Your parents are sick sons of bitches," Isabel growled.

Bence got up and dusted his knees. "We must get out of here quickly."

The two companions charged towards a score of rotting flesh and metal armor. Bence slashed through a few within seconds, but he struggled with each strike of his sword.

"Their blood, or whatever, is like molasses. Careful—" The symphony of groans drowned out his voice.

Isabel was trying to whip and rip an undead soldier's head off, but the purple goo seemed to attach itself to her whip The body came down, but head hung on by some tendon. She growled in frustration.

From the corner of her eye, the empty torches caught her attention. Isabel ducked the sluggish swing of an axe and dropped her whip. An idea popped into her head. She drew an arrow. Kai's Sapphire glowed fiercely, and droplets of water condensed over the arrow's tip. She shot it straight into the axe-wielder's heart, which immediately extinguished the purple flame. The creature fell. Isabel turned and repeated the maneuver to the soldier that clung to her whip. After retrieving her weapon, she took count of her arrows. Isabel knew she would not have enough to face future foes, so she pulled out her sai for close combat.

"Bence, lower their defenses, and I will strike their hearts with a blast of water!"

He gave her an odd look but ran to her side. Bence swung his sword to block attacks. Isabel charged her sai with a sheen of water as she drove them into each undead soldier's chest. One by one they fell. Soon Isabel was down to her last opponent. Bence slashed his sword and sliced off one of its arms. The undead soldier lost balance and fell on him.

It moaned at Bence, gazing at its prey with its with empty sockets. It took its remaining hand and placed an iron grip around Bence's neck. He gagged and flailed his arms and legs, but the animated corpse would not budge. Isabel tiptoed towards the struggling pair. Winding her arm, Isabel shot her fist downward. A loud crunch echoed in the cold room, and the undead soldier broke down into pieces under Isabel's sai.

"What took you so long?"

Isabel waved him off. She had already made her way to the door, but Bence was still sporting a wild smirk.

"What a woman," he chuckled to himself. Bence got up, kicked the pile of bones and ran out the other door. Another winding hallway greeted them. They jogged lightly until they found another door.

"We don't seem to have a lot of options," Isabel murmured. She reached for the nob, but stopped to see Bence signal to her. He motioned to slow down as he bit his lips. Holding her breath, Isabel continued to turn the knob, as silently as she could.

The next room revealed two gargantuan Veijari, one derived from the Foti and the other, Kai. They snoozed near the other entrance. A creak escaped from the door's hinges, startling Isabel and Bence into paralysis. Removing her hand as if the knob was burning hot, she waited for a sound. Bence took over and pushed the door open a few more inches. They both peered through the crack and observed the beasts. The Kai Veijari was snoring. The Foti Veijari slept with his head flung back behind the chair. His paws twitched. Isabel sighed.

Suddenly, the wolfish Foti Veijari jolted up. Blinking to focus his eyesight, he scratched at his mane. Isabel bit her lip and inched back behind the door. Bence turned towards her. Their eyes met for a brief moment. Bence dropped his gaze, and then peeked back at her, flushing red. Isabel elbowed him and peeked from the crevice.

"Hey, Tacari, you hear that?"

"Shut up, I am trying to sleep, Dreng."

"Tacari, the door is open!" With a thud, Dreng howled, hankering for a blood bath.

"This place has been playing tricks with us for too long. Remember, for years Cehennem has been trying to give us false hope of escape? Pay no mind," scolded the Kai Veijari.

"But *Tacari*, Damian and Echidna said that the Princess *is* coming..."

Tacari roared and whipped his tail at Dreng, who snarled back. Tacari finally stomped towards the open door. Isabel clambered backwards, eyes darting everywhere. She only had seconds to decide her next move. To run or fight. Bence gave her a knowing look, and she nodded. Tacari flung the door open, and Bence swiftly lodged his blade up and through Tacari's throat. No sound escaped, just gurgling.

"Tacari?"

Isabel swung around from behind the Kai Veijari's large body. She drew an arrow and shot it right into Dreng's heart. As soon as he fell, Bence release his blade, and Tacari's body tumbled forward, out the door. Isabel approached the Foti Veijari, still fighting for his last breath.

"What plans do Damian and Echinda have?"

Dreng hacked and smiled, but said nothing. Within seconds, Dreng was dead. Isabel's eyes welled up as she kicked at the lifeless Veijari. Silence dragged on, and Isabel only dug her nails into her palms deeper to keep from trembling. Bence paced back and forth behind her, cursing. Minutes went by, and when despair crept up Isabel's spine, she finally urged Bence onward.

"Something's off. I thought Damian would place Cehennem on a much higher alert than staffing two lazy Veijari by a door. An-and that ghoul... it called you a traitor, and yet nothing happened as a result? No troops to surround us?"

"Is that what you want?"

"Don't be a wise ass. Of course not," she spat. "But it just bothers me."

"Well, don't forget, we are dealing with both Damian and Echidna. And my mother is a patient woman. Just keep your guard up. We're almost at the central chamber."

Isabel and Bence continued through the next door, and

were greeted by, once again, another hallway. The same hallway made of soil and clay with a smattering of lamps. The purple mist had thickened to a fog. Isabel could only see a few feet ahead, but she pressed on with Bence leading the way. The hall opened up to the original entrance to Cehennem, except they were hundreds of feet below. The opening to the outdoors was the size of a fingernail. Isabel inhaled deeply — the fog was not so oppressive here. Her fragmented thoughts pieced together as she planned her next steps.

An ominous screeching echoed in the darkness disrupted her peace.

"Kana!" Isabel shouted.

The creatures seemed to appear from the shadows and dove towards the two companions. Isabel sliced at them, meeting their talons with her sai. But the force threw her on her back. Two Kana clawed and pecked at her. Isabel swung her arms wildly as she tried to focus on using any of her stones of power. But every time she tried to focus, the stale perfume-like smell of violet haze disoriented her. One of the Kana slashed through her leather arm bracer. Gritting her teeth, Isabel lifted her legs and kicked it away. The second Kana snagged her ankle and bit down.

Warm liquid washed up her leg. When Isabel looked down, it was the Kana's blood. Bence's sword sliced halfway down its neck. He pried it out, leapt into the air and swung his blade full circle, catching the second Kana in the face. It landed with a thud.

"Focus, Isabel!"

She teetered on her feet, holding the sai together with both hands. "I-I got it."

The second Kana thrashed about, gnashing its beak at her. It aimed for her other foot, but Bence drove his weapon into its skull before Isabel could blink.

"What are you doing? You're going to die! Do you understand me?" Bence cupped his hands around Isabel's face. They were ice cold.

Her head spun. She turned and started to dry heave. "I don't understand what's happening to me." Contents finally spilled forth from Isabel's mouth, burning her lips. "I was fine until we traveled through that last tunnel. I can't see straight. The air is better out here, but the Kana moved too quickly."

Bence furrowed his brow. "You got to fight it. The atmosphere is oppressive. Always has been. It's just getting worse. Even I feel its effects, but you have to stay with me. Stay with me!" He took her by the shoulders and shook.

"Elixir," she panted.

"What?" She gestured to a bulky pocket. Bence dug his hand and pulled out a glass vial. "From Jabin. He said it could help."

"With that ankle wound or your foggy mind?" he asked with doubt clouding his face.

"Give it," Isabel said, slurring. She pulled the cork off, spit it out, and gulped the contents.

Like static electricity, the elixir pricked every nerve ending, sending Isabel jumping into the air. A veil of clarity enveloped her mind, and both her previous ribcage injury and current Kana bite faded into nothingness.

Bence's eyes were wide open. "That was some impressive potion. You all right?"

Isabel nodded and surveyed her surroundings. The two dead Kana lie at her feet. A stone staircase veered up two flights.

"The structure of this building astounds me," Isabel said. How can we be traveling up when Cehennem extends into the earth?

Before Bence could respond, a rumble of voices expanded the cylindrical arena. Hordes of his siblings poured down from the flight above them. He raced past Isabel, waving his arms.

"Stop! It's me, Bence!"

"We do not recognize traitors," replied one of his sisters, exposing her rotten teeth.

"Don't lie and tell us you brought her to us. Your heart is too weak. And now that Farid is dead, I may as well be the new captain of my father's army," roared a brother.

"No, I want to be the new captain!" interrupted another sibling.

"I am older than *you*."

A small scuffle broke out, and Bence signaled to Isabel. "These are my kin. I don't know what to do."

"Thinking... I'm thinking," Isabel muttered.

All of a sudden, one of the brawling brothers fell off the stairwell and plummeted down the abyss.

"Rek, how could you?" roared one of the siblings.

Bence blinked and turned to Isabel. "Rek also is one of my sisters, but I thought she died in the battle at Zeyland."

She nodded. The name sounded familiar to her.

Rek came into view, eye patch over one eye, tuft of hair covering the other. She drew dual swords and Bence drew his. Damian's army erupted in gross cheers.

"Rek. You are alive?"

Rek brushed off her eye patch to reveal her slit pupil and winked. Isabel gaped in surprise as she watched the two circle each other while maneuvering towards the knot of onlookers.

It's a Zingari. How was she really able to keep the guise up for this long?

Bence and Rek tentatively clashed swords. Rek backed Bence into the crowd of siblings, when she abruptly tripped Bence with a sweep of a leg. As Bence crashed onto the floor, The Zingari wearing Rek's form leapt into the crowd and began slashing at the slew of Damian's offspring who all fell back in panic.

"Follow me!" Rek shouted.

Bence and Isabel followed the path the warrior was carving for them, and Isabel shot lines of fire from the palm of her hand at anyone who neared them. The trio made it up to the next platform, and the figure of Rek cleared all but the last two opponents.

"We were fooled by a Zingari?" spat one.

"Pathetic, you creatures are. Remember, you have no home. And Damian will keep it that way!" called the other Aeonian as he tried to lunge past her to reach Isabel. The Zingari grabbed a limb and flipped him over. The second Aeonian charged forward, and the Zingari did the same thing, but the momentum was so great the Zingari teetered at the edge of the platform. Isabel ran towards them, but the Zingari shook her head. The Zingari jumped off the platform, dragging both Aeonians with her.

"No!" Isabel sobbed.

Bence tried to pick her up, but she felt like stone.

"We must keep going," he insisted with a gentle tone.

"I didn't even know her name. I did not know what it took for her to hide out like that. Did she do this on her own or—" Isabel kept breaking into sobs. Bence shook her, but the tears would not stop.

"Isabel, I think that Zingari would be quite disappointed to have given her life for a Princess who gave up so quickly."

Isabel sniffed as Bence helped her to her feet. They proceeded through the next door. They entered a gigantic platform that dropped off with no walls connected to it. Only a rickety spiral staircase stood out in the corner.

"It is like a stage," Bence mused. "I surely do not remember this room."

A shrill laughter filled the arena. Isabel's hands flew to her ears while her eyes scouted for the offender.

"My son, home so soon? Have I not given you another chance to take care of that wench?"

"Hey!" Isabel stomped, still looking around.

An explosion of violet fog revealed a lean silhouette. Echidna was wrapped in a velvet gown, armed with only a dagger and her amethyst embedded in the only ring adorning her fingers.

"Mother, you will have to kill me then." Bence stepped forward and in front of Isabel. He swung his sword forward. His other hand balled into a fist behind his back. "Yes, you gave life to me, but love was not in your heart. I became ruthless because of that, and all the mind games you played.

All those years you drilled me with the false message that monsters lived in the outside world when we were the real monsters—"

"Cease your self-righteous whining!" Echidna cleared her throat. "So sorry, I am usually more composed than that, I assure you, Lady Isabel. You sure have your way with men, my dear. But I have to say, even *I* stick to one man. Because if you do not, you can stir up some dangerous jealousy…"

Isabel glanced at Bence. She saw his eyes travel down towards her hand. Isabel sheepishly played with the ring on her finger. Her heart was now pounding so loudly, she did not hear the door creaking. Bence then stretched his neck to look past her. Beads of sweat formed at the crown of his head. Isabel held her breath and turned around. A figure loomed in the doorway, face indeterminable in the dark. The approaching silhouette's breath rattled. Echidna cackled and clapped her hands. A light washed over the figure.

Lanky and blonde, it was Dante, wounded and bleeding. Seething in anger.

"Dante, you're awake?" Isabel gasped. She sprinted towards him, but he disappeared into a haze at her touch. When she turned back to Echidna, she saw her with one arm around Dante.

Echidna stroked his arm. She smiled with malevolent glee.

"I felt bad for him, so I decided to help. I roused him from his deep slumber, healed his major wounds… Oh, and put a little birdie in his ear that my son was trying to wreck his picture-perfect marriage."

Bence choked. "I bet you poisoned his mind is what you

did!"

"Hush now. He is upset enough as it is," Echidna cooed.

As she backed away, Dante remained still, body enveloped in lavender. The color darkened to a violet and smoldered at his shoulders, as if it were a fire. Color faded from his eye. Dante reared his head and roared, like a beast.

"Shit." Bence held his ground.

Ignoring Bence, Isabel pleaded with Dante. "What are you doing? Calm down. This place messes with your head. And now I know it's Echinda's enchantments." Dante did not falter his steps. He kept walking, limbs rigid. "There is *nothing* between Bence and I. Stop it. This is silly. Don't let this lie cloud your judgment!"

Dante quickened his pace every few feet until he was in a full sprint. Then, he made a sudden turn and threw his rage at Bence.

CHAPTER

41

The two clashed swords. Bence fended Dante's blows and stayed on the defensive. However, with each strike, Bence could feel Dante getting stronger and stronger. His muscles burned. Sweat beaded at the base of his neck. Bence wondered if the incantation his mother cast on Dante was sapping his energy as well.

"You stole my woman, you vile sack of shit. You belong in hell!"

Bence parried another one of Dante's blows.

"She is my *wife! And I will die to defend her from the likes of you!*" Dante's voice bellowed at a deafening decibel.

Swords locked, Bence pulled his face closer to observe Dante. His pupils dilated to the point where he couldn't distinguish the color of his eyes. His cheeks flushed red, spreading down his neck. He was like a rabid animal, consumed by one thought. "Snap out of it," Bence growled. "I've been there, Dante. I know what it feels like to be convinced who the enemy is. But I promise you, it's not me. At least, it is no longer."

"Dante, no!"

Jerking his head, Bence spotted Isabel approaching them. But Echidna snapped her hands and Isabel's limbs froze in place. She turned and twisted, but Isabel was immobilized by the witch's dark magic.

"My humblest apologies! This is their battle, sweetie!"

With a twist, Bence wrestled Dante's sword away from him. It clanged onto the floor a few feet away. Dante's elbow connected with Bence's jaw, sending him crashing onto the ground. Dante continued to punch Bence, showing no signs of fatigue. Bence tried to raise his other arm, but Dante knocked through his defense, grabbed his hair and slammed him against his knee. Every inch of Bence's body ached, and his breathing was painful and laborious. His sword spun away out of reach.

"Stop it!" cried Isabel. "Echidna, why do you want to kill your own son? Why not just kill me?"

"Because—" Her voice echoed somewhere in the distance. "I wanted you to suffer first before you die."

"Dante! Bence!" Isabel screamed.

"Isabel," Bence whispered. Specks of red clouded his vision, but he rolled to one side and avoided the latest blow. Dante's fists had become so strong his missed blows left marks on the stone floor. Bence flailed his arms, searching for his sword. He only had one final maneuver left. Bence used the rest of his strength and kicked his legs up, sending Dante up and over him. Dante landed hard and rolled back towards the backdrop. Bence got up and limped towards his sword. He spat blood, took a huge breath, and stalked towards Dante. Dante's fury grew, but Bence was timing it. Dante swung his arm in a clock-wise fashion. Bence ducked. As Dante's body spun with the momentum, Bence kicked out his legs and knocked Dante off his feet and over the edge.

Dante grabbed on the edge with his hands, and the violet glow flickered. He blinked and struggled to stay a hold.

"Dante! *Dante!*" Isabel kept screaming.

He blinked again, as if searching for her voice.

"Dante!"

"Isabel? Where are you? I have been looking for you!" The haze faded and his eyes focused. He locked eyes with Bence.

Bence extended his hand. "Grab ahold, and I will pull you to safety. And to Isabel. We will vanquish Damian and Echidna together."

Covered in grime, Dante's mouth fell agape. He scrutinized Bence in silence.

"Hurry. What are you waiting for? Isabel is waiting—"

"Bence!" cried Isabel.

Dante closed his eyes. He gave one last gasp and let go.

Bence stared down into the chasm. As if he could see him, as if he could still save his life. Isabel fell into a fit of hysterics somewhere behind him. Bence finally straightened out, looked at her, and shook his head. Isabel screamed, and Echinda nodded in silence.

"See you upstairs."

With an exaggerated bow, Echidna disappeared in a puff of purple smog.

CHAPTER
42

Pins and needles. This sensation crawled through her muscles as Isabel flexed her fingers. Her limbs grew warm as Echidna's spell wore off. Isabel shuddered as Bence laid his hand on her shoulder. She collapsed onto his chest, a hurricane of emotions exploded inside. Tears washed down Isabel's face as she slammed her fists onto Bence's chest. He stood like a pillar of stone.

"Isabel," Bence croaked.

She did not respond. Her thoughts were consumed by Dante.

Gone. He's just gone. Didn't he hear my voice?

"You killed him!" Isabel screamed. The platform shook as gusts of air blast upwards as if vents opened up from the earth, throwing Bence back.

"Isabel. No. He let go. I tried to save him!" Pressing against the gale, he pressed his two hands together. "Please believe me. I wanted to pull him to safety but he let go. I swear it!"

She wanted to smash his face in. Burn him alive. Another person she loved was now dead. Collapsing to her knees, she thrashed her arms, sending debris in Bence's direction. "Stay still. I'm going to kill you once and for all!" She tried launching fireballs, but Bence dodged and rolled from each one. However, all he did was pick up his sword and sheath it. He kept his hands high, palms facing outward.

"Please, Isabel—"

A sick confidence consumed her. She knew in the back of her mind she could bury everyone while protecting herself. Bury Bence, Damian, and Echidna with a snap of her fingers. Then she could walk away from the ruins and never look back. Dunyan's Amber glowed obediently. "You! You are nothing but a *monster*!"

When she uttered those last words, Bence froze, staring at her like a lost animal. His jaw moved but nothing came out. He lowered his arms and slumped his shoulders.

That's it. He surrendered! I've won!

Before Isabel summoned her powers for the killing blow, she noticed a faint haze clouding her vision. Isabel swallowed hard. She needed to focus.

"The monsters are outside. The monsters are outside waiting to kill you and your family," voices cackled in unison.

Through her blurred vision, she watched Bence drop to his hands and knees.

"We told you so! Eeh hee! The monster has come to kill you now!" Shadows danced along the walls. Some did somersaults of glee.

"Shut up!" Bence shouted. "Shut up!"

"If you want to live, you better fight back! The monster is here to kill you and your family! Just like we've been saying all these years!" The shadows chanted over and over.

Isabel paused. She shook her head and rubbed her eyes. Her heart beat slowed.

I am… the monster?

Isabel's head snapped up. The fog dissipated. Bence rolled on the floor in front of her, hands over his ears.

This is what Echinda wanted. To finish off her disobedient son. The one, single child of the hundreds she bore who realized his whole life was a lie.

A hand flew to her mouth. Isabel rushed to Bence and held him. She shushed in his ear to drown out the sounds of the shadows. His staccato shouts made her flinch.

"I'm sorry," she whispered, "I believe you. It was my fault for failing to save him."

The shadows hissed as their chants faded.

"It's not a matter of whose fault it is." Bence grit his teeth. He shifted his weight and sat up. "My mother, she is a manipulator. I do not doubt she poisoned his mind."

Extending her hand, Isabel wrangled a fragile smile. She pulled him onto his feet. They stood awkwardly for a brief moment before she leaned in and embraced Bence. Her heart weighed her down like an anchor. Her world was falling apart piece by piece and Isabel realized his world was too. Bence's arms remained by his side, body as rigid as a plank.

"We must move forward," he said, voice rumbling.

She squeezed tighter as tears fell from her eyes. "But they

are your parents…" Fatigue haunted her. There was too much death. Death to solve more death.

With one swift motion, Bence placed a hand on her chin and lifted her head. He rubbed tears from her eyes with his thumbs. She blinked repeatedly; her vision cleared from the haze. Turning her head, she noticed Echidna's violet fog retreated into the abyss.

"Dante was troubled. And my parents chose the path of violence. So, I stand by you. This is my decision." Bence swallowed hard. "I only knew one type of life when I was in Cehennem. Not long after our invasion, I began to see so many other sides, stories, endless possibilities… I met you." He nodded and pat a hand to his chest.

When Bence released Isabel, she felt weightless. A wave of calm rushed over her as she gazed into his eyes. There was something different about the way he looked at her. She couldn't put her finger on it, but it provided her with a level of comfort she had never known before. The playful malice that once flickered in his green orbs disappeared.

"Get ready. I am going to need you." Isabel locked hands with his and placed them over her heart.

Without a word, Bence nodded and drew his sword. They turned to the decrepit stairwell. The rusted handrail chipped at the touch. Each step creaked under every footstep. A stale breeze funneled downward. After climbing through the opening in the ceiling, she reached the top floor.

A vast floor consisting of stone expanded forth from the top of the stairs. A chill nipped at her skin. Every movement created an echo. The walls were caked in mud and moss. The same eerie violent glow radiated throughout the room, but Isabel was unable to locate its source. Bence hummed as he scanned the room.

"Where did she go?" she whispered.

He touched her arm.

"Bence—"

She no longer felt him. A whirring following by the sound of something dragging across the ground to her right caught Isabel's attention. An unknown force had pulled Bence feet first to the other side of the room. Flailing his arms, he opened his mouth to scream, but no sound came forth. Bence smashed into the stone wall, limbs stretched apart, and hung upside-down. Veins bulged in his neck as he struggled against the invisible binding. As Isabel ran towards him, bellowing laughter shook the room. She lost her balance and crashed against the floor. When she looked up, a tidal wave of violet smoke erupted all around her, masking two silhouettes. Damian and Echidna appeared, eyes ablaze with amusement.

"Isabel!" cackled Echidna. "Welcome!"

A flash of light stunned her, but when she regained her vision, Damian was no longer by Echidna's side. Isabel scanned the room. She backed up and bumped into something. She swallowed.

"Bence?"

All she could hear was a low, slow chuckle. Isabel revolved around the spot. Damian towered over her. His rusted headpiece wrapped around his forehead. She could barely make out fragments of amethyst forming in the four-pronged setting.

"Silly little girl." He brushed aside a loose strand of hair with a meaty hand.

Isabel flinched, but Damian snatched her hair and yanked her to the ground. The impact awakened her wounds. Isabel's ribs ached as jolts of pain zapped through her entire body. She bit her tongue to prevent herself from crying out.

"I cannot believe such a *puny child* delayed my mission for as long as you did!"

"I guess you are not as good as you thought you were. Pity, no?" Isabel hissed as she struggled to stand.

Damian roared and thrashed his arm out, sending her flying into the air like a rag doll. Isabel twisted around and broke her fall with her right arm. She wretched in pain, but rose quickly enough to spot Damian charging at her like an enraged bull. She dove out of the way and turned to catch him crashing into his wife, who shrieked hysterically.

"You lumbering idiot. Turn around! Get her! Get her!"

Before he could react, Isabel reached for her bow, aimed at his chest, and released an arrow. Echidna snatched it out of Damian's way with lightning speed and snapped it in half. Isabel drew another arrow, setting its tip ablaze and released without hesitation. It zoomed through the air with lightning speed and exploded upon contact with the ground a foot away from them. Flames engulfed the pair. Foti's Ruby flicked proudly; Isabel silently congratulated herself as she sprinted towards Bence.

When she passed the flames, she saw Damian holding his wife. He looked up at her and barked, emitting sound waves that tunneled through the fire and air towards Isabel. The pulsating energy knocked her off her feet, and she landed a few feet from Bence. The pounding of Damian's boots signaled his approach. He lunged at Isabel. Cries of struggle filled the air. Damian pinned her down with ease. Isabel wriggled underneath his weight, gasping for air beneath his huge palm. Damian's blackened fingernails dug into her face. He shouted, and she grunted. Damian eventually positioned her flat on her back, bending her neck backwards. Just enough to see Bence's still unconscious body above her. As the dust settled, the pitter-patter of Echinda's approach sent Isabel's mind into panic.

"And I thought watching Dante die would break your spirit. I thought maybe you would snap and kill my traitorous son. But I guess, bitch, you need to make things more difficult!" Echidna's face loomed over hers as she screamed. Her thin, bony fingers, which contrasted her husband's meaty hands, scratched her face. The searing pain caused tears to well in Isabel's eyes. Warm blood streamed from the cuts, trickling into her mouth. Even though Isabel tried to summon the powers from her armlet, none of the stones glowed. Echidna's stale perfume encased her mind, disorienting her.

The assault stopped. Echidna stood up and strolled to her son. Spitting out blood, Isabel twisted in vain as she watched her. The farther away Echidna walked, the less her mind was shrouded in confusion.

Come on. Air. No, fire. Maybe water? Can I combine them—

"My poor baby," Echidna cooed, twirling her son's locks. "You were poisoned by this she-devil. And to think you had such a promising military career. Mommy was so proud of you." She picked his head up and grazed his lips with hers.

Isabel gagged and squirmed under Damian's grip.

Earth. Knock her off her feet—

"Are you still watching?" Echidna purred. "Now," she turned back to Bence, "wake up, my son."

Her devilish haze lifted Bence from the wall and set him down. His eyes snapped open. First, he looked at his mother, then at Isabel. His lips curled into a sneer.

"Release her," he snarled. "She is mine."

"My boy!" Damian roared with delight, easing his grip on Isabel. He backed up and stood opposite of Echidna. Bence prowled towards Isabel, his parents watching proudly behind him.

"Bence, please." Isabel whimpered on the floor. "You promised!"

As she strained to sit up, energy surged from her armlet, ready to attack on command. Sparks erupted at her fingertips. Bence pressed Isabel back onto the ground with his boot. He knelt down and put his face next to hers.

"Isabel?"

The fine hairs stood on the back of her neck. She opened her mouth, but he slid his hands over her lips.

"Listen to me. You have the full power of the armlet now. Grab onto me and summon a wind storm so strong that will fling them into chaos and take this building down."

Without another word, Isabel's armlet lit up. Bence lunged and gripped her tightly. Howling winds erupted from it with a blast of blinding white. The tempest blew away Echidna and Damian with ease. Their cries drowned in the roaring gusts as they tumbled back and forth. Isabel looked up and smiled at them. Kai's Sapphire glowed next: rain from an undeterminable source began pouring into the arena. The room flooded at record speed. Damian and Echidna slammed onto the floor with a splash. Damian flailed around in the rising deluge. Every time he attempted an attack, a wave of ice cold water washed over his open mouth. He coughed and cried for his wife.

"You think a *little storm* will stop us? Be prepared to see our true power!" Echidna's voice drilled into the air. When she uttered the last syllable, everything slowed to a halt. Each raindrop froze, suspended in midair. The air was still. Waves stood statuesque. A deathly silence hung over the area a long moment as all objects slowed to a halt. Isabel's movements were sluggish, as if swimming in molasses.

As sound and fury slowly resumed, Cehennem began to quake. Chunks of wall broke apart. Isabel lost sight of Damian and Echidna. Bence fell backwards as the floor shifted, and he disappeared into the abyss. All Isabel could hear was his scream echoing as the collapsing structure swallowed her as well.

Falling, falling.

CHAPTER
43

It defied all logic. Isabel lost her sense of direction as her body was flung in multiple directions. After slamming against a pillar of wood, she felt the water-logged earth forced in between her fingers. Chunks of soil and stone rained on her.

I'm going to be buried alive.

But as soon as she finished the thought, the ground shuddered and launched her upwards. It was as if the earth was roaring — Isabel covered her ears as everything around her vibrated with sound. Debris pressed against every part of her body, squeezing the air from her lungs. Claustrophobia closed its jaws on her. But everything kept moving, swirling like quicksand in reverse.

A *pop.* Then, a *boom.*

Flung into the air, the world swirled around her. Sky, ground, sky, ground. Everything was a swirl of gray, brown, and purple until she landed back first onto the ground. Isabel moaned. Her neck burned when she strained to look around her. Rubble that had been flung into the sky came raining down.

A pair of arms looped under her armpits and dragged her backwards. Pillars and chunks of stone crashed before her one by one. Some too close for comfort.

"I got you," the voice said. Bence's voice.

Once out of range, the pair watched in amazement as bits of Cehennem flew about. Rays of violet light circled around. Eventually, nothing remained of the cursed prison. After the dust settled, Echidna and Damian stood at a distance; his amethyst glowed in full in his headpiece. Echidna admired the stone and stroked it with her hand that wore her ring.

"Behold, our own stones of power!" Damian bellowed.

Isabel and Bence looked at one another. He grinned.

"Let's do this," she shouted.

Isabel and Bence split up as the two enchanters charged at them. Bence veered off to grapple with his father, and Isabel turned her focus to Echidna who tackled her to the ground with lightning speed. Isabel wriggled and flipped Echidna over. With Echidna on the ground, Isabel snapped her fingers and soil loosened up and sucked the evil woman in. Sticky mud oozed over her hands and feet as Echidna screamed in frustration. Isabel landed a few blows to Echidna's face. When her knuckles bled, she got up and drew her sai. Foti's Ruby ignited the metal prongs. Echidna writhed and freed one of her legs with one loud *plop*. As Isabel aimed for her chest, Echidna kicked Isabel who missed and dug the two blades into her shoulders.

When Isabel backed up a few steps, Echidna's amethyst

flashed angrily. The sai glowed violet and slowly pulled from her chest. Echidna freed herself completely and took hold of the bloody sai. She swung the blades furiously at Isabel who ducked at each attempt, fumbling for Foti's whip.

Isabel cracked the whip at Echidna's leg. As it took hold, Isabel pulled. Echidna fell again, and the sai flung a few feet to her left. Isabel sent her burning rage down the leather, branding a thick line on Echidna's ankle. Isabel lunged at her, but Echidna's amethyst glowed once more, suspending Isabel in place and flinging her up and over Echidna. Isabel rolled onto her stomach but before she could catch a breath, Echidna wrapped her arm around her neck. Isabel gagged and gasped for air while hitting her fist weakly against her assailant, summoning the wind to tear them apart, but Echidna's grip was iron-clad.

"Isabel!" Somewhere Bence's voice echoed in the stormy, dark field.

Isabel's eyes traveled from Damian, who was raising some sort of spear.

"Hold her tight, dear!" Damian bellowed, taking aim.

It all happened in slow motion. Damian flung his spear. It rocketed towards the two women at an astonishing velocity, glowing with the same purple as the amethyst on his headpiece. The spear honed on Isabel, held in position by Echidna. When Isabel realized she couldn't move and that her mind was too cloudy to command the armlet, she bit Echidna's forearm. When the evil sorceress' grip loosened, Isabel bent forward.

Thud.

Isabel stood, her torso bent forward, and stared at the

ground, wincing at the piercing cries. Blood poured onto her. She wrestled herself free and turned to see Echidna crumple onto the ground, the spear lodged into her forehead. Isabel slammed a sai into her ring. The light from the amethyst flickered out, leaving colorless pieces of broken stone. She turned to Bence, who then turned to Damian. The giant man fell to his knees and tore his hair. His cries cracked through the air like thunder.

"Bence!" Isabel shouted.

He was at her side within moments. Bence held her up and grit his teeth.

"She had it coming. You okay?"

Isabel nodded, swallowing a lump in her throat. Her neck burned. Her ribs ached. Her feet were numb. But she couldn't complain right now. Bence and Isabel watched Damian's arms go limp. After a few heartbeats of silence, Damian stood up and glared at them. His stone of power blazed a brilliant purple, overpowering his blood red eyes, blinding Bence and Isabel. Before Isabel could reach for her sai, Damian charged at full speed. Bence took a step in front of Isabel.

"Father, no! Give up! You have lost!" Bence bellowed.

Damian was deaf to his son's pleas. He bound towards them and collided with Bence. Isabel could feel the pulse of energy as the pair tumbled past her, rolling hundreds of feet and into the mud. Isabel dashed over to retrieve her sai and pursued them. Her eyes darted back and forth, unable to lock onto Damian.

"Your mother—" Damian huffed. "—your eyes are like your mothers! How does it feel to kill her, matricidal beast!"

Bence bent his knees to his chest and sprung them out, kicking Damian back a few feet.

"I did not kill her. You did." Bence pounded his chest. "How does it feel to see everything you used for your own means just fall apart? Your sons and daughters have fallen. And now your wife—" Bence eyed Isabel who nodded.

Isabel lunged at him. Ear splitting howls erupted from Damian, as she slashed at him with her sai. Isabel's family weapons dug deep and she heard bones crack. She tried to dodge his flailing arms, but one of Damian's hands flew to her neck. The two were locked into position, neither of them able to budge. Damian grinned, exposing his yellow, rotten teeth. Through his cracked lips, he coughed up blood.

"I will take you with me if I must... I will not die alone." Damian slurped, blood and drool everywhere. "It... would be my pleasure."

Isabel's tears welled up. All seemed hopeless. She was going to die one way or another.

"Isabel!"

It was the last thing she heard when she closed her eyes, and commanded Foti's Ruby to awaken. The sai between them set ablaze, spreading to Damian, engulfing him in flames. In turn, the arm grappling Isabel's neck served as a bridge for the flames to consume her as well. Within seconds, the two bodies were swallowed up by red, orange, and yellow. She grit her teeth as the fire seared her flesh, turning her focus on Dante, her mother and father, and everyone who depended on her.

Isabel felt herself absorb into the atmosphere. Silence. Darkness.

CHAPTER

44

Beyond the fumes stood Bence. He dropped his sword and ran towards them. He tried to rip Isabel away and roll her body onto the wet mud. He furiously pat his hands around her, begging her to summon Kai's Sapphire. Upon the lack of response, he eyed her armlet and reached for the sapphire. As he hoped, the stone reacted, sending a monsoon of rain pouring upon them.

All flames were extinguished. Everything fell quiet. The only sound was the pitter-patter of rain washing over the exhausted desolation.

Bence's chest never felt so heavy, yet empty. In the years he trained in Cehennem, never had he expected to be cradling the head of his mortal enemy. Wet strands of her chestnut hair clung to her face. It was badly burned. Blisters bubbled down her neck, but Bence could still find beauty when he gazed at her. The flames spared her more so than his father, who lay like a charred lump a few feet away.

Tears mixed with rain drops as they fell from his lashes.

His life was fabricated by lies, with hate sewn into the fibers of his heart. And to ultimately turn on his parents tore him from reality. Bence shook his head. Again. Over and over.

This has to be another nightmare from the shadow ghouls. This can't be real.

A breath curled into the chill air before his eyes. Hands shaking, Bence brought his head close to Isabel's. He detected faint breathing. His heart leapt as heat flushed to his cheeks. Bence fumbled to adjust her body. He moved hair from her eyes, tilted her chin up to open her airway, and loosened her armor.

"Come on, come on," he muttered. "You're the only one I got left."

One thought nagged the back of his mind. Isabel is the only witness of what he had done. He was being selfish, but he knew if she died, Deran would obliterate him. Punish him to the highest extent of the law, and he would be the only Aeonian to suffer this consequence. And yet, even if Isabel did survive, could she really pardon him for all his past crimes?

But I chose a different path. I helped her. I'm not the same person as I was.

Bence was scared. He couldn't hide it. His whole body shivered; he fought hyperventilation.

"Isabel. Wake up."

He jumped in place when he heard shouting in the distance. Men wielding swords ran towards his direction. Bence looked at Isabel, then back at the men. She still didn't move. Cupping his hand on her cheek, he kissed her forehead. Her skin was still hot.

"Isabel. Thank you."

CHAPTER

45

Isabel's eyes shot open as she gasped for air. Clouds of smoke and ash hovered over patches of mud. Her body ached, covered in blisters. As Isabel stood, she winced as she wobbled her feet that burned like fire. There was no one around, except for a charred body in front of her. The face was almost indiscernible, other than the amethyst on his forehead. She wiped her lips with her sleeve as she stalked over Damian's body. After observing him for a few minutes with no signs of life, she turned back around to limp away.

"Bence?"

Her ankle snagged on something. She turned around to look at the offending branch. However, it was Damian's blackened hand. Isabel shouted, as the charred grip refused to release itself. Damian's empty sockets stared up at her. The amethyst glowed once more, pulsing life into the burnt body.

His grip pressed harder against the burns on her ankles.

Isabel grit her teeth. "Let go!"

Isabel fell to the ground, and she screamed in pain. She extended her arm, fingertips grazing the handle of her sai. Damian pulled her closer, but Isabel grabbed ahold of her weapon. She spun around and drove one sai into Damian's forehead. The amethyst shattered, and the body sputtered to a halt. Damian's last breath squeezed out of his body, dissipated as an ashy haze into thin air. Nothing remained but fragmented stone.

"Isabel?" There was a pause. "Isabel!" A voice echoed in the air.

"Bence?" Isabel got up and turned around. Harmon jogged through the clearing towards her.

"My Princess! You are alive!"

Harmon leaped into the air, laughing in disbelief. Isabel limped towards him and held his hands.

"Yes, Harmon. Damian and Echidna are gone, for good. We are safe now. We are all safe."

As Isabel finished her sentence, herds of people marched into view, led by Jabin. Faces of human and Zingari alike were filled with anticipation. Isabel raised her sai into the air, and everyone erupted into loud cheers. People hugged one another and shook hands.

"We can finally go home," shouted one Tuuli. "We can sail to Lea and see our families!"

"As with us," replied a man beside the Tuuli. "We can rebuild the castle and start over."

"Here, here! Three cheers to a new era of peace in Deran!" a Zingari interjected.

"Three cheers for Isabel, Princess of Deran!" echoed the

crowd in unison.

Isabel was drawn into the massive celebration. She was bumped left and right, shaking hands, and receiving pats on the back, wincing in pain. Soon, even all the adrenaline in her body could not stop her from trembling from exhaustion. Jabin pulled her aside and smiled.

"My friend. You need rest. Let's get you looked at, too," he whispered with a grin.

"Jabin." She panted. "I will give you Zeyland. The Dunya no longer inhabit the land, and your people deserve a home."

The short, floppy-eared Zingari blinked at her. His lip quivered in wonder as she bent down to hug him.

"Thank you, Jabin." His plush fur warmed her body.

"That is extremely generous. A small patch of land will do."

"Nonsense," Isabel asserted. Pulling back, she scratched the back of his ear. A frown spread across her face. "Jabin?"

"Yes?"

"Did you see anyone else? Any survivors of Cehennem?"

"No," Jabin answered with a wild shake of his head. "Should there have been?"

Heat rose up her neck. She scanned the horizon for a glint of emerald. "No," Isabel replied as her heart sank with a twinge of sorrow. "Of course not."

EPILOGUE

It was a ghost town. Isabel couldn't make out a single shadow in any of the windows. Releasing a breath, she closed the door behind her. The hinges emitted a squeak, scattering swallows from their trees. When silence resumed, she tip-toed down the walkway and pushed the gate open.

Turning her head, she rested her gaze on Dante's manor. She's spent twenty-six sleepless nights there since her final showdown with the Aeonians. Even when she was lulled into a false sense of security, she would wake up screaming, drenched in a cold sweat. The Deranian castle was far from complete. A candle lit the first floor window.

Must be Aysu.

Aysu suffered, perhaps more than Isabel, over Dante's death. Isabel had spared her the intimate details, feeling Dante's reputation should remain unsullied.

Dante would have wanted that.

Pulling the cloak over her head, she continued down the winding cobble-stone streets of Buryan. Her boots made faint imprints in the dusting of snow. Each shop, each home she passed, draped their windows with thick curtains. Her heart twisted in guilt. It took her a long time to realize the split opinion of Dante's leadership, and now with his sudden death, every citizen was uneasy for their future. That's why she put Harmon in charge. For now. He only accepted the position until an election could be held.

The wintry breeze danced around her cloak and nipped her nose. Her tears had already dried on her cheeks. Isabel took a swift turn down an alley, lit by only one lantern. Her shadow expanded and shrank, but Isabel avoided looking at it. Shadows were the things that haunted her dreams. After a few more feet, she arrived at the pier. The wooden boulevard stretched for miles.

Deserted. As I expected it to be.

She gingerly stepped down one of the docks and spotted a boat, enough to fit one. She had been eyeing this one for the last month. An elderly fisherman would take it out and be gone for hours. He never returned with fish. Just the same sullen look plastered over his face.

Grabbing the ropes, Isabel loosened the binding and steadied herself in it. Ice cold water sloshed around and spilled into the boat. Once things settled, she rose the singular sail and prayed for wind. Tuuli's Opal glowed to life and an invisible force gently pushed her away from shore.

Peace.

For the last few days, Isabel crept from the manor and borrowed the man's boat and sailed aimlessly until sunrise. Her fingertips scratched the edge of the boat as if trying to push out the nauseous sludge filling her chest. Her soul had been feeling heavy. It was difficult to escape the shock of the gore and death from her adventures. Isabel felt herself shutting herself away from everyone, afraid that the next person she became close to would die.

Her mother and father had looked so peaceful. While Isabel was covered in blood and blisters, they had lay in bed, eyes closed, skin dewy. They were dressed in satin and the pillows were perfumed with frankincense. She recalled turning to Aysu and asked, "How long?"

Aysu's response was, "Just this morning."

The morning she cleaned Deran of its evil. Isabel had fallen to her knees and had no idea how long she remained like that. Everything was a blur since then. Everyone attended the funeral, except Dover. There was a mention he was still fighting for his life.

There's so much to do after mourning ends.

Isabel wasn't ready to accept it. Even with the prospect of good news: The Foti were ready to tear down their walls and share their water supply with the Tuuli. She leaned back and stretched her arms behind her neck. The sky was a vast ocean of darkness; there wasn't a cloud in the sky. Adin stretched past Deva in a race across the horizon. The two gigantic orbs outshined the stars and mesmerized Isabel.

The two moons had no one left to worship them. The Dunyans, who always believed fate was intertwined with the two celestial beings, were the only ones. And now they were gone. The guilt still punched Isabel in the chest. A Zingari led search party couldn't find Avani or Kaj. Sighing, Isabel sat up and rested her chin on her hand. There was no escape from her thoughts. Even in the middle of the ocean.

A splash caught Isabel's attention. She spotted a handful of Kai swimming east. Isabel figured she was near the Sapphire Reefs. Rotating her arm, she directed the wind westwards. Towards Lea Island.

Isabel closed her eyes and breathed in the cool breeze. The boat jerked her back into reality as the craft bumped onto shore. She kicked off her shoes, hopped off the boat, and dug her toes into the cold sand. She reveled in the blissful silence. The white froth from the ocean tumbled playfully past her ankles. Isabel's tight face pulled up for a rare smile.

Isabel wandered down the beach, lost in thought. There was a memory of one more person that plagued her.

Bence.

The enigma who started as a man who hunted her and ended as an ally. She didn't have the chance to thank him. Deep down, she knew she couldn't have defeated Damian and Echidna without him.

And it must have killed him to make that decision.

But she didn't know if Bence was dead, or alive. Somewhere.

Isabel's musings were interrupted by the crackle and pop of a fire in the distance. When Isabel drew closer, she side-stepped behind a tree. Isabel peered curiously at the fire, but she did not see anyone. So, she crept from her hiding place and approached the fire. Branches were stacked onto one another, and palm leaves disintegrated into ash.

"Isabel?"

She flipped her head around, hair flying over her eyes. A man stood to the right of her, arms cradling chopped up wood. His tunic hung loosely over his wasted frame, and his pants were muddy and torn. Red-orange hair, coarse from the sea water, was tousled everywhere. A few strands fell over his stunned eyes. The deep green color seemed to be the only thing that had not faded.